W9-BON-938

WINNER OF COMMONWEALTH CLUB OF CALIFORNIA
GOLD MEDAL FOR FICTION

"An intelligent, carefully researched, richly imagined novel."
—*Boston Globe*

"Strong and authentic. The element of surprise is a magical,
jolting moment." —*Washington Post Book World*

"*When Nietzsche Wept* is the best dramatization of a great
thinker's thought since Sartre's *The Freud Scenario*."
—*Chicago Tribune*

"In this admirable novel, Irvin Yalom fulfills his promise as a
powerful storyteller and a brilliant diviner of the human
psyche." —Rollo May

"*When Nietzsche Wept* is Irvin Yalom's next (psycho)logical
step forward from *Love's Executioner*. Deep thought wrapped
up in superb storytelling. What more could one ask?"
—Theodore Roszak, author of *Flicker*

"A fascinating novel of what might have been the embryonic
geniuses of Sigmund Freud and Friedrich Nietzsche collided.
A fascinating story and a real page-turner."
—*Palo Alto Peninsula Times Tribune*

WHEN NIETZSCHE WEPT

IRVIN D. YALOM

PERENNIAL ■ CLASSICS

HARPER**PERENNIAL** ● MODERN**CLASSICS**

First HarperPerennial edition published 1993.
First Perennial Classics edition published 2005.
Perennial Classics are published by Perennial, an imprint of HarperCollins Publishers.

Designed by Ellen Levine
Hand Lettering by Honi Werner

Library of Congress Cataloging-in-Publication Data

Yalom, Irvin D.
   When Nietzsche wept / Irvin D. Yalom.
      p. cm.
   ISBN 978-0-06-074812-8
      1. Nietzsche, Friedrich Wilhelm, 1844–1900—Fiction. 2. Psychotherapist and patient—Fiction. 3. Breuer, Josef, 1842–1925—Fiction. 4. Depression, Mental—Fiction. 5. Suicidal behavior—Fiction. 6. Male friendship—Fiction. I. Title.

PS3575.A39W47 2005
813'.54—dc22   2004060574

08 09 10 11 12 13 RRD 15 14 13 12 11

To the circle of friends
who have sustained me over the years:

Mort, Jay, Herb, David,
Helen, John, Mary, Saul, Cathy, Larry,
Carol, Rollo, Harvey, Ruthellen, Stina,
Herant, Bea, Marianne, Bob, Pat.

To my sister, JEAN,
and to my best friend, MARILYN.

Some cannot loosen their own chains and can nonetheless redeem their friends.

You must be ready to burn yourself in your own flame: how could you become new, if you had not first become ashes?

—*Thus Spake Zarathustra*

WHEN NIETZSCHE WEPT

CHAPTER 1

THE CHIMES OF SAN SALVATORE broke into Josef Breuer's reverie. He tugged his heavy gold watch from his waistcoat pocket. Nine o'clock. Once again, he read the small silver-bordered card he had received the day before.

> 21 October 1882
>
> Doctor Breuer,
>
> I must see you on a matter of great urgency. The future of German philosophy hangs in the balance. Meet me at nine tomorrow morning at the Café Sorrento.
>
> Lou Salomé

An impertinent note! No one had addressed him so brashly in years. He knew of no Lou Salomé. No address on the envelope. No way to tell this person that nine o'clock was not convenient, that Frau Breuer would not be pleased to breakfast alone, that Dr. Breuer was on vacation, and that "matters of urgency" had no interest for him—indeed, that Dr. Breuer had come to Venice precisely to get *away* from matters of urgency.

Yet here he was, at the Café Sorrento, at nine o'clock, scanning the faces around him, wondering which one might be the impertinent Lou Salomé.

"More coffee, sir?"

Breuer nodded to the waiter, a lad of thirteen or fourteen with wet black hair brushed sleekly back. How long had he been daydreaming? He looked again at his watch. Another ten minutes of life squandered. And squandered on what? As usual he had been daydreaming about Bertha, beautiful Bertha, his patient for the past two years. He had been recalling her teasing voice: "Doctor Breuer, why are you so afraid of me?" He had been remembering her words when he told her that he would no longer be her doctor: "I will wait. You will always be the only man in my life."

He berated himself: "For God's sake, stop! Stop thinking! Open your eyes! Look! Let the world in!"

Breuer lifted his cup, inhaling the aroma of rich coffee along with deep breaths of cold Venetian October air. He turned his head and looked about. The other tables of the Café Sorrento were filled with breakfasting men and women—mostly tourists and mostly elderly. Several held newspapers in one hand and coffee cups in the other. Beyond the tables, steel-blue clouds of pigeons hovered and swooped. The still waters of the Grand Canal, shimmering with the reflections of the great palaces lining its banks, were disturbed only by the undulating wake of a coasting gondola. Other gondolas still slept, moored to twisted poles which lay askew in the canal, like spears flung down haphazardly by some giant hand.

"Yes, that's right—look about you, you fool!" Breuer said to himself. "People come from all over the world to see Venice—people who refuse to die before they are blessed by this beauty."

How much of life have I missed, he wondered, simply by failing to look? Or by looking and not seeing? Yesterday he had taken a solitary walk around the island of Murano and, at an hour's end, had seen nothing, registered nothing. No images had transferred from his retina to his cortex. All his attention had been consumed with thoughts of Bertha: her beguiling smile, her adoring eyes, the feel of her warm, trusting body and her rapid breathing as he examined or massaged her. Such scenes had power—a life of their own; whenever he was off guard, they invaded his mind and usurped his imagination. Is this to be my lot forever? he wondered. Am I destined to be merely a stage on which memories of Bertha eternally play out their drama?

Someone rose at the adjoining table. The shrill scrape of the metal chair against the brick roused him, and once again he searched for Lou Salomé.

There she was! The woman walking down the Riva del Carbon, entering the café. Only she could have written that note—that handsome woman, tall and slim, wrapped in fur, striding imperiously toward him now through the maze of tight-packed tables. And as she neared, Breuer saw that she was young, perhaps even younger than Bertha, possibly a schoolgirl. But that commanding presence—extraordinary! It would carry her far!

Lou Salomé continued toward him with no trace of hesitation. How could she be so sure it was he? His left hand quickly stroked the reddish bristles of his beard lest bits of breakfast roll still clung there. His right hand pulled down the side of his black jacket so that it didn't hunch up around his neck. When she was only a few feet away, she stopped for an instant and gazed boldly into his eyes.

Suddenly Breuer's mind ceased its chattering. *Now* looking required no concentration. *Now* retina and cortex cooperated perfectly, allowing the image of Lou Salomé to pour freely into his mind. She was a woman of uncommon beauty: powerful forehead, strong, sculpted chin, bright blue eyes, full and sensuous lips, and carelessly brushed silver-blond hair gathered lackadaisically in a high bun, exposing her ears and her long, graceful neck. He noticed with particular pleasure the wisps of hair that had escaped the gathering bun and stretched out recklessly in every direction.

In three more strides, she was at his table. "Doctor Breuer, I am Lou Salomé. May I?"—gesturing toward the chair. She sat down so quickly that Breuer had no time to offer her a proper greeting—to rise, to bow, to kiss her hand, to pull out her chair.

"Waiter! Waiter!" Breuer snapped his fingers crisply. "A coffee for the lady. Cafè latte?" He glanced toward Fräulein Salomé. She nodded and, despite the morning chill, removed her fur wrap.

"Yes, a cafè latte."

Breuer and his guest sat silent for a moment. Then Lou Salomé looked directly into his eyes and began: "I have a friend in despair. I'm afraid he'll kill himself in the very near future. It would be a great loss for me, and a great personal tragedy because I would bear some responsibility. Yet I could endure and overcome it. But"—she leaned toward him, speaking more softly—"such a loss could extend far beyond me: this man's death would have momentous consequences—for you, for European culture, for all of us. Believe me."

Breuer started to say, "Surely you exaggerate, Fräulein," but could not utter the words. What would have seemed adolescent hyperbole in any other young woman seemed different here, something to be taken seriously. Her sincerity, her flow of conviction were irresistible.

"Who is this man, your friend? Do I know of him?"

"Not yet! But in time we shall all know him. His name is Friedrich Nietzsche. Perhaps this letter from Richard Wagner to Professor Nietzsche may serve to introduce him." She extracted a letter from her bag, unfolded it, and offered it to Breuer. "I should first tell you that Nietzsche knows neither that I am here nor that I possess this letter."

Fräulein Salomé's last sentence gave Breuer pause. Should I read such a letter? This Professor Nietzsche doesn't know she's showing it to me—or even that she has possession of it! How has she obtained it? Borrowed it? Stolen it?

Breuer took pride in many of his attributes. He was loyal and generous. His diagnostic ingenuity was legend: in Vienna, he was the personal physician of great scientists, artists, and philosophers like Brahms, Brücke, and Brentano. At forty, he was known throughout Europe, and distinguished citizens from all over the West traveled great distances to consult him. Yet more than anything, he took pride in his *integrity*—not once in his life had he committed a dishonorable act. Unless perhaps he could be held accountable for his carnal thoughts of Bertha, thoughts that rightfully should be directed to his wife, Mathilde.

So he hesitated to take the letter in Lou Salomé's outstretched hand. But only briefly. Another glance into her crystalline blue eyes and he opened it. It was dated 10 January 1882 and began: "My friend, Friedrich"; several paragraphs had been circled.

You have now given to the world a work that is unequaled. Your book is characterized by an assurance so consummate as to betoken the most profound originality. In what other way could my wife and I have realized the most ardent wish of our lives, which was that some day something might come to us from without and take full possession of our hearts and souls! Each of us has read your book twice—once alone during the day, and then aloud in the evening. We fairly fight over the one copy and regret that the promised second one has not yet arrived.

But you are ill! Are you also discouraged? If so, how gladly would I do something to dispel your despondency! How shall I begin? I can do no other than lavish my unqualified praise upon you.

Accept it, at least, in a friendly spirit, even though it leave you unsatisfied.

Heartfelt greetings from yours,
Richard Wagner

Richard Wagner! For all his Viennese urbanity, for all his familiarity and ease with the great men of his time, Breuer was dazzled. A letter, and such a letter, written in the master's own hand! But he quickly regained his composure.

"Very interesting, my dear Fräulein, but now please tell me precisely what I can do for you."

Leaning forward again, Lou Salomé rested her gloved hand lightly on Breuer's hand. "Nietzsche is sick, very sick. He needs your help."

"But what's the nature of his illness? What are his symptoms?" Breuer, flustered by the touch of her hand, was now pleased to coast in familiar waters.

"Headaches. First of all, tormenting headaches. And continued bouts of nausea. And impending blindness—his vision has been gradually deteriorating. And stomach trouble—sometimes he cannot eat for days. And insomnia—no drug can offer him sleep, so he takes dangerous amounts of morphia. And dizziness—sometimes he is seasick on dry land for days at a time."

Long lists of symptoms were neither novelty nor enticement for Breuer, who usually saw twenty-five to thirty patients a day and had come to Venice precisely for a reprieve from such fare. Yet such was Lou Salomé's intensity that he felt compelled to attend closely.

"The answer to your question, my dear lady, is yes, *of course,* I will see your friend. That goes without saying. After all, I am a physician. But, please, allow *me* to pose a question. Why don't you and your friend take a more direct route to me? Why not simply write to my office in Vienna requesting an appointment?" And with that, Breuer looked around for the waiter to bring his check, and thought how pleased Mathilde would be by his returning to the hotel so quickly.

But this bold woman was not to be put off. "Doctor Breuer, a few more minutes, please. I can't exaggerate the seriousness of Nietzsche's condition, the depth of his despair."

"I don't doubt that. But I ask again, Fräulein Salomé, why doesn't Herr Nietzsche consult with me in my office in Vienna? Or visit a physician in Italy? Where is his home? Would you like me to provide a referral to a physician in his own city? And why *me?* For that matter, how did you know I was in Venice? Or that I am a patron of the opera and admire Wagner?"

Lou Salomé was unruffled, and smiled as Breuer began to fire questions at her, her smile growing mischievous as the fusillade went on.

"Fräulein, you are smiling as though you have a secret. I think you are a young lady who enjoys mysteries!"

"So many questions, Doctor Breuer. It's remarkable—we have conversed for only a few minutes, and yet there are so many perplexing questions. Surely that bodes well for future conversations. Let me tell you more about our patient."

Our patient! As Breuer marveled again at her audacity, Lou Salomé continued, "Nietzsche has exhausted the medical resources of Germany, Switzerland, and Italy. No physician has been able to comprehend his malady or relieve his symptoms. In the last twenty-four months, he tells me, he has seen twenty-four of Europe's best physicians. He has given up his home, left his friends, resigned his university professorship. He has become a wanderer in search of a tolerable climate, in quest of a day or two's relief from pain."

The young woman paused, lifting her cup to sip while keeping her gaze fixed on Breuer.

"Fräulein, in my consulting practice, I often see patients with unusual or puzzling conditions. But let me speak honestly: I have no miracles at my disposal. In such a situation as this—blindness, headaches, vertigo, gastritis, weakness, insomnia—where many excellent physicians have been consulted and found wanting, there is little likelihood I can do more than become his twenty-fifth excellent physician in as many months."

Breuer leaned back in his chair, took out a cigar, and lit it. He blew out a thin blue fume of smoke, waited for the air to clear, then continued, "Again, however, I extend my offer to examine Herr Professor Nietzsche in my office. But it well may be that the cause and cure of a condition as intractable as his seems to be are beyond the reach of eighteen hundred and eighty-two's medical science. Your friend may have been born a generation too soon."

"Born too soon!" She laughed. "A prescient remark, Doctor Breuer.

How often have I heard Nietzsche utter that very phrase! Now I am *certain* you are the right physician for him."

Despite his readiness to leave, and his recurring vision of Mathilde, fully dressed and impatiently pacing their hotel room, Breuer immediately expressed interest. "How so?"

"He often terms himself a 'posthumous philosopher'—a philosopher for whom the world isn't yet ready. In fact, the new book he is planning begins with that theme—a prophet, Zarathustra, bursting with wisdom, decides to enlighten the people. But no one understands his words. They aren't ready for him, and the prophet, realizing that he's come too soon, returns to his solitude."

"Fräulein, your words intrigue me—I have a passion for philosophy. But my time today is limited, and I have yet to hear a direct answer to the question of why your friend does not consult me in Vienna."

"Doctor Breuer"—and Lou Salomé looked directly into his eyes— "forgive my imprecision. Perhaps I am unnecessarily indirect. I've always enjoyed basking in the presence of great minds—perhaps because I need models for my own development, perhaps I simply like to collect them. But I do know I feel privileged to converse with a man of your depth and range."

Breuer felt himself flush. He could not hold her gaze any longer and looked away as she continued.

"What I mean to say is that perhaps I am guilty of being indirect simply to prolong our time here together."

"More coffee, Fräulein?" Breuer signaled the waiter. "And more of these droll breakfast rolls. Have you ever reflected upon the difference between German and Italian baking? Allow me to describe my theory about the concordance of bread and national character."

So Breuer did not hurry back to Mathilde. And as he took a leisurely breakfast with Lou Salomé, he mused upon the irony of his situation. How strange that he had come to Venice to undo the damage done by one beautiful woman and now sat tête-à-tête with another even more beautiful! He also observed that, for the first time in months, his mind was free of his obsession with Bertha.

Perhaps, he mused, there's hope for me, after all. Perhaps I can use this woman to crowd Bertha off the stage of my mind. Can I have discovered a psychological equivalent of pharmacologic replacement therapy? A benign drug like valerian can replace a more dangerous one like morphine. Likewise, perhaps Lou Salomé for Bertha—that would be a happy progression! After all, this woman is more sophisticated, more realized. Bertha is—how to say it?—presexual, a woman manqué, a child twisting awkwardly in a woman's body.

Yet Breuer knew that Bertha's presexual innocence was precisely what drew him to her. Both women excited him: thinking about them brought a warm vibration to his loins. And both women frightened him: each dangerous, but in different ways. This Lou Salomé frightened him because of her power—of what she might do to him. Bertha frightened him because of her submissiveness—because of what he might do to *her*. He trembled when he thought of the risks he had taken with Bertha—how close he had come to violating the most fundamental rule of medical ethics, to bringing ruin upon himself, his family, his entire life.

Meanwhile he was so deeply engaged in conversation and so entirely charmed by his young breakfast companion that at last it was she, not he, who reverted to her friend's illness—specifically to Breuer's comment about medical miracles.

"I am twenty-one years old, Doctor Breuer, and have given up all belief in miracles. I realize that the failure of twenty-four excellent physicians can only mean we have reached the limits of contemporary medical knowledge. But don't mistake me! I have no illusions that you can cure Nietzsche's medical condition. That was *not* why I sought your help."

Breuer put down his coffee cup and blotted his mustache and beard with his napkin. "Forgive me, Fräulein, now I am truly confused. You began, did you not, by saying you wanted my help because your friend is very sick?"

"No, Doctor Breuer, I said I had a friend who is in *despair*, who is in grave danger of taking his life. It is Professor Nietzsche's *despair*, not his *corpus*, that I ask you to heal."

"But, Fräulein, if your friend is in despair over his health and I have no medical therapeutics for him, what can be done? I cannot minister to a mind diseased."

Breuer took Lou Salomé's nod to mean she had recognized the words of Macbeth's physician, and continued, "Fräulein Salomé, there is no medicine for despair, no doctor for the soul. There is little that I can do except to recommend one of a number of excellent therapeutic spas in

Austria or Italy. Or perhaps a talk with a priest or some other religious counselor, a family member—perhaps a good friend."

"Doctor Breuer, I know that you can do more. I have a spy. My brother, Jenia, is a medical student who attended your clinic earlier this year in Vienna."

Jenia Salomé! Breuer tried to recall the name. There were so many students.

"Through him I learned of your love of Wagner, that you would be vacationing this week at the Amalfi Hotel in Venice, and also how to recognize you. But, most important of all, it was through him that I learned that you are, indeed, a doctor for despair. Last summer he attended an informal conference where you described your treatment of a young woman called Anna O.—a woman who was in despair and whom you treated with a new technique, a 'talking cure'—a cure based on reason, on the unraveling of tangled mental associations. Jenia says you are the only physician in Europe who can offer a true psychological treatment."

Anna O.! Breuer started at the name, and spilled coffee as he lifted the cup to his lips. He dried his hand with his napkin, hoping that Fräulein Salomé hadn't noticed the accident. Anna O., Anna O.! It was incredible! Everywhere he turned, he encountered Anna O.—his secret code name for Bertha Pappenheim. Fastidiously discreet, Breuer never used his patients' true names when discussing them with students. Instead, he constructed a pseudonym by moving a patient's initials back one letter in the alphabet: thus B.P. for Bertha Pappenheim became A.O., or Anna O.

"Jenia was extraordinarily impressed with you, Doctor Breuer. When he described your teaching conference and your cure of Anna O., he said he was blessed to be able to stand in the light of genius. Now, Jenia is no impressionable lad. I've never heard him speak like that before. I resolved then that I should one day meet you, know you, perhaps study with you. But my 'one day' became more immediate when Nietzsche's condition worsened over the past two months."

Breuer looked around. Many of the other patrons had finished and left, but here he sat, in full retreat from Bertha, speaking to an astonishing woman whom she had brought into his life. A shiver, a chill, passed through him. Was there to be no refuge from Bertha?

"Fräulein"—Breuer cleared his throat and forced himself to continue— "the case your brother described was just that—a single case in which I used a highly experimental technique. There is no reason to believe that this particular technique would be helpful with your friend. In fact, there is every reason to believe it wouldn't."

"Why so, Doctor Breuer?"

"I'm afraid time does not permit a long answer. For now I shall simply point out that Anna O. and your friend have very different illnesses. She was afflicted with hysteria and suffered from certain disabling symptoms, as your brother may have described to you. My approach consisted of systematically wiping out each symptom by helping my patient to recall, with the help of mesmerism, the forgotten psychic trauma in which it originated. Once the specific source was uncovered, the symptom dissolved."

"Suppose, Doctor Breuer, we consider despair to be a symptom. Couldn't you approach it in the same manner?"

"Despair is not a medical symptom, Fräulein; it is vague, imprecise. Each of Anna O.'s symptoms involved some discrete part of her body; each was caused by the discharge of intracerebral excitation through some neural causeway. Insofar as you've described it, your friend's despair is entirely ideational. No treatment approach exists for such a condition."

For the first time, Lou Salomé hesitated. "But, Doctor Breuer"—again she placed her hand on his—"before your work with Anna O., there was no psychological treatment for hysteria. As I understand it, physicians used only baths or that horrid electrical treatment. I'm convinced that you, perhaps only you, could devise such a new treatment for Nietzsche."

Suddenly Breuer noticed the time. He had to get back to Mathilde. "Fräulein, I shall do everything in my power to help your friend. Please allow me to give you my card. I shall see your friend in Vienna."

She glanced only briefly at the card before placing it in her purse.

"Doctor Breuer, I'm afraid it is not so simple. Nietzsche is not, shall I say, a cooperative patient. In fact, he doesn't know that I'm speaking to you. He is an intensely private person and a proud man. He'll never be able to acknowledge his need for help."

"But you say he speaks openly of suicide."

"In every conversation, in every letter. But he doesn't ask for help. Were he to know of our conversation, he would never forgive me, and I'm certain he would refuse to consult with you. Even if, somehow, I were to persuade him to consult with you, he'd limit the consultation to his bodily ailments. Never—not in a thousand years—would he place himself in the position of asking you to alleviate his despair. He has strong opinions about weakness and power."

Breuer began to feel frustrated and impatient. "So, Fräulein, the drama becomes more complex. You want me to meet with a certain Professor Nietzsche, whom you consider to be one of the great philosophers of our age, in order to persuade him that life—or, at least, *his* life—is worth living. And, moreover, I must accomplish this without our philosopher knowing it."

Lou Salomé nodded, exhaled deeply, and sat back in her chair.

"But how is it possible?" he continued. "Simply to accomplish the first goal—to cure despair—is in itself beyond the reach of medical science. But this second condition—that the patient be treated surreptitiously—transfers our enterprise to the realm of the fantastic. Are there other obstacles you have yet to reveal? Perhaps Professor Nietzsche speaks only Sanskrit—or refuses to leave his hermitage in Tibet?"

Breuer felt giddy but, noticing Lou Salomé's bemused expression, quickly controlled himself. "Seriously, Fräulein Salomé, how can I do this?"

"*Now* you see, Doctor Breuer! *Now* you see why I sought out *you* rather than a lesser man!"

The bells of San Salvatore pealed the hour. Ten o'clock. Mathilde would be anxious by now. Ah, but for her. . . . Breuer again motioned to the waiter. As they waited for the check, Lou Salomé issued an unusual invitation.

"Doctor Breuer, will you be my guest for breakfast tomorrow? As I mentioned before, I bear some personal responsibility for Professor Nietzsche's despair. There is a great deal more I must tell you."

"Tomorrow is, I regret, impossible. It's not every day that a lovely woman invites me to breakfast, Fräulein, but I am not free to accept. The nature of my visit here with my wife makes it inadvisable to leave her again."

"Let me then suggest another plan. I've promised my brother to visit him this month. In fact, until just recently I had planned to travel there with Professor Nietzsche. Permit me, when I am in Vienna, to provide you with more information. Meanwhile, I shall try to persuade Professor Nietzsche to consult with you professionally about his deteriorating physical health."

They walked together out of the café. Only a few patrons lingered as the waiters cleared away the tables. As Breuer prepared to take his leave, Lou Salomé took his arm and started to walk with him.

"Doctor Breuer, this hour has been too short. I am greedy and desire more of your time. May I walk with you back to your hotel?"

The statement struck Breuer as bold, masculine; yet from her lips it seemed right, unaffected—the natural way people should talk and live. If a woman enjoys a man's company, why shouldn't she take his arm and ask to walk with him? Yet what other woman he knew would have uttered those words? This was a different sort of woman. This woman was free!

"*Never* have I so regretted declining an invitation," Breuer said, pressing her arm closer to him, "but it is time for me to return, and to return alone. My loving but concerned wife will be waiting at the window, and I have a duty to be sensitive to her feelings."

"Of course, but"—and she drew her arm from his, to stand facing him, self-enclosed, forceful as a man—"to me, the word 'duty' is weighty and oppressive. I've pared down my duties to only one—to perpetuate my freedom. Marriage and its entourage of possession and jealousy enslave the spirit. They will never have dominion over me. I hope, Doctor Breuer, the time will come when neither men nor women are tyrannized by each other's frailties." She turned with all the assurance of her arrival. "Auf Wiedersehen. Till our next meeting—in Vienna."

CHAPTER 2

FOUR WEEKS LATER, Breuer sat at his desk in his office at Bäckerstrasse 7. It was four o'clock in the afternoon, and he was impatiently awaiting the arrival of Fräulein Lou Salomé.

It was unusual for him to have a hiatus during his workday, but in his eagerness to see her, he had quickly dispatched his previous three patients. All had straightforward ailments requiring little effort on his part.

The first two—men in their sixties—suffered from virtually identical conditions: severely labored breathing and a rasping, dry bronchial cough. For years Breuer had treated their chronic emphysema which, in cold, wet weather, became superimposed with acute bronchitis, resulting in severe pulmonary compromise. For both patients, he prescribed morphine for the cough (Dover's powder, five grains three times a day), small doses of an expectorant (ipecac), steam inhalations, and mustard plasters to the thorax. Though some physicians scoffed at mustard plasters, Breuer believed in them and often prescribed them—especially this year, when half of Vienna seemed to be down with respiratory illness. The city had seen no sun for three weeks, only a remorseless freezing drizzle.

The third patient, a house servant in the home of Crown Prince Rudolf, was a feverish, pockmarked young man with a sore throat, so shy that Breuer had to be imperious in ordering him to undress for an examination. The diagnosis was follicular tonsillitis. Though adept at quickly excising tonsils with scissors and forceps, Breuer decided these tonsils were not ripe enough to remove. Instead, he prescribed a cold compress to the neck, a potassium chlorate gargle, and carbonized water spray inhalations. Since this was the patient's third sore throat of the winter, Breuer also advised him to harden his skin and his resistance with daily cold baths.

Now, as he waited, he picked up the letter he had received three days ago from Fräulein Salomé. As boldly as in her previous note, she announced that she would arrive at his office today at four for a consultation. Breuer's nostrils flared: *"She* tells *me* what time she shall arrive. She issues the edict. She bestows upon me the honor of—"

But he quickly caught himself: "Don't take yourself so seriously, Josef. What difference does it make? Even though Fräulein Salomé had no way of knowing, it happens that Wednesday afternoon is an excellent time to see her. In the long skein of things, what difference does it make?"

"She tells *me . . ."* Breuer reflected upon his tone of voice: it was precisely this inflated self-importance that he detested in his medical colleagues like Billroth and the elder Schnitzler, and in many of his illustrious patients like Brahms and Wittgenstein. The quality he most liked in his closer acquaintances, most of whom were also his patients, was their unpretentiousness. That was what drew him to Anton Bruckner. Maybe Anton would never be the composer Brahms was, but at least he didn't worship the ground under his own feet.

Most of all, Breuer enjoyed the irreverent young sons of some of his acquaintances—the young Hugo Wolf, Gustav Mahler, Teddie Herzl, and that most improbable medical student, Arthur Schnitzler. He identified with them and, when other elders were out of hearing, delighted them with caustic jabs at the reigning class. For example, last week at the Polyklinik Ball, he had amused the group of young men crowding about him by pronouncing, "Yes, yes, it is true that the Viennese are a religious people—their god is named 'Decorum.' "

Breuer, ever the scientist, recalled the facility with which he had, in only a few minutes, switched from one mental state to another—from arrogance to unpretentiousness. What an interesting phenomenon! Could he replicate it?

Then and there he conducted a thought experiment. First he tried to slip into the Viennese persona with all the pomposity he had come to hate. By puffing himself up and silently muttering "How *dare* she!," squinting his eyes and gritting his frontal cerebral lobes, he re-experienced the pique and indignation that envelop those who take themselves too seriously. Then exhaling and relaxing, he let it all slip away and stepped back into his own skin—into a state of mind which could laugh at itself, at its own ridiculous posturing.

He noted that each of these states of mind had its own emotional coloring: the inflated one had sharp corners—a nastiness and irritability—as well as a loftiness and loneliness. The other state, in contrast, felt round, soft, and accepting.

These were definite, identifiable emotions, Breuer thought, but they were also *modest* emotions. What about more *powerful* emotions and the states of mind that brew *them?* Might there be a way to control those stronger emotions? Might that not lead to an effective psychological therapy?

He considered his own experience. His most labile states of mind involved women. There were times—today, ensconced in the fortress of his consulting room, was one of them—when he felt strong and safe. At such times, he saw women as they really were: struggling, aspiring creatures dealing with the endless pressing problems of everyday life; and he saw the reality of their breasts: clusters of mammary cells floating in lipoid pools. He knew about their leakages, dysmenorrheic problems, sciatica, and various irregular protrusions—prolapsed bladders and uteruses, and bulging blue hemorrhoids and varicosities.

But then there were other times—times of enchantment, of being captured by women who were larger than life, their breasts swelling into powerful, magical globes—when he was overcome by an extraordinary craving to merge with their bodies, to suckle at their nipples, to slip into their warmth and wetness. This state of mind could be overwhelming, could overturn an entire life—and had, in his work with Bertha, almost cost him everything he held dear.

It was all a matter of perspective, of switching frames of mind. If he could teach patients to do that at will, he might indeed become what Fräulein Salomé sought—a doctor for despair.

His reverie was interrupted by the sound of the door opening and closing in his outer office. Breuer waited a moment or two, so as not to appear overanxious, and then stepped into his waiting room to greet Lou Salomé. She was wet, the Viennese drizzle having become a downpour—but before he could help her out of her dripping outer coat, she was shrugging it off by herself and handing it to his nurse and receptionist, Frau Becker.

After ushering Fräulein Salomé into his office and motioning her toward a heavy black leather–upholstered chair, Breuer sat down in the chair next to her. He couldn't help remarking, "I see you prefer to do things for yourself. Doesn't that deprive men of the pleasure of serving you?"

"We both know that some of the services men provide are not necessarily good for women's health!"

"Your future husband will need extensive retraining. The habits of a lifetime are not easily extinguished."

"Marriage? No, not for me! I have told you. Oh, perhaps a part-time marriage—that might suit me, but nothing more binding."

Looking at his bold, beautiful visitor, Breuer could see much appeal in the idea of a part-time marriage. It was hard to keep in mind that she was only half his age. She wore a simple, long black dress buttoned high up to her neck, and a fur pelt with tiny fox face and feet was wrapped around her shoulders. Strange, Breuer thought, in cold Venice she discards her fur, yet clings to it in my overheated office. Still, it was time to get down to business.

"Now, Fräulein," he said, "let us take up the matter of your friend's illness."

"*Despair*—not illness. I have several recommendations. May I share them with you?"

Is there no limit to her presumption? he wondered indignantly. She speaks as though she were my confrère—the head of a clinic, a physician with thirty years of experience—not an inexperienced schoolgirl.

Calm down, Josef! he admonished himself. She is very young, she doesn't worship the Viennese god, Decorum. Besides, she knows this Professor Nietzsche better than I do. She's remarkably intelligent and may have something important to say. God knows I have no idea about curing despair: I can't cure my own.

He answered calmly, "Indeed, Fräulein. Please proceed."

"My brother, Jenia, whom I saw this morning, mentioned that you used mesmerism to help Anna O. recall the original psychological source of each of her symptoms. I remember your telling me in Venice that this uncovering of the origin of each symptom somehow dissolved it. The *how* of this 'somehow' intrigues me. Some day when we have more time, I hope that you will enlighten me about the precise mechanism through which arriving at the knowledge of the source eliminates the symptom."

Breuer shook his head and waved his hands, palms toward Lou Salomé.

"It's an empirical observation. Even had we all the time in the world to talk, I'm afraid I could not provide you with the precision you seek. But your recommendations, Fräulein?"

"My first recommendation is: *do not attempt this mesmerism method with Nietzsche*. It would not be successful with him! His mind, his intellect, is a miracle—one of the wonders of the world, as you will see for yourself. But he is, to borrow one of his favorite phrases, only human, all too human, and he has his own blind spots."

Lou Salomé now removed her fur, rose slowly, and walked across the office to place it on Breuer's sofa. She glanced for a moment at the framed diplomas hanging on the wall, adjusted one that hung slightly askew, and then sat down again and crossed her legs before going on.

"Nietzsche is extraordinarily sensitive to issues of power. He would refuse to engage in any process that he perceives as surrendering his power to another. He is attracted in his philosophy to the pre-Socratic Greeks, especially to their concept of Agonis—the belief that one develops one's natural gifts only through contest—and he is deeply distrustful of the motives of anyone who forgoes contest and claims to be altruistic. His mentor in these matters was Schopenhauer. No one desires, he believes, to help another: instead, people wish only to dominate and increase their own power. The few times when he surrendered his power to another, he's ended up feeling devastated and enraged. It happened with Richard Wagner. I believe it is happening now with me."

"What do you mean, it's happening with you? Is it true that you are, in some way, personally responsible for Professor Nietzsche's great despair?"

"He believes I am. That is why my *second* recommendation is: *do not ally yourself with me*. You look puzzled—for you to understand, I must tell you everything about my relationship to Nietzsche. I shall omit nothing and answer your every question with candor. This will not be easy. I place myself in your hands, but my words must remain our secret."

"Of course, you may count on that, Fräulein," he replied, marveling at her directness, at how refreshing it was to converse with someone so open.

"Well, then . . . I first met Nietzsche approximately eight months ago, in April."

Frau Becker knocked and entered with coffee. If she was surprised to see Breuer seated next to Lou Salomé rather than in his customary place behind the desk, she gave no evidence of it. Without a word, she deposited a tray containing china, spoons, and a gleaming silver pot of coffee and quickly left. Breuer poured the coffee as Lou Salomé continued.

"I left Russia last year because of my health—a respiratory condition which is now much improved. I first lived in Zurich and studied theology with Biederman and also worked with the poet Gottfried Kinkel—I don't think I've mentioned that I'm an aspiring poet. When my mother and I moved to Rome early this year, Kinkel provided a letter of introduction to Malwida von Meysenburg. You know her—she wrote *Memoirs of an Idealist*."

Breuer nodded. He was familiar with Malwida von Meysenbug's work, especially with her crusades for women's rights, radical political reform, and diverse transformations in the educational process. He was less comfortable with her recent antimaterialistic tracts, which he thought based on pseudo-scientific claims.

Lou Salomé continued, "So I went to Malwida's literary salon and there met a charming and brilliant philosopher, Paul Rée, with whom I became quite friendly. Herr Rée had attended Nietzsche's classes at Basel many years before, and thereafter the two had maintained a close friendship. I could see that Herr Rée admired Nietzsche over all other men. Soon he developed the notion that, if he and I were friends, then Nietzsche and I must also become friends. Paul—Herr Rée—but, Doctor"— she flushed for only an instant, but long enough for Breuer to notice, and for her to notice him noticing—"allow me to call him Paul, since that is how I address him, and today we have no time for social niceties. I'm very close to Paul, though I'll never immolate myself in marriage to him or to anyone!

"But," she went on impatiently, "I have spent enough time explaining a brief involuntary flushing of my face. Aren't we the only animals that blush?"

At a loss for words, Breuer could muster only a nod. For a while, surrounded by his medical paraphernalia, he had felt more powerful than during their last talk. But now, exposed to the power of her charm, he felt his strength slipping away. Her comment about her blush was remarkable: never in his life had he heard a woman, or anyone else for that matter, speak of social intercourse with such directness. And she was only twenty-one years old!

"Paul was convinced that Nietzsche and I would become fast friends," Lou Salomé continued, "that we were perfect for one another. He wanted me to become Nietzsche's student, protégée, and counterfoil. He wanted Nietzsche to be my teacher, my secular priest."

They were interrupted by a light knock on the door. Breuer rose to open it, and Frau Becker whispered loudly that a new patient had entered. Breuer sat down again and reassured Lou Salomé that they had ample time, for unannounced patients expect long delays, and urged her to go on.

"Well," she continued, "Paul arranged a meeting at Saint Peter's Basilica, the most unlikely place for the rendezvous of our unholy Trinity—the name we later adopted for ourselves, though Nietzsche often referred to it as a 'Pythagorean relationship.' "

Breuer caught himself gazing at his visitor's bosom rather than at her face. How long, he wondered, have I been doing that? Has she noticed? Have other women noticed me doing that? In his imagination, he grabbed a broom and swept away all sexual thoughts. He concentrated harder on her eyes and her words.

"I was immediately attracted to Nietzsche. He's not an imposing man physically—medium height, with a gentle voice and unblinking eyes that look inward rather than out, as if he were protecting some inner treasure. I didn't know then that he is three-quarters blind. Still, there was something extraordinarily compelling about him. The first words he spoke to me were: 'From what stars have we dropped down to each other here?'

"Then the three of us started to talk. And what talk! For a time, it appeared that Paul's hopes for a friendship or mentorship between Nietzsche and me would be realized. Intellectually, we were a perfect fit. We folded into each other's minds—he said we had twin brother-sister brains. Ah, he read aloud the jewels of his last book, he set my poems to music, he told me what he was going to offer the world during the next ten years—he believed that his health would grant him no more than a decade.

"Soon Paul, Nietzsche, and I decided we should live together in a *ménage à trois*. We began to make plans to spend this winter in Vienna or possibly Paris."

A *ménage à trois!* Breuer cleared his throat and shifted uneasily in his chair. He saw her smiling at his discomfiture. Is there *nothing* she misses? What a diagnostician this woman would make! Has she ever considered a career in medicine? Might she, as my student? *My* protégée? My colleague, working by my side in the consulting room, the laboratory? This fantasy had power, real power—but her words shook Breuer out of it.

"Yes, I know the world doesn't smile upon two men and a woman living chastely together." She accented "chastely" superbly—hard enough to set matters right, yet soft enough to avoid rebuke. "But we are free-thinking idealists who reject socially imposed restrictions. We believe in our capability to create our own moral structure."

As Breuer did not respond, his visitor appeared, for the first time, uncertain how to proceed.

"Shall I continue? Do we have time? Am I offending you?"

"Continue, please, *gnädiges* Fräulein. First, I have set aside the time for you." He reached across his desk, held up his calender, and pointed to the large L.S. scrawled across Wednesday, 22 November 1882. "You see I have nothing else scheduled this afternoon. And secondly, you are not offending me. On the contrary, I admire your candor, your forthrightness. Would that all friends spoke so honestly! Life would be richer and more genuine."

Accepting his praise without comment, Lou Salomé poured herself more coffee and continued with her story. "First, I should make clear that my relationship with Nietzsche, though intense, was brief. We met only four times, and were almost always chaperoned by my mother, by Paul's mother, or by Nietzsche's sister. In fact, Nietzsche and I were seldom alone for walks or conversations.

"The intellectual honeymoon of our unholy Trinity was also brief. Fissures appeared. Then romantic and lustful feelings. Perhaps they were present from the very beginning. Perhaps I should take responsibility for failing to recognize them." She shook herself as if to doff that responsibility, and went on to recount a crucial sequence of events.

"Toward the end of our first meeting, Nietzsche grew concerned about my plan for a chaste *ménage à trois*, thinking the world not ready for it, and asked me to keep our plan secret. He was especially concerned about his family: under no circumstances must his mother or his sister learn about us. Such conventionality! I was surprised and disappointed, and wondered if I'd been misled by his courageous language and his free-thinking proclamations.

"Shortly afterward, Nietzsche arrived at an even stronger position—that such a living arrangement would be socially dangerous for me, perhaps even ruinous. And, in order to protect me, he said he had decided to propose marriage, and asked Paul to convey his offer to me. Can you imagine the position that put Paul in? But Paul, out of loyalty to his friend—dutifully, though a bit phlegmatically—told me of Nietzsche's proposal."

"Did it surprise you?" Breuer asked.

"Very much—especially coming after our very first visit. It also unsettled me. Nietzsche is a great man and has a gentleness, a power, an extraordinary presence; I don't deny, Doctor Breuer, that I was strongly attracted to him—but not romantically. Perhaps he sensed my attraction to him and did not believe my assertion that marriage was as far from my mind as romance."

A sudden gust of wind rattling the windows distracted Breuer for a moment. He suddenly felt stiff in neck and shoulders. He had been listening so intently that for several minutes he had not moved a muscle. Occasionally patients had talked to him of personal issues, but never like this. Never face to face, never so unblinkingly. Bertha had revealed a great deal, but always in an "absent" state of mind. Lou Salomé was "present" and, even when describing remote events, created such moments of intimacy that Breuer felt they were lovers talking. He had no trouble understanding why Nietzsche would propose marriage to her after only a single meeting.

"And then, Fräulein?"

"Then I resolved to be more frank when we next met. But it turned out to be unnecessary. Nietzsche quickly realized that he was as frightened by the prospect of marriage as I was repelled by it. When I next saw him, two weeks later in Orta, his first words to me were that I must disregard his proposal. He urged me instead to join him in pursuit of the ideal relationship—passionate, chaste, intellectual, and nonmarital.

"The three of us reconciled. Nietzsche was in such high spirits about our *ménage à trois* that he insisted, one afternoon in Lucerne, that we pose for this—the only picture of our unholy Trinity."

In the photograph she handed Breuer, two men were standing before a cart; she was kneeling inside it, brandishing a small whip. "The man in the front, with the mustache, gazing upward—that's Nietzsche," she said warmly. "The other one is Paul."

Breuer inspected the photograph carefully. It disturbed him to see these two men—pathetic, shackled giants—harnessed by this beautiful young woman and her tiny whip.

"What do you think of my stable, Doctor Breuer?"

For the first time, one of her gay comments missed its mark, and Breuer was reminded suddenly that she was only a twenty-one-year-old girl. He felt uncomfortable—he did not like to see seams in this polished creature. His heart went out to the two men in bondage—his brothers. Surely he could have been one of them.

His visitor must have sensed her misstep, Breuer thought, noticing how she rushed to continue her narrative.

"We met twice more, in Tautenberg, about three months ago, with Nietzsche's sister and then in Leipzig with Paul's mother. But Nietzsche wrote me continually. Here's a letter, in which he responded to my telling him how moved I was by his book *Dawn*."

Breuer quickly read the short letter she handed him.

My dear Lou,

I, too, have dawns about me, and not painted ones! Something I no longer believed possible, to find a friend for my *ultimate happiness and suffering*, now seems to me possible—the *golden* possibility on the horizon of my whole future life. I am moved whenever I so much as think of the bold and rich soul of my dear Lou.

F.N.

Breuer kept silent. Now he felt an even greater bond of empathy with Nietzsche. To find dawns and golden possibilities, to love a rich, bold soul: everyone needs that, he thought, at least once in a lifetime.

"During this same time," Lou continued, "Paul began to write equally ardent letters. And despite my best mediating efforts, the tension within our Trinity increased alarmingly. The friendship between Paul and Nietzsche was disintegrating quickly. Ultimately they began to disparage each other in their letters to me."

"But surely," Breuer interjected, "this comes as no surprise to you? Two ardent men in an intimate relation with the same woman?"

"Perhaps I was naïve. I believed that we three could share a life of the mind, that we could do serious philosophical work together."

Apparently unsettled by Breuer's question, she rose, stretched slightly, and sauntered to the window, stopping on the way to inspect some of the objects on his desk—a Renaissance bronze mortar and pestle, a small Egyptian funerary figure, an intricate wooden model of the semicircular canals of the inner ear.

"Perhaps I'm obstinate," she said, looking out the window, "but I am still not convinced that our *ménage à trois* was impossible! It might have worked had it not been for the interference of Nietzsche's odious sister. Nietzsche invited me to spend the summer with him and Elisabeth in Tautenberg, a small village in Thüringen. She and I met at Bayreuth, where we met Wagner and attended a performance of *Parsifal.* Then together we journeyed to Tautenberg."

"Why do you call her odious, Fräulein?"

"Elisabeth is a divisive, mean-spirited, dishonest, anti-Semitic goose. When I made the mistake of telling her Paul is Jewish, she took pains to make this known to Wagner's entire circle in order to ensure that Paul would never be welcome in Bayreuth."

Breuer put down his coffee cup. While at first Lou Salomé had lulled him into the sweet safe realm of love, art, and philosophy, now her words jarred him back to reality, to the ugly world of anti-Semitism. That very morning he had read in the *Neue Freie Presse* a story about fraternities of youths roaming the university, entering the classrooms, shouting *"Juden hinaus!"* (Jews get out) and forcing all Jews out of the lecture halls—physically pulling anyone who resisted.

"Fräulein, I, too, am Jewish, and must inquire whether Professor Nietzsche shares his sister's anti-Jewish views?"

"I know you're Jewish. Jenia told me. It's important that you know Nietzsche cares only about truth. He hates the lie of prejudice—all prejudice. He *hates* his sister's anti-Semitism. He is appalled and disgusted that Bernard Förster, one of Germany's most outspoken and virulent anti-Semites, often visits her. His sister, Elisabeth . . ."

Now her words came faster, the pitch of her voice rising an octave. Breuer could tell that she knew she was straying from her prepared narrative, but could not stop herself.

"Elisabeth, Doctor Breuer, is a horror. She called me a prostitute. She lied to Nietzsche and told him that I showed everyone that photo and bragged about how he loves the taste of my whip. She always lies! She is a dangerous woman. Some day, mark my words, she will do Nietzsche great damage!"

Still standing, she held tightly to the back of a chair as she spoke these words. Then, sitting, she continued more calmly, "As you may imagine, my three weeks at Tautenberg with Nietzsche and Elisabeth were complex. My time alone with him was sublime. Wonderful walks and deep conversations about everything—sometimes his health permitted him to talk ten hours a day! I wonder if ever before there has been such *philosophical openness* between two persons. We talked about the relativity of good and evil, about the necessity to free oneself from public morality in order to live morally, about a freethinker's religion. Nietzsche's words seemed true: we *had* sibling brains—we could say so much to one another with half-words, half-sentences, mere gestures. Yet this paradise was spoiled, because all the while we were under the eye of his serpent sister—I could see her listening, always misunderstanding, scheming."

"Tell me, why would Elisabeth slander you?"

"Because she's fighting for her life. She is a small-minded, spiritually impoverished woman. She cannot afford to lose her brother to another woman. She realizes Nietzsche is, and will forever be, her sole source of significance."

She glanced at her watch and then at the closed door.

"I'm concerned about the time, so I'll tell you the rest quickly. Just last month, despite Elisabeth's objections, Paul, Nietzsche, and I spent three weeks in Leipzig with Paul's mother, where we once again had serious philosophical discussions, particularly about the development of religious belief. We parted only two weeks ago, with Nietzsche still believing we three would spend the spring living together in Paris. But it will never be, I know that now. His sister succeeded in poisoning his mind against me, and recently he began sending letters full of despair and hatred for both Paul and me."

"And now, today, Fräulein Salomé, where do things stand?"

"Everything has deteriorated. Paul and Nietzsche have become enemies. Paul grows angry every time he reads Nietzsche's letters to me, every time he hears of any tender feelings I have for Nietzsche."

"Paul reads your letters?"

"Yes, why not? Our friendship has grown deeper. I suspect I will always be close to him. We have no secrets from one another: we even read one another's diaries. Paul has been entreating me to break off with Nietzsche. Finally I acquiesced and wrote Nietzsche that though I shall always treasure our friendship, our *ménage à trois* was no longer possible. I told him that there was too much pain, too much destructive influence—from his sister, from his mother, from the quarrels between him and Paul."

"And his response?"

"Wild! Frightening! He writes crazed letters, sometimes insulting or threatening, sometimes deeply despairing. Here, look at these passages I've received just this past week!"

She held out two letters whose appearance even showed agitation: the uneven script, the many words abbreviated or underlined several times. Breuer squinted at the paragraphs she had circled, but then, unable to make out more than a few words, handed them back to her.

"I forgot," she said, "how difficult it is to read his script. Let me decipher this one addressed to both Paul and me: 'Don't let my outbreaks of megalomania or wounded vanity bother you too much—and if I should one day happen to take my own life in some fit of passion, there wouldn't be anything in that to worry about overmuch. What are my fantasies to you! . . . I came to this reasonable view of the situation after I had taken—from despair—an enormous dose of opium——' "

She broke off. "That's enough to give you an idea of his despair. I've been staying at Paul's family estate in Bavaria for several weeks now, so all my mail comes there. Paul has been destroying his most vitriolic letters in order to spare me pain, but this one to me alone slipped through: 'If I banish you from me now, it is a frightful censure of your whole being. . . . You have caused damage, you have done *harm*—and not only to me but to all the people who have loved me: this sword hangs over you.' "

She looked up at Breuer. *"Now,* Doctor, do you see why I so strongly recommend that you don't ally yourself with me in any way?"

Breuer drew deep upon his cigar. Though intrigued by Lou Salomé and absorbed in the melodrama she was unfolding, he was troubled. Was it wise to have agreed to enter into it? What a jungle! What primitive and powerful relationships: the unholy Trinity, Nietzsche's ruptured friendship with Paul, the powerful connection between Nietzsche and his sister. And the viciousness between her and Lou Salomé: I must take care, he told himself, to stay out of the way of *those* thunderbolts. Most explosive of all, of course, is Nietzsche's desperate love, now turned to hatred, for Lou Salomé. But it was too late to turn back. He had committed himself and in Venice had blithely told her, "I have never refused to treat the sick."

He turned back to Lou Salomé. "These letters help me understand your alarm, Fräulein Salomé. I share your concern about your friend: his stability seems precarious, and suicide a real possibility. But since you now have little influence over Professor Nietzsche, how can you persuade him to visit me?"

"Yes, *that* is a problem—one I have been considering at length. Even my name is poison to him now, and I shall have to work indirectly. That means, of course, that he must *never, never* know of my having arranged a meeting with you. You must never tell him! But now that I know you are willing to meet with him——"

She put down her cup and looked so intently at Breuer that he had to reply quickly: "Of course, Fräulein. As I said to you in Venice, 'I have never refused to treat the sick.' "

Upon hearing these words, Lou Salomé broke into a broad smile. Ah, she had been under more tension than he had imagined.

"With that assurance, Doctor Breuer, I shall begin our campaign to place Nietzsche in your office without his knowing my part in the matter. His behavior is now so disturbed that I'm certain all his friends are alarmed and would welcome any sensible plan to help. On my way back to Berlin tomorrow, I'll stop in Basel to propose our plan to Franz Overbeck, Nietzsche's lifelong friend. Your reputation as a diagnostician will help us. I believe Professor Overbeck can persuade Nietzsche to consult with you about his medical condition. If I am successful, you will hear from me by letter."

In speedy succession, she put Nietzsche's letters back into her purse, rose, flounced her long ruffled skirt, gathered up her fox stole from the couch, and reached out to clasp Breuer's hand. "And now, my dear Doctor Breuer——"

As she placed her other hand on his, Breuer's pulse quickened. Don't be an old fool, he thought, but gave himself up to the warmth of her hand. He wanted to tell her how he loved her touching him. Perhaps she knew, for she kept his hand in hers as she spoke.

"I hope we stay in frequent contact about this matter. Not only because of my deep feelings about Nietzsche and my fear that I am, unwittingly, responsible for some of his distress. There's something else. I hope, too, you and I will become friends. I have many faults, as you've seen: I am impulsive, I shock you, I am unconventional. But I also have strengths. I have an excellent eye for nobility of spirit in a man. And when I have found such a man I prefer not to lose him. So we shall write?"

She dropped his hand, strode to the door, then stopped abruptly. She reached into her bag to draw out two small volumes.

"Oh, Doctor Breuer, I almost forgot. I think you should have Nietzsche's last two books. They'll give you insight into his mind. But he must not know you have seen them. That would arouse his suspicion, since so few of these books have sold."

Again, she touched Breuer's arm. "And one more point. Despite having so few readers now, Nietzsche is convinced that fame will come. He told me once that the day after tomorrow belongs to him. So don't tell anyone you're helping him. Don't use his name to anyone. If you do and he finds out, he'd consider it a great betrayal. Your patient—Anna O.—that's not her real name, is it? You use a pseudonym?"

Breuer nodded.

"Then I'd advise you to do the same for Nietzsche. Auf Wiedersehen, Doctor Breuer," and she held out her hand.

"Auf Wiedersehen, Fräulein," said Breuer, as he bowed and pressed it to his lips.

Shutting the door behind her, he glanced at the two slim, paper-covered volumes and noted their strange titles—*Die Fröhliche Wissenschaft (The Gay Science)* and *Menschliches, Allzumenschliches (Human, All Too Human)*—before putting them down on his desk. He went to the window to catch one last glimpse of Lou Salomé. She raised her umbrella, walked quickly down his front steps, and, without looking back, entered a waiting fiacre.

CHAPTER 3

T URNING FROM THE WINDOW, Breuer shook his head to dislodge Lou Salomé from his mind. Then he tugged the cord hanging over his desk to signal Frau Becker to send in the patient waiting in the outer office. Herr Perlroth, a stooped, long-bearded Orthodox Jew, stepped hesitantly through the doorway.

Fifty years ago, Breuer soon learned, Herr Perlroth had undergone a traumatic tonsillectomy—his memory of that procedure so searing that, until this day, he had refused to consult a physician. Even now he had delayed his visit, but a "desperate medical situation," as he put it, had left him no choice. Breuer immediately doffed his medical demeanor, came out from behind his desk, and sat in the adjoining chair, just as he had with Lou Salomé, to chat casually with his new patient. They talked about the weather, the new wave of Jewish immigrants from Galicia, the Austrian Reform Association's inflammatory anti-Semitism, and their common origins. Herr Perlroth, like almost everyone in the Jewish community, had known and revered Leopold, Breuer's father, and, within minutes, had transferred this trust for the father onto the son.

"And so, Herr Perlroth," said Breuer, "how may I be of service to you?"

"I cannot make my water, Doctor. All day long, and night too, I have to go. I run to the toilet, but nothing comes. I stand and stand, and finally a few driblets come. Twenty minutes later, same thing. I have to go again, but . . ."

A few more questions, and Breuer was certain about the cause of Herr Perlroth's problems. The patient's prostate gland had to be obstructing the urethra. Now only one important question remained: Did Herr Perlroth have a benign enlargement of the prostate or did he have a cancer? On rectal examination, Breuer palpated no rock-hard cancer nodules but found instead a spongy, benign enlargement.

Upon hearing there was no evidence of cancer, Herr Perlroth broke into a jubilant smile and grabbed Breuer's hand and kissed it. But his mood darkened once again when Breuer described, as reassuringly as possible, the unpleasant nature of the required treatment: the urinary passageway would have to be dilated by the insertion into the penis of a graduated series of long metal rods, or "sounds." Because Breuer himself did not perform this treatment, he referred Herr Perlroth to his brother-in-law Max, a urologist.

After Herr Perlroth left, it was a little after six, time for Breuer's late-afternoon house calls. He restocked his large black leather medical bag, put on his fur-lined greatcoat and top hat, and stepped outside where his driver, Fischmann, and his two-horsed carriage were waiting. (While he had been examining Herr Perlroth, Frau Becker had hailed a *Dienstmann* stationed at the intersection next to the office—a red-eyed, red-nosed young errand man who wore a large official badge, a pointed hat, and an oversized khaki army coat with epaulets—and given him ten *Kreuzer* to run to fetch Fischmann. More affluent than most Viennese physicians, Breuer leased a fiacre by the year, rather than hire one when needed.)

As always, he handed Fischmann the list of patients to be visited. Breuer made house calls twice a day: early, after his small breakfast of coffee and crisp three-cornered *Kaisersemmel;* and again, at the end of his afternoon office consultations, as today. Like most internists of Vienna, Breuer sent a patient to a hospital only when there was no other recourse. Not only were people cared for better at home, but they were safer from the contagious diseases that often stormed through the public hospitals.

As a consequence, Breuer's two-horse fiacre was in frequent use: indeed, it was a mobile study, and kept well stocked with the latest medical journals and reference works. A few weeks ago, he had invited a young physician friend, Sigmund Freud, to accompany him for an entire day. A mistake perhaps! The young man had been attempting to decide on his choice of medical specialty, and that day may have frightened him away from the practice of general internal medicine. For, according to Freud's calculations, Breuer had spent six hours in his fiacre!

Now, after visiting seven patients, three of them desperately ill, Breuer had finished the day's work. Fischmann turned toward the Café Griensteidl, where Breuer usually shared a coffee with the group of physicians and scientists who, for fifteen years, had met each evening at the same *Stammtisch,* a large table reserved in the choicest corner of the café.

But tonight Breuer changed his mind. "Take me home, Fischmann. I'm too wet and tired for the café."

Resting his head on the black leather seat, he closed his eyes. This exhausting day had begun badly: he had been unable to return to sleep after a nightmare at 4:00 A.M. His morning schedule had been heavy: ten house calls and then nine office-consultation patients. In the afternoon, more office patients, and then the stimulating but enervating interview with Lou Salomé.

Even now, his mind was not his own. Insidious fantasies of Bertha seeped in: holding her arm, walking together with her in the warm sun, far from the icy gray slush of Vienna. Soon, however, discordant images intruded: his marriage shattered, his children left behind, as he sailed away forever, to start a new life with Bertha in America. The thoughts haunted him. He hated them: they robbed him of his peace; they were alien, neither possible nor desirable. Still, he welcomed them: the only alternative— banishing Bertha from his mind—seemed inconceivable.

The fiacre rattled crossing a plank bridge over the Wien River. Breuer looked out at the pedestrians hurrying home from work, mostly men, each carrying a black umbrella and dressed much as he was—dark fur-lined greatcoat, white gloves, and black top hat. Someone familiar caught his eye. The short, hatless man with the trim beard, passing the others, winning the race! That powerful stride—he'd know it anywhere! Many times in the Vienna woods, he had tried to keep pace with those churning legs, which never slowed except to search for *Herrenpilze*—the large pungent mushrooms that grew among the rootwork of the black firs.

Asking Fischmann to pull over, Breuer opened the window and called out, "Sig, where are you going?"

His young friend, wearing a coarse but honest blue coat, closed his umbrella as he turned to the fiacre; then, recognizing Breuer, grinned and replied, "I'm heading toward Bäckerstrasse seven. A most charming woman has invited me for supper tonight."

"Ach! I have disappointing news!" Breuer laughed in reply. "Her most charming husband is on his way home this very minute! Jump in, Sig, ride with me. I'm finished for the day, and too tired to go to the Griensteidl. We'll have time to talk before we eat."

Freud shook the water off his umbrella, stamped his feet on the curbstone, and climbed in. It was dark, and the candle burning in the carriage generated more shadows than light. After a moment of silence, he turned to look closely at his friend's face. "You look tired, Josef. A long day?"

"A hard one. It started and ended with a visit to Adolf Fiefer. You know him?"

"No, but I've read some of his pieces in the *Neue Freie Presse*. A fine writer."

"We played together as children. We used to walk to school together. He's been my patient since the first day of my practice. Well, about three months ago, I diagnosed liver cancer. It's spread like wildfire, and now he has advanced obstructive jaundice. Do you know the next stage, Sig?"

"Well, if his common duct is obstructed, then his bile will continue to back up into the bloodstream until he dies of hepatic toxicity. Before that, he'll go into liver coma, won't he?"

"Precisely. Any day now. Yet I can't tell him that. I keep up my hopeful, dishonest smile even though I want to say an honest goodbye to him. I'll never get used to my patients dying."

"Let's hope none of us do." Freud sighed. "Hope is essential, and who but we can sustain it? To me, it's the hardest part of being a physician. Sometimes I have great doubts whether I'm up to the task. Death is so powerful. Our treatments so puny—especially in neurology. Thank God, I'm almost finished with *that* rotation. Their obsession with localization is obscene. You should have heard Westphal and Meyer quarreling on rounds today about the precise brain localization of a cancer—*right in front of the patient!*

"But"—and he paused—"who am I to talk? Only six months ago, when I was working in the neuropathology lab, I was overjoyed at the arrival of a baby's brain so I could have the triumph of determining the precise site of the pathology! Maybe I'm getting too cynical, but more and more I grow convinced that our disputations about the location of the lesion drown out the *real* truth: that our patients die, and we doctors are impotent."

"And, Sig, the pity is that the students of physicians like Westphal never learn how to offer comfort to the dying."

The two men rode in silence as the fiacre swayed in the heavy wind. Now the rain was picking up again and splattered down on the carriage roof. Breuer wanted to give his young friend some advice, but hesitated, choosing his words, knowing Freud's sensitivity.

"Sig, let me say something to you. I know how disappointing it is for you to go into the practice of medicine. It must feel like a defeat, like settling for a lesser destiny. Yesterday at the café, I couldn't help overhearing you criticize Brücke for both refusing to promote you and advising you to give up your ambitions for a university career. But don't blame him! I know he thinks highly of you. From his own lips I heard that you are the finest student he's ever had."

"Then why not promote me?"

"To what, Sig? To Exner's or Fleischl's job—if they ever leave? At one hundred *Gulden* a year? Brücke's right about the money! Research is a rich man's work. You can't live on that stipend. And support your parents? You wouldn't be able to marry for ten years. Maybe Brücke wasn't too delicate, but he was right in saying that your only chance to remain in research is to marry for a large dowry. When you proposed six months ago to Martha, knowing she would bring you no dowry, *you*—not Brücke—decided your future."

Freud closed his eyes for a moment before answering.

"Your words wound me, Josef. I've always sensed your disapproval of Martha."

Breuer knew how difficult it was for Freud to speak forthrightly to him—a man sixteen years older than he and not only his friend, but his teacher, his father, his older brother. He reached out to touch Freud's hand.

"Not true, Sig! Not at all! We disagree only about timing. I felt you had too many hard years of training ahead of you to burden yourself with a fiancée. But we agree about Martha—I met her only once, at the party before her family left for Hamburg, and liked her immediately. She reminded me of Mathilde at that age."

"That's not surprising"—Freud's voice softened now—"your wife was my model. Ever since I met Mathilde, I've been looking for a wife like her. The truth, Josef, tell me the truth—if Mathilde had been poor, wouldn't you still have married her?"

"The truth, Sig—and don't hate me for this answer, it was fourteen years ago, times have changed—is that I would have done whatever my father required of me."

Freud remained silent as he took out one of his cheap cigars, then offered it to Breuer, who, as always, declined it.

As Freud lit up, Breuer continued, "Sig, I feel what you feel. *You* are *me*. You are me ten, eleven years ago. When Oppolzer, my chief of medicine, died suddenly of typhus, my university career ended just as abruptly, just as cruelly, as yours has. I, too, had considered myself a lad of great promise. I expected to succeed him. I *should* have succeeded him. Everyone knew that. But a gentile was chosen instead. And I, like you, was forced to settle for less."

"Then, Josef, you know how defeated I feel. It's unfair! Look at the chair of medicine—Northnagel, that brute! Look at the chair of psychiatry—Meynert! Am I less able? I could make great discoveries!"

"And so you will, Sig. Eleven years ago, I moved my laboratory and my pigeons into my home and continued my research. It can be done. You'll find a way. But it will never be the way of the university. And we both know it's not just the money. Every day the anti-Semites grow more shrill. Did you see the piece in this morning's *Neue Freie Presse*, about the gentile fraternities bursting into lectures and pulling Jews out of the classroom? They're threatening now to disrupt all classes taught by Jewish professors. And did you see yesterday's *Presse*? And the piece about the trial in Galicia of a Jew accused of a ritual murder of a Christian child? They actually claim he needed Christian blood for the matzo dough! Can you believe it? Eighteen hundred and eighty-two, and it still goes on! These are cavemen—savages coated with just the thinnest glaze of Christianity. *That's* why you have no academic future! Brücke dissociates himself personally from such prejudice, of course, but who knows how he really feels? I do know that in private he told me that anti-Semitism would ultimately destroy your university career."

"But I'm meant to be a researcher, Josef. I'm not as suited as you for medical practice. All Vienna knows of your diagnostic intuition. I don't have that gift. For the rest of my life, I shall be a journeyman doctor—Pegasus yoked to the plow!"

"Sig, I have no skills that I cannot teach you."

Freud sat back, out of the candle's light, grateful for the darkness. Never had he bared so much to Josef, or to anyone except Martha, to whom he wrote a letter every day about his most intimate thoughts and feelings.

"But, Sig, don't take it out on medicine. You *are* being cynical. Look at the advancements of just the last twenty years—even in neurology. Think of the paralysis of lead poisoning, or bromide psychosis, or cerebral trichinosis. These were mysteries twenty years ago. Science moves slowly, but in every decade we conquer another disease."

There was a long silence before Breuer continued.

"Let's change the subject. I want to ask you something. You're teaching a lot of medical students now. Have you run across a Russian student by the name of Salomé, Jenia Salomé?"

"Jenia Salomé? I don't think so. Why?"

"His sister came to see me today. A strange meeting." The fiacre passed through the small entranceway of Bäckerstrasse 7 and lurched to a sudden stop, making the carriage sway on its heavy springs for a moment. "Here we are. I'll tell you about it inside."

They dismounted in the imposing sixteenth-century cobblestone courtyard surrounded by high, ivy-draped walls. On each side, above open ground-level arches braced by stately pilasters, rose five tiers of large arched windows, each containing a dozen wood-framed panes. As the two men approached the vestibule portal, the *Portier,* always on duty, peered out through the small glass panel in his apartment door, then rushed to unlock the door, bowing to greet them.

They ascended the stairs, passing Breuer's office on the second story, to the family's spacious third-floor apartment, where Mathilde waited. At thirty-six, she was a striking woman. Her satiny, glowing skin set off a finely chiseled nose, blue-gray eyes, and thick chestnut hair, which she wore coiled in a long braid on the top of her head. In a white blouse and a long gray skirt wrapped tight around her waist, she cut a graceful figure, though she had given birth to her fifth child only a few months before.

Taking Josef's hat, she brushed his hair back with her hand, helped him off with his coat, and handed it to the house servant, Aloisia, whom they had called "Louis" ever since she had entered their service fourteen years before. Then she turned to Freud.

"Sigi, you're drenched and frozen. Into the tub with you! We've already heated the water, and I've laid out some of Josef's fresh linen for you on the shelf. How convenient the two of you are the same size! I can never offer such hospitality to Max." Max, her sister Rachel's husband, was enormous, weighing over two hundred sixty pounds.

"Don't worry about Max," said Breuer. "I make up for it with referrals to him." Turning to Freud, he added, "I sent Max another hypertrophied prostate today. That's four this week. *There's* a field for you!"

"No," Mathilde interjected, taking Freud's arm and leading him toward the bath, "urology is not for Sigi. Cleaning out bladders and water pipes all day! He'd go mad in a week!"

She stopped at the door. "Josef, the children are eating. Look in on them—but just for a minute. I want you to take a nap before dinner. I heard you rustling around all night. You hardly slept."

Without a word, Breuer headed toward his bedroom, then changed his mind and decided instead to help Freud fill the bath. Turning back, Breuer saw Mathilde lean toward Freud and heard her whisper, "You see what I mean, Sigi, he hardly talks to me!"

In the bathroom Breuer attached the nozzles of the petroleum pump to the tubs of hot water Louis and Freud were carrying in from the kitchen. The massive white tub, miraculously supported by dainty brass cat claws, quickly filled. As Breuer left and walked down the hall, he heard Freud's purr of pleasure as he lowered himself into the steaming water.

Lying on his bed, Breuer could not sleep for thinking about Mathilde confiding in Freud so intimately. More and more, Freud seemed like one of the family, now even dining with them several times a week. At first, the bond had been primarily between Breuer and Freud: perhaps Sig took the place of Adolf, his younger brother, who had died several years before. But over the past year Mathilde and Freud had grown close. Their ten years' difference in age allowed Mathilde the privilege of a maternal affection; she often said Freud reminded her of Josef when she had first met him.

So what, Breuer asked himself, if Mathilde does tell Freud of my disaffection? What difference does it really make? Most likely Freud already knows: he registers everything that goes on in the household. He's not an astute medical diagnostician, but he rarely misses anything pertaining to human relationships. And he must also have noticed how starved the children are for a father's love—Robert, Bertha, Margarethe, and Johannes swarming over him with ecstatic shrieks of "Uncle Sigi," and even little Dora smiling, whenever he appears. Without doubt Freud's presence in the household was a good thing; Breuer knew that he himself was too personally distracted to supply the kind of presence his family needed. Yes, Freud filled in for him; and, rather than shame, he, for the most part, felt gratitude to his young friend.

And Breuer knew he could not object to Mathilde's complaining about her marriage. She had grounds for complaint! Almost every evening, he worked until midnight in his laboratory. He spent Sunday mornings in his office preparing his Sunday-afternoon lectures to the medical students. Several nights a week, he stayed at the café until eight or nine, and he now played tarock twice a week, rather than once. Even the midday dinner, which had always been inviolate family time, was being encroached upon. At least once a week, Josef overscheduled himself and worked through most of the dinner break. And, of course, whenever Max came, they locked the door of the study and played chess for hours.

Giving up on the nap, Breuer went into the kitchen to ask about supper. He knew that Freud loved long hot soaks, but was anxious to get through the meal and still have time for work in the laboratory. He knocked on the bathroom door. "Sig, when you're finished, come to the study. Mathilde's agreed to serve us supper there in our shirtsleeves."

Freud quickly dried himself, donned Josef's underwear, left his soiled linen in the hamper to be washed, and hastened to help Breuer and Mathilde load trays for their evening meal. (The Breuers, like most Viennese, had their main meal at midday and ate a modest evening supper of cold leftovers.) The glass-paneled door to the kitchen dripped with mist. Pushing it open, Freud was assailed by the wonderful, warm fragrance of carrot-and-celery barley soup.

Mathilde, ladle in hand, greeted him. "Sigi, it's so cold out I've made some hot soup. It's what you both need."

Freud took the tray from her. "Only two bowls? You're not eating?"

"When Josef says he wants to eat in the study, that usually means he wants to talk to you alone."

"Mathilde," objected Breuer, "I did not say that. Sig will stop coming here if he doesn't get your company at dinner."

"No, I'm tired, and you two have had no time alone this week."

As they went down the long hallway, Freud popped into the children's bedrooms to kiss them good night; he resisted their entreaties for a story by promising to tell them two stories on his next visit. He joined Breuer in the study, a dark-paneled room with a large central window draped in rich maroon velvet. Stuffed in the lower part of the window, between the inner and the outer panes, were several pillows to serve as insulation

Guarding the window was a sturdy dark-walnut desk on which were heaped open books. On the floor was a thick blue-and-ivory-flowered Kashan carpet, and three walls were lined from floor to ceiling with bookcases crammed with books in heavy dark leather bindings. In a far corner of the room, on a Biedermeier card table with thin, tapering black-and-gold spiraled legs, Louis had already set a cold roast chicken, a salad of cabbage, caraway seeds, and sour cream, some *Seltstangerl* (salt and kemmelseed breadsticks), and *Giesshübler* (mineral water). Now Mathilde took the soup bowls from the tray Freud was carrying, placed them on the table, and prepared to leave.

Breuer, conscious of Freud's presence, reached out to touch her arm. "Stay for a while. Sig and I have no secrets from you."

"I've already eaten something with the children. You two can manage without me."

"Mathilde"—Breuer tried for lightness—"you say you don't see me enough. Yet here I am, and you desert me."

But she shook her head. "I'll stop back in a bit with some strudel." Breuer threw a look of entreaty toward Freud, as though to say, "What else can I do?" A moment later, just as Mathilde was closing the door behind her, he noticed her glance significantly toward Freud, as if to say, "You see what has become of our life together?" For the first time, Breuer became aware of the awkward and delicate role in which his young friend had been placed: to be a confidant to both members of a disaffected couple!

As the two men ate in silence, Breuer noticed Freud's eyes scanning the bookshelves.

"Shall I save a shelf for your future books, Sig?"

"How I wish! But not in this decade, Josef. I've no time even to think. The only thing a clinical aspirant at the Vienna General Hospital has ever written is a postcard. No, I was thinking, not of writing, but of *reading* these books. Oh, the endless labor of the intellectual—pouring all this knowledge into the brain through a three-millimeter aperture in the iris."

Breuer smiled. "A wonderful image! Schopenhauer and Spinoza distilled, condensed, and funneled through the pupil, along the optic nerve, and directly into our occipital lobes. I'd love to be able to eat with my eyes—I'm always too tired now for serious reading."

"And your nap?" Freud asked. "What happened to it? I thought you were going to lie down before supper."

"I can't nap anymore. I think I'm too tired to sleep. That same nightmare woke me again in the middle of the night—the one about falling."

"Tell me again, Josef, exactly how did it go?"

"It's the same every time." Breuer downed an entire glass of seltzer, put down his fork, and sat back to allow his food to settle. "And it's very vivid—I must have had it ten times in the last year. First I feel the earth tremble. I am frightened and go outside to search for . . ."

He deliberated a moment, trying to remember how he had described the dream previously. In it he was always searching for Bertha, but there were limits to what he was willing to reveal to Freud. Not only was he embarrassed by his infatuation with Bertha, but he also saw no reason to complicate Freud's relationship with Mathilde by telling him things he would be constrained to keep secret from her.

". . . to search for someone. The ground beneath my feet starts to liquefy, like quicksand. I sink slowly into the earth and fall forty feet— exactly that. Then I come to rest on a large slab. There is writing on the slab. I try to make it out, but I cannot read it."

"Such an enticing dream, Josef. One thing I'm sure of: the key to its meaning is that undecipherable writing on the slab."

"If, indeed, the dream has any meaning at all."

"It *must*, Josef. The same dream, ten times? Surely you wouldn't allow your sleep to be disturbed by something trivial! The other part that interests me is the forty feet. How did you know it was precisely that?"

"I know it—but don't know how I know it."

Freud, who had as usual quickly emptied his plate, quickly swallowed his last mouthful and said, "I'm sure the figure is accurate. After all, *you* designed the dream! You know, Josef, I'm still collecting dreams, and more and more I believe that precise numbers in dreams always have real significance. I have a new example I don't think I've told you about. Last week we had a dinner for Isaac Schönberg, a friend of my father's."

"I know him. It's his son Ignaz, isn't it, who's interested in your fiancée's sister?"

"Yes, that's the one, and he's more than 'interested' in Minna. Well, it was Isaac's sixtieth birthday, and he described a dream he'd had the night before. He was walking down a long dark road and had sixty gold pieces in his pocket. Like you, he was entirely certain of that precise figure. He tried to save his coins, but they kept falling out of a hole in his pocket, and it was too dark to find them. Now, I don't believe it was a coincidence that he dreamed of sixty coins on his sixtieth birthday. I'm certain—how could it be otherwise?—that the sixty coins represent his sixty years."

"And the hole in the pocket?" Breuer asked, picking up a second joint of chicken.

"The dream must be a wish to lose his years and become younger," replied Freud, as he, too, reached for more chicken.

"Or, Sig, maybe the dream expressed a fear—a fear that his years are running out and that he soon will have none left! Remember, he was on a long dark road and trying to recover something he'd lost."

"Yes, I suppose so. Perhaps dreams can express either wishes *or* fears. Or maybe both. But tell me, Josef, when did you first have this dream?"

"Let me see." Breuer recalled that the first time was shortly after he had began to doubt whether his treatment could help Bertha, and in a discussion with Frau Pappenheim had raised the possibility of Bertha's being transferred to the Bellevue Sanatorium in Switzerland. That would have been about the beginning of 1882, nearly a year ago, as he told Freud.

"And wasn't it last January, I came to your fortieth birthday dinner," asked Freud, "along with the entire Altmann family? So, if you've had the dream since then, doesn't it follow that the forty feet signifies forty *years?*"

"Well, in a couple of months, I'll be forty-one. If you're right, shouldn't I fall forty-*one* feet in the dream, beginning next January?"

Freud threw up his arms. "From here on, we need a consultant. I've come to the limits of my dream theory. Will a dream once dreamed change to accommodate changes in the dreamer's life? Fascinating question! Why are years disguised as feet anyhow? Why does the little dream maker residing in our minds go to all that trouble to disguise the truth? My guess is that the dream won't change to forty-one feet. I think the dream maker would be afraid that changing it one foot as you get one year older would be too transparent, would give away the dream code."

"Sig," Breuer chuckled, as he wiped his mouth and mustache with his napkin, "here's where we always part company. When you start talking of another, separate mind, a sentient elf inside of us designing sophisticated dreams and disguising them from our conscious mind—that seems ridiculous."

"I agree, it does seem ridiculous—yet look at the evidence for it, look at all the scientists and mathematicians who have reported solving important problems in dreams! And, Josef, there is no competing explanation.

No matter how ridiculous it seems, there *must* be a separate, unconscious intelligence. I'm sure——"

Mathilde entered with a pitcher of coffee and two pieces of her apple-raisin strudel, covered with a mound of *Schlag*. "What are you so sure of, Sigi?"

"The only thing I'm sure of is that we want you to sit down and stay awhile. Josef was just about to describe a patient he saw today."

"Sigi, I can't. Johannes is crying, and if I don't go in to him now, he'll wake the others."

As she departed, Freud turned to Breuer. "Now Josef, what about your strange meeting with that medical student's sister?"

Breuer hesitated, collecting his thoughts. He wanted to discuss Lou Salomé's proposal with Freud but feared it would lead into too much discussion of his treatment of Bertha.

"Well, her brother told her about my treatment of Bertha Pappenheim. Now she wants me to apply the same treatment to a friend of hers who is emotionally disturbed."

"How did this medical student, this Jenia Salomé, even know about Bertha Pappenheim? You've always been reluctant to talk to *me* about that case, Josef. I know nothing about it, aside from the fact that you used mesmerism."

Breuer wondered whether he detected a trace of jealousy in Freud's voice. "Yes, I haven't talked much about Bertha, Sig. Her family is too well known in the community. And I've especially avoided talking to you ever since I learned that Bertha is such a good friend of your fiancée. But, a few months ago, giving her the pseudonym of Anna O., I briefly described her treatment at a medical student case conference."

Freud leaned eagerly toward him. "I can't tell you how curious I am about the details of your new treatment, Josef. Can't you at least tell me what you told the medical students? You know I can keep professional secrets—even from Martha."

Breuer wavered. How much to tell? Of course, there was a great deal Freud knew already. Certainly, Mathilde had for months made no secret of her annoyance about her husband's spending so much time with Bertha. And Freud had been present in the house on the day Mathilde had finally exploded with anger and forbade Breuer ever again to mention his young patient's name in her presence.

Luckily Freud had not witnessed the final catastrophic scene of his treatment of Bertha! Breuer would never forget going to her house on that awful day when he found her writhing with the labor pains of a delusional pregnancy and proclaiming for all to hear: "Here comes Doctor Breuer's baby!" When Mathilde heard about *that*—such news rapidly making the rounds of Jewish housewives—she demanded that Breuer instantly transfer Bertha's case to another physician.

Had Mathilde reported all this to Freud? Breuer didn't want to ask. Not now. Perhaps later, when things had settled down. Accordingly, he chose his words carefully: "Well, you know, of course, Sig, that Bertha had all the typical symptoms of hysteria—sensory and motor disturbances, muscular contractures, deafness, hallucinations, amnesia, aphonia, phobias—and also unusual manifestations as well. For example, she had some bizarre linguistic disturbances, being unable—sometimes for weeks on end—to speak German, especially in the mornings. We held our conversations in English. Even more bizarre was her dual mental life: one part of her lived in the present; the other part of her responded emotionally to events that had occurred exactly one year before—as we discovered by checking her mother's diary for the preceding year. She also had severe facial neuralgia, which nothing but morphia could control—and, of course, she became addicted."

"And you treated her with mesmerism?" Freud asked.

"That was my original intent. I planned to follow Liebault's method of removing symptoms by hypnotic suggestion. But, thanks to Bertha—she's an extraordinarily creative woman—I discovered an entirely new principle of treatment. In the first few weeks, I visited her daily and invariably found her in such an agitated state that little effective work could be done. But then we learned that she could discharge her agitation by describing to me in detail every annoying event of the day."

Breuer stopped and closed his eyes to collect his thoughts. He knew this was important and wanted to include all the significant facts.

"This process took time. Often Bertha required an hour every morning of what she called 'chimneysweeping' just to clear her mind of dreams and unpleasant fantasies, and then, when I returned in the afternoon, new irritants had built up requiring further chimneysweeping. Only when we had entirely cleared this daily debris from her mind could we turn to the task of alleviating her more enduring symptoms. And at this point, Sig, we stumbled upon an astounding discovery!"

At Breuer's portentous tone, Freud, who had been lighting a cigar, froze and let the match burn his finger in his eagerness to hear Breuer's next words. "Ach, mein Gott!" he exclaimed, shaking out the match and sucking his finger. "Go on, Josef, the astounding discovery was———?"

"Well, we found that when she went back to the very source of a symptom and described it all to me, then that symptom disappeared on its own—*with no need for any hypnotic suggestion*———"

"Source?" asked Freud, now so fascinated that he dropped his cigar into the ashtray and left it there, smoldering and forgotten. "What do you mean, Josef, the *source* of the symptom?"

"The original irritant, the experience that gave rise to it."

"Please!" Freud demanded. "An example!"

"I'll tell you about her hydrophobia. Bertha had been unable or unwilling to drink water for several weeks. She had great thirst, but when she picked up a glass of water, she couldn't bring herself to drink and was forced to quench her thirst with melons and other fruits. Then one day in a trance—she was a self-mesmerizer and automatically entered a trance every session—she recalled how, weeks before, she had entered her nurse's room and witnessed her dog lap water from her drinking glass. No sooner did she describe this memory to me, along with discharging her considerable anger and disgust, than she requested a glass of water and drank it with no difficulty. The symptom never returned."

"Remarkable, remarkable!" Freud exclaimed. "And then?"

"Soon we were approaching every other symptom in this same systematic manner. Several symptoms—for example, her arm paralysis and her visual hallucinations of human skulls and snakes—were rooted in the shock of her father's death. When she described all the details and the emotions of that scene—to stimulate her recall, I even asked her to rearrange the furniture in the same way it was at the time of his death—then all these symptoms dissolved at once."

"It's beautiful!" Freud had risen and was pacing in his excitement. "The theoretical implications are breathtaking. And entirely compatible with Helmholtzian theory! Once the excess cerebral electrical charge responsible for symptoms is discharged through emotional catharsis, then the symptoms behave properly and promptly vanish! But you seem so calm, Josef. This is a *major* discovery. You *must* publish this case."

Breuer sighed deeply. "Perhaps, some day. But now is not the time. There are too many personal complications. I have Mathilde's feelings to consider. Perhaps now that I've described my treatment procedure, you can appreciate how much time I had to invest in Bertha's treatment. Well, Mathilde simply couldn't, or wouldn't, appreciate the scientific importance of the case. As you know, she grew to resent the hours I spent with Bertha—and, in fact, still is so angry she refuses to talk about it with me.

"And also," Breuer continued, "I cannot publish a case that ended so badly, Sig. At Mathilde's insistence, I removed myself from the case and transferred Bertha to Binswanger's sanatorium at Kreuzlingen last July. She is still undergoing treatment there. It's been hard to withdraw her from the morphia, and apparently some of her symptoms, like her inability to speak German, have returned."

"Even so"—Freud took care to avoid the topic of Mathilde's anger—"the case breaks new ground, Josef. It could open up a whole new treatment approach. Will you go over it with me when we have more time? I'd like to hear every detail."

"Gladly, Sig. In my office I have a copy of the summary I sent to Binswanger—about thirty pages. You can start by reading that."

Freud took out his watch. "Ach! It's late, and I still haven't heard the story of this medical student's sister. Her friend—the one she wants you to treat with your new talking cure—she's a hysteric? With symptoms like Bertha's?"

"No, Sig, that's where the story gets interesting. There is no hysteria, and the patient's not a 'she.' The friend is a man, who is, or was, in love with her. He fell into a suicidal love-sickness when she dropped him for another man, a former friend of his! Obviously she feels guilty, and she doesn't want his blood on her conscience."

"But, Josef"—Freud seemed shocked—"love-sickness! This is not a medical case."

"That was my first reaction as well. Exactly what I said to her. But wait until you hear the rest. The story gets better. Her friend, who is, incidentally, an accomplished philosopher and a close personal friend of Richard Wagner, doesn't want help, or at least is too proud to ask for it. She asks me to be a magician. Under the guise of consulting with him about his medical condition, she wants me to sneak in a cure for his psychological distress."

"That's impossible! Surely, Josef, you're not going to attempt this?"

"I'm afraid I have already agreed."

"Why?" Freud picked up his cigar again and leaned forward, frowning in his concern for his friend.

"I'm not sure myself, Sig. Since the Pappenheim case ended, I've felt restless and stagnant. Perhaps I need a distraction, a challenge like this. But there is another reason I took this case! The real reason! This medical student's sister is uncannily persuasive. You cannot say no to her. What a missionary she would make! I think she could convert a horse into a chicken. She is extraordinary, I can't describe to you just how. Perhaps one day you'll meet her. Then you'll see."

Freud rose, stretched, walked over to the window, and opened wide the velvet drapes. Unable to see through the vapor on the glass, he used his handkerchief to wipe a small section dry.

"Still raining, Sig?" Breuer asked. "Shall we fetch Fischmann?"

"No, it's almost stopped. I'll walk. But I have more questions about this new patient. When are you seeing him?"

"I've not heard from him yet. That's another problem. Fräulein Salomé and he are on bad terms now. Indeed, she showed me some of his enraged letters. Still, she assures me that she'll 'arrange' for him to consult me for his medical problems. And I have no doubt that, in this as in all things, she will do exactly what she sets out to do."

"And does the nature of this man's medical problems warrant a medical consultation?"

"Definitely. He is extremely ill and has already stumped two dozen physicians, many with excellent reputations. She described to me a long list of his symptoms—severe headaches, partial blindness, nausea, insomnia, vomiting, severe indigestion, equilibrium problems, weakness."

Seeing Freud shake his head in perplexity, Breuer added, "If you want to be a consultant, you've got to get used to such bewildering clinical pictures. Patients who are polysymptomatic and hop from one physician to another are an everyday part of my practice. You know, Sig, this might be a good teaching case for you. I'll keep you abreast." Breuer reflected for a moment. "In fact, let's have a quick one-minute quiz now. So far, just on the basis of these symptoms, what's your differential diagnosis?"

"I don't know, Josef, they don't fit together."

"Don't be so cautious. Just guess. Think out loud."

Freud flushed. However thirsty he was for knowledge, he hated to display ignorance. "Perhaps multiple sclerosis or an occipital brain tumor. Lead poisoning? I just don't know."

Breuer added, "Don't forget hemicrania. How about delusional hypo-chondriasis?"

"The problem," Freud said, "is that none of these diagnoses explains *all* the symptoms."

"Sig," said Breuer, rising and speaking in a confidential tone, "I'm going to give you a trade secret. One day it'll be your bread and butter as a consultant. I learned it from Oppolzer, who once said to me: 'Dogs can have fleas and lice, too.'"

"Meaning that the patient can——"

"Yes," Breuer said, putting his arm around Freud's shoulders. The two men began to walk down the long hallway. "The patient can have *two* diseases. If fact, those patients who reach a consultant generally do."

"But let's go back to the psychological problem, Josef. Your Fräulein says this man won't acknowledge his psychological distress. If he won't even admit he is suicidal, how will you proceed?"

"That shouldn't pose a problem," Breuer said confidently. "When I take a medical history, I can always find opportunities to glide into the psychological realm. When I inquire about insomnia, for example, I often ask about the type of thoughts that keep the patient awake. Or after the patient has recited the entire litany of his symptoms, I often sympathize and inquire, off-handedly, whether he feels discouraged by his illness, or feels like giving up, or doesn't want to live anymore. That rarely fails to persuade the patient to tell me everything."

At the front door, Breuer helped Freud on with his coat. "No, Sig, that's not the problem. I assure you I'll have no difficulty gaining our philosopher's confidence and getting him to confess everything. The problem is what to do with what I learn."

"Yes, what *will* you do if he's suicidal?"

"If I become convinced that he means to kill himself, I'll have him locked up immediately—either in the lunatic asylum at Brünnlfeld or perhaps in a private sanatorium like Breslauer's at Inzerdorf. But, Sig, that's not going to be the problem. Think about it—if he were truly suicidal, would he bother to consult with me?"

"Yes, of course!" Freud, looking flustered, tapped himself on the side of his head for his slowness of wit.

Breuer continued, "No, the real problem will be what to do with him if he is *not* suicidal, if he is simply suffering greatly."

"Yes," Freud said, "what then?"

"In that case, I'll have to persuade him to see a priest. Or perhaps to take a long cure at Marienbad. Or invent a way to treat him myself!"

"Invent a way to treat him? What do you mean, Josef? What kind of way?"

"Later, Sig. We shall talk later. Now, off with you! Don't stay in this heated room with that heavy coat on."

As Freud stepped out the door, he turned his head. "What did you say this philosopher's name is? Anyone I've heard of?"

Breuer hesitated. Remembering Lou Salomé's injunction for secrecy, on the spur of the moment he made up for Friedrich Nietzsche a name according to the code whereby he had devised Anna O. to represent Bertha Pappenheim. "No, he's an unknown. The name is Müller, Eckart Müller."

CHAPTER 4

Two weeks later, Breuer sat in his office, wearing his white consultation coat, and reading a letter from Lou Salomé:

23 November 1882

My dear Dr. Breuer,

Our plan is working. Professor Overbeck fully agrees with our view that the situation is indeed very dangerous. Never has he seen Nietzsche in worse condition. He will exert all possible influence to persuade him to consult with you. Neither I nor Nietzsche shall ever forget your kindness in this, the time of our need.

Lou Salomé

"*Our* plan, *our* view, *our* need. Our, our, our." Breuer put down the letter—having read it for perhaps the tenth time since its arrival a week ago—and picked up the mirror on his desk to watch himself say "our." He saw a thin pink sliver of lip encircling a small black hole in the midst of auburn bristles. He opened the hole wider and watched elastic lips stretch around yellowing teeth that stuck out of his gums like half-buried tombstones. Hair and hole, horn and teeth—hedgehog, walrus, ape, Josef Breuer.

He hated the sight of his beard. More often these days, clean-shaven men were to be seen on the street; when would *he* find the courage to shave off the whole hairy mess? He hated also the outcropping of gray that had insidiously appeared in his mustache, on the left side of his chin, and in his sideburns. These gray bristles were, he knew, the advance scouts of a relentless, wintry invasion. And there would be no stopping the march of the hours, the days, the years.

Breuer hated all the mirror reflected—not only the gray tide and the animalistic teeth and hair, but the hooked nose straining toward his chin, the absurdly large ears, and the massive naked forehead—the balding had begun there and had, without pity, cropped its way back, displaying the shame of his bare skull.

And the eyes! Breuer softened and looked into his eyes; he could always find youth there. He winked. He often winked and beckoned at himself—at his real self, at the sixteen-year-old Josef dwelling in those eyes. But no greeting today from young Josef! Instead, his father's eyes peered at him—old, tired eyes surrounded by wrinkled, reddened eyelids. Breuer watched with fascination as his father's mouth formed a hole to say, "Our, our, our." More and more often, Breuer thought about his father. Leopold Breuer had been dead for ten years. He had died at the age of eighty-two, forty-two years older than Josef was now.

He put down the mirror. Forty-two years left! How could he endure forty-two more years? Forty-two years of waiting for the years to pass. Forty-two years of staring into his aging eyes. Was there no escape from the prison of time? Ah, to be able to begin again! But how? Where? With whom? Not with Lou Salomé. She was free, and she might flutter, when she so chose, in and out of his prison. But it would never be "our" with her—never "our" life, "our" new life.

Nor, he knew, would it ever again be "our" with Bertha. Whenever he could escape the old, circular remembrances about Bertha—the almond fragrance of her skin, the mighty swell of her breasts under her gown, the heat of her body as she leaned against him when entering a trance—whenever he succeeded in stepping back and gaining perspective on himself, he realized that, all along, Bertha had been a fantasy.

Poor, unformed, mad Bertha—what a foolish dream it was to think I could complete her, form her, so that she, in turn, could give me . . . what? That was the question. What was I searching for from her? What did I lack? Did I not have the good life? To whom can I complain that my life has led irrevocably into an ever-narrowing chute? Who can comprehend my torment, my sleepless nights, my flirtation with suicide? After all, haven't I everything one could wish: money, friends, family, a beautiful and charming wife, renown, respectability? Who will comfort me? Who refrain from asking the obvious question: "What more can you want?"

Frau Becker's voice, announcing the arrival of Friedrich Nietzsche, startled Breuer, even though he had been expecting it.

Stout, short, gray-haired, vigorous, and bespectacled, Frau Becker ran Breuer's consulting office with astonishing precision. In fact, she filled her role so consummately that there were no visible leftovers of the private Frau Becker. In the six months since he had hired her, they had not exchanged a personal word. Though he tried, he could not remember her first name or imagine her doing anything but nursely duties. Frau Becker on a picnic? Reading the morning *Neue Freie Presse*? In the bathtub? Pudgy Frau Becker naked? Mounted? Breathing hard in passion? Inconceivable!

Still, despite his dismissal of her as a woman, Frau Becker was an astute observer, and Breuer had come to value her initial impressions.

"How does this Professor Nietzsche strike you?"

"Herr Doctor, he has a gentleman's bearing but not a gentleman's grooming. He seems shy. Almost humble. And a gentle manner, very different from many of the gentlefolk who come here—for example, that Russian grand lady, two weeks ago."

Breuer had himself noted a gentleness to Professor Nietzsche's letter requesting a consultation, at Dr. Breuer's convenience, within the next two weeks, if at all possible. Nietzsche would, he explained in his letter, journey to Vienna expressly for the purpose of a consultation. Until he received word, he would remain in Basel with his friend, Professor Overbeck. Breuer smiled to himself when he contrasted Nietzsche's letter with Lou Salomé's dispatches ordering him to be available at her convenience.

As he waited for Frau Becker to bring Nietzsche in, Breuer scanned his desk and suddenly noted with alarm the two books given him by Lou Salomé. During a free half-hour yesterday, he had skimmed them and left them carelessly in plain view. He realized that if Nietzsche were to see them, the treatment would end before it began, as it would be all but impossible to explain them without mentioning Lou Salomé. How uncommonly careless of me, Breuer thought. Am I trying to sabotage this enterprise?

Quickly slipping the books into a desk drawer, he rose to greet Nietzsche. The professor was not at all what he had expected from Lou's description. His demeanor was gentle, and while of solid physique—about five-foot eight or nine, and one hundred and fifty or sixty pounds—there was something curiously insubstantial about his body, as though you could pass your hand through it. He was dressed in a heavy, almost military-weight, black suit. Under his jacket he wore a heavy brown peasant sweater which almost entirely covered his shirt and his mauve cravat.

As they shook hands, Breuer noted Nietzsche's cold skin and limp clasp.

"Good day, Herr Professor—but not such a good one for travelers, I should imagine."

"No, Doctor Breuer, not good for traveling. Nor for the condition that brings me to you. I have learned to avoid such weather. It is only your excellent reputation that lures me this far north in winter."

Before sitting down in the chair to which Breuer directed him, Nietzsche fussily put a bulging, scuffed briefcase first on one side of the chair and then on the other, apparently seeking some suitable resting place for it.

Breuer sat quietly and continued to inspect his patient as the latter made himself comfortable. Despite Nietzsche's unassuming appearance, he conveyed a strong presence. It was the powerful head that commanded attention. Especially his eyes, soft brown, but extraordinarily intense and deeply set beneath a prominent orbital ridge. What had Lou Salomé said about his eyes? That they seemed to stare inward, as though at some hidden treasure? Yes, Breuer could see that. His patient's brown, gleaming hair was carefully brushed. Aside from a long mustache, which fell like an avalanche over his lips and on either side of his mouth, down to his chin, he was clean-shaven. The mustache evoked in Breuer a sense of hairy kinship: he had a quixotic impulse to warn the professor not to eat a Viennese pastry in public, especially one heaped high with *Schlag*, or he would be combing it out of his mustache long afterward.

Nietzsche's soft voice was surprising: the voice in his two books had been forceful, bold and authoritative, almost strident. Again and again, Breuer was to encounter this same discrepancy between the Nietzsche of flesh and blood and the Nietzsche of pen and paper.

Aside from his brief talk with Freud, Breuer had given little thought to this unusual consultation. Now, for the first time, he seriously questioned the wisdom of being involved in this matter. Lou Salomé, the bewitcher, the major conspirator, was long gone, and in her place sat this unsuspecting, duped Professor Nietzsche. Two men maneuvered into meeting under false pretenses by a woman who was now, no doubt, off to some new intrigue. No, he had little heart for this venture.

Still, it's time to put all that behind me, Breuer thought. A man who has threatened to take his own life is now my patient, and I must give him my total attention.

"How was your journey, Professor Nietzsche? I understand you've just come from Basel?"

"That was but my last stop," Nietzsche said, sitting stiffly. "My whole life has become a journey, and I begin to feel that my only home, the only familiar place to which I always return, is my illness."

Not a man for small talk, Breuer reflected. "Then, Professor Nietzsche, let us proceed immediately to investigate your illness."

"Would it be more efficient for you first to peruse these documents?" And Nietzsche drew from his briefcase a heavy folder crammed with papers. "I have been ill perhaps all my life, but most severely so for the last decade. Here are the full reports of my previous consultations. May I?"

Breuer nodded, and Nietzsche opened the folder, reached across the desk, and placed the contents—letters, hospital charts, and laboratory reports—in front of Breuer.

Breuer scanned the first page, containing a list of twenty-four physicians and the dates of each consultation. He recognized several prominent Swiss, German, and Italian names.

"Some of these names are known to me. Excellent physicians all! Here I see three—Kessler, Turin, and Koenig—whom I know well. They trained in Vienna. As you imply, Professor Nietzsche, it would be unwise to ignore the observations and conclusions of these excellent men—yet there is great *disadvantage* in my beginning with them. Too much authority, too many prestigious opinions and conclusions oppress one's own imaginative synthetic powers. For much the same reason, I prefer to read a play before seeing it performed and certainly before reading reviews. Have you not found that to be the case in your own work?"

Nietzsche seemed startled. Good, thought Breuer. Professor Nietzsche must see that I am a different kind of physician. He is not accustomed to physicians who converse about psychological constructs or inquire, knowledgeably, about his work.

"Yes," Nietzsche replied, "it is an important consideration in my work. My original field is philology. My first appointment, my *only* appointment, was that of professor of philology at Basel. I have an especially strong interest in the pre-Socratic philosophers, and with them I have always found it crucial to return to the original text. Interpreters of texts are *always* dishonest—not intentionally, of course—but they cannot step outside their own historical frame. Nor, for that matter, out of their autobiographical frame."

"But does not an unwillingness to pay homage to interpreters make one unpopular in the academic philosophical community?" Breuer felt confident. This consultation was on course. He was well embarked on the process of successfully persuading Nietzsche that he, his new physician, was a kindred spirit with kindred interests. It was not going to be difficult to seduce this Professor Nietzsche—and Breuer viewed it as seduction indeed, as enticing his patient into a relationship he had not sought in order to obtain help he had not requested.

"Unpopular? Without question! I had to resign my professorship three years ago because of illness—the very illness, yet undiagnosed, that brings me to you today. But even were I perfectly healthy I believe my distrust of interpreters would have ultimately made me an unwelcome guest at the academic table."

"But, Professor Nietzsche, if all interpreters are limited by their autobiographical frame, how do you escape the same limitation in your own work?"

"First," Nietzsche responded, "one must identify the limitation. Next, one must learn to see oneself from afar—although sometimes, alas, the severity of my illness impairs my perspective."

It did not escape Breuer that it was Nietzsche, not he, who was keeping their discussion focused on his illness, which was, after all, the *raison d'être* of their meeting. Was there perhaps a subtle rebuke in Nietzsche's words? "Don't try too hard, Josef," he reminded himself. "A patient's confidence in a physician should not be explicitly pursued; it will ensue naturally from a competent consultation." While often self-critical in many areas of his life, Breuer had supreme confidence in himself as a physician. "Do not pander, patronize, scheme, or strategize," his instincts told him. "Simply go about your business in your usual professional manner."

"But let us return to our task, Professor Nietzsche. What I have been meaning to say is that I should prefer to take a medical history and conduct an examination *before* I examine your records. Then, at our next meeting, I shall try to provide you with as comprehensive a synthesis as possible."

Breuer placed a blank pad of paper on the desk before him. "Your letter told me a few things about your condition: that you have had headaches and visual symptoms for at least ten years; that you are rarely free of your illness; that, as you put it, your illness always awaits you. And now today you inform me that at least twenty-four physicians have failed to be of help. That is all I know about you. So, shall we begin? First, please tell me in your own words everything about your illness."

CHAPTER 5

FOR NINETY MINUTES, the two men talked. Breuer, sitting in his high-backed leather chair, was taking rapid notes. Nietzsche, who occasionally paused to allow Breuer's pen to keep pace, sat in a chair of the same leather, equally comfortable but smaller than Breuer's. Like most physicians of the day, Breuer preferred to have his patients look up to him from below.

Breuer's clinical evaluation was thorough and methodical. After first listening carefully to the patient's free-form description of the illness, he next systematically investigated each symptom—its first appearance, its transformation over time, its response to therapeutic efforts. His third step was to check every organ system in the body. Starting from the top of the head, Breuer worked his way down to the feet. First the brain and nervous system. He began by inquiring about the functioning of each of the twelve cranial nerves—the sense of smell, vision, eye movements, hearing, facial and tongue movement and sensation, swallowing, balance, speech.

Descending the body, Breuer reviewed, one by one, every other functional system: respiratory, cardiovascular, gastrointestinal, and genital-urinary. This painstaking organ review jostled the patient's memory and ensured that nothing was overlooked: Breuer never omitted any part of it, even if he was certain beforehand of the diagnosis.

Next, a careful medical history: the patient's childhood health, his parents' and siblings' health, and an investigation of all other aspects of his life—occupational choice, social life, military service, geographic moves, dietary and recreational preferences. Breuer's final step was to allow his intuition full rein and to make all other inquiries that his data thus far suggested. Thus, the other day, in a puzzling case of respiratory distress, he had made a correct diagnosis of diaphragmatic trichinosis by inquiring into the thoroughness with which the patient cooked her smoked salt pork.

Throughout this procedure, Nietzsche remained deeply attentive: indeed, he nodded appreciatively at each of Breuer's questions. No surprise, of course, to Breuer. He had never encountered a patient who did not secretly enjoy a microscopic examination of his life. And the greater the power of magnification, the more the patient enjoyed it. The joy of being observed ran so deep that Breuer believed the real pain of old age, bereavement, outliving one's friends, was the absence of scrutiny—the horror of living an unobserved life.

Breuer *was* surprised, however, at the complexity of Nietzsche's ailments and at the thoroughness of his patient's own observations. Breuer's notes filled page after page. His hand began to weary as Nietzsche described a gruesome assemblage of symptoms: monstrous, crippling headaches; seasickness on dry land—vertigo, disequilibrium, nausea, vomiting, anorexia, disgust for food; fevers, heavy night sweats which necessitated two or three nightly changes of nightshirt and linen; crushing bouts of fatigue which at times approximated generalized muscular paralysis; gastric pain; hematemesis; intestinal cramps; severe constipation; hemorrhoids; and disabling visual problems—eye fatigue, inexorable fading of vision, frequent watering and pain in his eyes, visual blurring, and great sensitivity to light, especially in the mornings.

Breuer's questions added a few more symptoms Nietzsche had either neglected or been reluctant to mention: visual scintillations and scotomata, which often preceded a headache; intractable insomnia; severe nocturnal muscle cramps; generalized tension; and rapid, inexplicable mood shifts.

Mood shifts! The words Breuer had been waiting for! As he had described to Freud, he always sniffed for a propitious point of entry into a patient's psychological state. These "mood shifts" might be just the key that would lead to Nietzsche's despair and suicide intention!

Breuer proceeded gingerly, asking him to elaborate on his mood shifts. "Have you noticed alterations in your feelings which seem related to your illness?"

Nietzsche's demeanor did not change. He seemed unconcerned that this question might lead into a more intimate realm. "There have been times when, on the day before an attack, I have felt particularly good—I have come to think of it as feeling *dangerously good.*"

"And after the attack?"

"My typical attack lasts from twelve hours to two days. After such an attack, I generally feel fatigued and leaden. Even my thoughts are sluggish for a day or two. But sometimes, especially after a longer attack of several days, it is different. I feel refreshed, cleansed. I explode with energy. I cherish these times—my mind swarms with the rarest of ideas."

Breuer persisted. Once he found the trail, he did not easily give up the chase. "Your fatigue and the leaden feeling—how long do they last?"

"Not long. Once the attack lessens and my body belongs to itself again, I assume control. Then I will myself to overcome the heaviness."

Perhaps, Breuer reflected, this might be more difficult than he first thought. He would have to be more direct. Nietzsche, it was clear, was not going to volunteer any information about despair.

"And melancholia? To what extent does it accompany or succeed your attacks?"

"I have black periods. Who has not? But they do not have *me*. They are not of my illness, but of my being. One might say I have the courage to have them."

Breuer noted Nietzsche's slight smile and his bold tone. Now, for the first time, Breuer recognized the voice of the man who had written those two audacious, enigmatic books concealed in his desk drawer. He considered, but only for a moment, a direct challenge to Nietzsche's ex-cathedra distinction between the realms of illness and being. And that statement about having the courage to have black periods, what did he *mean* by that? But patience! Best to maintain control of the consultation. There would be other openings.

Carefully, he continued. "Have you ever kept a detailed diary of your attacks—their frequency, their intensity, their duration?"

"Not this year. I've been too preoccupied with momentous events and changes in my life. But last year I had one hundred and seventeen days of absolute incapacitation and almost two hundred days in which I was partially incapacitated—with milder headaches, eye pain, stomach pain, or nausea."

Here were two promising openings—but which to follow? Should he inquire about the nature of those "momentous events and changes"—

surely Nietzsche was referring to Lou Salomé—or strengthen the doctor-patient rapport by being empathic? Knowing that it was impossible to have *too* much rapport, Breuer chose the latter.

"Let's see, that leaves only forty-eight days without illness. That is very little 'well' time, Professor Nietzsche."

"Thinking back over several years, rarely have I had times of well-being that have persisted for over two weeks. I think I can remember each one of them!"

Hearing a wistful, forlorn tone in Nietzsche's voice, Breuer decided to gamble. Here was an opening that could lead directly into his patient's despair. He put down his pen and, in his most earnest and professionally concerned voice, remarked, "Such a situation—the majority of one's days a torment, a handful of healthy days a year, one's life consumed by pain—seems a natural breeding place for despair, for pessimism about the point of living."

Nietzsche stopped. For once he did not have a ready answer. His head swayed from side to side as if he were pondering whether to permit himself to be consoled. But his words said something else.

"Undoubtedly that is true, Doctor Breuer, for some people, perhaps for most—here I must defer to your experience—but it is *not* true for me. Despair? No, perhaps once true, but not now. My illness belongs to the domain of my body, but it is not *me*. I am my illness and my body, but they are not me. Both must be overcome, if not physically, then metaphysically.

"As for your other comment, my 'point of living' is something entirely divorced from this"—here he thumped his abdomen—"sorry protoplasm. I have a *why* of living and can put up with any *how*. I have a ten-year point of living, a mission. I am pregnant, here"—he tapped his temple—"with books, books almost fully formed, books only I can deliver. Sometimes I think of my headaches as cerebral labor pains."

Nietzsche apparently had no intention of discussing or even acknowl-edging despair; and it would be futile, Breuer realized, to attempt to snare him. He suddenly recalled feeling being outmaneuvered when-ever he played chess with his father, the best player in the Jewish Viennese community.

But perhaps there was nothing to acknowledge! Perhaps Fräulein Salomé was wrong. Nietzsche sounded as though his spirit had overcome this monstrous illness. As for suicide, Breuer had an absolutely infallible test for the risk of suicide. Does the patient project himself into the future? Nietzsche had passed that test! He was *not* suicidal: he spoke of a ten-year mission, of books he had yet to extract from his mind.

Yet with his own eyes, Breuer had seen Nietzsche's suicidal letters. Was he dissimulating? Or was it that he did not now feel despair because he had *already decided upon suicide*? Breuer had known patients like that before. They were dangerous. They appear improved—in a sense, *are* improved; their melancholia lightens; they smile, eat, sleep once more. But their improvement means they have discovered an escape from their despair— the escape of death. Was that Nietzsche's plan? Had he decided to kill himself? No, Breuer remembered what he had told Freud: If Nietzsche intended suicide, why was he here? Why take the trouble to visit yet another physician, to journey from Rapallo to Basel, and thence to Vienna?

Despite his frustration at not obtaining the information he sought, Breuer could not fault his patient's cooperation. Nietzsche responded fully to each medical question—if anything, *too* fully. Many headache sufferers report sensitivity to diet and weather, so Breuer was not surprised to learn that this was true for Nietzsche as well. But he was astonished by the exquisite detail of his patient's report. Without pausing, Nietzsche spoke for twenty minutes about his response to atmospheric conditions. His body, he said, was like an aneroid barometer–thermometer reacting violently to every oscillation of atmospheric pressure, temperature, or altitude. Gray skies depressed him, leaden clouds or rain enervated him, drought invigorated him, winter represented a form of mental "lockjaw," the sun opened him up again. For years his life had consisted of a search for the perfect climate. Summers were endurable. The cloudless, windless, sunny plateau of the Engadine suited him; and for four months every year, he resided in a small *Gasthaus* in the little Swiss village of Sils Maria. But winters were a curse. He had never found a friendly wintering spot; and during the cold months, he lived in southern Italy, moving from city to city in search of salubrious climate. Vienna's wind and wet gloom poisoned him, Nietzsche said. His nervous system cried out for sun and dry, still air.

When Breuer asked about diet, Nietzsche delivered another lengthy discourse on the relationship between diet, gastric distress, and headache attacks. What remarkable precision! Never before had Breuer encountered a patient who answered every question so comprehensively. What did it mean?

Was Nietzsche an obsessional hypochondriac? Breuer had seen many boring, self-pitying hypochondriacs who relished describing their innards. But these patients had a *"Weltanschauung* stenosis," a narrowing of world view. And how tedious it was to be in their presence! They had no thoughts but those of corpus, no interests or values but those of health.

No, Nietzsche was not one of these. His range of interest was extensive, his persona engaging. Certainly Fräulein Salomé had found him so, *still* found him so, even if she found Paul Rée more romantically congenial. Furthermore, Nietzsche did not describe his symptoms to elicit sympathy or even support—this Breuer had learned early in their interview.

So why this exquisite detail about his bodily functions? Perhaps it was simply that Nietzsche had a good mind, with perfect retention, and approached a medical evaluation in a fundamentally rational manner, providing comprehensive data to an expert consultant. Or, he was uncommonly introspective. Before the end of his evaluation, Breuer obtained still another answer: Nietzsche had so little contact with other human beings that he spent an extraordinary amount of time in conversation with his own nervous system.

His history taking complete, Breuer proceeded to the physical examination. He accompanied his patient to his examining office, a small, sterile room containing only a dressing screen and chair, an examining table covered with a starched white sheet, a sink, a scale, and a steel cabinet containing Breuer's instruments. A few minutes after leaving Nietzsche to strip and change, Breuer returned to find him, though already wearing the open-backed dressing gown, still in his high black socks and garters and carefully folding his clothes. He apologized for the delay, saying, "My nomadic life dictates that I can have only a single suit. Hence, I make certain it's comfortable whenever I put it to rest."

Breuer's physical exam was as methodical as his medical history. Beginning with the head, he slowly worked his way down the body, listening, tapping, touching, smelling, feeling, looking. Despite his patient's abundance of symptoms, Breuer found no physical abnormalities aside from a large scar over the sternum—a result of a riding accident while in the military; a minute oblique dueling scar on the bridge of the nose; and some signs of anemia: pale lips, conjunctiva, and creases of the palm.

The cause of the anemia? Probably nutritional. Nietzsche had said that he often avoided meat for weeks at a time. But later Breuer remembered that Nietzsche had said he occasionally vomited blood, and thus might be losing blood from gastric bleeding. He drew some blood for a red-cell count and, after a rectal examination, collected a stool specimen from his glove which he would later examine for occult blood.

What of Nietzsche's visual complaints? First, Breuer noted a unilateral conjunctivitis which could be easily managed with eye salve. Despite considerable effort, Breuer was unable to focus his ophthalmoscope on Nietzsche's retina: something was obstructing the view, probably a corneal opacity, perhaps an edema of the cornea.

Breuer particularly focused on Nietzsche's nervous system, not only because of the nature of the headaches but also because his father had died, when he was four, of "softening of the brain"—a generic term which might refer to any of a number of abnormalities, including stroke, tumor, or some form of inherited cerebral degeneration. But after testing every aspect of brain and nerve function—balance, coordination, sensation, strength, proprioception, hearing, smell, swallowing—Breuer found no evidence whatsoever of structural nervous system disease.

While Nietzsche dressed, Breuer returned to his office to chart the results of his examination. When, a few minutes later, Frau Becker brought Nietzsche back into the office, Breuer realized that, though their time was drawing to a close, he had failed utterly to elicit any mention of melancholia or suicide. He tried another approach, an interview device that rarely failed to yield results.

"Professor Nietzsche, I would like you to describe, in detail, a typical day of your life."

"Now you have me, Doctor Breuer! That's the most difficult question you have posed. I move so much, my surroundings are inconstant. My attacks dictate my life——"

"Choose any ordinary day, a day between attacks in the past few weeks."

"Well, I awaken early—if, indeed, I have slept at all——"

Breuer felt encouraged. Already he had an opening. "Allow me to interrupt, Professor Nietzsche. You say *if* you have slept?"

"My sleep is dreadful. Sometimes it is muscle cramps, sometimes stomach pain, sometimes a tension that invades every part of my body, sometimes my thoughts—usually malignant, nocturnal thoughts; sometimes I lie awake all night, sometimes drugs give me two or three hours' sleep."

"Which drugs? How much of each?" Breuer asked quickly. Though it was imperative that he learn about Nietzsche's self-medication, he realized immediately that he had not chosen the best option. Better, much better, to have inquired about those dark nocturnal thoughts!

"Chloral hydrate, almost every night, at least one gram. Sometimes, if my body is desperate for sleep, I add morphia or Veronal, but then I am in stupor the next day. Occasionally hashish, but it also blunts my thinking the following day. I prefer chloral. Shall I continue with this day, which has already dawned badly?"

"Please."

"I take some breakfast in my room—you want this much detail?"

"Yes, exactly. Tell me everything."

"Well, breakfast is a simple affair. The *Gasthaus* owner brings me some hot water. That's all. Occasionally, if I feel particularly well, I ask for weak tea and dry bread. Then I bathe in cold water—necessary if I am to work with any vigor—and spend the rest of the day at work—writing, thinking, and occasionally, if my eyes permit, a little reading. If I feel well, I will walk, sometimes for hours. I scribble as I walk and often do my best work, have my finest thoughts, while walking——"

"Yes, I too," Breuer rushed to add. "After four or five miles, I find I have clarified the most puzzling problems."

Nietzsche paused, apparently thrown off balance by Breuer's personal comment. He started to acknowledge it, stuttered, and, in the end, ignored it and continued his account. "I dine always at the same table at my hotel. I've described my diet to you—always unspiced food, preferably boiled, no alcohol, no coffee. Often for weeks I can tolerate only boiled unsalted vegetables. No tobacco, either. I speak a few words to other guests at my table but rarely engage in prolonged conversation. If I am particularly fortunate, I encounter a thoughtful guest who will offer to read to me or take dictation. My funds are limited, and I am unable to pay for such services. The afternoon is the same as the morning—walking, thinking, scribbling. In the evening I take supper in my room—again, hot water or weak tea and biscuits—and then I work until the chloral says, 'Halt, you may rest.' Such is my corporeal life."

"You speak only of hotels? And your home?"

"My home is my steamer trunk. I am a tortoise and carry my home on my back. I place it in the corner of my hotel room, and when the weather becomes oppressive, I hoist it and move to higher, drier skies."

Breuer had planned to return to Nietzsche's "malignant nocturnal thoughts" but now saw an even more promising line of inquiry—one that could not fail to lead directly to Fräulein Salomé.

"Professor Nietzsche, I am aware that your description of your typical day contains little mention of other people! Pardon my inquiry—I know these are not typical medical questions, but I adhere to a belief in organismic totality. I believe that physical well-being is not separable from social and psychological well-being."

Nietzsche flushed. He took out a small tortoiseshell mustache comb and for a short time slouched in silence, nervously grooming his ponderous mustache. Then, apparently having reached a decision, he sat up, cleared his throat, and spoke firmly: "You are not the first physician who has made this observation. I assume you are referring to sex. Doctor Lanzoni, an Italian consultant whom I saw several years ago, suggested that my condition was aggravated by isolation and abstinence and recommended that I acquire a regular sexual outlet. I followed his advice and worked out an arrangement with a young peasant woman in a village near Rapallo. But at the end of three weeks I was almost moribund with head pain—a little more of such Italian treatment, and the patient would have expired!"

"Why was it such noxious advice?"

"A flash of bestial pleasure followed by hours of self-loathing, of cleansing myself of the protoplasmic stink of rutting, is not, in my view, the route to—how did you put it?—'organismic totality.' "

"Nor in my view either," Breuer quickly agreed. "Yet can you deny that all of us are embedded in a social context, a context that historically has facilitated survival and provided the pleasure inherent in human connectedness?"

"Perhaps such herd pleasures are not for everyone," Nietzsche said, shaking his head. "Thrice have I reached out and attempted to build a footbridge to others. And thrice I have been betrayed."

At last! Breuer could scarcely conceal his excitement. Certainly one of Nietzsche's three betrayals was Lou Salomé. Perhaps Paul Rée was another. Who was the third? Finally, finally, Nietzsche had opened the door. Without doubt, the path was now clear for a discussion of betrayal, and the despair betrayal induced.

Breuer mustered his most empathic tone of voice. "Three attempts, three terrible betrayals—and since then a retreat into painful isolation. You have suffered, and perhaps, in some manner, this suffering bears upon your illness. Would you be willing to trust me with the details of these betrayals?"

Again, Nietzsche shook his head. He appeared to retreat into himself. "Doctor Breuer, I have trusted you with a great a deal of myself. Today

I have shared more of the intimate details of my life than I have done with anyone in a very long time. But trust *me* when I say my illness has long antedated these personal disappointments. Remember my family history: my father died of brain disease—perhaps a familial disease. Remember that headaches and ill health have plagued me since my schooldays, long before these betrayals. It is also true that my illness was never ameliorated by the brief intimate friendships I have enjoyed. No, it is not that I have trusted too little: my mistake was to trust too much. I am not prepared to, cannot *afford* to, trust again."

Breuer was stunned. How could he have miscalculated? Only a moment ago, Nietzsche had seemed willing, almost eager, to confide in him. And now to be so rebuffed! What had happened? He tried to recall the sequence of events. Nietzsche had mentioned trying to build a footbridge to another and then having been betrayed. At that point Breuer had sympathetically reached out to him and then—and then—*footbridge*—the term struck some chord. Nietzsche's books! Yes, almost certainly there was a vivid passage involving a footbridge. Perhaps the key to obtaining Nietzsche's confidence lay in those books. Breuer also vaguely recalled another passage that argued for the importance of psychological self-scrutiny. He resolved to read the two books more carefully before their next meeting: perhaps he might be able to influence Nietzsche with his own arguments.

Yet what could he really do with any argument he found in Nietzsche's books? How even explain how he happened to have them? None of the three Viennese bookstores where he had inquired for his books had even heard of the author. Breuer hated duplicity and, for a moment, considered telling Nietzsche everything: Lou Salomé's visit to him, his knowledge of Nietzsche's desperation, his promise to Fräulein Salomé, her gift of his books.

No, that could lead only to failure: without doubt Nietzsche would feel manipulated and betrayed. Breuer was certain that Nietzsche was in despair because of his entanglement in—to use Nietzsche's fine term—a *Pythagorean* relationship with Lou and Paul Rée. And if Nietzsche were to learn of Lou Salomé's visit, he would undoubtedly view her and Breuer as two sides of another triangle. No, Breuer was convinced that honesty and sincerity, his natural solution to life's dilemmas, would in this case make matters far worse. Somehow he would have to find a way to obtain the books *legitimately*.

It was late. The wet gray day was turning into darkness. In the silence,

Nietzsche stirred uneasily. Breuer was tired. His prey had eluded him, and he had run out of ideas. He decided to temporize.

"I believe, Professor Nietzsche, that we can proceed no further today. I need time to study your past medical records and to perform the necessary laboratory tests."

Nietzsche sighed softly. Did he look disappointed? Did he want their meeting to continue longer? Breuer thought so but, no longer trusting his judgment regarding Nietzsche's reactions, suggested further consultation later in the week. "Friday afternoon? Same time?"

"Yes, of course. I am entirely at your disposal, Doctor Breuer. I have no other reason to be in Vienna."

The consultation over, Breuer arose. But Nietzsche hesitated and then abruptly sat back in his chair.

"Doctor Breuer, I've taken much of your time. Please do not make the mistake of underestimating my appreciation for your efforts—but indulge me for a moment more. Allow me, in my own behalf, to ask you three questions!"

CHAPTER 6

"ASK YOUR QUESTIONS, please, Professor Nietzsche," said Breuer, settling back in his chair. "Considering the barrage of questions I have directed at you, three is a modest request. If your questions lie within my realm of knowledge, I shall not fail to answer you."

He was tired. It had been a long day, and ahead of him were still a six o'clock teaching conference and his evening calls. But even so, he did not mind Nietzsche's request. On the contrary, he felt unaccountably exhilarated. Perhaps the opening he had sought was at hand.

"When you hear my questions, you may, like many of your colleagues, regret that promise. I have a trinity of questions, three questions, but perhaps only one. And that one question—a plea as well as a question—is: Will you tell me the truth?"

"And the three questions?" Breuer asked.

"The first is: Will I go blind? The second: Will I have these attacks forever? And finally, the most difficult question: Do I have a progressive brain disease which will kill me young like my father, drive me into paralysis or, worse, into madness or dementia?"

Breuer was speechless. He sat in silence, aimlessly leafing through the pages of Nietzsche's medical dossier. No patient, in fifteen years of medical practice, had ever posed such brutally direct questions.

Nietzsche, noting his discomfiture, continued, "Forgive me for confronting you so. But I have had many years of indirect discourse with physicians, especially German physicians who anoint themselves as sextons of the truth, yet withhold their knowledge. No physician has the right to withhold from the patient what is rightfully his."

Breuer couldn't help smiling at Nietzsche's characterization of German physicians. Or bristling at the pronouncement about the rights of the patient. This little philosopher with the large mustache stimulated his mind.

"I am most willing to discuss these issues of medical practice, Professor Nietzsche. You ask forthright questions. I shall attempt to respond with equal directness. I agree with your position about the rights of the patient. But you have omitted an equally important concept: *the obligations of the patient.* I prefer a completely honest relationship with my patients. But it must be a reciprocal honesty: the patient, too, must be committed to honesty with me. Honesty—honest questions, honest answers—makes for the best medicine. Under this condition, then, you have my word: I shall share with you all my knowledge and my conclusions.

"But, Professor Nietzsche," Breuer went on, "I do *not* agree that it should *always* be thus. There are patients and there are situations when the good physician *must,* for the sake of the patient, withhold the truth."

"Yes, Doctor Breuer, I've heard many physicians say that. But who has the right to make that decision for another? That posture can only violate the patient's autonomy."

"It is my duty," Breuer replied, "to offer comfort to patients. And it is not a duty to be taken lightly. Sometimes it's a thankless duty: sometimes there's bad news I cannot share with a patient; sometimes it's my duty to remain silent and bear the pain for both patient and family."

"But, Doctor Breuer, that type of duty obliterates a more fundamental duty: each person's duty to oneself to discover truth."

For a moment, in the heat of the dialogue, Breuer had forgotten that Nietzsche was his patient. These were enormously interesting questions, and he was completely absorbed. He rose and began to pace behind his chair while he spoke.

"Is it my duty to impose a truth on others that they do not wish to know?"

"Who can determine what one wishes *not* to know?" Nietzsche demanded.

"That" said Breuer firmly, "is what may be called the art of medicine. One learns such things not from texts but from the bedside. Allow me to use, as an example, a patient whom I shall visit in the hospital later this evening. I tell you this in complete confidence and shall, of course, withhold his identity. This man has a fatal disease, a far advanced cancer of the liver. He is jaundiced because of liver failure. His bile is rising in his bloodstream. His prognosis is hopeless. I doubt that he will live more than two or three weeks. When I saw him this morning, he listened calmly to my explanation of why his skin has turned yellow, and then he put his hand on mine as though to ease *my* burden, as though to silence me. Then he changed the subject. He inquired after my family—I have known him for over thirty years—and talked about the business awaiting him when he returned home.

"But"—Breuer drew a deep breath—"I know he will *never* return home. Shall I tell him that? You see, Professor Nietzsche, it is not so easy. Usually what is *not* asked is the important question! If he had wanted to know, he would have asked me the cause of his liver's malfunctioning or when I planned to discharge him from hospital. But on these matters he is silent. Shall I be so hard as to tell him what he does not wish to know?"

"Sometimes," Nietzsche responded, "teachers must be hard. People must be given a hard message because life is hard, and dying is hard."

"Should I deprive people of their choice of how they wish to face their death? By what right, by what mandate, do I assume that role? You say that teachers must sometimes be hard. Perhaps. But the physician's task is to reduce stress and to enhance the body's ability to heal."

A hard rain slashed against the window. The pane rattled. Breuer walked over and peered out. He wheeled about. "In fact, as I think about it, I'm not sure I even agree with you about a *teacher's* hardness. Perhaps only a special kind of teacher—perhaps a prophet."

"Yes, yes"—Nietzsche's voice rose an octave in his excitement—"a teacher of bitter truths, an unpopular prophet. I think that this is what I am." He punctuated each word of this sentence by pointing his finger into his chest. "You, Doctor Breuer, dedicate yourself to making life easy. I, on the other hand, am dedicated to making things difficult for my invisible body of students."

"But what is the virtue of an unpopular truth, of making things difficult? When I left my patient this morning, he said to me, 'I place myself in God's hands.' Who can dare to say that this, too, is not a form of the truth."

"Who?" Now Nietzsche, too, had risen and paced on one side of the desk while Breuer paced on the other. "Who dares to say it?" He stopped, held to the back of his chair, and pointed toward himself. *"I dare to say it!"*

He might, Breuer thought, have been speaking from a pulpit, exhorting a congregation—but, of course, his father had been a minister.

"Truth," Nietzsche continued, "is arrived at through disbelief and skepticism, not through a childlike wishing something were so! Your patient's wish to be in God's hands is not truth. It is simply a child's wish—and nothing more! It is a wish not to die, a wish for the everlastingly bloated nipple we have labeled 'God'! Evolutionary theory scientifically demonstrates God's redundancy—though Darwin himself had not the courage to follow his evidence to its true conclusion. Surely, you must realize that we created God, and that all of us together now have killed him."

Breuer dropped this line of argument as though it were a hot ingot. He could not defend theism. A freethinker since adolescence, he had often, in discussions with his father and with religious teachers, taken Nietzsche's identical position. He sat down, and spoke in a softer, more conciliatory tone, as Nietzsche, too, returned to his own chair.

"Such fervor for the truth! Forgive me, Professor Nietzsche, if I sound challenging, but we agreed to speak truthfully. You speak about the truth in a holy tone, as though to substitute one religion for another. Allow me to play devil's advocate. Allow me to ask: Why such *passion,* such *reverence,* for the truth? How will it profit my patient of this morning?"

"It is not the truth that is holy, but the search for one's own truth! Can there be a more sacred act than self-inquiry? My philosophical work, some say, is built on sand: my views shift continually. But one of my granite sentences is: 'Become who you are.' And how can one discover *who* and *what* one is without the truth?"

"But the truth is that my patient has only a short time to live. Shall I offer him that self-knowledge?"

"True choice, full choice," Nietzsche responded, "can blossom only in the sunshine of truth. How can it be otherwise?"

Realizing that Nietzsche could discourse persuasively—and interminably—in this abstract realm of truth and choice, Breuer saw he had to force him to speak more concretely. "And my patient this morning? What is *his* range of choices? Perhaps trust in God *is* his choice!"

"That is not a choice for *man.* It is not a human choice, but a grasp for an illusion outside oneself. Such a choice, a choice for the other, for the supernatural, is always enfeebling. It always makes man less than he is. I love that which makes us more than we are!"

"Let us not talk about man in the abstract," Breuer insisted, "but about a single flesh-and-blood *man*—this patient of mine. Consider his situation. He has only days or weeks to live! What sense is there in talking choice to him?"

Undaunted, Nietzsche responded instantly. "If he doesn't *know* he is about to die, how can your patient make a decision about *how* to die?"

"How to die, Professor Nietzsche?"

"Yes, he must decide *how* to face death: to talk to others, to give advice, to say the things he has been saving to say before his death, to take his leave of others, or to be alone, to weep, to defy death, to curse it, to be thankful to it."

"You still discuss an ideal, an abstraction, but I am left to minister to the singular man, to the man of flesh and blood. I know that he will die, and die in great pain in a short time. Why bludgeon him with that? Above all, hope must be preserved. And who else but the physician can sustain hope?"

"Hope? *Hope is the final evil!*" Nietzsche all but shouted. "In my book *Human, All Too Human,* I suggested that when Pandora's box was opened, and the evils Zeus had placed therein had escaped into man's world, there still remained, unbeknownst to anyone, one final evil: hope. Ever since then, man has mistakenly regarded the box and its contents of hope as a coffer of good fortune. But we have forgotten Zeus's wish that man continue to allow himself to be tormented. Hope is the worst of evils because it protracts torment."

"Your implication, then, is that one should shorten one's dying if one wishes."

"That is one possible choice, but only in the light of full knowledge."

Breuer felt triumphant. He had been patient. He had allowed things to take their course. And now he would see the rewards of his strategy! The discussion was moving precisely in the direction he had wished.

"You are referring to suicide, Professor Nietzsche. Should suicide be a choice?"

Again, Nietzsche was firm and clear. "Each person owns his own death. And each should enact it in his own way. Perhaps—only perhaps—there is a right by which we can take a man's life. But there is no right by which we can take a man's death. That is not comfort. That is cruelty!"

Breuer persisted. "Would suicide ever be your choice?"

"Dying is hard. I've always felt the final reward of the dead is to die no more!"

"The final reward of the dead: to die no more!" Breuer nodded appreciatively, walked back to his desk, sat down, and picked up his pen. "May I jot that down?"

"Yes, of course. But let me not plagiarize myself. I did not just create that phrase. It appears in another book of mine, *The Gay Science.*"

Breuer could hardly believe his good fortune. In the past few minutes Nietzsche had mentioned both of the books Lou Salomé had given him. Though excited by this discussion and reluctant to interrupt its momentum, Breuer could not pass up the opportunity to resolve the dilemma of the two books.

"Professor Nietzsche, what you say about these two books of yours interests me greatly. How may I purchase them? A bookseller in Vienna perhaps?"

Nietzsche could hardly hide his pleasure at the request. "My publisher, Schmeitzner in Chemnitz, is in the wrong profession. His proper destiny would have been international diplomacy or, perhaps, espionage. He is a genius at intrigue, and my books are his greatest secret. In eight years he has spent nothing—not one pfennig—on publicity. He has not sent out one copy for review, nor placed one book in one bookstore.

"So, you will not find my books in any Viennese bookstore. Nor even in a Viennese home. So few have been sold I know the name of most purchasers, and I recall no Viennese among my readers. You must, therefore, contact my publisher directly. Here is his address." Nietzsche opened his briefcase, jotted down a few lines on a scrap of paper, and handed it to Breuer. "Although I could write him for you, I would prefer, if you don't mind, that he receive a letter from you directly. Perhaps an order from an eminent medical scientist may incite him to reveal the existence of my books to others."

Tucking the paper into his vest pocket, Breuer replied, "This very evening I'll send in an order for your books. But what a pity I cannot, more quickly, purchase—or even borrow—copies of them. Since I'm interested in the entire life of my patients, including their work and beliefs, your books might instruct my investigation of your condition—to say nothing of the pleasure it would be to read your work and discuss it with you!"

"Ah," Nietzsche replied, "in that request I can assist you. My personal copies of these books are in my luggage. Let me lend them to you. I'll bring them to your office later today."

Grateful that his ploy had worked, Breuer wanted to give something back to Nietzsche. "To devote one's life to writing, to pour one's life into one's books and then to have so few readers—awful! For the many writers I know in Vienna, that would be a fate worse than death. How have you borne it? How *do* you bear it now?"

Nietzsche did not acknowledge Breuer's overture, either by smile or by tone of voice. Looking straight ahead, he said, "Where is there a Viennese who remembers there is space and time outside of the Ringstrasse? I have patience. Perhaps by the year two thousand, people will dare to read my books." He rose abruptly. "Friday, then?"

Breuer felt rebuffed and dismissed. Why had Nietzsche so quickly grown cold? This was the second time today it had happened, the first being the footbridge incident—and each rebuff, Breuer realized, had followed his extending a sympathetic hand. What does this mean? he pondered. That Professor Nietzsche cannot tolerate others coming close or offering help? Then he recalled Lou Salomé's warning not to try to hypnotize Nietzsche, something to do with his strong feelings about power.

Breuer allowed himself to imagine, for a moment, her response to Nietzsche's reaction. She would not have let it pass but would have addressed it immediately and directly. Perhaps she would have said, "Why is it, Friedrich, that every time someone says something kind to you, you bite their hand?"

How ironic, Breuer reflected, that though he had resented Lou Salomé's impertinence, here he was conjuring up her image so that she might instruct him! But he quickly let these thoughts drift away. Perhaps *she* could say these things. But he could not. Certainly not when the frosty Professor Nietzsche was moving toward the door.

"Yes, Friday at two, Professor Nietzsche."

Nietzsche bowed his head slightly and strode quickly out of the office. Breuer watched from the window as he descended the steps, irritably refused a fiacre, glanced up at the darkened sky, wrapped his scarf around his ears, and trudged off down the street.

CHAPTER 7

A T THREE THE NEXT MORNING, Breuer once again felt the ground liquefy beneath him. Once again, while trying to find Bertha, he fell forty feet to the marble slab adorned with mysterious symbols. He awoke in a panic, his heart racing, his nightshirt and pillow drenched with perspiration. Taking care not to awaken Mathilde, he climbed out of bed, tiptoed to the toilet to urinate, changed into another nightshirt, turned his pillow over to the dry side, and tried to coax himself back to sleep.

But there would be no more sleep that night. He lay awake listening to Mathilde's deep breathing. Everyone slept: all five children, as well as Louis the house servant, Marta the cook, and Gretchen the children's nurse—all asleep but him. He stood guard for the entire house. He—the one who worked hardest and most needed rest—it fell to him to stay awake and to worry for everyone.

Now he suffered an onslaught of anxieties. Some he fended off, others kept coming. Dr. Binswanger had written from the Bellevue Sanatorium that Bertha was worse than ever. Even more unsettling was his news that Dr. Exner, a young staff psychiatrist, had fallen in love with her and transferred her care to another physician after proposing marriage to her! Had she returned his love? Surely she must have given him some sign! At least Dr. Exner had enough sense to be unmarried and to resign from the case with alacrity. The thought of Bertha smiling at young Exner in the same special way she had once smiled at him seared Breuer's thoughts.

Bertha worse than ever! How stupid he had been to have boasted to her mother about his new hypnotic method! What must she think of him *now*? What must the whole medical community be saying behind his back? If only he hadn't touted her treatment in that case conference—the very one Lou Salomé's brother had attended! Why couldn't he learn to keep his mouth shut? He shivered with humiliation and remorse.

Had someone guessed that he was in love with Bertha? Surely everyone had wondered why a physician would spend one to two hours every day with a patient month after month! He had known that Bertha was unnaturally attached to her father. Yet hadn't he, her physician, exploited this attachment for his own benefit? Why else would she have loved a man of his years, of his homeliness?

Breuer cringed when he thought about the erection that always popped up whenever Bertha entered a trance. Thank God he had never given in to his feelings, never declared his love, never caressed her breasts. And then he imagined giving her a medical massage. Suddenly he was clasping her wrists firmly, extending her arms over her head, raising her nightgown, spreading her legs apart with his knees, putting his hands under her buttocks, and lifting her toward him. He had loosened his belt, and was opening his trousers when suddenly a horde of people—nurses, colleagues, Frau Pappenheim—burst into the room!

He sank deeper into the bed, ravaged and defeated. Why did he torment himself so? Over and over, he surrendered and let worries swarm over him. There was plenty of Jewish worry—the rising anti-Semitism which had blocked his university career; the emergence of Schönerer's new party, the German National Association; the vicious anti-Semitic speeches at the meeting of the Austrian Reform Association, inciting the artisan guilds to attack Jews: finance Jews, press Jews, railway Jews, theater Jews. Only this week, Schönerer had demanded the reinstatement of the old legal restrictions on Jewish life and incited riots throughout the city. It would, Breuer knew, only worsen. Already it had invaded the university. Student bodies had recently decreed that since Jews were born "without honor," they would henceforth not be permitted to obtain satisfaction through a duel for insults suffered. Invectives about Jew doctors had not yet been heard, but it was just a matter of time.

He listened to Mathilde's light snores. There lay his real worry! She had folded her life into his. She was loving, she mothered his children. Her dowry from the Altmann family had made him a wealthy man. Though she was bitter about Bertha, who could blame her? She had a right to her bitterness.

Breuer looked again at her. When he married her, she was the most beautiful woman he had ever seen—and still was. She was more beautiful than the empress, or than Bertha or even Lou Salomé. What man in Vienna did not envy him? Why, then, could he not touch her, kiss her? Why did her open mouth frighten him? Why this frightening notion that he had to escape her grasp? That she was the source of his anguish?

He watched her in the darkness. Her sweet lips, the graceful dome of her cheekbones, her satiny skin. He imagined her face aging, wrinkling, her skin hardening into leathery plaques, falling away, exposing the ivory skull beneath. He watched the swell of her breasts, resting upon the rib bars of her thoracic cage. And recalled once, walking on a windswept beach, coming upon the carcass of a giant fish—its side partially decomposed, its bleached, bare ribs grinning up at him.

Breuer tried to wash death from his mind. He hummed his favorite incantation, Lucretius' phrase: "Where death is, I am not. Where I am, death is not. Why worry?" But it didn't help.

He shook his head, trying to shake off these morbid thoughts. Where had they come from? From speaking with Nietzsche about death? No, rather than inserting these thoughts into his mind, Nietzsche simply *released* them. They had always been there; he had thought them all before. Yet where in his mind were they housed when he wasn't thinking about them? Freud was right: there *had* to be a reservoir of complex thoughts in the brain, beyond consciousness but on alert, ready at any time to be mustered and marched onto the stage of conscious thinking.

And not just thoughts in this nonconscious reservoir, but feelings as well! A few days ago, while riding in a fiacre, Breuer had glanced at the fiacre next to him. Its two horses trotted along pulling the cab in which sat two passengers, a dour-faced elderly couple. *But there was no driver.* A ghost fiacre! Fear flashed through him, and he had had an instantaneous diaphoresis: his clothes drenched within seconds. And then the driver of the fiacre came into view: he had simply been bending over to adjust his boot.

At first, Breuer had laughed at his foolish reaction. But the more he thought about it, the more he realized that, rationalist and freethinker though he might be, his mind nonetheless harbored clusters of supernatural terror. And not too deep either: they were "on call," only seconds from the surface. Ah, for a tonsil forceps that could rip out these clusters, roots and all!

Still no sleep on the horizon. Breuer stood up to adjust his twisted nightshirt and to fluff the pillows. He thought again about Nietzsche. What a strange man! What stirring talks they'd had! He liked such talking, it made him feel at ease, in his element. What was Nietzsche's "granite sentence"? "Become who you are!" But who am I? Breuer asked himself. What was I meant to become? His father had been a Talmudic scholar; perhaps philosophic disputation was in his blood. He was glad for the few philosophy courses he had taken at university—more than most physicians because, at his father's insistence, he had spent his first year there in the faculty of philosophy before entering his medical studies. And glad he had maintained his relationship with Brentano and Jodl, his philosophy professors. He really should see them more often. There was something cleansing about discourse in the realm of pure ideas. It was there, perhaps *only* there, that he was unsullied by Bertha and carnality. What would it be like to dwell all the time, like Nietzsche, in that realm?

And the way Nietzsche dared to say things! Imagine! To say that hope is the greatest evil! That God is dead! That truth is an error without which we cannot live! That the enemies of truth are not lies, but convictions! That the final reward of the dead is to die no more! That physicians have no right to deprive a man of his own death! Evil thoughts! He had debated Nietzsche on each. Yet it was a mock debate: deep in his heart, he knew Nietzsche was right.

And Nietzsche's freedom! What would it be like to live as he lived? No house, no obligations, no salaries to pay, no children to raise, no schedule, no role, no place in society. There was something alluring about such freedom. Why did Friedrich Nietzsche have so much of it and Josef Breuer so little? Nietzsche has simply seized his freedom. Why can't I? groaned Breuer. He lay in bed growing dizzy with such thoughts until the alarm rang at six.

"Good morning, Doctor Breuer," Frau Becker greeted him when he arrived at his office at ten thirty after his morning round of home visits. "That Professor Nietzsche was waiting in the vestibule when I arrived to open the office. He brought these books for you and asked me to tell you that they are his personal copies with handwritten marginal notations containing ideas for future work. They are very private, he said, and you should show them to no one. He looked terrible, by the way, and acted very strangely."

"How so, Frau Becker?"

"He kept blinking his eyes as though he couldn't see or didn't want to see what he was seeing. And his face was pallid, as though he were going to faint. I asked him if he needed any help, some tea, or whether he wanted to lie down in your office. I thought I was being kind, but he seemed displeased, almost angry. Then he wheeled around without a word and went stumbling down the stairs."

Breuer took Nietzsche's packet from Frau Becker—two books tidily wrapped in a sheet of yesterday's *Neue Freie Presse* and tied with a short piece of cord. He unwrapped them and placed them on his desk next to the copies given to him by Lou Salomé. Nietzsche may have exaggerated by saying that he would have the only copies of these books in Vienna, but undoubtedly he was now the only Viennese with *two* copies of them.

"Oh, Doctor Breuer, aren't these the same books that grand Russian lady left?" Frau Becker had just brought in the morning mail and, removing the newspaper and cord from his desk, noticed the titles of the books.

How lies breed lies, Breuer thought, and what a vigilant life a liar is forced to live. Frau Becker, though formal and efficient, also liked to "visit" with patients. Was she capable of mentioning to Nietzsche "the Russian lady" and her gift of books? He had to warn her.

"Frau Becker, there's something I must tell you. That Russian woman, Fräulein Salomé—the one you've taken such a liking to—is, or *was,* a close friend of Professor Nietzsche's. She was worried about the professor and was responsible for his referral to me through friends. Only he doesn't know that, as now he and Fräulein Salomé are on the worst of terms. If I am to have any chance of helping him, he must *never* learn of my meeting with her."

Frau Becker nodded with her usual discretion, then glanced out the window to see two patients arriving. "Herr Hauptmann and Frau Klein. Whom do you wish to see first?"

Giving Nietzsche a specific appointment time had been unusual. Ordinarily Breuer, like other Viennese physicians, merely specified a day and saw patients in the order of their arrival.

"Send in Herr Hauptmann. He needs to return to work."

♦ ♦ ♦

After his last morning patient, Breuer decided to study Nietzsche's books before his visit the next day, and asked Frau Becker to tell his wife that he'd not come upstairs until dinner was actually on the table. Then he picked up the two cheaply bound volumes, each less than three hundred pages. He would have preferred to read the copies Lou Salomé had given him so that he could underline and write in the margins as he read. But he felt compelled to read Nietzsche's own copies, as if to minimize his duplicity. Nietzsche's personal markings were distracting: much underlining and, in the margins, many exclamation points and cries of "YES! YES!" and occasionally "NO!" or "IDIOT!" Also many scribbled notes, which Breuer could not make out.

They were strange books, unlike any others he had ever seen. Each book contained hundreds of numbered sections, many of which bore little relation to one another. The sections were brief, at the most two or three paragraphs, often only a few sentences, and sometimes simply an aphorism: "Thoughts are the shadows of our feelings—always darker, emptier and simpler." "No one ever dies of fatal truths nowadays—there are too many antidotes." "What good is a book that does not carry us beyond all books?"

Evidently Professor Nietzsche felt qualified to discourse on every subject—music, art, nature, politics, hermeneutics, history, psychology. Lou Salomé had described him as a great philosopher. Perhaps. Breuer wasn't ready to render judgment on the content of his books. But it was clear that Nietzsche was a poetic writer, a true *Dichter*.

Some of Nietzsche's declarations appeared ridiculous—a silly pronouncement, for example, that fathers and sons always have more in common than mothers and daughters. But many of the aphorisms stung him into self-reflection: "What is the seal of liberation?—No longer being ashamed in front of oneself!" He was struck by one particularly arresting passage:

> Just as the bones, flesh, intestines and blood vessels are enclosed in a skin that makes the sight of man endurable, so the agitations and passions of the soul are enveloped in vanity; it is the skin of the soul.

What to make of these writings? They defied characterization except that, as a body, they seemed deliberately provocative; they challenged all!

conventions, questioned, even denigrated conventional virtues, and extolled anarchy.

Breuer glanced at his watch. One fifteen. No more time for leisurely browsing. Knowing he would be summoned for dinner any minute, he sought passages that might offer him practical help in tomorrow's meeting with Nietzsche.

Freud's hospital schedule did not usually allow him to come to dinner on Thursdays. But today Breuer had invited him especially so they could go over the consultation with Nietzsche. After a full Viennese dinner of savory cabbage and raisin soup, wiener schnitzel, spätzle, Brussels sprouts, baked breaded tomatoes, Marta's home-made pumpernickel, baked apple with cinnamon and *Schlag,* and seltzer water, Breuer and Freud retired to the study.

As he described the medical history and symptoms of the patient he was calling Herr Eckart Müller, Breuer noticed Freud's eyelids slowly closing. He had confronted Freud's postprandial lethargy before and knew how to deal with it.

"So, Sig," he said briskly, "let's get you prepared for your medical matriculation examinations. I'll pretend I'm Professor Northnagel. I couldn't sleep last night, I've got some dyspepsia, and Mathilde is after me again for being late to dinner, so I'm cross enough today to imitate the brute."

Breuer adopted a thick North-German accent and the rigid, authoritarian posture of a Prussian: "All right, Doctor Freud, I have given you the medical history on Herr Eckart Müller. Now you're ready for your physical examination. Tell me, what will you be looking for?"

Freud's eyes opened fully, and he ran his finger around his collar to loosen it. He did not share Breuer's fondness for these mock exams. Though he agreed they were good pedagogically, they always agitated him.

"Undoubtedly," he began, "the patient has a lesion in his central nervous system. His cephalgia, his deteriorating vision, his father's neurological history, his disturbances in equilibrium—all point to that. I'm suspicious of a brain tumor. Possibly disseminated sclerosis. I'd do a thorough neurological examination, checking the cranial nerves with great care, especially the first, second, fifth, and eleventh. I'd also check the visual fields carefully—the tumor may be pressing on the optic nerve."

"What about the other visual phenomena, Doctor Freud? The scintillations, the blurred vision in the morning which improves later in the day? Do you happen to know of a cancer that can do this?"

"I'd get a good look at the retina. He may have some macular degeneration."

"Macular degeneration that improves in the afternoons? Remarkable! That's a case we should write up for publication! And his periodic fatigue, his rheumatoid symptoms, and his vomiting of blood? That's caused by a cancer, too?"

"Herr Professor Northnagel, the patient may have two diseases. Fleas and lice, too, as Oppolzer used to say. He may be anemic."

"How would you examine for anemia?"

"Do a hemoglobin and a stool guiac."

"Nein! Nein! Mein Gott! What do they teach you in the Viennese medical schools? Examine with your five senses? Forget the laboratory tests, your Jewish medicine! The laboratory only confirms what your physical examination already tells you. Suppose you're on the battlefield, Doctor—you're going to call for a stool test?"

"I'd check the patient's color, especially the creases of his palms and his mucosal membranes—gums, tongue, conjuctiva."

"Right. But you forgot the most important one, the fingernails."

Breuer cleared his throat, continuing to play Northnagel. "Now, my aspiring young doctor," he said, "I give you the results of the physical. First, the neurological examination is completely and absolutely normal—not a *single* negative finding. So much for a brain tumor or disseminated sclerosis, which, Doctor Freud, were unlikely possibilities in the first place, unless you know of cases that persist for years and erupt periodically with severe twenty-four- to forty-eight-hour symptomatology and then dissolve entirely with no neurological deficit. No, no, no! This is not structural disease but an episodic physiological disorder." Breuer drew himself up and, exaggerating his Prussian accent, pronounced, "There's only one possible diagnosis, Doctor Freud."

Freud flushed deeply. "I don't know." He looked so forlorn that Breuer halted the game, dismissed Northnagel, and softened his tone.

"Yes, you do, Sig. We discussed it last time. Hemicrania, or migraine. And don't feel ashamed about not thinking of it: migraine is a house-call disease. Clinical aspirants rarely ever see it because migraine sufferers seldom go into the hospital. Without question, Herr Müller has a severe case of hemicrania. He has all the classic symptoms. Let's review them: intermittent attacks of unilateral throbbing headaches—often familial, by the way—accompanied by anorexia, nausea and vomiting, and visual aberrations—prodromal light flashing, even hemianopsia."

Freud had taken a small notebook from his inside coat pocket and was jotting down notes. "I'm beginning to remember some of my reading about hemicrania, Josef. Du Bois-Reymond's theory is that it's a vascular disease, the pain caused by a spasm of the brain arterioles."

"Du Bois-Reymond is right about it being vascular, but not all patients have arteriole spasm. I've seen many with the opposite—a dilation of the vessels. Mollendorff thinks the pain is caused not by spasm but by a stretching of the relaxed blood vessels."

"What about his loss of vision?"

"*There's* your fleas and lice! It's the result of something else, not the migraine. I couldn't focus my ophthalmoscope on his retina. Something obstructs the view. It's not in the lens, not a cataract, but in the cornea. I don't know the cause of this corneal opacity, but I've seen it before. Perhaps it's edema of the cornea—that would account for the fact that his vision is worse in the morning. Corneal edema is greatest after the eyes have been closed all night and gradually resolves when fluid is evaporated from the opened eyes during the day."

"His weakness?"

"He *is* slightly anemic. Possibly gastric bleeding, but probably dietary anemia. His dyspepsia is so great that he can't tolerate meat for weeks at a time."

Freud continued to take notes. "What about prognosis? Did the same disease kill his father?"

"He asked me the same question, Sig. In fact, I've never had a patient before who absolutely insists on all the blunt facts. He made me promise to be truthful with him and then posed three questions: Will his disease be progressive, will he go blind, will he die of it? Have you ever heard of a patient talking like that? I promised I'd answer him in our session tomorrow."

"What will you tell him?"

"I can give him a lot of reassurance based on an excellent study by Liveling, a British physician, the best medical research I've seen coming out of England. You should read his monograph." Breuer held up a thick volume and handed it to Freud, who slowly leafed through the pages.

"It's not translated yet," Breuer continued, "but your English is good enough. Liveling reports on a large sample of migraine sufferers and concludes that migraine becomes *less* potent as the patient ages and also that it is *not* associated with any other brain disease. So, even though the disease is inherited, it's highly unlikely that his father died of the same disease.

"Of course," Breuer continued, "Liveling's research method is sloppy. The monograph doesn't make it clear whether his results are based on longitudinal or cross-sectional data. Do you understand what I mean by that, Sig?"

Freud responded immediately, apparently more at home with research method than with clinical medicine. "The longitudinal method means following individual patients for years and discovering that their attacks lessen as they grow older, does it not?"

"Precisely," said Breuer. "And the cross-sectional method—"

Freud interrupted like an eager schoolboy in the front row of the class. "The cross-sectional method is a single observation at one point in time—in this case, that the older patients in the sample show fewer migraine attacks than younger ones."

Enjoying his friend's pleasure, Breuer gave him another opportunity to shine. "Can you guess which method is more accurate?"

"The cross-sectional method can't be very accurate: the sample may contain very few old patients with severe migraine, not because the migraine gets better, but because such patients are too sick or too discouraged with medical doctors to agree to be studied."

"Exactly, and a shortcoming I don't think Liveling realized. An excellent answer, Sig. Shall we have a celebratory cigar?" Freud eagerly accepted one of Breuer's fine Turkish cigars, and the two men lit up and savored the aroma.

"Now," Freud commented, "can we talk about the rest of the case?" He then added in a loud whisper, *"The interesting part."*

Breuer smiled.

"Maybe I shouldn't say this," Freud continued, "but since Northnagel's left the room, I'll confess to you privately that the psychological aspects of this case intrigue me more than the medical picture."

Breuer noticed that his young friend did indeed appear more animated. Freud's eyes were sparkling with curiosity as he asked, "How suicidal is this patient? Were you able to advise him to seek counsel?"

Now it was Breuer's turn to feel sheepish. He flushed as he remembered how, in their last talk, he had exuded confidence in his interviewing skills. "He's a strange man, Sig. I've never met such resistance. It was like a brick wall. A *smart* brick wall. He gave me plenty of good openings. He spoke of feeling well only fifty days last year, of black moods, of being betrayed, of living in total isolation, of being a writer without readers, of having severe insomnia with malignant nocturnal thoughts."

"But, Josef, those are just the types of openings you said you were looking for!"

"Exactly. Yet every time I pursued one of them, I came up empty-handed. Yes, he acknowledges often being ill, but insists it's his body that is ill—not *him*, not his essence. As for black moods, he says he is proud of having the courage to experience black moods! 'Proud of the courage to have black moods'—can you believe it? Crazy talk! Betrayal? Yes, I suspect he refers to what happened with Fräulein Salomé, but he claims to have overcome it and does not wish to discuss it. As for suicide, he denies being suicidal, but defends the patient's right to choose his own death. Though he might welcome death—he says that the final reward of the dead is to die no more!—he has too much still to accomplish, too many books to write. In fact, he says his head is pregnant with books, and he thinks that his cephalgia is cerebral labor pain."

Freud shook his head in sympathy with Breuer's consternation. "Cerebral labor pain—what a metaphor! Like Minerva born from the brow of Zeus! Strange thoughts—cerebral labor pain, choosing one's death, the courage to have black moods. He's not without wit, Josef. Is it, I wonder, a crazy wit or a wise craziness?"

Breuer shook his head. Freud sat back, exhaled a long fume of blue smoke, and watched it ascend and fade away before he spoke again. "This case becomes more fascinating every day. So, what about the Fräulein's report of suicidal despair? Is he lying to her? Or to you? Or to himself?"

"Lying to himself, Sig? How do you lie to yourself? Who is the liar? Who is being lied to?"

"Perhaps part of him is suicidal, but the conscious part doesn't know it."

Breuer turned to look more closely at his young friend. He had expected to see a grin on his face, but Freud was entirely serious.

"Sig, more and more you talk of this little unconscious homunculus living a separate life from its host. Please, Sig, follow my advice: speak about this theory only to me. No, no, I won't call it a theory even—there's no evidence whatsoever for it—let's call it a fanciful notion. Don't talk about this fanciful notion to Brücke: it would relieve his guilt for not having the courage to promote a Jew."

Freud responded with unusual resoluteness. "It will remain between us until it is proven by sufficient evidence. Then I shall not refrain from publication."

For the first time Breuer became aware that there was not much boyishness left in his young friend. Instead, there was germinating an audaciousness, a willingness to stand up for his convictions—qualities he wished he had himself.

"Sig, you speak of *evidence,* as though this could be a subject for scientific inquiry. But this homunculus has no concrete reality. It's simply a construct, like a Platonic ideal. What would possibly constitute evidence? Can you give me even one example? And don't use dreams, I won't accept *them* as evidence—they, too, are insubstantial constructs."

"You yourself have supplied evidence, Josef. You tell me that Bertha Pappenheim's emotional life is dictated by events that occurred precisely twelve months ago—past events of which she has no conscious knowledge. And yet they are described accurately in her mother's diary of a year before. To my mind, this is equivalent to laboratory proof."

"But this rests on the assumption that Bertha is a reliable witness, that she really does not recall these past events."

But, but, but, but—there it is again, Breuer thought—that "demon but." He felt like punching himself. All his life he had taken vacillating "but" positions, and now he had done it again with Freud as well as with Nietzsche—when, in his heart, he suspected they were both right.

Freud jotted down a few more sentences in his notebook. "Josef, do you think I can see Frau Pappenheim's diary sometime?"

"I've returned it to her, but I believe I can retrieve it again."

Freud took out his watch. "I've got to get back to the hospital soon for Northnagel's rounds. But before I go, tell me what you're going to do with your reluctant patient."

"You mean, what I'd like to do? Three steps. I'd like to establish a good doctor-patient rapport with him. Then I'd like to hospitalize him at a clinic for a few weeks to observe his hemicrania and regulate his medication. And then, during these weeks, I'd like to meet with him frequently for in-depth discussions of his despair." Breuer sighed. "But, knowing him, there's little likelihood he'll cooperate with any of this. Any ideas, Sig?"

Freud, who was still looking through Liveling's monograph, now held up a page for Breuer to scan. "Here, listen to this. Under 'Etiology,' Liveling says, 'Episodes of migraine have been induced by dyspepsia, by eyestrain, and by stress. Prolonged bed rest may be advisable. Young migraine sufferers may have to be removed from the stress of school and tutored in the peace of the home. Some physicians advise changing one's occupation to a less demanding one.' "

Breuer looked quizzical. "So?"

"I believe that's our answer! Stress! Why not make stress the key to your treatment plan? Take the position that, to overcome his migraine, Herr Müller must reduce his stress, including mental stress. Suggest to him that stress is stifled emotion, and that, as in the treatment of Bertha, it can be reduced by providing an outlet. Use the chimneysweeping method. You can even show him this statement by Liveling and invoke the power of medical authority."

Freud noticed Breuer smiling at his words, and asked, "You think this is a foolish plan?"

"Not at all, Sig. In fact, I think it's excellent advice, and I shall follow it carefully. The part that made me smile was the last thing you said—'invoke the power of medical authority.' You'd have to know this patient to appreciate the joke, but the idea of expecting him to bow to medical, or to any other type of, authority strikes me as comical."

And opening Nietzsche's *The Gay Science,* Breuer read aloud several passages he'd marked. "Herr Müller contests *all* authority and conventions. For example, he stands virtues on their head and renames them vices—as in this view of faithfulness: 'Obstinately, he clings to something he has come to see through; but he calls it faithfulness.'

"And of politeness: 'He is so polite. Yes, he always carries a biscuit for Cerberus and is so timid that he thinks everyone is Cerberus, even you and I. That is his politeness.'

"And listen to this fascinating metaphor for both visual impairment and despair: 'To find everything profound; that is an inconvenient trait. It makes one strain one's eyes all the time, and in the end one finds more than one might have wished.' "

Freud had been listening with interest. "To see more than one wishes," he murmured. "I wonder what he has seen. May I take a look at the book?"

But Breuer had his answer ready: "Sig, he made me give an oath that I show this book to no one, since it has personal notations. My rapport with him is so tenuous that for now I had better honor his request. Later, perhaps.

"One of the strange things about my interview with Herr Müller," he went on, stopping at the last of his markers, "was that whenever I tried to express empathy with him, he took offense, and broke the rapport between us. Ah! 'Footbridge'! Yes, here's the passage I'm looking for."

As Breuer read, Freud closed his eyes the better to concentrate.

" 'There was a time in our lives when we were so close that nothing seemed to obstruct our friendship and brotherhood, and only a small footbridge separated us. Just as you were about to step on it, I asked you: "Do you want to cross the footbridge to me?"—Immediately you did not want to any more; and when I asked you again you remained silent. Since then mountains and torrential rivers and whatever separates and alienates have been cast between us, and even if we wanted to get together, we couldn't. But when you now think of that little footbridge, words fail you and you sob and marvel.' "

Breuer put the book down. "What do you make of it, Sig?"

"I'm not sure." Freud rose and paced before the bookcase as he talked. "It's a curious little story. Let's reason it out. One person is about to cross the footbridge—that is, get closer to the other—when the second person invites him to do the very thing he planned. Then the first person cannot take the step because now it would seem as though he were submitting to the other—power apparently getting in the way of closeness."

"Yes, yes, you're right, Sig. Excellent! I see it now. That means that Herr Müller will interpret any expression of positive sentiment as a bid for power. A peculiar notion: it makes it almost impossible to get close to him. In another section somewhere in here, he says that we feel hatred toward those who see our secrets and catch us in tender feelings. What we need at that moment is not sympathy but to regain our power over our own emotions."

"Josef," said Freud, sitting down again and tapping off his ash into the ashtray, "last week I observed Bilroth using his ingenious new surgical technique to remove a cancerous stomach. Now, as I listen to you, it seems to me you have to perform a psychological surgical procedure equally complex and delicate. You know he's suicidal from the Fräulein's report, yet you cannot tell him you know. You must persuade him to reveal his despair; yet, if you succeed, he will hate you for shaming him. You must gain his confidence; yet, if you act in a sympathetic manner toward him, he will accuse you of trying to gain power over him."

"Psychological surgery—it's interesting to hear you put it that way," said Breuer. "Perhaps we're developing a whole medical subspecialty. Wait, there's something else I wanted to read you that seems relevant."

He turned the pages of *Human, All Too Human* for a couple of minutes. "I can't find the passage now, but its point is that the seeker after truth must undergo a personal psychological analysis—he terms it 'moral dissection.' In fact, he goes so far as to say that the errors of even the greatest philosophers were caused by ignorance of their own motivation. He claims that in order to discover the truth, one must first know oneself fully. And to do that, one must remove oneself from one's customary point of view, even from one's own century and country—and then examine oneself from a distance!"

"To analyze one's own psyche! Not an easy task," said Freud, rising to leave, "but a task that obviously would be facilitated by the presence of an objective, informed guide!"

"My thought, exactly!" Breuer responded as he escorted Freud down the hallway. "Now, the hard part—to persuade him of that!"

"I don't think it will be difficult," said Freud. "You have on your side both his own arguments about psychological dissection and the medical theory about stress and migraine—subtly invoked, of course. I don't see how you can fail to persuade your reluctant philosopher of the wisdom in a course of self-examination under your guidance. Good night, Josef."

"Thank you, Sig"—and Breuer clasped his shoulder briefly. "It's been a good talk. The student has taught the teacher."

Letter from Elisabeth Nietzsche to Friedrich Nietzsche

26 November 1882

My dear Fritz,

Neither Mother nor I have heard from you in weeks. This is no time for you to disappear! Your Russian simian continues to spread her lies about you. She shows that disgraceful picture of you and that Jew, Rée, in harness to her and jokes to everyone that you like the taste of her whip. I warned you to retrieve that picture—she will blackmail us with it all our lives! She mocks you everywhere and her paramour, Rée, joins in the chorus. She says that Nietzsche, the otherworldly philosopher, is only interested in one thing: her . . . —a part of her anatomy—I cannot bring myself to repeat her words—her filth. I leave it to your imagination. She is now living with your friend, Rée, in open vice before the eyes of his mother—a fine lot, all of them. None of this is unexpected behavior, not unexpected by *me* anyway (I still smart at the way you dismissed my warnings at Tautenberg), but it is now becoming a more deadly game—she is infiltrating Basel with her lies. I have learned that she has written letters both to Kemp and to Wilhelm! Fritz, hear me: *she will not stop until she has cost you your pension.* You may choose silence but I will not: I shall call for an official police investigation of her behavior with Rée! If I am successful, *and I must have your backing,* she will be deported for immorality within the month! Fritz, send me your address.

Your only sister,
Elisabeth

ARLY MORNINGS NEVER VARIED in the Breuer household. At six, the corner baker, a patient of Breuer's, delivered *Kaisersemmel*, fresh from the oven. While her husband dressed, Mathilde set the table, made his cinnamon coffee, and laid out the crisp three-hatted rolls with sweet butter and black cherry preserves. Despite the tension in their marriage, Mathilde always prepared his breakfast while Louis and Gretchen attended to the children.

Breuer, preoccupied this morning with his upcoming meeting with Nietzsche, was so busy leafing through *Human, All Too Human* that he scarcely looked up as Mathilde poured his coffee. He finished his breakfast in silence and then muttered that his noon interview with his new patient might extend into the dinner hour. Mathilde was not pleased.

"I hear so much talk about this philosopher I begin to worry. You and Sigi spend hours talking about him! You worked through dinner on Wednesday, yesterday you stayed in your office reading his book until the food was on the table, and today again you read him at breakfast. And now you talk again about missing dinner! The children need to see their father's face. Please, Josef, don't make too much of him. Like the others."

Breuer knew Mathilde was referring to Bertha, but not *only* to Bertha: she had often objected to his failure to set reasonable limits on the time he spent with patients. To him, commitment to a patient was inviolable. Once he took on a patient, he never shirked from providing that person with all the time and energy he felt necessary. His fees were low and, for a patient who was hard-pressed financially, he charged nothing at all. At times, Mathilde felt she had to protect Breuer from himself—that is, if she was to have any of his time and attention.

"The others, Mathilde?"

"You know what I mean, Josef." She still would not speak Bertha's name. "Some things, of course, a wife can understand. Your *Stammtisch* at the café—I know you must have a place to meet your friends—the tarock, the pigeons in your laboratory, the chess. But the other times—why give so much of yourself unnecessarily?"

"When? What are you talking about?" Breuer knew he was being perverse, that he was guiding them toward an unpleasant confrontation.

"Think about the time you used to give to Fräulein Berger."

With the exception of Bertha, this—of all the examples Mathilde could have given—was the one guaranteed to irritate him most. Eva Berger, his previous nurse, had worked for him for ten years or so, since the day he began his practice. His unusually close relationship with her had caused Mathilde almost as much consternation as had his relationship with Bertha. Over their years together, Breuer and his nurse had developed a friendship that transcended professional roles. Often they confided deeply personal things to one another; and when they were alone, they addressed one another by first name—possibly the only physician and nurse in all Vienna to do so, but that was Breuer's way.

"You always misunderstood my relationship with Fräulein Berger," Breuer replied in an icy tone. "To this day, I regret listening to you. Firing her remains one of the great shames of my life."

Six months ago, on the fateful day when the delusional Bertha had announced that she was pregnant by Breuer, Mathilde had demanded not only that he take himself off Bertha's case but also that he fire Eva Berger. Mathilde was enraged and mortified and wanted to cleanse every stain of Bertha from her life. And of Eva, too, whom Mathilde, knowing that her husband discussed everything with his nurse, regarded as an accomplice in the whole awful Bertha affair.

During that crisis, Breuer was so overcome with remorse, so humiliated and self-accusatory, that he acceded to all of Mathilde's demands. Though he knew Eva was a sacrificial victim, he could not find the courage to defend her. The very next day, he not only transferred Bertha's care to a colleague but fired the innocent Eva Berger.

"I'm sorry I brought it up, Josef. But what am I to do when I watch you withdraw more and more from me and from our children? When I ask for something from you, it's not to plague you, but because I—*we*—want your presence. Consider it a compliment, an invitation." Mathilde smiled at him.

"I like invitations—but I hate commands!" Breuer immediately regretted his words, but did not know how to retract them. He finished his breakfast in silence.

Nietzsche had arrived fifteen minutes before his twelve-o'clock appointment. Breuer found him sitting quietly in a corner of the waiting room, his wide-brimmed green felt hat on his head, his coat buttoned to his neck, his eyes closed. As they walked back into his office and settled into their chairs, Breuer attempted to put him at ease.

"Thank you for trusting me with your personal copies of your books. If any of your marginal notes contained confidential material, have no fear—I cannot decipher your script. You have a physician's handwriting—almost as illegible as mine! Have you ever considered a career in medicine?"

When Nietzsche merely raised his head at Breuer's weak joke, Breuer continued, undaunted, "But allow me to comment on your excellent books. I did not have time to finish them yesterday, but I was fascinated and stirred by many of your passages. You write extraordinarily well. Your publisher is not only lazy, but a fool: these are books a publisher should champion with his life blood."

Nietzsche again made no reply, only bowing his head slightly to acknowledge the compliment. Careful, Breuer thought, perhaps he is offended by compliments as well!

"But, to the business at hand, Professor Nietzsche. Forgive me for prattling on. Let us discuss your medical condition. Based on your previous physicians' reports and my examination and laboratory studies, I am certain that your major condition is hemicrania, or migraine. I assume you have heard this before—two of your previous physicians mention it in their consultation notes."

"Yes, other physicians have told me that I have headaches with migraine characteristics: great pain, often in only one side of the head, preceded by an aura of flashing lights and accompanied by vomiting. These I certainly have. Does your use of the term go beyond that, Doctor Breuer?"

"Perhaps. There have been a number of new developments in our understanding of migraine—my guess is that by the next generation we will have it under complete control. Some of the recent research addresses the three questions you posed. First, in respect to whether it will always be your fate to suffer such dreadful attacks, the data strongly indicate that migraine becomes *less* potent as a patient ages. You must understand that these are statistics only, referring simply to the odds—they provide no certainty about any individual case.

"Let us turn to the 'hard one,' as you put it, of your questions—that is, whether you have a constitutional condition like your father's that will eventuate in death, madness, or dementia—I believe that's the order in which you listed them?"

Nietzsche's eyes widened, apparently in surprise at hearing his questions being so directly addressed. Good, good, Breuer thought, keep him off guard. He's probably never had a physician who can be just as bold as he himself is.

"There is *no evidence whatsoever,*" he continued emphatically, "from any published study or from my own extensive clinical experience, that migraine is progressive or associated with any other brain disease. I don't know what disease your father had—my guess is a cancer, possibly a brain hemorrhage. But there is no evidence that migraine progresses to these diseases or to any other." He paused.

"So, before proceeding further, have I addressed your questions honestly?"

"Two of the three, Doctor Breuer. There was one other: Will I go blind?"

"I'm afraid that's a question that cannot be answered. But I'll tell you what I can. First, there is no evidence that your deteriorating vision is related to your migraine. I know it's tempting to consider all symptoms as manifestation of one underlying condition, but that's not the case here. Now, visual strain may aggravate, even precipitate a migraine attack—that's another issue to which we will return later—but your visual problem is something entirely different. I do know that your cornea, the thin covering over the iris—here let me draw this picture . . ."

On his prescription pad, Breuer sketched the anatomy of the eye, showing Nietzsche that his cornea was more opaque than it should be, most likely because of edema, accumulated fluid.

"We don't know the cause of this condition, but we do know that progression is very gradual and that, though your vision may become more hazy, it is unlikely you will ever be blind. I cannot be entirely certain, because the opaque condition of your cornea makes it impossible for me to see and examine your retina with my ophthalmoscope. So you understand my problem in answering your question more completely?"

Nietzsche, who a few minutes before had taken off his coat and laid it in his lap along with his hat, now stood to hang both on the coat rack by the office door. As he sat down again, he exhaled loudly and appeared more relaxed.

"Thank you, Doctor Breuer. You are indeed a man of your word. Have you concealed nothing from me?"

A good opportunity, Breuer thought, to encourage Nietzsche to reveal more about himself. But I must be subtle.

"Concealed? A great deal! Many of my thoughts, feelings, reactions to you! Sometimes I wonder what a conversation would be like with a different social convention—with nothing concealed! But I give you my word I have concealed nothing of your medical condition. And you? Remember we have a reciprocal contract of honesty. Tell me, what do you conceal from me?"

"Certainly nothing of my medical condition," Nietzsche replied. "But I do conceal as much as possible of those thoughts that are not meant to be shared! You wonder about a conversation with nothing concealed—its real name is hell, I believe. To disclose oneself to another is the prelude to betrayal, and betrayal makes one sick, does it not?"

"A provocative position, Professor Nietzsche. But while we are discussing disclosure, let me reveal one private thought. Our discussion on Wednesday was enormously stimulating to me, and I would welcome the opportunity for future talks with you. I have a passion for philosophy, yet studied far too little of it at university. My everyday medical practice rarely offers satisfaction for my passion—it smolders and longs for combustion."

Nietzsche smiled but made no comment. Breuer felt confident; he had prepared himself well. The rapport was building, and the interview was on course. Now he would discuss treatment: first drugs, and then some form of "talking treatment."

"But let us turn to the treatment of your migraine. There are many new medications which have been reported effective for some patients. I am speaking of such drugs as bromides, caffeine, valerian, belladonna, amyl nitrate, nitroglycerine, colchicine, and ergot, to name but a few on the list. I see from your records that you yourself have tried some of these. Certain of them have proven effective for reasons no one understands, some because of their general analgesic or sedative properties, and some because they attack the basic mechanism of migraine."

"Which is?" Nietzsche asked.

"Vascular. Every observer agrees that the blood vessels, especially the temporal arteries, are involved in a migraine attack. They constrict vigorously and then seem to engorge. The pain may emanate from the walls of the stretched or constricted vessels themselves, or from the organs which cry for their normal blood supply, especially the membranes covering the brain—the dura mater and the pia mater."

"And the reason for this anarchy of the blood vessels?"

"Still unknown," Breuer responded. "But I believe we will have the solution shortly. Until then, we can only speculate. Many physicians, and among these I include myself, are impressed with the underlying pathology of rhythmicity in hemicrania. In fact, some go so far as to say that the disorder in rhythm is more fundamental than the headache."

"I don't understand, Doctor Breuer."

"I mean that the rhythm disorder may express itself through any of a number of organs. Thus the headache itself need not be present in an attack of migraine. There may be such a thing as abdominal migraine, characterized by sharp attacks of abdominal pain, without head pain. Other patients have reported sudden episodes in which they feel suddenly despondent or elated. Some patients periodically have a sense that they have already experienced their current experiences. The French call it *déjà vu*—perhaps that, too, is a variant of migraine."

"And underlying the disorder of rhythm? The cause of causes? Shall we ultimately arrive at God—the final error in the false search for ultimate truth?"

"No, we may arrive at medical mysticism, but not God! Not in this office."

"That's good," Nietzsche said with some relief. "It suddenly occurred to me that in speaking freely I have possibly been insensitive to your religious sentiments."

"No danger of that, Professor Nietzsche. I suspect I am as devout a Jewish freethinker as you are a Lutheran one."

Nietzsche smiled, more broadly than ever before, and settled even more comfortably into his chair. "If I still smoked, Doctor Breuer, now would be the time for me to offer you a cigar."

Breuer felt decidedly encouraged. *Freud's suggestion that I emphasize stress as an underlying cause of migraine attacks is brilliant,* he thought, *and bound to succeed. Now I have properly set the stage. The time has come for action!*

He leaned forward in his chair and spoke confidently and deliberately. "I am most interested in your question about the cause of a disordered biological rhythm. I believe, as do most authorities on migraine, that a fundamental cause of migraine lies in one's general level of stress. Stress can be caused by a number of psychological factors—for example, upsetting events in one's work, family, personal relationships, or sexual life. Though some consider this viewpoint unorthodox, I believe it is the wave of the future for medicine."

Silence. Breuer was unsure of Nietzsche's reaction. On the one hand, he was nodding his head as though agreeing—but also flexing his foot, always a sign of tension.

"How does my answer strike you, Professor Nietzsche?"

"Does your position imply that the patient chooses his illness?"

Be wary, Josef, of that question! Breuer thought.

"No, that was not at all my meaning, Professor Nietzsche, although I have known patients who in some strange way profited from medical illness."

"You mean, for example, young men who injure themselves to escape military service?"

A treacherous question. Breuer grew even more wary. Nietzsche had said that he had served in the Prussian artillery for a short time and been discharged because of a clumsy peacetime injury.

"No, something more subtle"—*ach, a clumsy mistake,* Breuer instantly realized. *Nietzsche would take offense at the phrase.* But seeing no way to rectify it, he continued. "I refer to a young man of military age who escapes the military because of the advent of some actual disease. For example"— Breuer stretched for something completely removed from Nietzsche's experience—"tuberculosis or a debilitating skin infection."

"You have seen such things?"

"Every physician has seen such strange 'coincidences.' But to return to your question, I do *not* mean that you choose your illness—unless, of course, you profit in some way from your migraine. Do you?"

Nietzsche was silent, apparently deeply immersed in reflection. Breuer relaxed and commended himself. *A good response! That's the way to* handle him. Be direct and challenging; he likes that. And phrase questions in a way that engages his intellect!

"Do I in any way profit from this misery?" Nietzsche finally responded. "I have reflected on that very question for many years. Perhaps I *do* profit. In two ways. You suggest that the attacks are caused by stress, but sometimes the opposite is true—that the attacks *dissipate* stress. My work is stressful. It requires me to face the dark side of existence, and the migraine attack, awful as it is, may be a cleansing convulsion that permits me to continue."

A powerful answer! One Breuer had not anticipated, and he scrambled to regain his balance.

"You say you profit from illness in two ways. The second?"

"I believe I profit from my poor vision. For years now, I have been unable to read the thoughts of other thinkers. Thus, separate from others, I think my own thoughts. Intellectually I have had to live off my own fat! Perhaps that's a good thing. Perhaps that's why I have become an honest philosopher. I write only from my own experience. I write in blood, and the best truth is a bloody truth!"

"You have thus been cut off from all colleagueship in your profession?"

Another mistake! Again, Breuer caught it immediately. His question was off the point and reflected only his own preoccupation with recognition from colleagues.

"That's of little concern to me, Doctor Breuer, especially when I consider the shameful state of German philosophy today. I long ago walked out of the halls of the academy, and did not neglect to slam the door behind me. But as I think about it, perhaps this is yet another advantage of my migraine."

"How so, Professor Nietzsche?"

"My illness has emancipated me. It was because of my illness I had to resign my position at Basel. If I were still there, I'd be preoccupied with defending myself from my colleagues. Even my first book, *The Birth of Tragedy,* a relatively conventional work, evoked so much professional censure and controversy that the Basel faculty discouraged students from signing up for my courses. In my last two years there, I—perhaps the best lecturer in Basel history—spoke to audiences of only two or three. I am told Hegel lamented on his deathbed that he had only one student who understood him, and even that one student *mis*understood him! I am unable to claim even one misunderstanding student."

Breuer's natural inclination was to offer support. But fearing to offend Nietzsche again, he settled for a nod of comprehension, taking care not to convey sympathy.

"And still another advantage of my illness occurs to me, Doctor Breuer: my medical condition resulted in my release from the military. There was a time when I was foolish enough to seek a dueling scar"—here Nietzsche pointed to the small scar on the bridge of his nose—"or to demonstrate how much lager I could contain. I was even so foolish to consider a military career. Remember in those early days I was without a father's guidance. But my illness spared me all this. Even now, as I speak, I begin to think of even more fundamental ways my illness had helped me . . ."

Despite his interest in Nietzsche's words, Breuer grew impatient. His objective was to persuade his patient to engage in a talking treatment, and he had made the offhanded comment about profiting from illness only as a prelude to his proposal. He hadn't counted on the fertility of Nietzsche's mind. Any question tossed to him, the smallest grain of a question, sprouted lush foliage of thought.

Nietzsche's words flowed now. He seemed prepared to discourse for hours on the subject. "My illness has also confronted me with the actuality of death. For some time, I have believed that I had an incurable disease which would kill me at an early age. The spectre of imminent death has been a great boon: I have worked without rest because I feared I would die before I could finish what I need to write. And isn't a work of art greater if the end is catastrophic? The taste of my death in my mouth gave me perspective and courage. It's the courage to be *myself* that is the important thing. Am I a professor? A philologist? A philosopher? Who cares?"

Nietzsche's tempo increased. He seemed pleased with his flow of thoughts. "Thank you, Doctor Breuer. Talking to you has helped me consolidate these ideas. Yes, I should bless my illness, bless it. For a psychologist, personal suffering is a blessing—the training ground for facing the suffering of existence."

Nietzsche seemed fixed on some inward wision, and Breuer no longer felt that they were engaged in a conversation. He expected, at any minute, his patient to take out pen and paper and begin composing.

But, then, Nietzsche looked up and spoke to him more directly. "Do you remember, on Wednesday, my sentence of granite: 'Become he who you are'? Today I tell you my second granite sentence: *'Whatever does not kill me, makes me stronger.*' Thus I say again, 'My illness is a blessing.' "

Gone, now, was Breuer's sense of command and conviction. He had intellectual vertigo as Nietzsche, once again, had turned everything topsy-turvy. White is black, good is bad. His miserable migraine, a blessing. Breuer felt the consultation slipping away from him. He struggled to regain control.

"A fascinating perspective, Professor Nietzsche, one I've never heard expressed before. But certainly we agree, do we not, that you have already reaped the major benefit of your illness? Now, today, in midlife, armed with the wisdom and the perspective that the illness begat, I am sure you can work more effectively without its interference. It has served its function, has it not?"

While he was talking and collecting his thoughts, Breuer rearranged the objects on his desk: the wooden model of the inner ear, the Venetian swirled blue-and-gold glass paperweight, the bronze mortar and pestle, the prescription pad, the massive pharmaceutical formulary.

"Besides, as I understand you, Professor Nietzsche, you do not describe choosing an illness so much as you describe conquering and benefiting from one. Am I correct?"

"I *do* speak of conquering, or *overcoming,* an illness," Nietzsche replied, "but as to *choosing*—I'm not sure; perhaps one *does* choose an illness. It depends on who the 'one' is. The psyche does not function as a single entity. Parts of our mind may operate independently of others. Perhaps 'I' and my body formed a conspiracy behind the back of my own mind. The mind is, you know, fond of back alleys and trapdoors."

Breuer was startled at the similarity of Nietzsche's statement to Freud's position the day before. "You suggest that there are independent walled-off mental kingdoms within our mind?" he asked.

"It is impossible to escape that conclusion. In fact, much of our life may be lived by our instincts. Perhaps the conscious mental representations are afterthoughts—ideas thought *after* the deed to provide us with the illusion of power and control. Doctor Breuer, once again I thank you—our conversation has presented me with an important project to consider this winter. Please forgive me for a moment."

Opening his briefcase, Nietzsche took out a pencil stub and notebook and jotted down a few lines. Breuer stretched his head, trying, in vain, to read them upside down.

Nietzsche's complex line of thought had gone far beyond the little point

Breuer wanted to make. Still, though he felt like a poor simpleton, he had no recourse but to press on. "As your physician, I shall take the view that even though benefit has accrued from your illness, as you have argued so lucidly, the time has come for us to declare war upon it, to learn its secrets, to discover its weaknesses, and to eradicate it. Will you humor me and entertain this point of view?"

Nietzsche looked up from his notebook and nodded in acquiescence.

"I believe it is possible," Breuer went on, "for one to choose illness inadvertently by choosing a way of life which produces stress. When this stress becomes great enough or chronic enough, it triggers in turn some susceptible organ system—in the case of migraine, the vascular system. So, you see, I speak of indirect choice. One does not, strictly speaking, choose or select a disease; but one *does* choose stress—*and it is stress that chooses the disease!*"

Nietzsche's nod of comprehension encouraged Breuer to continue. "Thus *stress* is our enemy, and my task, as your physician, is to help you reduce the stress in your life."

Breuer felt relieved to be back on track. Now, he thought, I've prepared the soil for the next, and last, short step: to propose that I help Nietzsche alleviate the psychological sources of stress in his life.

Nietzsche placed his pencil and notebook back into his briefcase. "Doctor Breuer, I have for several years now addressed the issue of stress in my life. Reduce stress, you say! It was precisely for that reason I left the University of Basel in eighteen seventy-nine. I lead a stress-free life. I have given up teaching. I manage no estate. I have no home to look after, no servants to supervise, no wife to quarrel with, no children to discipline. I live frugally on a small pension. I have no obligations to anyone. I have pared stress in my life to the barest minimum, to an irreducible level. How can it be cut further?"

"I don't agree that it is irreducible, Professor Nietzsche. It is precisely this question I should like to explore with you. You see——"

"Keep in mind," Nietzsche interrupted, "that I have inherited an exquisitely sensitive nervous system. I know this from my profound responsiveness to music and to art. When I heard *Carmen* for the first time, every nerve cell in my brain fired at once: my entire nervous system was ablaze. For the same reason, I respond violently to every nuance of change in weather and barometric pressure."

"But," Breuer countered, "such neuronal hyperalertness may not be constitutional. It may itself be a function of stress from other sources."

"No, no!" Nietzsche protested, shaking his head impatiently, as though Breuer had missed the point. "My point is that hyperalertness, as you put it, is not *undesirable:* it is *necessary* to my work. I *want* to be alert. I do not want to be excluded from any part of my internal experience! And if tension is the price of insight, so be it! I am rich enough to pay that price."

Breuer did not respond. He had not expected such massive and immediate resistance. He had not yet even described his treatment proposal; yet the arguments he had prepared had been anticipated and were already battered. Silently he sought a way to marshal his troops.

Nietzsche continued: "You have looked at my books. You understand that my writing succeeds not because I am intelligent or scholarly. No, it's because I have the daring, the willingness, to detach myself from the comfort of the herd and to face strong and evil inclinations. Inquiry and science start with disbelief. Yet disbelief is inherently stressful! Only the strong can tolerate it. Do you know what the real question for a thinker is?" He did not pause for an answer. "The real question is: How much truth can I stand? It is no occupation for those of your patients who wish to eliminate stress, to live the tranquil life."

Breuer had no suitable rejoinder. Freud's strategy was in shreds. Base your approach on the elimination of stress, he had advised. But here is a patient who insists that his life work, the very thing that keeps him alive, *requires* stress.

Drawing himself up, Breuer reverted to medical authority. "I understand your dilemma precisely, Professor Nietzsche, but hear me out. You may see that there may be ways for you to suffer less while continuing to conduct your philosophical inquiries. I've thought much about your case. In my many years of clinical experience with migraine, I have helped many patients. I believe I can help you. Please let me present my treatment plan."

Nietzsche nodded and leaned back in his chair—feeling safe, Breuer imagined, behind the barricade he had erected.

"I propose that you be admitted to the Lauzon Clinic in Vienna for a month of observation and treatment. There are certain advantages to such an arrangement. We will be able to conduct systematic trials with several of the new migraine medications. I see by your chart that you have never had a clinical trial of ergotamine. It's a promising new treatment for migraine, but it requires precautions. It must be taken immediately at the onset of an attack; furthermore, if used incorrectly it may produce serious side effects. I much prefer to regulate the proper dosage while the patient is in the hospital and under close surveillance. Such observation may also give us valuable information about the trigger to the migraine. I see that you are a keen observer of your own condition—but, still, there's real advantage in the observations of trained professionals.

"I've often used the Lauzon for my patients," Breuer hurried on, permitting no interruptions. "It's comfortable and competently run. The new director has introduced many innovative features, including the serving of waters from Baden-Baden. Moreover, since it's within range of my office, I can visit you daily, Sundays excepted, and together we shall explore the sources of stress in your life."

Nietzsche was shaking his head, slightly but determinedly.

"Allow me," Breuer continued, "to anticipate your objection—the one you have just presented, that stress is so intrinsic to your work and to your mission that, even were it possible to extirpate it, you would not agree to such a procedure. I have it right?"

Nietzsche nodded. Breuer was pleased to see a glimmer of curiosity in his eyes. Good, good! he thought. The professor believes he has uttered the final word on stress. He is surprised to see me drag in its carcass!

"But my clinical experience has taught me that there are many sources of tension, sources that may be beyond the ken of the individual who is stressed, and that require an objective guide for elucidation."

"And the sources of tension are what, Doctor Breuer?"

"At one point in our discussion—it was when I asked whether you keep a diary of the events around your migraine attacks—you alluded to momentous and disturbing events in your life that distracted you from your diary keeping. I assume that these events—you are yet to be explicit about them—are sources of stress that might be alleviated through discussion."

"I have already resolved these distractions, Doctor Breuer," said Nietzsche with finality.

But Breuer persisted. "Surely there are other stresses. For example, on Wednesday you alluded to a recent betrayal. Certainly that betrayal begat stress. As no human being is free of *Angst,* so no one escapes the pain of friendship gone awry. Or the pain of isolation. To be honest, Professor Nietzsche, as your physician I am concerned by the daily schedule you described. Who can tolerate such isolation? Earlier you presented your lack of wife, children, and colleagues as evidence that you had eliminated stress from your life. But I see it differently: extreme isolation doesn't eliminate stress but is, in *itself*, stress. Loneliness is a breeding ground for sickness."

Nietzsche shook his head vigorously. "Allow me to disagree, Doctor Breuer. Great thinkers always choose their own company, think their own thoughts, undisturbed by the herd. Consider Thoreau, Spinoza, or the religious ascetics like Saint Jerome, Saint Francis, or the Buddha."

"I don't know Thoreau, but as for the rest—are they paragons of mental health? Besides"—here Breuer smiled broadly, hoping to lighten the discussion—"your argument must be in grave peril if you turn to the religious elders for support."

Nietzsche was not amused. "Doctor Breuer, I am grateful to you for your efforts in my behalf, and have already profited from this consultation: the information you offered about migraine is precious to me. But it is not advisable for me to go into a clinic. My extended stays at the baths—weeks at Saint-Moritz, at Hex, at Steinabad—have always come to naught."

Breuer was tenacious. "You must understand, Professor Nietzsche, that our treatment at the Lauzon Clinic would have no similarity to a cure at any of the European baths. I regret I even mentioned the Baden-Baden waters. They represent the smallest part of what the Lauzon, under my supervision, has to offer."

"Doctor Breuer, were you and your clinic located elsewhere I would give your plan serious consideration. Tunisia perhaps, Sicily, or even Rapallo. But a Vienna winter would be an abomination for my nervous system. I do not believe I would survive."

Although Breuer knew from Lou Salomé that Nietzsche had expressed no such objections when she had proposed that she and Nietzsche and Paul Rée spend the winter together in Vienna, it was, of course, information he could not use. Still, he had a much better response.

"But, Professor Nietzsche, you make my point precisely! If we hospitalized you in Sardinia or Tunisia and you were migraine-free for a month, we would have accomplished naught. Medical inquiry is no different from philosophical inquiry: *risk must be taken!* Under our supervision at the Lauzon, a developing migraine attack would be not a cause for alarm but rather a *blessing*—a treasure trove of information about the cause and the treatment of your condition. Let me assure you that I will be immediately available to you and can quickly abort an attack with ergotamine or nitroglycerine."

Here Breuer paused. He knew his response was powerful. He tried not to beam.

Nietzsche swallowed before replying. "Your point is well taken, Doctor Breuer. However, it is quite impossible for me to accept your recommendation. My objection to your plan and formulation of treatment stems from the deepest, most fundamental levels. But these are beside the point owing to a mundane but pre-eminent obstacle—money! Even under the best of circumstances, my resources would be strained by a month of intensive medical care. At this moment, it is impossible."

"Ach, Professor Nietzsche, isn't it strange that I ask so many questions about intimate aspects of your body and life, yet refrain, as do most physicians, from intruding upon your financial privacy?"

"You were unnecessarily discreet, Doctor Breuer. I have no reluctance to discussing finances. Money matters little to me—as long as there is enough of it for me to continue my work. I live simply and, aside from a few books, spend nothing except what I need for my bare subsistence. When I resigned from Basel three years ago, the university granted me a small pension. That is my money! I have no other funds or source of income—no estate from my father, no stipend from patrons—powerful enemies have seen to that—and, as I indicated to you, my writing has never yielded me a penny. Two years ago the University of Basel voted me a small increase in my pension. I think the first award was so that I would go away, and the second so that I would stay away."

Nietzsche reached into his jacket and extracted a letter. "I always assumed that the pension would be for life. However, this very morning Overbeck forwarded a letter from my sister in which she suggests that my pension is in jeopardy."

"Why is that, Professor Nietzsche?"

"Someone whom my sister does not like is slandering me. At the moment I do not know whether the charges are true, or whether my sister exaggerates—as she often does. Be that as it may, the important point is I cannot at this time possibly undertake a significant financial obligation."

Breuer was delighted and relieved by Nietzsche's objection. This was an obstacle easily overcome. "Professor Nietzsche, I believe we have similar attitudes toward money. I, like you, have never attached emotional importance to it. However, by sheer chance, my circumstances differ from yours. Had your father lived to leave you an estate, you would have money. Although my father, a prominent teacher of Hebrew, left me only a modest estate, he arranged a marriage for me with the daughter of one of the wealthiest Jewish families in Vienna. Both families were satisfied: a handsome dowry in exchange for a medical scientist with great potential.

"All of this, Professor Nietzsche, is by way of saying that your financial obstacle is no obstacle at all. My wife's family, the Altmanns, have endowed the Lauzon with two free beds which I may use at my discretion. Thus, there would be no clinic charges, nor any fees for my services. I emerge wealthier from each of our discussions! So then, good! All is settled! I shall notify the Lauzon. Shall we arrange for admission today?"

CHAPTER 9

B UT ALL WAS *NOT* SETTLED. Nietzsche sat with his eyes closed for a long time. Then, suddenly opening them, he said decisively, "Doctor Breuer, I've taken enough of your valuable time. Your offer is a generous one. I shall long remember it, but I cannot—I will not accept it. There are reasons beyond reasons"—words spoken with finality, as though he did not intend further explanation. In preparation for departure, he closed the clasps on his briefcase.

Breuer was astonished. This interview resembled more a chess contest than a professional consultation. He had made a move, proposed a plan, which Nietzsche immediately countered. He had responded to the objection, only to face still another of Nietzsche's objections. Was there no end to them? But Breuer, an old hand at clinical impasses, turned now to a ploy that rarely failed.

"Professor Nietzsche, be my consultant for a moment! Please imagine this interesting situation; perhaps you can help me understand it. I have encountered a patient who has been very sick for some time. He enjoys even tolerable health less than one day out of three. He then undertakes a long, arduous journey to consult with a medical expert. The consultant performs his task competently. He examines the patient and makes a proper diagnosis. Patient and consultant apparently develop a relationship of recip-rocal respect. The consultant then proposes a comprehensive treatment plan in which he has complete confidence. Yet the patient shows no interest whatsoever, not even curiosity, in the treatment plan. On the contrary, he rejects it instantaneously and raises obstacle after obstacle. Can you help me understand this mystery?"

Nietzsche's eyes widened. Though he appeared intrigued by Breuer's droll gambit, he did not respond.

Breuer persisted. "Perhaps we should start at the beginning of this riddle. Why does this patient who does not want treatment seek consultation in the first place?"

"I came because of strong pressure from my friends."

Breuer was disappointed that his patient declined to enter into the spirit of his little artifice. Though Nietzsche wrote with great wit and extolled laughter in the written word, it was clear the Herr Professor did not like to play.

"Your friends in Basel?"

"Yes, both Professor Overbeck and his wife are close to me. Also, a good friend in Genoa. I don't have many friends—a consequence of my nomadic life—and the fact that every one of them urged me to seek consultation was remarkable! As was the fact that Doctor Breuer's name seemed to be on all their lips."

Breuer recognized the adroit hand of Lou Salomé. "Surely," he said, "their concern must have been ignited by the gravity of your medical condition."

"Or perhaps from my speaking of it too often in my letters."

"But your speaking of it must reflect your own concern. Why else write them such letters? Surely not to evoke concern? Or sympathy?"

A good move! Check! Breuer was pleased with himself. Nietzsche was forced to retreat.

"I have too few friends to risk losing them. It occurred to me that, as a mark of friendship, I should do what I could to alleviate their concern. Hence my arrival in your office."

Breuer decided to press his advantage. He moved more boldly.

"You have no concern for yourself? Impossible! Over two hundred days a year of punishing incapacitation! I have attended too many patients in the midst of a migraine attack to accept any minimization of your pain."

Excellent! Another file on the chessboard closed off. Where would his opponent move now? Breuer wondered.

Nietzsche, apparently realizing he had to develop some of his other pieces, turned his attention back to the center of the board. "I have been called many things—philosopher, psychologist, pagan, agitator, antichrist. I have even been called some *unflattering* things. But I prefer to call myself a scientist, because the cornerstone of my philosophic method, as of the scientific method, is *disbelief*. I always maintain the most rigorous possible skepticism, and I am skeptical now. I cannot accept your recommendation for psychic exploration on the basis of medical authority."

"But, Professor Nietzsche, we are entirely in agreement. The only authority to be followed is reason, and my recommendation is supported by reason. I claim only two things. First, that stress may make one sick—and much scientific observation supports this claim. Second, that considerable stress exists in your life—and I speak of a stress *different* from that inherent in your philosophic inquiry.

"Let us examine the data together," Breuer continued. "Consider the letter you described from your sister. Surely there is stress in being slandered. And, incidentally, you violated our contract of reciprocal honesty by failing to mention this slanderer to me earlier." Breuer moved more boldly yet. There was no other way—he had nothing to lose.

"And surely there is stress in the thought of losing your pension, your sole source of support. And if that is mere alarmist exaggeration by your sister, then there is the stress of having a sister willing to alarm you!"

Had he gone too far? Nietzsche's hand, Breuer noticed, had slid down the side of his chair and was slowly inching its way to the handle of his briefcase. But there was no turning back now. Breuer went for checkmate.

"But I have even more powerful support for my position—a brilliant recent book"—he reached out and tapped his copy of *Human, All Too Human*—"by a soon-to-be, if there be any justice in this world, eminent philosopher. Listen!"

Opening the book to the passage he had described to Freud, he read: " *'Psychological observation is among the expedients by means of which one can alleviate the burden of living.'* A page or two farther, the author asserts that psychological observation is essential and that—here, in his words— *'Mankind can no longer be spared the cruel sight of the moral dissecting table.'* A couple of pages later, he points out that the errors of the greatest philosophers usually stem from a false explanation of human actions and sensations which ultimately results in *'the erection of a false ethics and religious and mythological monsters.'*

"I could go on"—and Breuer flipped through the pages—"but the point made by this excellent book is that, if human belief and behavior are to be understood, one must first sweep away convention, mythology, and religion. Only then, with *no preconceptions whatsoever,* should one presume to examine the human subject."

"I am quite familiar with that book," said Nietzsche sternly.

"But will you not follow its prescription?"

"I devote my life to its prescription. But you have not read far enough. For years now, I alone have performed such a psychological dissection: I have been the subject of my own study. But I am not willing to be *your* subject! Would you yourself be willing to be the subject of another? Allow me to put a direct question to you, Doctor Breuer. What is *your* motivation in this treatment project?"

"You come to me for help. I offer it. I am a doctor. That's what I do."

"Far too simple! Both of us know that human motivation is far more complex, and at the same time more primitive. I ask again, what is your motivation?"

"It *is* a simple matter, Professor Nietzsche. One practices one's profession—a cobbler cobbles, a baker bakes, and a doctor doctors. One earns one's living, one practices one's calling, and my calling is to be of service, to alleviate pain."

Breuer tried to convey confidence but began to feel queasy. He did not like Nietzsche's latest move.

"These are not satisfactory answers to my question, Doctor Breuer. When you say a doctor doctors, a baker bakes, or one practices one's calling, that is not motivation: that is habit. You've omitted from your answer consciousness, choice, and self-interest. I prefer it when you say one earns one's living—that, at least, one can understand. One strives to put food in one's stomach. But you don't request money from me."

"I might pose you the same question, Professor Nietzsche. You say you earn nothing from your work: Why, therefore, do you philosophize?" Breuer tried to stay on the offensive but felt his momentum ebbing.

"Ah, but there is one important distinction between us. I do not claim that I philosophize *for you,* whereas you, Doctor, continue to pretend that your motivation is to serve me, to alleviate my pain. Such claims have nothing to do with human motivation. They are part of the slave mentality artfully engineered by priestly propaganda. Dissect your motives deeper! You will find that no one has *ever* done anything wholly for others. All actions are self-directed, all service is self-serving, all love self-loving."

Nietzsche's words came faster, and he rushed on.

"You seem surprised by that comment? Perhaps you think of those you love. Dig deeper, and you will learn that you do not love *them:* what you love is the pleasant sensations such love produces in you! You love desire, not the desired. So, may I ask again why you wish to serve me? Again, I ask, Doctor Breuer"—here Nietzsche's voice grew stern—*"what are your motives?"*

Breuer felt dizzy. He choked back his first impulse: to comment on the ugliness and crassness of Nietzsche's formulation, and thus inevitably put an end to the aggravating case of Professor Nietzsche. He imagined, for a moment, the sight of Nietzsche's back as he stomped out of his office. God, what a relief! Free at last of this whole sorry, frustrating business. Yet it saddened him to think he would not see Nietzsche again. He was drawn to this man. But why? Indeed, what *were* his motives?

Breuer found himself thinking again of chess games with his father. He had always made the same error—of concentrating too much on attack, pressing it beyond his own supply lines, and ignoring his defense until, like lightning, his father's queen struck behind his lines and threatened mate. He brushed the fantasy away, not failing, however, to take note of its meaning: he must never, never again underestimate this Professor Nietzsche.

"Again, I ask, Doctor Breuer, *what are your motives?"*

Breuer struggled to respond. What were they? He marveled at the way his mind resisted Nietzsche's question. He forced himself to concentrate. His desire to help Nietzsche—when had it begun? In Venice, of course, bewitched by Lou Salomé's beauty. So charmed had he been that he had readily agreed to help her friend. To undertake the healing of Professor Nietzsche had provided not only an ongoing link with her but an opportunity to elevate himself in her eyes. Then there was the link with Wagner. Of course, that was conflicted: Breuer loved Wagner's music but hated his anti-Semitism.

What else? Over the weeks, Lou Salomé had dimmed in his mind. She was no longer the reason for his engagement with Nietzsche. No, he knew he was intrigued by the intellectual challenge before him. Even Frau Becker the other day had said no other physician in Vienna would have taken on such a patient.

Then there was Freud. Having proposed Nietzsche to Freud as a teaching case, he'd look foolish if the professor spurned his help. Or was it that he wished to be near greatness? Perhaps Lou Salomé was right in saying that Nietzsche represented the future of German philosophy: those books by Nietzsche—they had the smell of genius.

None of these motives, Breuer knew, had any relevance to the man Nietzsche, to the flesh-and-blood person before him. And so he had to remain silent about his contact with Lou Salomé, his glee at going where other physicians feared to tread, his craving for the touch of greatness. Perhaps, Breuer grudgingly acknowledged, Nietzsche's ugly theories about motivation have merit! Even so, he had no intention of abetting his patient's outrageous challenge to his claim of service. But how, then, to respond to Nietzsche's annoying and inconvenient question?

"My motives? Who can answer such a question? Motives exist in many layers. Who decrees that only the first layer, the animalistic motives, are the ones that count? No, no—I see you're ready to repeat the question; let me attempt to answer the spirit of your inquiry. I spent ten years in medical training. Shall I waste those years of training because I no longer need money? Doctoring is my way of justifying the effort of those early years—a way of providing consistency and value to my life. And of providing meaning! Should I sit all day and count my money? Would *you* do that? I am certain you would not! And then there is another motive. I enjoy the intellectual stimulation I receive from my contacts with you."

"These motives have at least the aroma of honesty," Nietzsche conceded.

"And I've just thought of another—I like that granite sentence: 'Become who you are.' What if what I am, or what I was destined for, is to be of service, to aid others, to contribute to medical science and the relief of suffering?"

Breuer felt much better. He was regaining his composure. Perhaps I've been too argumentative, he thought. Something more conciliatory is needed. "Here's still another motive. Let us say—and I believe it to be so—that your destiny is to be one of the great philosophers. Thus my treatment not only may help your physical being but will also aid you in your project of becoming who *you* are."

"And if I am, as you say, to become great, then *you* as my animator, my saviour, become even greater!" Nietzsche exclaimed as if he knew he'd just fired the telling shot.

"No! I didn't say that!" Breuer's patience, generally inexhaustible in his professional role, was beginning to shred. "I am the physician to many individuals who are eminent in their field—the leading scientists, artists, musicians in Vienna. Does that make me greater than they? No one even knows I treat them."

"But you have told me, and now use their eminence to enhance your authority with me!"

"Professor Nietzsche, I don't believe what I'm hearing. Do you actually believe that, if your destiny is fulfilled, I shall go about proclaiming that it is I, Josef Breuer, who created you?"

"Do *you* actually believe that such things do *not* happen?"

Breuer tried to settle himself. Careful, Josef, keep your temper. Consider things from *his* standpoint. Try to understand the source of his distrust.

"Professor Nietzsche, I know you have been betrayed in the past and are therefore justified to anticipate betrayal in the future. You have my word, however, that it will not happen here. I promise you that your name will never be mentioned by me. Nor shall it even appear in clinic records. Let us invent a pseudonym for you."

"It's not what you may tell others, I accept your word on that. What matters is what you will tell *yourself,* and what I will tell *myself.* In all that you have told me of your motives, there was, despite your continuing claims of service and the alleviation of distress, nothing really of *me* in it. That is how it should be. You will use me in your self-project: that, too, is expected—it is the way of nature. But do you not see, *I will be used up by you!* Your pity for me, your charity, your empathy, your techniques to help me, to manage me—the effects of all these make you stronger at the expense of my strength. I am not rich enough to afford such help!"

This man is impossible, Breuer thought. He dredges up the worst, the basest, motives for everything. Breuer's few remaining tatters of clinical objectivity fluttered away. He could no longer contain his feelings.

"Professor Nietzsche, allow me to speak frankly. I have seen much merit in many of your arguments today, but this last assertion, this fantasy about my wishing to weaken you, about my strength feeding on yours, is total nonsense!"

Breuer saw Nietzsche's hand slipping farther down toward the handle of his briefcase, but could not stop himself! "Don't you see, here's a perfect example of why you *cannot* dissect your own psyche. Your vision is blurred!"

He saw Nietzsche grasp his briefcase and start to rise. Nonetheless, he continued, "Because of your own unfortunate problems with friendships, you make bizarre mistakes!"

Nietzsche was buttoning up his coat, but Breuer could not hold his tongue: "You assume your own attitudes are universal and then you try to comprehend for all mankind what you cannot comprehend about yourself."

Nietzsche's hand was on the doorknob.

"I apologize for interrupting you, Doctor Breuer, but I must arrange for this afternoon's train to Basel. May I return in two hours to pay my bill and collect my books? I shall leave a forwarding address for your consultation report." He bowed stiffly and turned. Breuer winced at the sight of his back as he walked out of the office.

CHAPTER 10

B REUER DIDN'T MOVE when the door shut—and was still sitting, frozen, at his desk when Frau Becker hurried in.

"What happened, Doctor Breuer? Professor Nietzsche just bolted out of your office, muttering that he'd return shortly to get his bill and his books."

"Somehow I botched everything this afternoon," said Breuer, and briefly recounted the events of his last hour with Nietzsche. "When, at the end, he picked up and left, I was almost shouting at him."

"He must have goaded you into it. A sick man comes for treatment, you do your best, then he fights with you about everything you say. My last employer, Doctor Ulrich, would have thrown him out long before, I swear it."

"The man needs help badly." Breuer got up and, going to the window, mused softly, almost to himself, "Yet he's too proud to accept it. But this pride of his—it's part of his illness, just as much as if it were a diseased body organ. So stupid of me to raise my voice at him! There must have been a way to have approached him—to have engaged him, and his pride, in some treatment program."

"If he's too proud to accept help, how can you treat him? At night, while he's sleeping?"

There was no response from Breuer, who stood looking out the window, rocking slightly back and forth, full of self-recrimination.

Frau Becker tried again. "Remember a couple of months ago, when you were trying to help that old woman, Frau Kohl, the one who was afraid to leave her room?"

Breuer nodded, still with his back to Frau Becker. "I remember."

"And then she suddenly broke off treatment just as you had gotten her to the point where she'd walk into another room if you were holding her hand. When you told me about it, I remarked how frustrated you must feel to bring her so close to cure and then have her quit."

Breuer nodded impatiently; he wasn't clear about the point, if there was one. "So?"

"Then you said something very good. You said that life is long and patients often have long careers in treatment. You said they may learn something from one doctor, carry it inside their heads, and, sometime in the future, be ready to do more. And that meanwhile you had played the role she was ready for."

"So?" Breuer asked again.

"So, maybe that's true for Professor Nietzsche. Maybe he'll hear your words when he's ready—perhaps sometime in the future."

Breuer turned to look at Frau Becker. He was moved by what she had said. Not so much by the content, for he doubted whether anything that had transpired in his office would ever prove useful to Nietzsche. But by what she had tried to do. When he was in pain, Breuer—unlike Nietzsche—welcomed help.

"I hope you're right, Frau Becker. And thanks for trying to cheer me up—that's a new role for you. A few more patients like Nietzsche, and you'll be an expert at it. Who are we seeing this afternoon? I could do with something simpler—perhaps a case of tuberculosis or congestive heart failure."

Several hours later, Breuer presided over the Friday evening family supper. In addition to his three older children, Robert, Bertha, and Margarethe (Louis had already fed Johannes and Dora), the party of fifteen included three of Mathilde's sisters, Hanna and Minna—still unmarried—and Rachel with her husband, Max, and their three children, Mathilde's parents, and an elderly widowed aunt. Freud, who had been expected, was not present—he had sent word that he would be dining alone on bread and water while working up six late hospital admissions. Breuer was disappointed. Still agitated by Nietzsche's departure, he had looked forward to a discussion with his young friend.

Although Breuer, Mathilde, and all her sisters were partially assimilated "three-day Jews," observing only the three highest holidays, they sat in respectful silence while Aaron, Mathilde's father, and Max—the two practicing Jews in the family—chanted prayers over the bread and wine. The Breuers followed no dietary restrictions; but for Aaron's sake, Mathilde served no pork that evening. Ordinarily, Breuer enjoyed pork, and his favorite dish, a prune-latticed pork roast, was often served at his table. Moreover, Breuer, and Freud as well, were great devotees of the crisp juicy pork wieners sold at the Prater. While walking there, they never failed to stop for a sausage snack.

This meal, like all Mathilde's meals, began with hot soup—tonight a thick one of barley and lima beans—and was followed by a large carp baked with carrots and onions, and the main course, a succulent goose stuffed with Brussels sprouts.

When the cinnamon-cherry strudel, hot and crisp from the oven, was served, Breuer and Max picked up their plates and walked down the hall to Breuer's study. For fifteen years after Friday-night dinners, they had always taken their dessert and played chess in the study.

Josef had known Max long before they had married the Altmann sisters. But had they not been brothers-in-law, they would never have remained friends. Though Breuer admired Max's intelligence, surgical skills, and chess virtuosity, he disliked his brother-in-law's limited ghetto mentality and vulgar materialism. Sometimes Breuer disliked even looking at Max: not only was he ugly—bald, blotchy-skinned, and morbidly obese—but he looked old. Breuer tried to forget that he and Max were the same age.

Well, there would be no chess tonight. Breuer told Max he was too agitated and wished to talk instead. He and Max rarely talked intimately; but aside from Freud, Breuer had no other male confidant—in fact, no confidant at all since the departure of Eva Berger, his previous nurse. Now, though he had misgivings about the extent of Max's sensitivity, he nevertheless plunged in and, for twenty minutes without pause, spoke about Nietzsche, referring to him, of course, as Herr Müller and unburdening himself of everything, even the meeting with Lou Salomé in Venice.

"But, Josef," Max began in an abrasive, dismissive tone, "why blame yourself? Who could treat such a man? He's crazy, that's all! When his head hurts bad enough, he'll come begging!"

"You don't understand, Max. Part of his disease is *not* to accept help. He's almost paranoid: he suspects the worst of everybody."

"Josef, Vienna is filled with patients. You and I could work one hundred fifty hours a week and still have to refer patients out every day. Right?"

Breuer didn't reply.

"Right?" Max asked again.

"That's not the point, Max."

"It *is* the point, Josef. Patients are banging at your door to get in, and here you are begging someone to let you help him. It doesn't make sense! Why should you beg?" Max reached for a bottle and two small glasses. "Some slivovitz?"

Breuer nodded, and Max poured. Despite the fact that the Altmann fortune was founded on wine sales, their small glass of chess slivovitz was the only alcohol either man ever drank.

"Max, listen to me, suppose you have a patient with—Max, you're not listening. You're turning your head."

"I'm listening, I'm listening," Max insisted.

"Suppose you have a patient with prostatic enlargement and a totally obstructed urethra," Breuer continued. "Your patient has urinary retention, his retrograde renal pressure is rising, he's going into uremic poisoning, and yet he absolutely refuses help. Why? Maybe he has senile dementia. Maybe he's more terrified of your instruments, your catheters, and your tray of steel sounds than of uremia. Maybe he's psychotic and thinks you're going to castrate him. So what then? What are you going to do?"

"Twenty years in practice," Max replied, "it's never happened."

"But it *could*. I'm using it to make a point. *If* it happened, what would you do?"

"It's his family's decision, not mine."

"Max, come on—you're avoiding the question! Suppose there *were* no family?"

"How should I know? Whatever they do in the asylums—put him in restraints, anesthetize him, catheterize him, try to dilate his urethra with sounds."

"Every day? Catheterize him in restraints? Come on, Max, you'd kill him in a week! No, what you would do is try to change his attitude toward you and toward treatment. It's the same thing when you treat children. Does a child ever *want* to be treated?"

Max ignored Breuer's point. "And you say you want to hospitalize him and talk to him every day—Josef, look at the time involved! Can he afford so much of your time?"

When Breuer spoke of his patient's poverty and his plan to use the family-endowed beds and to treat him without a fee, Max grew even more concerned.

"You worry me, Josef! I'll be frank. I'm truly worried about you. Because a pretty Russian girl whom you don't even know talks to you, you want to treat a crazy man who doesn't want to be treated for a condition he denies having. And now you say you want to do it for free. Tell me," said Max, wagging his finger at Breuer, "who's crazier, you or him?"

"I'll tell you what's crazy, Max! What's crazy is for you always to bring up the money. The interest on Mathilde's dowry keeps accumulating in the bank. And later, when we each get our share of the Altmann inheritance, you and I both will be swimming in money. I can't begin to spend all the money that comes in now, and I know you've got a lot more than I have. So why bring up money? What's the point of worrying about whether such-and-such a patient can pay me? Sometimes, Max, you don't see past money."

"All right, forget the money. Maybe you're right. Sometimes I don't know *why* I'm working or what's the point of charging anyone. But, thank God, no one hears us: they'd think we were both crazy! Aren't you going to eat the rest of your strudel?"

Breuer shook his head, and Max lifted his plate and slid the pastry onto his own.

"But, Josef, this is not medicine! The patients you treat—this professor—what's he got? The diagnosis? A cancer of his pride? That Pappenheim girl who was afraid of drinking water, wasn't she the one who suddenly couldn't speak German any more, only English? And every day developed a new paralysis? And that young boy who thought he was the emperor's son, and that lady who was afraid to leave her room. Craziness! You didn't have the best training in Vienna to work with craziness!"

After eating Breuer's strudel in one mammoth bite and washing it down with a second glass of slivovitz, Max resumed. "You're the finest diagnostician in Vienna. No one in this city knows more than you about respiratory diseases or about equilibrium. Everyone knows your research! Mark my words—some day they'll have to invite you into the National Academy. If you weren't a Jew, you'd be a professor now, everyone knows that. But if you keep treating these crazy conditions, what will happen to your reputation? The anti-Semites will say, *'See, see, see!'* "—Max stabbed the air with his finger—"*That's* why! *That's* why he's not the professor of medicine. He is not fit, he is not sound!"

"Max, let's play chess." Breuer jerked open the chess box and angrily spilled the pieces onto the board. "Tonight I say I want to talk to you because I'm upset, and look how you help me! I'm crazy, my patients are crazy, and I should throw them out the door. I'm ruining my reputation, I should squeeze florins I don't need——"

"No, no! I took the money part back!"

"Is this a way to help? You don't listen to what I ask."

"Which is? Tell me again. I'll listen better." Max's large, mobile face grew suddenly earnest.

"I had in my office today a man who needs help, who is a suffering patient—and I handled him poorly. I can't correct the situation with this patient, Max, it's finished with him. But I'm seeing more neurotic patients, and I have to understand how to work with them. It's a whole new field. No textbooks. There are thousands of patients out there who need help— but no one knows how to help them!"

"I don't know anything about this, Josef. More and more you work with thinking and the brain. I'm at the opposite end, I——" Max chortled. Breuer braced himself. "The apertures I talk to don't talk back. But I can tell you one thing—I get the feeling you were competing with this professor, just like you used to do with Brentano in philosophy class. Do you remember the day he snapped at you? Twenty years ago and I remember like yesterday. He said, 'Herr Breuer, why don't you try to learn what I have to teach rather than prove how much I don't know?' "

Breuer nodded. Max continued, "Well, that's what your consultation sounds like to me. Even your ploy of trying to trap this Müller by quoting his own book. That wasn't smart—how could you win? If the trap fails, *he* wins. If the trap works, then he's so angry he wouldn't cooperate anyway."

Breuer sat silent, fingering the chess pieces while he considered Max's words. "Maybe you're right. You know, I felt even at the time that probably I shouldn't have tried quoting his book. I shouldn't have listened to Sig. I had a premonition that quoting his words to him wasn't clever, but he kept parrying me, goading me into a competitive relationship. It's funny, you know—all during my consultation I kept thinking of playing chess. I'd spring this trap on him, he'd get out of it and spring one on me. Maybe it was me; you say I was like that at school. But I haven't been that way with a patient in years, Max. I think it's something in him—he pulls it from me, maybe from everyone, and then calls it human nature. And he believes that it is! That's where his whole philosophy goes wrong."

"See, Josef, you're still doing it, trying to punch holes in his philosophy. You say he's a genius. If he's such a genius, maybe *you should learn from him* instead of trying to beat him!"

"Good, Max, that's good! I don't like it, but it sounds right. It helps." Breuer drew a deep breath and exhaled noisily. *"Now* let's play. I've been thinking about a new answer to the queen's gambit."

Max played a queen's gambit, and Breuer responded with a bold center-counter gambit, only to find himself in deep trouble eight moves later. Max cruelly forked Breuer's bishop and knight with a pawn and, without looking up from the board, said, "Josef, as long as we talk such talk tonight, let me talk, too. Maybe it's not my business, but I can't close my ears. Mathilde tells Rachel that you haven't touched her in months."

Breuer studied the board for a few more minutes and, after realizing he had no escape from the fork, took Max's pawn before answering him. "Yes, it's bad. Very bad. But, Max, how can I talk to you about it? I might as well talk directly into Mathilde's ear, because I know you talk to your wife, and she talks to her sister."

"No, believe me, I can keep secrets from Rachel. I'll tell *you* a secret: if Rachel knew about what's going on with me and my new nurse, Fräulein Wittner, I'd be out on my ass—last week! It's like you and Eva Berger—screwing around with nurses must run in the family."

Breuer studied the chessboard. He was troubled by Max's comment. So that was how the community viewed his relationship with Eva! Though the charge was untrue, he felt guilty nonetheless about one moment of great sexual temptation. In a momentous conversation several months ago, Eva had told him she feared he was on the brink of entering a ruinous liaison with Bertha, and had offered "to do anything" to help him free himself from his obsession with his young patient. Hadn't Eva been offering herself sexually? Breuer had been certain of it. But the demon "but" had intervened, and in this, as in so many other ways, he could not bring himself to act. Yet he often thought about Eva's offer and sorely regretted his missed opportunity!

Now Eva was gone. And he had never been able to set things right with her. After he discharged her, she never spoke to him again and had ignored his offers of money or assistance in obtaining a new position. Though he could never undo his failure to defend her against Mathilde, he determined now that he could at least defend her against Max's accusations.

"No, Max, you've got it wrong. I'm no angel, but I swear I never touched Eva. She was just a friend, a good friend."

"Sorry, Josef, I guess I just put myself in your place and then assumed that you and Eva——"

"I can see how you'd think that. We had an unusual friendship. She was a confidante, we spoke about everything together. She got a terrible reward after all those years of working for me. I should never have knuckled under to Mathilde's anger. I should have stood up to her."

"Is that why you and Mathilde are—you know—estranged?"

"Maybe I do hold that against Mathilde, but that's not the real problem in our marriage. It's much more than that, Max. But I don't know *what* it is. Mathilde is a good wife. Oh, I hated the way she acted about Bertha and Eva. But in one way she was right—I paid more attention to them than to her. What happens now, though, is strange. When I look at her, I still think she's beautiful."

"And?"

"And I just can't touch her. I turn away. I don't want her to come close."

"Maybe that's not so uncommon. Rachel's no Mathilde, but she's a good-looking woman, and yet I have more interest in Fräulein Wittner—who, I must admit, looks a little like a frog. Some days when I walk down the Kirstenstrasse and see twenty, thirty whores lined up, I'm very tempted. None of them are prettier than Rachel, many have gonorrhea or syphilis, but still I'm tempted. If I knew for sure no one would recognize me, who knows? I might! Everyone gets tired of the same meal. You know, Josef, for every beautiful woman out there, there exists some poor man who is tired of *shtupping* her!"

Breuer never liked to encourage Max in his vulgar mode, but couldn't help smiling at his aphorism—true in its own gross way. "No, Max, it's not boredom. That's not the problem for me."

"Maybe you should get yourself checked out. Several urologists are writing about sex function. Did you read Kirsch's paper about diabetes causing impotence? Now that the taboo about talking about it is lifted, it's obvious that impotence is far more common than we thought."

"Impotent I'm not," replied Breuer. "Even though I've stayed away from sex, there's lots of juice flowing. That Russian girl, for example. And I've had the same kind of thoughts as you about the prostitutes on Kirstenstrasse. In fact, part of the problem is I have so many sexual thoughts about another woman that I feel guilty touching Mathilde." Breuer noticed how Max's self-revelations made it easier for him to talk. Perhaps Max, in his own crude way, could have handled Nietzsche better than he.

"But even that's not the main thing," Breuer found himself continuing, "it's something else! Something more diabolical inside me. You know, I think about leaving. I would never do it, but over and over again I think of just picking up and leaving—Mathilde, the children, Vienna—everything. I keep getting this crazy thought, and I know it's crazy—you don't have to tell me, Max—that all my problems would be solved if I could only find a way to get away from Mathilde."

Max shook his head, sighed, then captured Breuer's bishop, and began to mount an invincible queen's side attack. Breuer settled back heavily into his chair. How was he going to live through ten, twenty, thirty more years of losing to Max's French defense and the infernal queen's gambit?

CHAPTER 11

REUER LAY IN BED that night still thinking about the queen's gambit and Max's commentary on beautiful women and tired men. His troubled feelings about Nietzsche had diminished. Somehow the talk with Max had helped. Perhaps, all these years, he had underestimated Max. Now Mathilde, returning from the children, climbed into bed, moved close to him, and whispered, "Good night, Josef." He pretended to be asleep.

Rap! Rap! Rap! A pounding on the front door. Breuer looked at the clock. Four forty-five. He roused himself quickly—he never slept deeply—grabbed his robe, and started down the hall. Louis came out of her room, but he waved her back. As long as he was awake, he would answer the door.

The *Portier*, apologizing for waking him, said there was a man outside who wanted him for an emergency. Downstairs Breuer found an elderly man standing in the vestibule. He wore no hat and had obviously walked a long way—his breath came quickly, his hair was covered with snow, and the mucus leaking from his nose had frozen his thick mustache into a great icy broom.

"Doctor Breuer?" he asked, his voice trembling with agitation.

At Breuer's nod, he introduced himself as Herr Schlegel, bowing his head and touching the fingers of his right hand to his forehead in an atavistic remnant of what undoubtedly had been, in better times, a smart salute. "A patient of yours in my *Gasthaus* is sick, very sick," he said. "He cannot talk, but I found this card in his pocket."

Examining the formal card Herr Schlegel handed him, Breuer found his own name and address written on one side and on the reverse:

PROFESSOR FRIEDRICH NIETZSCHE
Professor of Philology
University of Basel

His decision was instantaneous. He gave Herr Schlegel explicit instructions for fetching Fischmann and the fiacre. "And when you get back here, I'll be dressed. You can tell me about my patient on the way to the *Gasthaus*."

Twenty minutes later, Herr Schlegel and Breuer were wrapped in blankets and being driven through the cold, snowy streets. The innkeeper explained that Professor Nietzsche had been at the *Gasthaus* since the beginning of the week. "A very good guest. Never any problems."

"Tell me about his sickness."

"All week he spends most days in his room. I don't know what he does up there. Whenever I bring his tea in the morning he's sitting at his table scribbling. That puzzled me because, you know, I'd found out he can't see well enough to read. Two or three days ago, a letter came for him postmarked Basel. I took it up to him, and a few minutes later he came downstairs squinting and blinking. He said he was having some eye trouble and asked if I'd read it to him. Said it was from his sister. I started, but after the first couple of lines—something about a Russian scandal—he seemed upset and asked for it back. I tried to catch a glimpse of the rest before handing it over but had time only to see the words 'deportation' and 'police.'

"He takes his meals out, though my wife offered to cook for him. I don't know where he eats—he didn't ask me for advice. He scarcely talked, though one night he said he was going to a free concert. But he wasn't shy, that's not why he was quiet. I observed several things about his quietness——"

The innkeeper, who had once served ten years in military intelligence, missed his old trade and amused himself by regarding his guests as mysteries and attempting to construct a character profile from small housekeeping details. On his long walk to Breuer's home, he had gathered together all his clues about Professor Nietzsche and rehearsed his presentation to the doctor. It was a rare opportunity: ordinarily he had no suitable audience, his wife and the other *Gasthaus* owners being too lumpish to appreciate real inductive skill.

But the doctor interrupted him. "His sickness, Herr Schlegel?"

"Yes, yes, Doctor." And swallowing his disappointment, Herr Schlegel reported how around nine on Friday morning Nietzsche had paid his bill and gone out, saying he would be leaving that afternoon and would come back before noon to collect his baggage. "I must have been away from my desk for a bit because I didn't see him come back. He walks very softly, you know, as if he doesn't want to be followed. And he doesn't use an umbrella, so I can't tell from the downstairs umbrella stand if he's in or not. I don't think he wants anyone to know where he is, when he's in, when he's out. He's good, he is—suspiciously good—at getting in and out without attracting notice."

"And his sickness?"

"Yes, yes, Doctor. I only thought some of these points might be important for diagnosis. Well, later in the afternoon, around three o'clock, my Frau, like always, went in to clean his room, and there he was—he hadn't left on the train at all! He was stretched out on his bed moaning, his hand on his head. She called me, and I told her to replace me at the desk—I never leave it unguarded. That's why, you see my point, I was surprised that he got back into the room without my seeing him."

"And then?" Breuer was impatient now—Herr Schlegel had, he decided, read one too many pulp mystery stories. Yet there was still plenty of time to indulge his companion's obvious wish to tell all he knew. The *Gasthaus* in the third, or Landstrasse, district was still a mile or so ahead, and in the thickening snow visibility was so poor that Fischmann had climbed down and was now walking his horse slowly through the frozen streets.

"I went into his room and asked if he was sick. He said he wasn't feeling well, a little headache—he'd pay for another day and leave tomorrow. He told me he often had headaches like this, and it was best if he didn't talk or move. Nothing to be done, he said, but wait it out. He was quite frosty—he usually is, you know, but today more so, icy. No doubt about it, he *wanted* to be left alone."

"What next?" Breuer shivered. The cold was seeping into his marrow. However irritating Herr Schlegel was, Breuer nonetheless liked hearing that others had found Nietzsche difficult.

"I offered to get a doctor, but he got *very* agitated at that! You should have seen him. 'No! No! No doctors! They only make things worse! No doctors!' He wasn't exactly rude—he never is, you know—just frosty! Always well mannered. You can see he's well born. Good private school, I'd bet. Travels in good circles. At first I couldn't figure out why he didn't stay at a more expensive hotel. But I checked his clothes—you can tell a lot from clothes, you know—good labels, good cloth, well tailored, good Italian leather shoes. But everything, even underclothing, is well worn, very well worn, often mended, and jackets haven't been that length in ten years. I said to my wife yesterday that he's a poor aristocrat with no idea of how to get along in today's world. Earlier in the week I took the liberty of asking him about the origin of the name Nietzsche, and he mumbled something about old Polish nobility."

"What happened then, after he refused a doctor?"

"He continued to insist he'd be all right if he were left alone. In his well-mannered way, he got the message across I should mind my own damn business. He's the silent-suffering type—or he's got something to hide. And stubborn! If he hadn't been so stubborn, I could have summoned you yesterday, before the snow started, and not have to get you up at this hour."

"What else did you notice?"

Herr Schlegel brightened at the question. "Well, for one thing he refused to leave a forwarding address, and the previous address was suspicious: General Delivery, Rapallo, Italy. I've never heard of Rapallo, and when I asked where it was, he just said, 'On the coast.' Naturally the police must be notified: his secrecy, sneaking about with no umbrella, no address, and that letter—Russian trouble, deportation, the police. Naturally, I searched for the letter when we cleaned his room, but I never found it. Burned it, I think, or hidden it."

"You haven't called in the police?" Breuer asked anxiously.

"Not yet. Best wait for daybreak. Bad for business. Don't want the police disturbing my other clients in the middle of the night. And, then, on top of everything else, he gets this sudden illness! You want to know what I think? Poison!"

"Good God, no!" Breuer almost shouted. "No, I'm sure not. Please, Herr Schlegel, forget about the police! I assure you, there's nothing to be concerned about. I know this man. I'll speak for him. He is not a spy. He is exactly what the card says, a university professor. And he *does* have these headaches often; that's why he came to see me. Please relax your suspicions."

In the flickering light of the fiacre's candle, Breuer could see that Herr Schlegel was *not* relaxing, and added, "However, I can understand how an acute observer could reach that conclusion. But trust me on this matter. The responsibility will be mine." He tried to get the innkeeper back to Nietzsche's illness. "Tell me, after you saw him in the afternoon, what else happened?"

"I check back twice more to see if he needs anything—you know, tea or something to eat. Each time he thanks me and refuses, not even turning his head. He seemed weak, and his face was pale."

Herr Schlegel paused for a minute, then—unable to stop himself from commentary—added, "No gratitude at all for my or my Frau's looking in on him—he's not a warm person, you know. He actually seemed annoyed at our kindness. We help him, and he gets annoyed! That didn't sit well with my Frau. She got annoyed back and won't have anything more to do with him—she wants him out tomorrow."

Ignoring his complaint, Breuer asked, "What happened next?"

"The next time I saw him was about three in the morning. Herr Spitz, the guest in the room next to him, was awakened—the noise of furniture being knocked over, he said, then moaning, even screaming. Getting no response to his knock and finding the door locked, Herr Spitz woke me up. He's a timid soul and kept apologizing for waking me. But he did the right thing. I told him that immediately.

"The professor had locked the door from inside. I had to break the lock—and I have to insist on his paying for a new one. When I entered, I found him unconscious, moaning and lying in his underwear on the bare mattress. All his clothes and all the bed coverings had been thrown about. My guess is he hadn't moved from the bed but had undressed and thrown everything on the floor—nothing was more than two or three feet from the bed. It was out of character for him, all out of character, Doctor. He's usually a tidy man. The Frau was shocked at the mess—vomit everywhere, it'll take a week before the room is rentable, before the stink clears out. He should, by rights, pay for that week. And bloodstains on the sheet, too—I rolled him over and looked, but no wound—the blood must have been in the vomit."

Herr Schlegel shook his head. "That's when I searched his pockets, found your address, and came to get you. My wife said to wait for dawn, but I thought he might die by then. I don't have to tell you what that means—undertaker, formal inquest, the police around all day. I've seen it many times—the other guests will clear out in twenty-four hours. In my brother-in-law's *Gasthaus* in the Schwarzwald, two guests died in one week. Do you know that, *ten* years later, people still refuse to take those death rooms? And he's completely redone them—curtains, paint, wallpaper. And people avoid them still. Word just gets around, the villagers talk, they never forget."

Herr Schlegel put his head out the window, looked around, and shouted to Fischmann: "Right turn—coming up, next block!" He turned back to Breuer. "Here we are! Next building, Doctor!"

Telling Fischmann to wait, Breuer followed Herr Schlegel into the *Gasthaus* and up four narrow flights of stairs. The stark landscape of the stairwells bore witness to Nietzsche's claim of being concerned only about sheer subsistence: Spartan clean; a threadbare carpet runner, with a different faded pattern on each flight; no bannisters; no furniture on the landings. Recently whitewashed walls softened by neither picture nor ornament—not even an official certificate of inspection.

Breathing hard from the climb, Breuer followed Herr Schlegel into Nietzsche's room. He took a moment to accommodate to the lush, acrid-sweet smell of vomit, then quickly scanned the scene. It was as Herr Schlegel had described. In fact, precisely so—the innkeeper not only being an accurate observer, but also having left everything untouched so as not to disturb some precious clue.

On a small bed in one corner of the room lay Nietzsche, clad only in his underwear, deeply asleep, perhaps in coma. Certainly he didn't stir in response to the sounds of their entering the room. Breuer gave Herr Schlegel leave to collect Nietzsche's strewn clothes and vomit-soaked and bloodstained bedsheets.

Once they were gone, the brutal bareness of the room emerged. It was not unlike a prison cell, Breuer thought: along one wall was a flimsy wooden table on which rested only a lantern and a half-filled water pitcher. Before the table stood a straight wooden chair, and under the table sat Nietzsche's suitcase and briefcase—both wrapped with a light chain and padlocked. Over the bed was a small grimy window with pathetic, faded and streaked yellow curtains, the room's sole concession to aesthetics.

Breuer asked to be left alone with his patient. His curiosity being stronger than his fatigue, Herr Schlegel protested, then acquiesced when Breuer reminded him of his obligations to his other guests: to be a good host, he would have to salvage some sleep.

Once alone, Breuer turned up the gaslight and surveyed the scene more carefully. The enamel basin on the floor next to the bed was half filled with blood-tinged, light green vomitus. The mattress and Nietzsche's face and chest glistened with drying vomitus—no doubt he had become too ill, or too stuporous, to reach for the basin. Next to the basin was a glass half filled with water, and next to that a small bottle three quarters filled with large oval tablets. Breuer inspected and then tasted a tablet. Most likely chloral hydrate—that would account for his stupor; but he couldn't be certain because he did not know when Nietzsche had taken the tablets. Had he time to absorb them into his bloodstream before he vomited all the contents of his stomach? Calculating the number of tablets missing from the jar, Breuer rapidly concluded that even had Nietzsche taken all the tablets that evening, and his stomach absorbed all the chloral, he had consumed a dangerous, but not lethal, dose. Had it been larger, Breuer knew there was little he could have done: gastric lavage was pointless, since Nietzsche's stomach was now empty, and he was far too stuporous—and probably too nauseated—to ingest any stimulant Breuer might give him.

Nietzsche looked moribund: face gray; eyes shrunken; his entire body cold, pallid, and pockmarked with goose pimples. His breathing was labored, and his pulse feeble and racing at one hundred fifty-six per minute. Now Nietzsche shivered, but when Breuer tried to cover him with one of the blankets Frau Schlegel had left, he moaned and kicked it away. Probably extreme hyperesthesia, Breuer thought: everything feels painful to him, even the merest touch of a blanket.

"Professor Nietzsche, Professor Nietzsche," he called. No response. Nor did Nietzsche stir when he, more loudly, called, "Friedrich, Friedrich." Then, "Fritz, Fritz." Nietzsche flinched at the sound, and flinched yet again as Breuer tried to lift his eyelids. Hyperesthesia even to sound and light, Breuer noted, and rose to turn the light down and the gas heater up.

Closer inspection confirmed Breuer's diagnosis of bilateral spastic migraine: Nietzsche's face, especially his forehead and ears, was cool and pale; his pupils were dilated; and both temporal arteries were so constricted they felt like two slender frozen cords in his temple.

Breuer's first concern, however, was not the migraine but the life-threatening tachycardia; and he proceeded, despite Nietzsche's thrashing, to apply firm thumb pressure to the left carotid artery. In less than a minute, his patient's pulse slowed to eighty. After closely observing his cardiac status for about fifteen minutes, Breuer felt satisfied and turned his attention to the migraine.

Reaching into his medical bag for nitroglycerine troches, he asked Nietzsche to open his mouth, but got no response. When he tried to pry open his mouth, Nietzsche clenched his teeth so hard that Breuer abandoned the effort. Perhaps amyl nitrate will do it, Breuer thought. He poured four drops on a cloth and held it under Nietzsche's nose. Nietzsche took a breath, flinched, and turned away. Resistive to the end, even in unconsciousness, thought Breuer.

He placed both hands on Nietzsche's temples and began, lightly at first and then with gradual increasing pressure, to massage his entire head and neck. He concentrated particularly on those areas that seemed, from his patient's reactions, to be most tender. As he proceeded, Nietzsche screamed and frantically shook his head. But Breuer persisted and calmly held his position, all the while whispering gently in his ear, "Take the pain, Fritz, take the pain—this will help." Nietzsche thrashed less, but continued to moan—deep, agonized, guttural "Noooos."

Ten, fifteen minutes passed. Breuer continued to massage. After twenty minutes, the moans softened and then became inaudible, but Nietzsche's lips were working, muttering something inaudible. Breuer bent his ear to Nietzsche's mouth but still could not make out the words. Was it "Leave me, leave me, leave me"? Or perhaps "Let me, let me"? He couldn't be certain.

Thirty, thirty-five minutes passed. Breuer continued to massage. Nietzsche's face felt warmer, and his color was returning. Perhaps the spasm was ending. Even though he was still stuporous, Nietzsche seemed to be resting easier. The mumbling continued, a little louder, a little clearer. Again, Breuer bent his ear close to Nietzsche's lips. He could distinguish the words now, though at first doubted his ears. Nietzsche was saying, "Help me, help me, help me, help me!"

A wave of compassion swept over Breuer. "Help me!" So, he thought, all along that's what he's been asking of me. Lou Salomé was wrong: her friend *is* capable of asking for help, but this is another Nietzsche, one I am meeting for the first time.

Breuer rested his hands and paced for a few minutes around Nietzsche's small cell. Then he soaked a towel in the cool water in the pitcher, placed the compress to his sleeping patient's brow, and whispered, "Yes, I will help you, Fritz. Count on me."

Nietzsche winced. Perhaps touch is still painful, Breuer thought, but held the compress in place nonetheless. Nietzsche opened his eyes slightly, looked at Breuer, and raised his hand to his brow. Perhaps he intended simply to remove the compress, but his hand approached Breuer's and for a moment, just for a moment, their hands touched.

Another hour passed. Daylight was breaking, almost seven thirty. Nietzsche's condition seemed stable. There was little more to be done at this time, Breuer thought. It was best now to attend to his other patients and return later when Nietzsche had slept off the chloral. After covering his patient with a light blanket, Breuer wrote a note saying he would return before noon, moved a chair next to the bed, and left the note on the chair in plain view. Descending the stairs, he directed Herr Schlegel, who was at his post at the front desk, to look in on Nietzsche every thirty minutes. Breuer woke Fischmann, who had been napping on a stool in the vestibule, and together they went out into the snowy morning to begin their round of house calls.

When he returned four hours later, he was greeted by Herr Schlegel, sitting at his post at the front desk. No, there had been no new developments: Nietzsche had been sleeping continuously. Yes, he seemed more comfortable, and he had behaved better—an occasional moan, but no screaming, thrashing, or vomiting.

Nietzsche's eyelids fluttered when Breuer entered his room, but he continued to sleep deeply even when Breuer addressed him. "Professor Nietzsche, can you hear me?" No response. "Fritz," Breuer called. He knew he was justified in addressing his patient informally—often stuporous patients will respond to younger, earlier names—but he still felt guilty, knowing he was also doing it for himself: he enjoyed calling Nietzsche by the familiar "Fritz." "Fritz! Breuer here. Can you hear me? Can you open your eyes?"

Almost immediately, Nietzsche's eyes opened. Did they contain a look of reproach? Breuer reverted at once to formal address.

"Professor Nietzsche. Back among the living, I am pleased to see. How do you feel?"

"Not pleased"—Nietzsche's voice was soft, and his words slurred—"to be living. Not pleased. No fear of darkness. Awful, feel awful."

Breuer put his hand on Nietzsche's brow, partly to feel his temperature, but also to offer comfort. Nietzsche recoiled, jerking his head back several inches. Perhaps he still has hyperesthesia, Breuer thought. But later, when he made a cold compress and held it to Nietzsche's brow, the latter, in a weak, weary voice, said, "I can do that," and, taking the compress from Breuer, comforted himself.

The rest of Breuer's examination was encouraging: his patient's pulse was now seventy-six, his complexion was ruddier, and the temporal arteries were no longer in spasm.

"My skull feels shattered," Nietzsche said. "My pain has changed—no longer sharp, more now like a deep, aching brain bruise."

Though his nausea was still too extreme for him to swallow medication, he was now able to accept the nitroglycerine troche Breuer placed under his tongue.

Over the next hour, Breuer sat and conversed with his patient, who gradually grew more responsive.

"I was concerned about you. You might have died. That much chloral is more poison than cure. You need a drug that will either attack the headache at its source or attenuate the pain. Chloral does neither—it's a sedative, and to render yourself unconscious in the face of that much pain requires a dose that might well be fatal. It almost was, you know. And your pulse was dangerously irregular."

Nietzsche shook his head. "I don't share your concern."

"Meaning——?"

"About outcome," Nietzsche whispered.

"About it's being fatal, you mean?"

"No, about anything—about anything."

Nietzsche's voice was almost plaintive. Breuer gentled his voice as well. "Were you hoping to die?"

"Am I living? Dying? Who cares? No slot. No slot."

"What do you mean?" Breuer asked. "That there's no slot, or place, for you? That you'd not be missed? That no one would care?"

A long silence. The two men remained together quietly, and soon Nietzsche was breathing deeply as he lapsed back into sleep. Breuer watched him for another few minutes, then left a note on the chair saying he would return later that afternoon or early evening. Once again, he instructed Herr Schlegel to check on his patient frequently, but not to bother offering food—perhaps hot water, but the professor would not be able to stomach anything solid for another day.

When he returned at seven o'clock, Breuer shuddered as he entered Nietzsche's room. The plaintive light of a single candle cast flickering shadows on the walls and revealed his patient lying in the darkness, eyes closed, hands folded on his chest, fully dressed in his black suit and heavy black shoes. Was this, Breuer wondered, a prevision of Nietzsche lying in state, alone and unmourned?

But he was neither dead nor asleep. He quickened at the sound of Breuer's voice and, with effort and in obvious pain, raised himself to a sitting position, with his head in his hands and his legs hanging over the side of the bed. He motioned to Breuer to seat himself.

"How are you feeling now?"

"My head is still squeezed by a steel vise. My stomach hopes it will never again encounter food. My neck and back—here"—Nietzsche pointed to the back of his neck and to the upper margins of his scapulae—"are excruciatingly tender. Aside from these things, however, I feel dreadful."

Breuer was slow to smile. Nietzsche's unexpected irony caught up with him only a minute later, when he noticed his patient's grin.

"But at least I am in familiar waters. I have visited this pain many times before."

"This was a typical attack, then?"

"Typical? Typical? Let me think. For sheer intensity, I'd say this was a strong attack. Of my last hundred attacks, perhaps only fifteen or twenty were more severe. Still, there were many worse attacks."

"How so?"

"They lasted much longer, the pain often continuing for two days. That's rare, I know, as other doctors have said."

"How do you explain the brevity of this one?" Breuer was fishing, trying to discover how much of the last sixteen hours Nietzsche remembered.

"We both know the answer to that question, Doctor Breuer. I am grateful to you. I know I'd still be writhing in pain on this bed if not for you. I wish there were some meaningful way I could repay you. That failing, we must rely on the currency of the realm. My feelings about debts and payment are unchanged, and I expect a bill from you commensurate with the time you have devoted to me. According to Herr Schlegel's account—which does not suffer from lack of precision—the bill should be considerable."

Though dismayed to hear Nietzsche return to his formal, distancing voice, Breuer said he would instruct Frau Becker to prepare the bill on Monday.

But Nietzsche shook his head. "Ach, I forgot your office is not open on Sunday, but tomorrow I plan to take the train to Basel. Is there no way we can settle my account now?"

"To Basel? Tomorrow! Surely not, Professor Nietzsche, not till this crisis is over. Despite our disagreements this past week, allow me now to function properly as your physician. Only a few hours ago, you were comatose and in a dangerous heart arrhythmia. It is more than *unwise* for you to travel tomorrow, it is *perilous*. And there's another factor: many migraines may recur immediately if sufficient rest is not taken. Surely you have made that observation."

Nietzsche was silent for a moment, obviously thinking over Breuer's words. Then he nodded. "Your advice will be heeded. I agree to stay over another day and leave on Monday. May I see you on Monday morning?"

Breuer nodded. "For the bill, you mean?"

"For that, and I'd be grateful also for your consultation note and a description of the clinical measures you employed to abort this attack. Your methods should be useful to your successors, primarily Italian physicians, since I will be spending the next several months in the south. Surely the power of this attack proscribes another winter in Central Europe."

"This is a time for rest and tranquillity, Professor Nietzsche, not for us to engage in further disputation. But please permit me to make two or three observations for you to mull over until we meet on Monday."

"After what you have done for me this day, I am bound to listen carefully."

Breuer weighed his words. He knew this would be his last chance. If he failed now, Nietzsche would be on the Basel train Monday afternoon. He quickly reminded himself not to repeat any of his previous mistakes with Nietzsche. Stay calm, he told himself. Don't try to outwit him; he's too clever by half. Don't argue: you will lose, and even if you win, you lose. And that other Nietzsche, the one who wants to die but pleads for help, the one you promised to help—that Nietzsche is not here now. Don't try to speak to him.

"Professor Nietzsche, let me begin by underscoring how critically ill you were last night. Your heartbeat was dangerously irregular and could have failed at any time. I don't know the cause, I need time to evaluate it. But it was not the migraine, nor do I believe it was the overdose of chloral. I have never seen chloral produce this effect before.

"That's the first point I want to make. The second is the chloral. The amount you took could have been fatal. It's possible the vomiting from the migraine saved your life. I, as your physician, must be concerned about your self-destructive behavior."

"Doctor Breuer, forgive me." Nietzsche spoke with his head cupped in his hands and his eyes closed. "I'd resolved to hear you out entirely without interrupting, but I fear my mind is too sluggish to retain thoughts. I had best speak when ideas are still fresh. I was unwise about the chloral and should have known better from similar previous experiences. I intended to take only a single chloral tablet—it does dull the blade of the pain—and then put the bottle back in my suitcase. What undoubtedly occurred last night was that I took one pill and forgot to put the bottle away. Then as the chloral took effect, I became confused, forgot I had already taken one tablet, and took another. I must have gone through this sequence several times. This has happened before. It was foolish behavior, but not suicidal—if that's what you mean to imply."

A plausible hypothesis, thought Breuer. The same thing had happened to many of his elderly, forgetful patients, and he always instructed their children to dispense medications. But he did not believe the explanation sufficiently accounted for Nietzsche's behavior. For one thing, *why,* even in his pain, did he forget to put the chloral back in his suitcase? Doesn't one have responsibility even for one's forgetfulness. No, Breuer thought, this patient's behavior is more malignantly self-destructive than he claims. In fact, there was proof: the soft voice that said, "Living or dying—who cares?" Yet it was proof that he could not use. He had to let Nietzsche's comment stand unchallenged.

"Even so, Professor Nietzsche, even if that *were* the explanation, it does not mitigate the risk. You must have a complete evaluation of your medication regime. But permit me another observation—this one about the onset of your attack. You attribute it to the weather. Without doubt that played a role: you have been a keen observer of the influence of atmospheric conditions on your migraine. But several factors are likely to act in concert to initiate a migraine attack, and for this episode I believe I bear a responsibility: it was shortly after I confronted you in a rude and aggressive fashion that your headache began."

"Again, Doctor Breuer, I must interject. You said nothing that a good physician should not have said, that other physicians would not have said earlier and with less tact than you. You do not deserve the blame for this attack. I sensed it coming long before our last talk. In fact, I had a premonition of it even on my way to Vienna."

Breuer hated to yield on this point. But this was not time for debate.

"I don't want to tax you further, Professor Nietzsche. Let me merely say, then, that on the basis of your overall medical condition, I feel even more strongly than before that an extended period of thorough observation and treatment is necessary. Even though I was called in hours after its onset, I was still successful in shortening this particular attack. Had you been under observation in a clinic, I feel confident that I could have developed a regimen to abort your attacks even more completely. I urge you to accept my recommendation to enter the Lauzon Clinic."

Breuer stopped. He had said all that was possible. He had been temperate, lucid, clinical. He could do no more. There was a long silence. He waited it out, listening to the sounds in the tiny room: Nietzsche's breathing, his own, the whining of the wind, a footstep and a creaking board in the room above.

Then Nietzsche responded in a gentle, almost inviting, voice. "I have never met a physician like you, not one as capable, not one as concerned. Nor as personal. Perhaps you could teach me much. When it comes to learning how to live with people, I believe I must start from scratch. I *am* indebted to you, and believe me, I know *how* indebted."

Nietzsche paused—"I'm tired and must lie down"—and stretched out on his back, his hands folded on his chest, his eyes fixed on the ceiling. "Being so indebted, I am distressed to go against your recommendation. But the reasons I gave you yesterday—was it just yesterday? It seems we've talked for months—those reasons were not frivolous, not simply dreamed up on the spot to oppose you. If you choose to read further in my books, you'll see how my reasons are rooted in the very ground of my thinking, hence of my being.

"These reasons feel even stronger now—stronger today than yesterday. I don't know why that should be. I cannot understand much about myself today. Doubtless you are right, chloral is not good for me, certainly not a tonic for my cerebration—I'm not thinking clearly even yet. But those reasons I offered you, they feel tenfold stronger now, a hundredfold stronger."

He turned his head to look at Breuer. "I urge you, Doctor, to cease your efforts on my behalf! To refuse your advice and your offer now, and to continue to refuse you again and again, only increases the humiliation of being so indebted to you.

"Please"—and he turned his head away again—"it is best for me to rest now—and perhaps best for you to return home. You mentioned once you have a family—I fear they will resent me, and with good cause. I know you have spent more time this day with me than with them. Until Monday, Doctor Breuer." Nietzsche closed his eyes.

Before departing, Breuer said that should Nietzsche require him, a messenger from Herr Schlegel would bring him within the hour, even on Sunday. Nietzsche thanked him, but did not open his eyes.

As Breuer walked down the stairs of the *Gasthaus*, he marveled at Nietzsche's control and resilience. Even from a sickbed, in a tawdry room still reeking with the odors of the violent upheaval of only hours ago, at a time when most migraine sufferers would be grateful simply to sit in a corner and breathe, Nietzsche was thinking and functioning: concealing his despair, planning his departure, defending his principles, urging his physician to return to his family, requesting a consultation report and a bill that was fair to his physician.

When he got to the waiting fiacre, Breuer decided that an hour's walk home would clear his head. He dismissed Fischmann, handing him a gold florin for a hot supper—waiting in the cold was hard work—and set off through the snow-covered streets.

Nietzsche would leave for Basel on Monday, he knew. Why did that matter so much? No matter how hard he pondered this question, it seemed beyond understanding. He knew only that Nietzsche mattered to him, that he was drawn to him in some preternatural way. Perhaps, he wondered, I see something of myself in Nietzsche. But what? We differ in every fundamental way—background, culture, life design. Do I envy his life? What is there to envy in that cold, lonely existence?

Certainly, Breuer thought, my feelings about Nietzsche have nothing to do with guilt. As a physician, I have done all that duty calls for; I cannot fault myself in that regard. Frau Becker and Max were right: What other physician would have put up for any length of time with such an arrogant, abrasive, and exasperating patient?

And vain! How naturally he had said *en passant*—and not in empty boasting but out of full conviction—that he was the best lecturer in the history of Basel, or that perhaps people might have the courage, might dare, to read his work by the year two thousand! Yet Breuer took offense at none of this. Perhaps Nietzsche was right! Certainly his speech and his prose were compelling, and his thoughts powerfully luminous—even his wrong thoughts.

Whatever the reasons, Breuer did not object to Nietzsche's mattering so much. Compared with the invasive, pillaging Bertha fantasies, his preoccupation with Nietzsche seemed benign, even benevolent. In fact, Breuer had a premonition that his encounter with this bizarre man might lead to something redemptive for himself.

Breuer walked on. That other man housed and hidden in Nietzsche, that man who pleaded for help: Where was he now? "That man who touched my hand," Breuer kept saying to himself, "how can I reach *him*? There must be a way! But he's determined to leave Vienna on Monday. Is there no stopping him? There *must* be a way!"

He gave up. He stopped thinking. His legs took over, and continued walking, toward a warm, well-lit home, toward his children and loving, unloved Mathilde. He concentrated only on breathing in the cold, cold air, warming it in the cradle of his lungs, and then releasing it in steamy clouds. He listened to the wind, to his steps, to the bursting of the fragile icy crust of snow underfoot. And suddenly, he knew a way—the *only* way!

His pace quickened. All the way home, he crunched the snow and, with every step, chanted to himself, "I know a way! I know a way!"

CHAPTER 12

ON MONDAY MORNING, Nietzsche came to Breuer's office for the final stages of their business together. After carefully studying Breuer's itemized bill to be sure nothing had been omitted, Nietzsche filled out a bank draft and handed it to Breuer. Then Breuer gave Nietzsche his clinical consultation report and suggested he read it while still in the office in case he had any questions. After scrutinizing it, Nietzsche opened his briefcase and placed it in his folder of medical reports.

"An excellent report, Doctor Breuer, comprehensive and comprehensible. And unlike many of my other reports, it contains no professional jargon, which, though offering the illusion of knowledge, is in reality the language of ignorance. And now, back to Basel. I have taken too much of your time."

Nietzsche closed and locked his briefcase. "I leave you, Doctor, feeling more indebted to you than to any man ever before. Ordinarily, leavetaking is accompanied by denials of the permanence of the event: people say, 'Auf Wiedersehen'—until we meet again. They are quick to plan for reunions and then, even more quickly, forget their resolutions. I am *not* one of those. I prefer the truth—which is that we shall almost certainly not meet again. I shall probably never return to Vienna, and I doubt you will ever be in such want of a patient like me as to track me down in Italy."

Nietzsche tightened his grip on his briefcase and started to get up.

It was a moment for which Breuer had prepared carefully. "Professor

Nietzsche, please, not just yet! There is another matter I wish to discuss with you."

Nietzsche tensed. No doubt, Breuer thought, he has been expecting another plea to enter the Lauzon Clinic. And dreading it.

"No, Professor Nietzsche, it's not what you think, not at all. Please relax. It is quite another matter. I've been procrastinating in raising this issue for reasons that will soon be apparent."

Breuer paused and took a deep breath.

"I have a proposition to make you—a rare proposition, perhaps one never before made by a doctor to a patient. I see myself delaying. This is hard to say. I'm not usually at a loss for words. But it's best simply to say it.

"I propose a professional exchange. That is, I propose that for the next month I act as physician to your body. I will concentrate only on your physical symptoms and medications. And you, in return, will act as physician to my mind, my spirit."

Nietzsche, still gripping his briefcase, seemed puzzled, then wary. "What do you mean—your mind, your spirit? How can I act as physician? Is this not but another variation of our discussion last week—that you doctor me and I teach you philosophy?"

"No, this request is entirely different. I do not ask you to teach me, but to *heal* me."

"Of what, may I ask?"

"A difficult question. And yet I pose it to my patients all the time. I asked it of *you*, and now it is my turn to answer it. I ask you to heal me of despair."

"Despair?" Nietzsche relaxed his hold on his briefcase and leaned forward. "What kind of despair? I see no despair."

"Not on the surface. *There* I seem to be living a satisfying life. But, underneath the surface, despair reigns. You ask what kind of despair? Let us say that my mind is not my own, that I am invaded and assaulted by alien and sordid thoughts. As a result, I feel self-contempt, and I doubt my integrity. Though I care for my wife and my children, I don't *love* them! In fact, I resent being imprisoned by them. I lack courage: the courage either to change my life or to continue living it. I have lost sight of *why* I live—the point of it all. I am preoccupied with aging. Though every day I grow closer to death, I am terrified of it. Even so, suicide sometimes enters my mind."

On Sunday, Breuer had rehearsed this answer often. But today it had been—in a strange way, considering the underlying duplicity of the plan—*sincere*. Breuer knew he was a poor liar. Though he had to conceal the big lie—that his proposal was a ploy to engage Nietzsche in treatment—he had resolved to tell the truth about everything else. Hence, in his speech, he presented the truth about himself in slightly exaggerated form. He also tried to select concerns that might in some way interlace with some of Nietzsche's own, unspoken concerns.

For once, Nietzsche appeared truly astounded. He shook his head slightly, obviously wanting no part of this proposal. Yet he was having difficulty formulating a rational objection.

"No, no, Doctor Breuer, this is impossible. I cannot do this, I've no training. Consider the risks—everything might be made worse."

"But, Professor, there is no such thing as training. Who is trained? To whom can I turn? To a physician? Such healing is not part of the medical discipline. To a religious leader? Shall I take the leap into religious fairy tales? I, like you, have lost the knack for such leaping. You, a *Lebens-philosopher*, spend your life contemplating the very issues that confound my life. To whom can I turn if not to you?"

"Doubts about yourself, wife, children? What do *I* know about these?"

Breuer responded at once. "And aging, death, freedom, suicide, the search for purpose—you know as much as anyone alive! Aren't these the precise concerns of your philosophy? Aren't your books entire treatises on despair?"

"I can't cure despair, Doctor Breuer. I study it. Despair is the price one pays for self-awareness. Look deeply into life, and you will always find despair."

"I know that, Professor Nietzsche, and I don't expect cure, merely relief. I want you to advise me. I want you to show me how to tolerate a life of despair."

"But I don't know how to show such things. And I have no advice for the singular man. I write for the race, for humankind."

"But, Professor Nietzsche, you believe in scientific method. If a race, or a village, or a flock has an ailment, the scientist proceeds by isolating and studying a single prototypic specimen and then generalizing to the whole. I spent ten years dissecting a tiny structure in the inner ear of the pigeon to discover how pigeons maintain their equilibrium! I could not work with pigeonkind. I had to work with individual pigeons. Only later was I able to generalize my findings to all pigeons, and then to birds and mammals, and humans as well. That's the way it has to be done. You can't conduct an experiment on the whole human race."

Breuer paused, awaiting Nietzsche's rebuttal. None came. He was rapt in thought.

Breuer continued. "The other day you described your belief that the specter of nihilism was stalking Europe. You argued that Darwin has made God obsolete, that just as we once created God, we have all now killed him. And that we no longer know how to live without our religious mythologies. Now I know you didn't say this directly—correct me if I'm mistaken—but I believe you consider it your mission to demonstrate that out of disbelief one can create a code of behavior for man, a new morality, a new enlightenment, to replace one born out of superstition and the lust for the supernatural." He paused.

Nietzsche nodded for him to continue.

"I believe, though you may disagree with my choice of terms, that your mission is to save humankind from both nihilism and illusion?"

Another slight nod from Nietzsche.

"Well, save *me!* Conduct the experiment with *me!* I'm the perfect subject. I have killed God. I have no supernatural beliefs, and am drowning in nihilism. I don't know *why* to live! I don't know *how* to live!"

Still no response from Nietzsche.

"If you hope to develop a plan for all mankind, or even a select few, try it on me. Practice on me. See what works and what doesn't—it should sharpen your thinking."

"You offer yourself as an experimental lamb?" Nietzsche replied. *"That* would be how I repay my debt to you?"

"I'm not concerned about risk. I believe in the healing value of talking. Simply to review my life with an informed mind like yours—that's what I want. That cannot fail to help me."

Nietzsche shook his head in bewilderment. "Do you have a specific procedure in mind?"

"Only this. As I proposed before, you enter the clinic under an assumed name, and I observe and treat your migraine attacks. When I make my daily visits, I shall first attend to you. I shall monitor your physical condition and prescribe any medication that may be indicated. For the rest of our visit, you become the physician and help me talk about my life concerns. I ask only that you listen to me and interject any comments you wish. That is all. Beyond that, I don't know. We'll have to invent our procedure along the way."

"No." Nietzsche shook his head firmly. "It is impossible, Doctor Breuer. I admit your plan is intriguing, but it is doomed from the onset. I am a writer, not a talker. And I write for the few, not the many."

"But your books are not for the few," Breuer quickly responded. "In fact, you express scorn for philosophers who write only for one another, whose work is removed from life, who do not *live* their philosophy."

"I don't write for other philosophers. But I do write for the few who represent the future. I am not meant to mingle, to live *among*. My skills for social intercourse, my trust, my caring for others—these have long atrophied. If, indeed, such skills were ever present. I have always been alone. I shall always remain alone. I accept that destiny."

"But, Professor Nietzsche, you want more. I saw sadness in your eyes when you said that others might not read your books until the year two thousand. You *want* to be read. I believe there is some part of you that still craves to be with others."

Nietzsche sat still, rigid in his chair.

"Remember that story you told me about Hegel on his deathbed?" Breuer continued. "About the only one student who understood him being one who *mis*understood him—and ended by saying that, on your own deathbed, you couldn't claim even one student. Well, why wait for the year two thousand? Here I am! You have your student right here, right now. And I'm a student who will listen to you, because my life depends on understanding you!"

Breuer paused for breath. He was very pleased. In his preparation the day before, he had correctly anticipated each of Nietzsche's objections and countered each of them. The trap was elegant. He could hardly wait to tell Sig.

He knew he should stop at this juncture—the first object being, after all, to ensure that Nietzsche did not take the train to Basel today—but could not resist adding one further point. "And, Professor Nietzsche, I remember how you said the other day that nothing disturbed you more than to be in debt to another with no possibility of equivalent repayment."

Nietzsche's response was quick and sharp. "You mean that you do this for *me*?"

"No, that's just the point. Even though my plan might in some way serve you, that is *not* my intention! My motivation is entirely self-serving. I need help! Are you strong enough to help me?"

Nietzsche stood up from his chair.

Breuer held his breath.

Nietzsche took a step toward Breuer and extended his hand. "I agree to your plan," he said.

Friedrich Nietzsche and Josef Breuer had struck a bargain.

Letter from Friedrich Nietzsche to Peter Gast

My dear Peter,

A change of plans. Again. I shall be in Vienna for an entire month and, hence, must, with regret, postpone our Rapallo visit. I will write when I know my plans more precisely. A great deal has happened, most of it interesting. I am having a slight attack (which would have been a two-week monster were it not for the intervention of your Dr. Breuer) and am too weak now to do more than give you a précis of what has transpired. More to follow.

Thank you for finding me the name of this Dr. Breuer—he is a great curiosity—a thinking, *scientific* physician. Is that not remarkable? He is willing to tell me what he knows about my illness and—even *more* remarkable—what he does *not* know!

He is a man who greatly wishes to dare and I believe is attracted to my daring to dare greatly. He has dared to offer me a most unusual proposition, and I have accepted it. For the next month he proposes to hospitalize me at the Lauzon Clinic, where he will study and treat my medical illness. (And all this to be at *his* expense! This means, dear friend, that you need not concern yourself about my subsistence this winter.)

And I? What must I offer in return? I, who none believed would ever again be gainfully employed, I am asked to be Dr. Breuer's personal philosopher for one month to provide personal philosophic counsel. His life is a torment, he contemplates suicide, he has asked me to guide him out of the thicket of despair.

How ironic, you must think, that your friend is called upon to muffle death's siren call, the same friend who is so enticed by that rhapsody, the very friend who wrote you last saying that the barrel of a gun seemed not an unfriendly sight!

Dear friend, I tell you this about my arrangement with Dr. Breuer in *total* confidence. This is for no one else's ear, not even Overbeck. You are the *only one* I entrust with this. I owe the good doctor total confidentiality.

Our bizarre arrangement evolved to its present form in a complex manner. First he offered to counsel *me* as part of my medical treatment! What a clumsy subterfuge! He pretended that he was interested only in my welfare, his only wish, his only reward, to make *me* healthy and whole! But we know about those priestly healers who project their weakness into others and then minister to others only as a way of increasing their own strength. We know about "Christian charity"!

Naturally, I saw through it and called it by its true name. He choked on the truth for a while—called me blind and base. He swore to elevated motives, mouthed fake sympathy and comical altruisms, but finally, to his credit, he found the strength to seek strength openly and honestly from me.

Your friend, Nietzsche, in the marketplace! Are you not appalled by the thought? Imagine my *Human, All Too Human,* or my *The Gay Science,* caged, tamed, housebroken! Imagine my aphorisms alphabetized into a practicum of homilies for daily life and work! At first, I, too, was appalled! But no longer. The project intrigues me—a forum for my ideas, a vessel to fill when I am ripe and overflowing, an opportunity—indeed, a laboratory, to test ideas on an individual specimen before positing them for the species (that was Dr. Breuer's notion).

Your Dr. Breuer, incidentally, seems a superior specimen, with the perceptiveness and the desire to stretch upward. Yes, he has the desire. And he has the head. But does he have the eyes—and the heart—to see? We shall see!

So today I convalesce and think quietly about *application*—a new venture. Perhaps I was in error to think that my sole mission was truth finding. For the next month, I shall see if my wisdom will enable another to live through despair. Why does he come to *me*? He says that after tasting my conversation and nibbling a bit of *Human, All Too Human,* he has developed an appetite for my philosophy. Perhaps, given the burden of my physical disease, he thought that I must be an expert on survival.

Of course he doesn't know the half of my burden. My friend, the Russian bitch-demon, that monkey with false breasts, continues her course of betrayal. Elisabeth, who says Lou is living with Rée, is campaigning to have her deported for immorality.

Elisabeth also writes that friend Lou has moved her hate-and-lie campaign to Basel, where she intends to imperil my pension. Cursed be that day in Rome when I first saw her. I have often said to you that every adversity—even encounters with pure evil—makes me stronger. But if I can turn *this* shit into gold, I shall . . . I shall . . . —we shall see.

I have not the energy to make a copy of this letter, dear friend. Please return it to me.

Yours,
F.N.

CHAPTER 13

N THE FIACRE on their way to the clinic later that day, Breuer raised the question of confidentiality, and proposed that Nietzsche might feel more comfortable being admitted under a pseudonym—specifically as Eckart Müller, the name he had used when discussing his patient with Freud.

"Eckart Müller, Eckkkkkkart Müuuller, Eckart Müuuuuuuller," Nietzsche, obviously in high spirits, caroled the name to himself slowly in a soft whisper as if to discern its melody. "It's as good a name as any other, I suppose. Does it have special significance? Perhaps," he speculated mischievously, "it's the name of some other notoriously obstinate patient?"

"It's simply a mnemonic," Breuer said. "I form a pseudonym for a patient's name by substituting for each initial the letter in the alphabet immediately preceding it. Thus, I got E.M. And Eckart Müller was simply the first E.M. that occurred to me."

Nietzsche smiled. "Perhaps, some medical historian will one day write a book on famous physicians of Vienna, and wonder why the distinguished Doctor Josef Breuer so often visited a certain Eckart Müller, a mysterious man without past or future."

It was the first time Breuer had seen Nietzsche being playful. It boded well for the future, and Breuer reciprocated. "And pity the philosophic biographers of the future when they attempt to trace the whereabouts of Professor Friedrich Nietzsche during the month of December in the year eighteen eighty-two."

A few minutes later, when he had thought more about it, Breuer began to regret having suggested a pseudonym. Having to address Nietzsche by a false name in the presence of the clinic staff imposed a wholly unnecessary subterfuge upon an already duplicitous situation. Why had he added to his burden? After all, Nietzsche did not need the protection of a pseudonym for the treatment of hemicrania, a straightforward medical condition. If anything, their present arrangement demanded that he, Breuer, take the risks, and hence, *he*, not Nietzsche, needed the sanctuary of confidentiality.

The fiacre entered the eighth district, known as Josefstadt, and stopped at the gates of the Lauzon Clinic. The gatekeeper, recognizing Fischmann, discreetly avoided peering into the cab and scurried to open the swinging iron gates. The fiacre lurched and bounced over the hundred-meter cobblestone driveway to the white-columned portico of the central building. The Lauzon Clinic, a handsome, four-story structure of white stone, housed forty neurological and psychiatric patients. When it was built three hundred years before as the city home of the Baron Friedrich Lauzon, it lay immediately outside the city walls of Vienna and was encircled by its own walls, along with stables, a coach house, servants' cottages, and twenty acres of garden and orchard. Here, generation after generation of young Lauzons were born, reared, and sent out to hunt the great wild boar. Upon the death of the last Baron Lauzon and his family in the typhoid epidemic of 1858, the Lauzon estate had passed to Baron Wertheim, a distant, improvident cousin who rarely left his country estate in Bavaria.

Advised by the estate executives that he could divest himself of the burden of his inherited property only by transforming it into a public institution, Baron Wertheim decided that the building should become a convalescent hospital, with the stipulation that his family receive perpetual free medical care. A charity trust was established, and a board of trustees enlisted—the latter unusual for including not only several leading Viennese Catholic families but two Jewish philanthropic families, the Gomperzes and the Altmanns. Though the hospital, which had opened in 1860, ministered primarily to the wealthy, six of its forty beds were endowed and made available to poor, but clean patients.

It was one of these six beds that Breuer, who represented the Altmann family on the hospital board, commandeered for Nietzsche. Breuer's influence at the Lauzon extended beyond his board membership; he was also the personal physician of the hospital director and several other members of the administration.

When Breuer and his new patient arrived at the clinic, they were greeted with great deference. All formal intake and registration procedures were waived, and the director and the chief nurse personally conducted doctor and patient on a tour of the available rooms.

"Too dark," Breuer said about the first room. "Herr Müller needs light for reading and correspondence. Let's look at something on the south side."

The second room was small but bright, and Nietzsche commented, "This will do. The light is much better."

But Breuer quickly overruled him. "Too small, no air. What else is free?"

Nietzsche also liked the third room. "Yes, this is entirely satisfactory."

But Breuer again was not pleased. "Too public. Too noisy. Can you make something available farther from the nursing desk?"

When they entered the next room, Nietzsche did not wait for Breuer's comment but immediately put his briefcase into the closet, took off his shoes, and lay down on the bed. There was no argument, since Breuer also approved of this bright, spacious third-floor corner room, with its large fireplace and excellent view of the gardens. Both men admired the large, slightly bald, but still regal salmon-and-blue Isfahan carpet, obviously a remnant of happier, healthier days at the Lauzon estate. Nietzsche nodded in appreciation of Breuer's request that a writing table, a gas desk lamp, and a comfortable chair be placed in the room.

As soon as they were alone, Nietzsche acknowledged that he had gotten up too quickly from his last attack: he felt fatigued, and his head pain was returning. Without protest, he agreed to spend the next twenty-four hours resting quietly in bed. Breuer walked down the hall to the nursing desk to order medications: colchicine for pain, chloral hydrate for sleep. So heavily addicted was Nietzsche to chloral that withdrawal would require several weeks.

When Breuer leaned into Nietzsche's room to take his leave, Nietzsche lifted his head from his pillow and, holding out the small glass of water by his bed, proposed a toast: "Until the official beginning of our project tomorrow! After a brief rest, I plan to spend the rest of the day developing a strategy for our philosophic counseling. Auf Wiedersehen, Doctor Breuer."

A strategy! Time, Breuer thought in the fiacre on the way home, time for *me, too,* to think about a strategy. So consumed had he been with ensnaring Nietzsche that he had given no thought whatsoever to how he was to tame his quarry, now in room 13 of the Lauzon Clinic. As the fiacre swayed and rattled, Breuer tried to concentrate on his own strategy. It all seemed a muddle, he had no real guidelines, no precedents. He would have to devise an entirely new treatment procedure. Best to discuss this with Sig; it was the kind of challenge he loved. Breuer told Fischmann to stop at the hospital and locate Doctor Freud.

The Allgemeine Krankenhaus, the Vienna General Hospital, where Freud, a clinical aspirant, was preparing himself for a career as a medical practitioner, was a small city unto itself. It housed two thousand patients and consisted of a dozen quadrangle buildings, each a separate department—each with its own courtyard and wall, each connected by a maze of subterranean tunnels to all the other quadrangular buildings. A four-meter stone wall separated the entire community from the outside world.

Fischmann, long familiar with the secrets of the maze, ran to fetch Freud from his medical ward. A few minutes later, he returned alone: "Doctor Freud's not there. Doctor Hauser said he went to his *Stammlokal* an hour ago."

Freud's coffeehouse, the Café Landtmann on Franzens-Ring, was only a few blocks from the hospital; and there Breuer found him, sitting alone, drinking coffee, and reading a French literary journal. The Café Landtmann was frequented by physicians, clinical aspirants, and medical students; and though far less fashionable than Breuer's Café Griensteidl, it subscribed to over eighty periodicals, perhaps more than any other Vienna coffeehouse.

"Sig, let's go to Demel's for a pastry. I've got some interesting things to tell you about the case of the migrainous professor."

Freud had his coat on in seconds. Though he loved Vienna's premier pastry shop, he couldn't afford to go except as someone's guest. Ten minutes later, they were seated at a quiet corner table. Breuer ordered two coffees, a chocolate torte for himself, and a lemon torte *mit Schlag* for Freud, which he finished so quickly that Breuer persuaded his young friend to choose another from the three-tiered silver pastry wagon. When Freud had finished a chocolate custard mille-feuille and a second coffee, both men lit cigars. Then Breuer described in detail everything that had happened with his Herr Müller since their last talk: the professor's refusal to enter psychological treatment, his angry departure, the middle-of-the-night migraine, the strange house call, his overdose and peculiar state of consciousness, the small, plaintive voice calling for help, and, finally, the remarkable bargain they had struck in Breuer's office that morning.

Freud stared at Breuer with great intensity as he told this tale—a look Breuer knew. It was Freud's total-recall look: he was not only contemplating and registering everything but recording it as well; six months hence, he would be able to repeat this conversation with perfect accuracy. But Freud's demeanor changed abruptly when Breuer described his final proposal.

"Josef, you offered him *WHAT*? You are to treat this Herr Müller's migraine, and he should treat *your despair*? You can't be serious! What does this mean?"

"Sig, believe me, it was the only way. If I had tried *anything* else, *poof!*—he'd be on his way to Basel. Remember that excellent strategy we planned? To persuade him to investigate and reduce his life stress? He demolished that in minutes by utterly eulogizing stress. He sang rhapsodies about it. Whatsoever does not kill him, he claims, makes him stronger. But the more I listened and thought about his writings, the more I was convinced he fancies himself a physician—not a personal one but a physician to our entire culture."

"So," Freud said, "you snared him by suggesting he begin to heal Western civilization by starting with a single specimen—you?"

"That's true, Sig. But first he snared *me!* Or, that homunculus you claim is active in each of us snared me with his pitiful plea of 'Help me, help me.' That, Sig, was almost enough to make me a believer in your ideas about there being an unconscious part of the mind."

Freud smiled at Breuer and enjoyed a long draw on his cigar. "Well, now that you've snared him, what next?"

"The first thing we've got to do, Sig, is get rid of this term 'snare.' The idea of snaring Eckart Müller is incongruous—like catching a thousand-pound gorilla with a butterfly net."

Freud smiled more broadly. "Yes, let's drop 'snare' and just say that you've got him in the clinic and will see him daily. What's your strategy? No doubt he's busy designing a strategy to help *you* with *your* despair, starting tomorrow."

"Yes, that's exactly what he said to me. He's probably working on it this very moment. So it's time for me to plan as well, and I hope you can help.

I haven't thought it through, but the strategy is clear. *I must persuade him he is helping me—while I slowly, imperceptibly, switch roles with him until he becomes the patient and I, once again, the physician."*

"Exactly," Freud agreed. "That's precisely what must be done."

Breuer marveled at Freud's ability always to sound so sure of himself, even in situations where there was no certainty whatsoever.

"He expects," Freud continued, "to be your doctor of despair. And that expectation must be met. Let us lay plans—one step at a time. The first phase obviously will be to persuade him of your despair. Let's plan this phase. What will you talk about?"

"I have no concerns about it, Sig. I can imagine many things to discuss."

"But really, Josef, how are you going to make that believable?"

Breuer hesitated, wondering how much of himself to reveal. Still, he answered, "Easy, Sig. All I have to do is tell the truth!"

Freud looked at Breuer in astonishment. "The truth? What do you mean, Josef? You have no despair, you have everything. You're the envy of every doctor in Vienna—all Europe clamors for your services. Many excellent students, like the promising young Doctor Freud, cherish your every word. Your research is remarkable, your wife the most beautiful, sensitive woman in the empire. Despair? Why, Josef, you're atop the very crest of life!"

Breuer put his hand on Freud's. "The crest of life! You've put it just right, Sig. The crest, the summit of the life climb! But the problem with crests is *that they lead downhill.* From the crest I can see all the rest of my years stretched out before me. And the view doesn't please me. I see only aging, diminishment, fathering, grandfathering."

"But, Josef"—the alarm in Freud's eyes was almost palpable—"how can you say that? I see success, not downhill! I see security, acclaim—your name attached in perpetuity to two major physiological discoveries!"

Breuer winced. How could he admit to having wagered his whole life only to find that the final prize was, after all, not to his liking? No, these things he must keep to himself. There are things you don't tell the young ones.

"Let me just put it this way, Sig. One feels things about life at forty that one cannot know at twenty-five."

"Twenty-six. On the far side of twenty-six."

Breuer laughed. "Sorry, Sig, I don't mean to be patronizing. But take my word that there are many private things I can discuss with Müller. For example, there are troubles in my marriage, troubles I'd prefer not to share with you, so you don't have to keep things from Mathilde and hurt the closeness you two share. Just believe me: I shall find much to say to Herr Müller, and I can make it convincing by sticking largely to the truth. It's the next step I worry about!"

"You mean what happens after he turns to you as a source of help for *his* despair? What you can do to lessen his burden?"

Breuer nodded.

"Tell me, Josef, suppose you could design the next phase in any way you wish. What would you like to happen? What is it one person can offer another?"

"Good! Good! You prod my thinking. You're magnificent at this, Sig!" Breuer reflected for several minutes. "Though my patient's a man—and not, of course, a hysteric—still, I think I'd like him to do exactly what Bertha did."

"To chimneysweep?"

"Yes, to reveal everything to me. I'm convinced there's something healing in unburdening. Look at the Catholics. The priests have been offering confessional relief for centuries."

"I wonder," said Freud, "whether the relief comes from the unburdening or from the belief in divine absolution?"

"I've had as patients agnostic Catholics who still benefited from going to confession. And on a couple of occasions in my own life, years ago, I experienced relief from confessing everything to a friend. How about you, Sig? Have you ever been relieved by confession? Ever unburdened yourself fully to anyone?"

"Of course, my fiancée. I write Martha every day."

"Come now, Sig." Breuer smiled and put his hand on his friend's shoulder. "You *know* there are things you can never tell Martha—*especially* Martha."

"No, Josef, I tell her *everything*. What couldn't I tell her?"

"When you're in love with a woman, you want her to think well of you in all ways. Naturally, you're going to keep things hidden about yourself—things that might present you in a bad light. Your sexual lusts, for example."

Breuer noted Freud's deep blush. Never before had he and Freud had such a conversation. Probably Freud had *never* had one.

"But my sexual feelings involve only Martha. No other woman attracts me."

"Then let's say *before* Martha."

"There was no 'before Martha.' She is the only woman I have ever craved."

"But, Sig, there *must* have been others. Every medical student in Vienna keeps a *Süssmädchen.* Young Schnitzler seems to have a new one every week."

"This is exactly the part of the world I want to shield Martha from. Schnitzler is dissolute—as everyone knows. I have no appetite for such dalliance. Nor time. Nor money—I need every florin for books."

Best to leave this topic quickly, Breuer thought. I have learned something important, however: I now know the limits of what I can ever hope to share with Freud.

"Sig, I've gotten us off the track. Let's go back five minutes. You asked what I want to happen. I'm saying that I hope Herr Müller will talk about his despair. I hope he'll use me as a father confessor. Maybe that in itself will be healing, maybe bring him back into the human fold. He's one of the most solitary creatures I've ever met. I doubt he's ever revealed himself to *anyone.*"

"But you told me he's been betrayed by others. No doubt he trusted and revealed himself to *them.* Otherwise, there could be no betrayal."

"Yes, you're right. Betrayal is a big issue for him. In fact, I think that should be a basic principle, perhaps the fundamental principle, for my procedure: *primum non nocere*—do no harm, do nothing he could possibly interpret as betrayal."

Breuer thought about his words for a few moments and then added, "You know, Sig, I treat all patients this way, so this should pose no problem in my future work with Herr Müller. But there's my past duplicity with him—*that* he might view as betrayal. Yet I can't undo it. I wish I could cleanse myself and share everything with him—my meeting with Fräulein Salomé, the conspiracy among his friends to steer him to Vienna, and, above all, my pretense that it is I, myself, and not he who is the patient."

Freud shook his head vigorously. "Absolutely not! This cleansing, this confession, would be for *your* sake and not for his. No, I think if you really want to help your patient, you will have to live with the lie."

Breuer nodded. He knew Freud was right. "All right, let's take stock. What do we have so far?"

Freud responded quickly. He loved this type of intellectual exercise. "We have several steps. *First*, engage him by disclosing yourself. *Second*, reverse the roles. *Third,* help him disclose *himself* fully. And we have one fundamental principle: to retain his trust and avoid any semblance of betrayal. Now, what's the next step? Suppose he *does* share his despair, then what?"

"Maybe," Breuer replied, "there doesn't have to be a next step? Perhaps simply revealing himself would constitute such a major achievement, such a change in his way of life, that it would be in itself sufficient?"

"Simple confession isn't that powerful, Josef. If it were, there'd be no neurotic Catholics!"

"Yes, I'm sure you're right. But perhaps"—Breuer took out his watch—"this is as much as we can plan for now." He signaled the waiter for the check.

"Josef, I've enjoyed this consultation. And I appreciate the way we confer—it's a honor for me to have you take my suggestions seriously."

"Actually, Sig, you're very good at this. Together we make a good team. Yet I can't imagine a great clamor for our new procedures. How often do patients come along who require such a Byzantine treatment plan? In fact, I've felt today that we were not so much devising a medical treatment as planning a conspiracy. You know whom I'd prefer as a patient? That other one—the one who called for help!"

"You mean the unconscious consciousness trapped inside your patient."

"Yes," said Breuer, handing the waiter a florin note without checking the tally—he never did. "Yes, it'd be a lot simpler to work with him. You know, Sig, maybe *that* should be the goal of treatment—to liberate that hidden consciousness, to allow him to ask for help in the daylight."

"Yes, that's good, Josef. But is 'liberation' the term? After all, he has no separate existence; he's an unconscious part of Müller. Isn't *integration* what we're after?" Freud seemed impressed with his own idea and pounded his fist softly upon the marble table as he repeated, "Integration of the unconscious."

"Ach, Sig, that's it!" The idea excited Breuer. "A major insight!" Leaving the waiter a few copper *Kreuzer,* he and Freud walked onto Michaelerplatz. "Yes, if my patient could *integrate* this other part of himself, that would be a real achievement. If he could learn how natural it is to crave comfort from another—surely *that* would be enough!"

Walking down the Kohlmarkt, they reached the busy thoroughfare of the Graben and parted. Freud turned down Naglergasse toward the hospital, while Breuer strolled through Stephansplatz toward Bäckerstrasse 7, which lay just beyond the looming Romanesque towers of the Church of Saint Stephen. The talk with Sig had left him feeling more confident about meeting tomorrow morning with Nietzsche. Nonetheless, he had a worrisome premonition that all this elaborate preparation might be only illusion—that *Nietzsche's* preparation, not his own, would govern their encounter.

CHAPTER 14

NIETZSCHE WAS INDEED PREPARED. The following morning, as soon as Breuer completed his physical exam, Nietzsche took control.

"You see," he told Breuer, displaying a large new notebook, "how well organized I am! Herr Kaufmann, one of your orderlies, was kind enough to purchase this for me yesterday."

He rose from his bed. "I also ordered another chair for the room. Shall we move over to them and begin our work?"

Breuer, silently bemused by his patient's grave assumption of authority, followed the suggestion and took a seat next to Nietzsche. Both chairs faced the fireplace, in which an orange blaze crackled. After warming himself for a moment, Breuer rotated his chair so that he could more easily see Nietzsche and persuaded Nietzsche to do the same.

"Let us begin," Nietzsche said, "by establishing the major categories for analysis. I've listed the issues you mentioned yesterday when you asked for my help."

Opening his notebook, Nietzsche showed how he had written on a separate page each of Breuer's complaints, and read them aloud: " 'One, general unhappiness. Two, besieged by alien thoughts. Three, self-hatred. Four, fear of aging. Five, fear of death. Six, urges toward suicide.' Is that complete?"

Taken aback by Nietzsche's formal tone, Breuer did not enjoy hearing his innermost concerns condensed to a list and described so clinically. But, for the moment, he responded cooperatively. "Not quite. I have serious trouble relating to my wife. I feel unaccountably distant from her—as though I were trapped in a marriage and a life not of my own choosing."

"Do you consider that *one* additional problem? Or *two?*"

"It depends on your unit definition."

"Yes, that is a problem, as is the fact that the items aren't on the same logical level. Some may be a result, or a cause, of others." Nietzsche leafed through his notes. "For example, 'unhappiness' may be a result of 'alien thoughts.' Or, 'urges toward suicide' may be either a result *or* a cause of death fears."

Breuer's discomfort grew. He did not like the direction this exchange was taking.

"Why do we need to establish a list at all? Somehow the whole idea of a list makes me uncomfortable."

Nietzsche looked troubled. His air of confidence was obviously tissue-thin. One demurral from Breuer, and his whole demeanor changed. He responded in a conciliatory tone.

"I thought we could proceed more systematically by establishing some priority of complaints. To be frank, however, I'm not certain whether to begin with the most *fundamental* problem—let us for the moment say, fear of death—or the *least fundamental,* or most derivative, one—let us say arbitrarily, invasion by alien thoughts. Or should we begin with the most *clinically urgent,* or *life-threatening,* one—let us say, suicidal urges. Or with the most *troublesome* problem, the one that most disturbs your everyday life—let us say, self-hatred."

Breuer's uneasiness grew. "I'm not at all sure this is a good approach."

"But I've based it on your own medical method," Nietzsche replied. "To the best of my recollection, you asked me to talk in general about my condition. You developed a list of my problems and then proceeded systematically—very systematically, as I recall—to explore each in turn. Is that not true?"

"Yes, that *is* the way I do a medical examination."

"Then, Doctor Breuer, why do you resist such an approach now? Can you suggest an alternative?"

Breuer shook his head. "When you put it this way, I'm inclined to agree with your suggested procedure. It's just that it seems forced or artificial to speak about my innermost life concerns in tidy categories. In my mind, all the problems are inextricably intertwined. Also, your list seems so *cold*. These are delicate, tender things—not so easy to talk about as back pain or skin rashes."

"Do not mistake awkwardness for callousness, Doctor Breuer. Remember, I am a solitary person, as I warned you. I'm not accustomed to easy and warm social exchange."

Closing his notebook, Nietzsche stared out the window for a moment. "Let me take another approach. I recall your saying yesterday that we must invent our procedure *together*. Tell me, Doctor Breuer, have you had any similar experience in your practice from which we can draw?"

"Similar experiences? Hmm . . . there's no real precedent in medical practice for what you and I are doing. I don't even know what to call it—maybe despair therapy or philosophic therapeutics, or some name yet to be invented. It's true that physicians are called upon to treat certain types of psychological disturbance: for example, ones that have a physical basis, like the delirium of brain fever, the paranoia of brain syphilis, or the psychosis of lead poisoning. We also take the responsibility for patients whose psychological condition damages their health or threatens life—for example, severe involutional melancholia or mania."

"Threatening to life? How so?"

"Melancholics starve themselves or may commit suicide. Manics often exhaust themselves to death."

Nietzsche did not respond, but sat silent, staring at the fire.

"But obviously," Breuer continued, "these are far removed from my personal situation, and the treatment for each of these conditions is not philosophic or psychological but instead some physical approach, such as electrical stimulation, baths, medication, enforced rest, and so on. Occasionally, with patients who have an irrational fear, we must devise some psychological method to calm them. Recently I was called to see an elderly woman who was terrified of going outside—she had not left her room in months. What I did was to speak to her kindly until she trusted me. Then, each time I saw her, I held her hand to increase her sense of safety and escorted her a little farther out of her room. But this is common-sense improvisation—like training a child. Such work hardly requires a physician."

"All this seems far removed from our task," said Nietzsche. "Is there nothing more relevant?"

"Well, of course, there are the many patients who have recently been coming to physicians for physical symptoms—such as paralysis, speech defect, or some form of blindness or deafness—whose cause lies entirely in psychological conflict. We call this condition 'hysteria'—from the Greek word for the uterus, *hysterus*."

Nietzsche nodded quickly as though to indicate there was no need to translate the Greek for him. Remembering that he had been a professor of philology, Breuer hurried on. "We used to think these symptoms were caused by a wandering uterus, an idea that, of course, makes no sense anatomically."

"How did they explain the disease in men?"

"For reasons still to be understood, it's a female disease; there are still no documented cases of hysteria in males. Hysteria, I've always thought, is a disease that should be of particular interest to philosophers. Perhaps it is they, not physicians, who will explain why the symptoms of hysteria do not conform to anatomical pathways."

"What do you mean?"

Breuer felt more relaxed. To explain medical issues to an attentive student was a comfortable and familiar role for him.

"Well, to take one example, I have seen patients whose hands are anesthetized in a way that could not possibly be caused by a disorder of the nerves. They have a 'glove' anesthesia—no sensation below their wrist—just as if an anesthetic band had been tied around their wrist."

"And that doesn't conform to the nervous system?" asked Nietzsche.

"Right. The nervous supply to the hand doesn't work that way: the hand is supplied by three different nerves—radial, ulnar, and median—each of which has a different origin in the brain. In fact, half of some fingers are supplied by one nerve, and the other half by another. But the patient doesn't know this. It's as though the patient imagines the entire hand is supplied by a single nerve, the 'hand nerve,' and then develops a disorder to conform with her imagination."

"Fascinating!" Nietzsche opened his notebook and jotted down a few words. "Suppose there were a woman expert in human anatomy, and she developed hysteria. Would she have an anatomically correct form of the disease?"

"I'm certain she would. Hysteria is an ideational disorder, not an anatomical one. There is much evidence that it involves no real anatomical damage to the nerves. In fact, some patients can be mesmerized, and the symptoms vanish in minutes."

"So, removal by mesmerism is the current treatment?"

"No! Unfortunately, mesmerism is not medically fashionable, at least not in Vienna. It has a bad reputation—primarily, I believe, because many of the early mesmerists were charlatans with no medical training. Furthermore, the mesmerism cure is always transient. But the fact that it works even briefly offers proof of the psychic cause of the illness."

"Have you, yourself," asked Nietzsche, "treated such patients?"

"A few. There is one patient I worked with extensively, whose case I should describe to you. Not because I recommend that you use this treatment with me, but because it will start us working on your list—your item number two, I think."

Nietzsche opened his notebook and read aloud, " 'Besieged by alien thoughts'? I don't understand. Why *alien*? And what's the connection with hysteria?"

"Let me clarify. First, I call these thoughts 'alien' because they appear to invade me from without. I don't want to think them, but when I order them away, they flee only briefly and soon, insidiously, infiltrate my mind again. And the types of thoughts? Well, they're thoughts about a beautiful woman—the patient whom I treated for hysteria. Shall I start at the beginning and tell you the entire story?"

Far from being curious, Nietzsche appeared uncomfortable at Breuer's question. "As a general rule, I suggest you reveal only enough for me to comprehend the issue. I urge you not to embarrass or humiliate yourself; nothing good can come of that."

Nietzsche was a secretive man. That Breuer knew. But he hadn't anticipated that Nietzsche would want him, too, to remain secretive. Breuer realized he had to take a stand on this issue: he had to reveal himself as fully as possible. Only then, he thought, can Nietzsche learn there is no horror in openness and honesty between people.

"You may be right, but it seems to me that the more I am able to tell of my innermost feelings, the more relief I will gain."

Nietzsche stiffened, but nodded for Breuer to continue.

"The story begins two years ago, when one of my patients asked me to take over the medical care of her daughter, whom I shall refer to as Anna O. so as not to disclose her real identity."

"But you've told me your pseudonym method, so her real initials must be B.P."

Breuer smiled, thinking, "This man is like Sig. He forgets nothing"—

and went on to describe the details of Bertha's illness. "It's also important that you know that Anna O. was twenty-one years old, extraordinarily intelligent, well educated, and astonishingly beautiful. A breath—no, a *cyclone*—of fresh air to a rapidly aging forty-year-old man! Do you know the kind of woman I describe?"

Nietzsche ignored the question. "And you became her physician?"

"Yes, I agreed to become her physician—and have never betrayed that trust. All the transgressions I am about to reveal consist of thoughts and fantasies rather than deeds. First, let me concentrate upon the psychological treatment.

"During our daily meetings she automatically entered a light trance state in which she discussed—or, as she put it, 'discharged'—all the disturbing events and thoughts of the last twenty-four hours. This process, which she referred to as 'chimneysweeping,' proved useful in helping her to feel better for the next twenty-four hours but had no effect on her hysterical symptoms. Then, one day, I stumbled upon an *effective* treatment."

And Breuer proceeded to describe how he had erased not only each of Bertha's symptoms by tracking down its original cause but, finally, every part of her illness when he helped her discover and re-experience its fundamental cause—the horror of her father's death.

Nietzsche, who had been eagerly taking notes, exclaimed, "Your treatment of this patient strikes me as extraordinary! Perhaps you've made a momentous discovery in psychological therapeutics. Perhaps, too, it may be of value for your own problems. I like the possibility of your being helped by your own discovery. For one can never really be helped by another; one must find the strength to help *oneself*. Perhaps you, like Anna O., must discover the original cause of each of your psychological problems. Yet you said that you don't recommend this treatment approach for yourself. Why not?"

"For a number of reasons," Breuer responded with the certainty of medical authority. "My condition is very different from Anna's. For one thing, I have no hypnoidal propensities: I have never experienced any unusual states of consciousness. That's important, because I believe that hysteria is caused by a traumatic experience occurring while the individual is in an aberrant state of consciousness. Because the traumatic memory and the increased cortical excitation exist in an alternate consciousness, they cannot therefore be 'handled,' or integrated, or worn away during everyday experience."

Without interrupting his account, Breuer rose, stoked the fire, and laid on another log. "Also, and perhaps even more important, my symptoms are not hysterical: they do not affect the nervous system or some part of the body. Remember, hysteria is a female disease. My condition is, I think, *qualitatively* closer to normal human *Angst* or misery. Quantitatively it is, of course, greatly magnified!

"Another thing, my symptoms are not acute: they have developed slowly over years. Look at your list. I cannot identify a precise beginning to any one of those problems. But there is another reason why the therapy I employed on my patient may not be useful to me—a rather disturbing reason. When Bertha's symptoms——"

"Bertha? I was right when I guessed her first initial was B."

Breuer closed his eyes in distress. "I fear I've blundered. It's terribly important to me that I not violate my patient's right to privacy. Especially *this* patient. Her family is very well known in the community, and it is also widely known I was her physician. Hence, I have been careful to speak little to other physicians of my work with her. But it is cumbersome to use a false name here, with you."

"You mean it's difficult to speak freely and unburden yourself while at the same time having to remain on guard with your words lest you use the wrong name?"

"Exactly." And Breuer sighed. "Now I have no choice but to continue to speak of her by her true name, Bertha—but you must swear to reveal it to no one."

At Nietzsche's ready "Of course," Breuer took a leather cigar case from his jacket pocket, extracted a cigar, and, his companion refusing it, lit it for himself. "Where was I?" he asked.

"You were talking about why your new treatment method might not be relevant to your own problems—something about a 'disturbing' reason."

"Yes, the disturbing reason," and Breuer exhaled a long fume of blue smoke before continuing. "I was fool enough to boast of having made an important discovery when I presented her case to a few colleagues and medical students. Yet only a few weeks later, when I transferred her care to another physician, I learned that almost all her symptoms had recurred. You see how awkward my position is?"

"Awkward," Nietzsche replied, "because you've announced a cure that may not be real?"

"I often daydream of finding the people who attended that conference and telling each one that my conclusions were wrong. A concern not unusual for me—my perception of my colleagues' opinions really distresses me. Even though I have evidence of their respect, I continue to feel like a fraud—that's another issue that plagues me. Add it to your list."

Nietzsche dutifully opened his notebook and wrote for a moment.

"But to continue with Bertha, I'm not entirely clear about the cause of her relapse. It may be that, like the mesmerism cure, my treatment is only temporarily successful. But it may also be that the treatment was effective but was undone by its catastrophic ending."

Nietzsche again picked up his pencil. "What do you mean, 'catastrophic ending'?"

"For you to understand, I must first tell you what transpired between Bertha and me. There's no sense in being delicate about it. Let me come right out and say it. I, old fool that I am, fell in love with her! I became obsessed with her. She was never out of my mind." Breuer was surprised by how easy—in fact, exhilarating—it was to reveal so much.

"My day was divided into two segments—being with Bertha and waiting to be with her again! I met with her for an hour every day of the week, and then even began visiting her twice a day. Whenever I saw her, I felt great passion. Whenever she touched me, I felt sexually aroused."

"Why did she touch you?"

"She had difficulty walking and clutched my arm as we strolled. Often sudden, severe contractures required me to do a deep massage of her thigh muscles. Sometimes she cried so pitifully I was forced to hold her in my arms to comfort her. Sometimes when I sat next to her, she spontaneously entered into a trance, put her head on my shoulder, and 'chimneyswept' for an hour. Or she'd put her head in my lap and sleep like a baby. There were many, many times when it was all I could do to contain my sexual feelings."

"Perhaps," said Nietzsche, "only by being a man does a man release the woman in woman."

Breuer's head jerked up. "Perhaps I misunderstand you! You know, of course, that any sexual activity with a patient is wrong—anathema to the physician's Hippocratic oath."

"And woman? What is woman's responsibility?"

"But this is not woman—this is *patient!* I must be missing your point."

"Let us return to it later," Nietzsche replied calmly. "I still haven't heard the catastrophic end."

"Well, it seemed to me Bertha was improving, her symptoms were clearing up, one by one. But her physician was not doing too well. My wife, Mathilde, who has always been understanding and even-tempered, began to resent, first, the amount of time I was spending with Bertha, and then, even more, my talking about her. Fortunately I was not so foolish as to tell Mathilde about the nature of my feelings, but I believe she suspected them. One day she spoke to me in anger and forbade me ever to mention Bertha again. I began to resent my wife and even developed the irrational idea that she stood in my way—that, were it not for her, I could start a life with Bertha."

Breuer stopped, noticing that Nietzsche had closed his eyes. "Are you all right? Have you had enough for one day?"

"I'm listening. Sometimes I see better with closed eyes."

"Well, there was another complicating factor. I had a nurse, Eva Berger, Frau Becker's predecessor, who, during our ten years together, had become a close friend and confidante. Eva became very concerned. She worried that my mad infatuation with Bertha might lead to ruin, that I might be unable to resist my impulses and do something foolish. In fact, out of her friendship for me, she offered herself as a sacrifice."

Nietzsche's eyes shot open. Breuer saw a lot of eyewhite.

"What do you mean, 'sacrifice'?"

"Her words were that she would do *anything* to prevent me from ruining myself. Eva knew that Mathilde and I were having virtually no sexual contact, and thought that was why I clove to Bertha. I believe she was offering to release my sexual tension."

"And you believe she was doing this for *you?*"

"I'm convinced of it. Eva is a very attractive woman and had her choice of many men. I assure you she did not make the offer because of my good looks: this balding head, this briar-patch beard, and these 'handles' "—and he touched his large, protruding ears—"as my playmates always called them. Also, once she confided to me that she had had, years before, an intimate and disastrous relationship with an employer that had ultimately cost her her job, and had sworn, 'Never again!' "

"And did Eva's sacrifice help?"

Ignoring the skepticism, possibly scorn, in the pronunciation of "sacrifice," Breuer answered matter-of-factly. "I never accepted her offer. I was fool enough to think that lying with Eva would be a betrayal of Bertha. Sometimes I regret that very much."

"I don't understand." Nietzsche's eyes, though still wide with interest, showed signs of weariness, as though he had now seen and heard far too much. "What is it that you regret?"

"Not accepting Eva's offer, of course. I think about that lost opportunity very often. It is another of those unwelcome thoughts that plague me." Breuer pointed to Nietzsche's notebook. "Put it on the list."

Nietzsche picked up his pencil again and, as he added another item to Breuer's expanding list of problems, asked, "This regret—I still don't understand it. If you had accepted Eva, how would you now be different?"

"Different? What does being different have to do with it? It was a unique opportunity—one that will never come my way again."

"It was *also* a unique opportunity to say no! To say a blessed 'no' to a predator. And *that* opportunity you grasped."

Breuer was stunned by Nietzsche's comment. Obviously Nietzsche knew nothing about the intensity of sexual yearning. But there was no point yet in debating this issue. Or, perhaps he hadn't made it clear that Eva might have been his for the asking. Couldn't Nietzsche understand that one must seize opportunities when they present themselves? Yet, there was something intriguing about his "blessed no" statement. He's a curious mixture, Breuer thought, of massive blind spots and lightning originality. Again, Breuer had an intimation that this strange man might have something of value to offer him.

"Where were we? Oh yes, the final calamity! All along I had thought that my sexual affair with Bertha was entirely autistic—that is, as transpiring only in *my* mind—and that I had entirely concealed it from her. Imagine my shock, then, when one day I was informed by her mother that Bertha had proclaimed she was pregnant with Dr. Breuer's baby!"

Breuer described Mathilde's outrage when she heard about the false pregnancy and her angry demands that he immediately transfer Bertha to another physician and discharge Eva as well.

"So what did you do?"

"What could I do? My whole career, my family, my whole life was at stake. It was the worst day of my life. I had to tell Eva to leave. Of course, I offered to allow her to continue to work for me until I could help her find another position. Although she said she understood, she didn't return to work the next day, and I've never seen her again. I've written her several times, but she never answered.

"And with Bertha, things were even worse. When I visited her the next day, her delirium had cleared, and with it her delusion that I had impregnated her. In fact, she had complete amnesia for the entire episode and responded catastrophically to my announcement that I could no longer be her physician. She cried—pleaded with me to change my mind—begged me to tell her what she had done wrong. And, of course, *she had done nothing wrong.* Her outburst about 'Doctor Breuer's baby' was part of her hysteria. Those were not *her* words, that was her delirium speaking."

"And *whose* delirium was it?" asked Nietzsche.

"Well, of course it was *her* delirium, but *not* her responsibility, any more than one has responsibility for the random, bizarre happenings of a dream. People say strange, incoherent things in such a state."

"Her words do not strike *me* as incoherent or random. You suggested, Doctor Breuer, that I should simply interject any comments that occur to me. Let me make an observation: I find it remarkable that *you* are responsible for *all* of your thoughts and *all* of your deeds, whereas *she*"— Nietzsche's voice was stern, and he shook his finger at Breuer—*"she,* by virtue of her illness, is exonerated from *everything."*

"But, Professor Nietzsche, *as you yourself say,* power is the important thing. I had the power by virtue of my position. She looked to me for help. I was aware of her vulnerability, aware that she loved her father very much, perhaps *too* much, and that her illness was precipitated by his death. I also knew that she imbued me with the love she had felt for him, and I exploited it. I wanted her to love me. Do you know what her last words to me were? After telling her I was transferring her care to another doctor, I walked away, and she called out, *'You will always be the only man for me—there will never be another man in my life!'* Terrible words! Evidence of how much I had harmed her. But there was something even more terrible: *I enjoyed those words!* I *enjoyed* hearing her acknowledge my power over her! So you see, I left her weakened. Crippled. I might as well have bound and maimed her feet!"

"And since you last saw her," Nietzsche asked, "what has been the fate of this cripple?"

"She was admitted to another sanatorium, in Kreuzlingen. Many of her original symptoms have recurred—her mood fluctuations, her loss of her mother tongue every morning, and her pain, which can be controlled only by morphine, to which she is addicted. One fact of interest: her doctor there fell in love with her, removed himself from her case, and has subsequently proposed marriage to her!"

"Ah, the same pattern repeats itself with the next doctor, you notice?"

"I notice only that I am devastated by the thought of Bertha together with another man. Please add 'jealousy' to your list: it's one of my major problems. I am infested with visions of the two of them talking, touching, even making love. Though such visions inflict great pain, I continue to torment myself. Can you understand that? Have you ever experienced such jealousy?"

This question marked a turning point in the session. At first, Breuer had deliberately revealed himself in order to set a model for Nietzsche, hoping to encourage him to reciprocate. But soon he had become entirely immersed in the confessional process. There was, after all, no risk—Nietzsche, believing he was *Breuer's* counselor, had given his oath of confidentiality.

It was a new experience: never before had Breuer shared so much of himself. There was Max—but with Max, he had wished to preserve his image and had chosen his words carefully. And even with Eva Berger, he had always held back, concealing his age creaks, his vacillations and self-doubts, all those qualities that might make an older man appear weak or stodgy to an attractive young woman.

But when he began to describe his jealous feelings about Bertha and her new doctor, Breuer had changed back into the role of Nietzsche's physician. He did not lie—indeed, there were rumors about Bertha and another doctor, and, indeed, he had suffered from jealousy—but he exaggerated his feelings in an attempt to orchestrate Nietzsche's self-revelation. For Nietzsche must have felt jealousy in the "Pythagorean" relationship involving himself, Lou Salomé, and Paul Rée.

But this strategy was without effect. At least, Nietzsche gave no evidence of unusual interest in this theme. He merely nodded vaguely, turned the pages of his notebook, and scanned his notes. The two men lapsed into silence. They stared at the dying fire. Then Breuer reached into his pocket and took out his heavy gold watch—a gift from his father. The back was inscribed, "To Josef, my son. Bear the spirit of my spirit into the future." He looked at Nietzsche. Did those weary eyes reflect the hope that this interview might be nearing its end? It was time to go.

"Professor Nietzsche, it does me good to talk to you. But I have a responsibility to you as well, and it occurs to me that I prescribed rest to avoid inflaming your migraine and then snatched it away by forcing you to listen for so long. Another thought: I remember the description you once gave me of your typical day, a day containing little close contact with others. Is this too large a dose all at once? Not only too much time, too much talk and listening, but also too much of another's intimate life?"

"Our agreement calls for honesty, Doctor Breuer, and it would not be honest to disagree with you. It *has* been a great deal today, and I *am* fatigued." He slumped back in his chair. "But no, I *don't* hear too much of your intimate life. I learn from you, too. I meant it when I said that when it comes to learning how to relate to other people, I have to start from scratch!"

As Breuer stood and reached for his coat, Nietzsche added, "One final comment. You've talked a great deal about the second item on our list: 'besieged by alien thoughts.' Perhaps we have today exhausted that category, for I now have an appreciation of how these unworthy thoughts invade and possess your mind. Yet they are nonetheless *your* thoughts, and it is *your* mind. I wonder what benefit there is to you in permitting this to occur—or, to put it more strongly—in *making* it occur."

Breuer, who had one arm in his coat sleeve, froze. *"Making* it occur? I don't know. All I can say is that, *from the inside,* it *doesn't* feel that way. It feels like it happens *to* me. Your claim that I *make* it happen has—how shall I say?—no *emotional* meaning for me."

"We must find a way to *give* it meaning." And Nietzsche rose and walked to the door with Breuer. "Let us try a thought experiment. For tomorrow's discussion, please consider this question: If you were *not* thinking these alien thoughts, what would you be thinking?"

༄

Excerpts from Dr. Breuer's Case Notes on Eckart Müller, 5 December 1882

An excellent beginning! Much accomplished. He developed a list of my problems and plans to focus on one at a time. Good. Let him think this is what we are doing. To encourage him to confess, I bared myself today.

He did not reciprocate but, in time, it will come. Certainly he was astounded, and impressed, by my openness.

I have an interesting tactical idea! I shall describe his situation as if it were my own. Then I let him counsel me and, in so doing, he will silently counsel himself. Thus, for example, I can help him work on his triangle—with Lou Salomé and Paul Rée—by asking for help with my triangle with Bertha and her new doctor. He is so secretive that this may be the only way to help him. Perhaps he will never be honest enough to ask for help directly.

He has an original mind. I cannot predict his responses. Perhaps Lou Salomé is right; perhaps he is destined to be a great philosopher. As long as he avoids the subject of human beings! In most aspects of human relatedness he has prodigious blind spots. But when it comes to the subject of women, he is barbaric, hardly human. No matter who the woman or what the situation, his response is predictable: the woman is predatory and scheming. And his advice about women is equally predictable: blame them, punish them! Oh yes, one other mode—avoid them!

As for sexual feelings: Does he have any at all? Does he view women as too dangerous? He must have sexual desire. But what happens to it? Is it dammed up, exerting pressure that must somehow burst out? Can that be, I wonder, the source of the migraine?

Excerpts from Friedrich Nietzsche's Notes on Dr. Breuer, 5 December 1882

The list grows. To my list of six, Doctor Breuer added five more.

7. *Feelings of being trapped—by marriage, by life*
8. *Feeling distant from wife*
9. *Regret about refusing Eva's sexual "sacrifice"*
10. *Overconcern about other physicians' opinions of him*
11. *Jealousy—Bertha and another man*

Will the list ever end? Will each day spawn new problems? How do I make him see that his problems clamor for attention only in order to obscure that which he does not wish to see? Petty thoughts infiltrate his mind like a fungus. They will eventually rot his body. As he left today, I asked him, what he would see if he were not blinded by trivia. Thus I pointed the way. Will he take it?

He is a curious mix—intelligent yet blind, sincere yet devious. Does he know of his own insincerity? He says I help him. He praises me. Does he know how I hate gifts? Does he know gifts scratch my skin and destroy my sleep? Is he one of those who pretends to give—only to elicit gifts? I shall not give them. Is he one who reveres reverence? Is he one who wants to find me rather than himself? I must give him nothing! When a friend needs a resting place, it is best to offer a hard cot!

He is engaging, sympathetic. Beware! About some things he has persuaded himself to reach upward, but his entrails have not been persuaded. About women, he is hardly human. A tragedy—to wallow in that muck! I know that muck: it is good to look down and see what I have overcome.

The greatest tree reaches for the highest heights and sinks the deepest roots, into darkness—even into evil; but he neither reaches up nor thrusts downward. Animal lust drains his strength—and his reason. Three women rend him, and he is grateful to them. He licks their bloody fangs.

One of them sprays him with her musk and pretends to sacrifice. She offers the "gift" of bondage—his bondage.

The other torments him. She pretends weakness so as to press herself against him as she walks. She pretends to sleep so as to place her head against his manhood and, when bored with these small torments, she humiliates him publicly. When that game is up, she moves on and continues her tricks with the next victim. And he is blind to all this. No matter what, he loves her. Whatever she does, he pities her patienthood, and he loves her.

The third woman binds him into permanent captivity. But that one I prefer. At least she does not hide her claws!

Letter to Lou Salomé from Friedrich Nietzsche, Decembe. 1882

My dear Lou,

. . . You have in me the best advocate but also the most merciless judge! I demand you judge yourself and that you determine your own punishment. . . . I had decided for myself back in Orta to reveal my whole philosophy to you. Oh you have no idea what a decision that was: I believed I couldn't make a better present to anyone. . . .

I tended back then to consider you a vision and manifestation of my earthly ideal. Please note I have terrible eyesight!

I think no one can think better of you, but also not worse.

If I had created you I would have given you better health and much more beyond that which is far more worthy . . . and perhaps a bit more love for me (although that has the absolute least importance) and it would have been the same with friend Rée. Neither with you nor with him can I speak even a single word about matters of my heart. I imagine you don't know at all what I want?—but this forced noiselessness is almost suffocating because I am fond of you people.

F.N.

CHAPTER 15

FOLLOWING THEIR FIRST SESSION, Breuer devoted only a few more minutes of his official time to Nietzsche: he wrote a note in Eckart Müller's chart, briefed the nurses about the status of his migraine, and, later in his office, wrote a more personal report in a notebook identical to the one Nietzsche used for his own notes.

But over the next twenty-four hours, Nietzsche claimed much of Breuer's unofficial time—time pilfered from other patients, from Mathilde, from his children, and, most of all, from his sleep. Sleeping only fitfully during the early hours of the night, Breuer dreamed vividly, disquietingly.

He dreamed that he and Nietzsche were talking together in a room that had no walls—perhaps a theater set. Workers who passed by carrying furniture listened to their conversation. The room felt temporary, as though it could all be folded up and carted away.

In a second dream, he sat in the bathtub and opened the water faucet. Out poured a stream of insects, small pieces of machinery, and large globules of slime which dangled from the faucet's mouth in long, odious strands. The machinery parts puzzled him. The slime and insects disgusted him.

At three o'clock, he was awakened by his recurrent nightmare: the ground trembling, the search for Bertha, the earth liquefying beneath his feet. He slipped into the earth, sinking forty feet before coming to rest on a white slab inscribed with an illegible message.

Breuer lay awake, listening to the pounding of his heart. He tried to calm himself with intellectual tasks. First, he wondered why things that seem sunny and benign at twelve noon so often drip with fear at three in the morning. Obtaining no relief, he turned to another diversion and tried to recall everything he had revealed to Nietzsche earlier that day. But the more he remembered, the more agitated he became. Had he said too much? Had his disclosures repulsed Nietzsche? What had possessed him to blurt out all his secret, shameful feelings about Bertha and Eva? At the time it had seemed right, even expiating, to share everything; but now he cringed to think of Nietzsche's opinion of him. Though knowing Nietzsche had puritanical feelings about sex, he had nonetheless assaulted him with sexual talk. Perhaps intentionally. Perhaps, hiding behind the mantle of patient-hood, he had meant to shock and outrage him. But why?

Soon Bertha, the empress of his mind, glided into view, flattening and scattering other thoughts, demanding his sole attention. Her sexual allure was unusually powerful that night: Bertha slowly and shyly unbuttoning her hospital gown; a naked Bertha entering trance; Bertha cupping her breast and beckoning him; his mouth filled with her soft, jutting nipple; Bertha parting her legs, whispering, "Take me," and tugging him to her. Breuer throbbed with desire; he considered reaching out to Mathilde for relief, but could not bear the duplicity and the guilt of, once again, using her body while imagining Bertha beneath him. He rose early to relieve himself.

"It seems," Breuer said to Nietzsche later that morning while reviewing his hospital chart, "Herr Müller had a much better night's sleep than did Doctor Breuer." He then recounted the events of his night: the fitful sleep, the dread, the dreams, the obsessions, his concerns about having revealed too much.

Nietzsche nodded knowingly throughout Breuer's statement and re-corded the dreams in his notebook. "As you know, I, too, have known such nights. Last night, with only one gram of chloral, I slept for five consecutive hours—but such a night is rare. Like you, I dream, I choke on night-dread. Like you, I have often wondered why fears reign at night. After twenty years of such wondering, I now believe that fears are not born of darkness; rather, fears are like the stars—always there, but obscured by the glare of daylight.

"And dreams," Nietzsche continued as he rose from the bed and walked with Breuer across the room to their chairs by the fireplace, "dreams are a glorious mystery which beg to be understood. I envy you your dreams. I rarely capture mine. I do not agree with the Swiss physician who once advised me not to waste my time thinking about dreams because they were nothing but random waste material, the nightly excretions of the mind. He claimed the brain cleanses itself every twenty-four hour by defecating the day's excess thoughts into dreams!"

Nietzsche paused to read his notes on Breuer's dreams. "Your nightmare is entirely baffling, but I believe your other two dreams emerged from our discussion yesterday. You tell me you worry that you might have revealed too much—and then you dream of a public room without walls. And the other dream—the spigot and mucus and insects—does it not corroborate your fear that you spewed out too much of the dark, unpleasant parts of yourself?"

"Yes, it was strange how that notion grew larger and larger as the night progressed. I worried that I had offended you, shocked or disgusted you. I worried how you might regard me."

"But did I not predict it?" Nietzsche, sitting cross-legged in the chair opposite Breuer, tapped his pencil against his notebook for emphasis. "This worry about *my* feelings is what I had feared; it was *precisely* for this reason I urged you not to reveal more than was necessary for my comprehension. I wish to help you stretch and grow, not weaken yourself by confessing your failings."

"But, Professor Nietzsche, here we have a major area of disagreement. In fact, last week we quarreled about this very issue. Let's try to reach a more amiable conclusion this time. I remember your saying, and also I read in your books, that all relationships must be understood on the basis of power. Yet that's simply not true for me. I'm not competing: I have no interest in defeating you. I only want your help in recapturing my life. The balance of power between us—who wins, who loses—seems trivial and irrelevant."

"Then why, Doctor Breuer, do you feel ashamed of having shown me your weaknesses?"

"Not because I've lost some contest with you! Who cares about that? I feel bad for one reason only: I value your opinion of me, and I fear that, after yesterday's sordid confession, you think far less of me! Consult your list"—Breuer gestured toward Nietzsche's notebook. "Remember the item about self-hatred—number three, I believe. I keep my true self hidden because there are so many despicable things about me. Then I dislike myself even more because I'm cut off from other people. If I'm ever to break this vicious cycle, I must be able to reveal myself to others!"

"Perhaps, but look"—and Nietzsche pointed toward item 10 in the notebook. "Here you say you are overconcerned with the opinions of your colleagues. I have known many who dislike themselves and try to rectify this by first persuading *others* to think well of them. Once that is done, then they begin to think well of *themselves*. But this is a false solution, this is submission to the authority of others. Your task is to accept *yourself*—not to find ways to gain *my* acceptance."

Breuer's head began to spin. He had a quick, penetrating mind and was not accustomed to being systematically outreasoned. But, obviously, rational debate with Nietzsche was inadvisable; he could never defeat him or persuade him of anything contrary to his position. Perhaps, Breuer concluded, he might do better with an impulsive, irrational approach.

"No, no, no! Believe me, Professor Nietzsche, while that makes sense, it won't work with me! I know only that I need your acceptance. You are right: the *ultimate* goal *is* to be independent of others' opinions, but the *route* to that goal—and I speak for *myself*, not for you—is to know that I am not beyond the pale of decency. I need to be able to reveal *everything* about myself to another and to learn that I, too, am . . . simply human."

As an afterthought, he added, "Human, all too human!"

The title of his book brought a smile to Nietzsche's face. "Touché, Doctor Breuer! Who can quarrel with that felicitous phrase? I understand now your feelings, but still I'm not clear about their implications for our procedure."

Breuer chose his words carefully in this delicate area.

"Nor am I. But I *do* know that I must be able to relax my guard. It will not work for me to feel I must be careful about what I reveal to you. Let me tell you about a recent incident that may be relevant. I was speaking to my brother-in-law, Max. Now I have never been intimate with Max because I have regarded him as psychologically insensitive. My marriage, however, had deteriorated to the point where I needed to discuss it with someone. I attempted to bring it up in a conversation with Max but was so overcome with shame that I found it hard to go on. Then, in a way I never expected, Max reciprocated by revealing similar difficulties he was encountering in *his* life. Somehow his revelation freed *me*, and, for the first time ever, he and I had a *personal* discussion. It helped enormously."

"When you say 'helped,' " Nietzsche immediately asked, "do you mean your despair diminished? Or your relationship with your wife improved? Or did you have a discussion that was momentarily expiating?"

Ach! Breuer realized he was caught! If he claimed his discussion with Max was truly helpful, then Nietzsche would raise the question why he needed *his,* Nietzsche's, counsel. Careful, careful.

"I don't know what I mean. I only know I felt better. That night I didn't lie awake and cringe with shame. And since then I've felt more open, more ready to pursue an investigation of myself."

This is not going well, Breuer thought. Perhaps a simple direct appeal would be better.

"I am certain, Professor Nietzsche, that I could express myself more honestly if I could be *assured* of your acceptance. When I talk about my obsessive love or my jealousy, it would help to know if you have experienced such things, too. I suspect, for example, that you find sex disagreeable and disapprove greatly of my sexual preoccupation. Naturally, this makes me uneasy about revealing these facets of myself."

A long pause. Nietzsche stared at the ceiling in deep thought. Breuer felt expectant, for he had been skillful in increasing the pressure. He hoped Nietzsche was now finally about to give something of himself.

"Perhaps," Nietzsche replied, "I have not been clear enough about my position. Tell me, have the books you ordered arrived from my publisher?"

"Not yet. Why do you ask? Are there passages relevant to our discussion today?"

"Yes, particularly in *The Gay Science.* There I state that sexual relationships are no different from other relationships in that they, too, involve a struggle for power. Sexual lust is, at bottom, lust for total dominance over the mind and body of the other."

"That doesn't ring true. Not for *my* lust!"

"Yes, yes!" Nietzsche insisted. "Look deeper, and you will see that lust is also a lust for dominance over *all others*. The 'lover' is not one who 'loves': instead, he aims for sole possession of his loved one. His wish is to exclude the entire world from some precious good. He is as mean-spirited as the dragon guarding his golden hoard! He does not love the world—on the contrary, he is utterly indifferent to all other living creatures. Did you not say this yourself? This is why you were pleased at—I've forgotten her name—the cripple?"

"Bertha, but she's not a cripp——"

"Yes, yes, you were pleased when Bertha said you would always be the only man in her life!"

"But you take the sex out of sex! I feel my sexual urge in my genitals, not in some abstract mental arena of power!"

"No," stated Nietzsche, "I merely call it by its right name! I do not object to a man who takes sex when he needs it. But I hate the man who begs for it, who gives up his power to the dispensing woman—to the crafty woman who turns her weakness, and his strength, into *her* strength."

"Ach, how can you deny the truly erotic? You ignore the impulse, the biological craving that is built into us, that permits us to reproduce! Sensuality is a part of life, of nature."

"*Part*, but not the *high* part! Verily, the mortal enemy of the high part. Here, let me read you a phrase I wrote early this morning."

Nietzsche put on his thick spectacles, reached over to his desk, picked up a worn notebook, and flipped through pages filled with an illegible scrawl. He stopped at the last page and, his nose almost touching it, read, " 'Sensuality is a bitch that nips at our heels! And how nicely this bitch knows how to beg for a piece of spirit when denied a piece of meat.' "

He closed the book. "So the problem is *not* that sex is *present*, but that it makes something else vanish—something more valuable, infinitely more precious! Lust, arousal, voluptuousness—they are the enslavers! The rabble spend their lives like swine feeding in the trough of lust."

"The trough of lust!" Breuer repeated to himself, astonished by Nietzsche's intensity. "You have strong feelings about this matter. I hear more passion in your voice than ever before."

"Great passion is required to defeat passion! Too many men have been broken on the wheel of lesser passion."

"And your *own* experiences in this domain?" Breuer was fishing. "Have you yourself had unfortunate experiences that helped shape your conclusions?"

"Your earlier point, about the primal goal of reproduction—let me ask you *this*:"—Nietzsche stabbed the air thrice with his finger—"Should we not *create*—should we not *become*—*before* we reproduce? Our responsibility to life is to create the higher, not to reproduce the lower. Nothing must interfere with the development of the hero inside of you. And if lust stands in the way, then it, too, must be overcome."

Face reality! Breuer told himself. You have virtually no control over these discussions, Josef. Nietzsche simply ignores any question he doesn't wish to answer.

"You know, Professor Nietzsche, I agree, intellectually, with much you say, but our level of discourse is too *abstract*. It's not *personal* enough to be helpful to me. Maybe I am too wedded to the practical—after all, my entire professional life has focused upon eliciting a complaint, making a diagnosis, and then addressing that complaint with a specific remedy."

He leaned forward, to look directly at Nietzsche. "Now, I know my type of malady cannot be addressed so pragmatically—but, in our discussion we veer too far to the opposite extreme. I can't *do* anything with your words. You tell me to overcome my lust, my lesser passions. You tell me to nurture the higher parts in myself—but you don't tell me *how* to overcome, *how* to nurture the hero in myself. These are fine poetic constructs, but right now, to me, they are just airy words."

Apparently unaffected by Breuer's plea, Nietzsche responded like a teacher to an impatient schoolboy. "In time I shall teach you *how* to overcome. You want to fly, but you cannot begin to fly by flying. I must first teach you to walk, and the first step in learning to walk is to understand that he who does not obey himself is ruled by others. It is easier, far easier, to obey another than to command oneself." With that, Nietzsche took out his small comb and began to groom his mustache.

"Easier to obey another than command oneself? Once again, Professor Nietzsche, why not address me more personally? I get the sense of your statement, but do you speak to *me*? What can I *do* with it? Forgive me if I sound earthbound. Right now my desires are mundane. I wish for simple things—to sleep a nightmare-free sleep past three in the morning, to feel some relief from precordial tension. Here is where my *Angst* sets up housekeeping, right here——" He pointed to the center of his sternum.

"What I need now," he went on, "is not an abstract, poetic statement but something human, direct. I need personal engagement: Can you share with me what it has been like for you? Did *you* have a love or an obsession like mine? How did *you* get past it? Overcome it? How long did it take?"

"There is one more thing I've planned to discuss with you today," said Nietzsche, putting away his comb and, once again, ignoring Breuer's question. "Do we have time?"

Breuer settled dispiritedly back in his chair. Obviously Nietzsche was going to continue to ignore his questions. He urged himself to be patient. He looked at his watch and said he could stay another fifteen minutes. "I'll be here every day at ten for thirty to forty minutes, though there will undoubtedly be days when an emergency will force me to leave sooner."

"Good! There's something important I want to say to you. Many times I have heard you complain of unhappiness. In fact"—Nietzsche opened his notebook to Breuer's list of problems—" 'general unhappiness' is the first problem on your list. Also today you have spoken of your *Angst*, your cordial tension——"

"*Pre*cordial—the region on top of the *cor*, the heart."

"Yes, thank you, we teach one another. Your *pre*cordial tension, your night fears, your insomnia, your despair—you speak much of these complaints, and you describe your 'earthbound' desire for immediate relief from discomfort. You lament that your discussion with me does not provide it in the way your discussion with Max did."

"Yes. And——"

"And you want me to address your tension directly, you want me to provide comfort."

"Exactly." Breuer leaned forward again in his chair. He nodded, urging Nietzsche along.

"I resisted your proposal, two days ago, that I become your—what shall we call it?—your counselor and help you deal with your despair. I disagreed when you claimed I was a world expert because I had studied these matters for many years.

"But, now as I reflect upon it, I realize you were right: I *am* an expert. I *do* have much to teach you: I have devoted much of my life to the study of despair. How much of my life, I can easily show you. A few months ago, my sister, Elisabeth, showed me a letter I had written to her in eighteen sixty-five, when I was twenty-one. Elisabeth never returns my letters—she stores everything away and says that some day she will build a museum to house my effects and charge admission. No doubt, knowing Elisabeth, she'll have me stuffed, mounted, and displayed as the main attraction. In that letter, I stated that there was a basic division of the ways of men: those who wish for peace of soul and happiness must believe and embrace faith, while *those who wish to pursue the truth must forsake peace of mind* and devote their life to inquiry.

"This I knew at twenty-one, half a life ago. It is time for *you* to learn it: it must be your basic starting place. You must choose between comfort and true inquiry! If you choose science, if you choose to be liberated from the soothing chains of the supernatural, if, as you claim, you choose to eschew belief and embrace godlessness, then you cannot in the same breath yearn for the small comforts of the believer! If you kill God, you must also leave the shelter of the temple."

Breuer sat quietly, looking out of Nietzsche's window into the sanatorium garden, where an elderly man in a wheelchair sat with closed eyes while a young nurse pushed him around a circular path. Nietzsche's comments were compelling. It was hard to slough them off as mere airy philosophizing. Yet, once more, he tried.

"You make it sound more choiceful than it was. My choice was not so deliberate, nor so deep. My choice for godlessness was less an active choice than a matter of being unable to believe in religious fairy tales. I chose science simply because it was the only mode possible to master the secrets of the body."

"Then you conceal your will from yourself. You must *now* learn to acknowledge your life and to have the courage to say, 'Thus I chose it!' The spirit of a man is constructed out of his choices!"

Breuer squirmed in his chair. Nietzsche's preaching tone made him uncomfortable. Where could he have learned it? Not from his preacher-father, who had died when Nietzsche was five. Could there be genetic transmission of preaching skills and inclinations?

Nietzsche continued the sermon. "If you choose to be one of those few who partake of the pleasure of growth and the exhilaration of godless freedom, then you must prepare yourself for the greatest pain. They are bound together and cannot be experienced apart! If you want less pain, then you must shrink, as the stoics did, and forgo the highest pleasure."

"I'm not sure, Professor Nietzsche, that one must accept that morbid *Weltanschauung*. That sounds like Schopenhauer, but there are other, less gloomy points of view."

"Gloomy? Ask yourself, Doctor Breuer, why are all the great philosophers gloomy? Ask yourself, 'Who are the secure ones, the comfortable, the eternally cheerful?' I'll tell you the answer: *only those with dull vision*—the common people and the children!"

"You say, Professor Nietzsche, that growth is the reward of pain——"

Nietzsche interrupted. "No, not *just* growth. There is also strength. A tree requires stormy weather if it is to attain a proud height. And creativity and discovery are begotten in pain. Here, allow me to quote myself from my notes of just a few days ago."

Again, Nietzsche thumbed through his notes, and then read, " 'One must have chaos and frenzy within oneself to give birth to a dancing star.' "

Breuer was now growing more irritated by Nietzsche's reading. His poetic speech felt like a barricade between them. On balance, Breuer was certain that things would be better if he could bring Nietzsche down from the stars.

"Again, you are too abstract. Please don't misunderstand me, Professor Nietzsche, your words are beautiful and powerful, but when you read them to me, I no longer feel that we're relating *personally*. I grasp your meaning intellectually: yes, there *are* rewards of pain—growth, strength, creativity. I understand it *here*"—Breuer gestured to his head—"but it doesn't get into *here*"—he gestured to his abdomen. "If this is to help me, it's got to reach me where my experience is rooted. *Here*, in my entrails, I experience no growth, I give birth to no dancing stars! I have only the frenzy and the chaos!"

Nietzsche smiled broadly and wagged his finger in the air. "Exactly! Now you've said it! That's the problem precisely! And *why* no growth? *Why* no worthier thoughts? That was the point of my final question yesterday, when I asked what you'd be thinking if you were *not* preoccupied with those alien thoughts? Please, sit back, close your eyes, and try this thought experiment with me.

"Let us take a distant perch, perhaps on a mountain peak, and observe together. There, over there, far away, we see a man, a man with a mind both intelligent and sensitive. Let us watch him. Perhaps once he looked deeply into the horror of his own existence. Perhaps he saw too much! Perhaps he encountered time's devouring jaws, or his own insignificance—mere speck that he is—or life's transiency and contingency. His fear was raw and terrible until the day he discovered that lust soothes fear. Therefore, he welcomed lust into his mind, and lust, a ruthless competitor, soon crowded out all other thoughts. But lust does not think; it craves, it recollects. So this man began to recollect lustfully of Bertha, the cripple. He no longer looked into the distance, but spent his time recollecting such miracles as how Bertha moved her fingers, her mouth, how she undressed, how she talked and stuttered, walked and limped.

"Soon his whole being was consumed with such pettiness. The great boulevards of his mind that were built for noble ideas became clogged with trash. His recollection of having once thought great thoughts grew dimmer and soon faded away. And his fears faded also. He was left with only a gnawing anxiety that something was amiss. Puzzled, he sought for the source of his anxiety amidst the trash of his mind. And that is how we find him today, rummaging through the rubbish, as if *it* contains the answer. He even asks *me* to rummage with him!"

Nietzsche stopped, awaiting Breuer's response. Silence.

"Tell me," Nietzsche urged, "what do you think of this man we observe?"

Silence.

"Doctor Breuer, what do you think?"

Breuer sat on in silence, his eyes closed, as if he had been mesmerized by Nietzsche's words.

"Josef! Josef, what do you think?"

Rousing himself, Breuer slowly opened his eyes and turned to look at Nietzsche. Still, he did not speak.

"Don't you see, Josef, that the problem is *not* that you feel discomfort? What importance is tension or pressure in your chest? Who ever promised you comfort? So you sleep poorly! So? Who ever promised you good sleep? No, the problem is *not* discomfort. The problem is that you have *discomfort about the wrong thing!*"

Nietzsche glanced at his watch. "I see I am keeping you too long. Let us end with the same suggestion I offered yesterday. Please think about what you would be thinking about if Bertha did not clog your mind. Agreed?"

Breuer nodded and took his leave.

Excerpts from Dr. Breuer's Case Notes on Eckart Müller, 6 December 1882

Strange things happened in our talk today. And none of it as I had planned. He answered none of my questions, revealed nothing of himself. He takes his role as counselor so solemnly that at times I find it comical. And yet, as I examine it from his perspective, his behavior is entirely correct:

he is honoring his contract and trying, as best he can, to help me. I respect him for that.

It is fascinating to observe his intelligence grappling with the problem of how to be helpful to a single individual, to a flesh-and-blood creature—to me. So far, however, he remains strangely unimaginative and relies completely on rhetoric. Can he truly believe that rational explanation or sheer exhortation will cure the problem?

In one of his books, he argues that a philosopher's personal moral structure dictates the type of philosophy he creates. I believe now that the same principle is true in this type of counseling: the counselor's personality dictates his counseling approach. Thus, because of Nietzsche's social fears and misanthropy, he selects an impersonal, distant style. He is, of course, blind to this: he proceeds to develop a theory to rationalize and legitimize his counseling approach. Thus, he offers no personal support, never holds out a comforting hand, lectures to me from a lofty platform, refuses to admit to his own personal problems, and declines to engage me in a human fashion. Except for one moment! Toward the end of our talk today—I forget what we were discussing—he suddenly referred to me as "Josef." Perhaps I am more successful than I thought in establishing rapport.

We are in a strange struggle. To see who can most help the other. I am troubled by this competition: I fear it will confirm for him his inane "power" model of social relations. Maybe I should do what Max says: stop competing and learn what I can from him. It is important for him to be in control. I see many signs that he feels victorious: he tells me how much he has to teach me, he reads his notes to me, he looks at the time and cavalierly dismisses me with an assignment for our next meeting. All this is irritating! But then I remind myself that I am a physician: I do not meet with him for my personal pleasure. After all, what is the personal pleasure in removing a patient's tonsils or dislodging a fecal impaction?

There was one moment today when I experienced a strange absence. I almost felt as though I were in a trance. Maybe I am, after all, susceptible to mesmerism.

Friedrich Nietzsche's Notes on Dr. Breuer, 6 December 1882

Sometimes it is worse for a philosopher to be understood than to be misunderstood. He tries to understand me too well; he attempts to wheedle specific directions from me. He wants to discover my way and use that as his way also. Not yet does he understand that there is a my way and a your way, but that there is no "the" way. And he does not ask for directions forthrightly but instead wheedles and pretends his wheedling is something else: he tries to persuade me that my revelation is essential to the process of our work, that it will help him talk, will make us more "human" together, as though wallowing in muck together is what it means to be human! I try to teach him that lovers of truth do not fear stormy or dirty water. What we fear is shallow water!

If medical practice is to serve as a guide in this endeavor, then must I not arrive at a "diagnosis"? Here is a new science—the diagnosis of despair. I diagnose him as one who longs to be a free spirit but cannot shed the fetters of belief. He wants only the yes, the acceptance, of choice, none of the no, the relinquishment. He is a self-deceiver: he makes choices but refuses to be the one who chooses. He knows he is miserable, but he does not know that he is miserable about the wrong thing! He expects from me relief, comfort, and happiness. But I must give him more misery. I must change his trivial misery back into the noble misery it once was.

How to detach trivial misery from its perch? To make suffering honest again? I used his own technique—the third-person technique that he employed with me last week in his clumsy attempt to entice me to put myself into his care; I instructed him to look at himself from above. But it was too strong; he almost fainted. I had to speak to him as a child, to call him "Josef," to revive him.

My burden is great. I work for his liberation. And my own as well. But I am not a Breuer: I comprehend my misery and I welcome it. And Lou Salomé is no cripple. Yet I know what it is to be besieged by one whom I love and hate!

CHAPTER 16

A GREAT PRACTITIONER of the *art* of medicine, Breuer usually began his hospital visits with bedside small talk which he gracefully guided into medical inquiry. But there was to be no small talk when he entered room 13 of the Lauzon Clinic the following morning. Nietzsche immediately announced that he felt unusually healthy and wished to waste none of their precious time talking about his nonexistent symptoms. He suggested that they get right down to business.

"My time will come again, Doctor Breuer; my illness never strays too long or too far. But now that it's *en vacance,* let's continue our work on *your* problems. What progress have you made on the thought experiment I proposed yesterday? What would you think about were you not preoccupied with fantasies of Bertha?"

"Professor Nietzsche, let me speak of something else first. There was a moment yesterday when you dropped my professional title and called me Josef. I liked it. I felt closer to you, and I liked *that.* Even though we have a professional relationship, the nature of our discourse requires that we speak intimately. Would you, therefore, be willing for us to use one another's first names?"

Nietzsche, who had arranged his life to avoid such personal interaction, was nonplused. He squirmed and stuttered but, apparently finding no gracious way to refuse, finally nodded grudgingly. To Breuer's further question whether to address him as Friedrich or Fritz, Nietzsche all but barked, "Friedrich, please. And now to work!"

"Yes, to work! Back to your question. What's behind Bertha? I know there is a stream of deeper and darker concerns, which I'm convinced intensified several months ago when I passed my fortieth year. You know, Friedrich, a crisis around the forty-year mark is not unusual. Take care, you have only two years to prepare yourself."

Breuer knew that his familiarity made Nietzsche uncomfortable, but that also parts of him yearned for closer human contact.

"I am not very concerned," said Nietzsche tentatively. "I think I have been forty since I was twenty!"

What was this? An approach! Without question, an approach! Breuer thought of a kitten his son Robert had recently found in the street. Set out some milk, he had told Robert, and back away. Let it drink safely and become used to your presence. Later, when it feels secure, you may be able to caress it. Breuer backed away.

"How to best describe my thoughts? I think morbid, dark things. Often I feel as if my life has crested." Breuer paused, remembering how he had put it to Freud. "I've climbed to the peak, and when I peer over the edge to view what lies ahead, I see only deterioration—descent into aging, grandparenting, white hair, or, indeed"—tapping the bald center of his scalp—"no hair at all. But no, that's not quite right. It's not *descending* that troubles me—it's the *not ascending.*"

"Not ascending, Doctor Breuer? Why can't you continue to ascend?"

"Friedrich, I know it's hard to break the habit, but please call me Josef."

"Josef, then. Tell me, Josef, about not ascending."

"Sometimes I imagine everyone has a secret phrase, Friedrich, a deep motif that becomes the central myth of one's life. When I was a child, someone once called me 'the lad of infinite promise.' I loved that phrase. I've hummed it to myself thousands of times. Often I've imagined myself as a tenor singing it at a high pitch: 'the laaaaaad of in-fin-ite prom-ise.' I liked to say it slowly and dramatically, emphasizing each syllable. Even now the words move me!"

"And what has happened to that lad of infinite promise?"

"Ah, *that* question! I ponder it often. What *has* become of him? I know now that there is no more promise—it's been used up!"

"Tell me, precisely what do you mean by 'promise'?"

"I'm not sure I know. I used to think I did. It meant the potential to climb, to spiral upward; it meant success, acclaim, scientific discoveries. But I've tasted the fruit of these promises. I'm a respected physician, a respectable citizen. I've made some important scientific discoveries—as long as historical records exist, my name will always be known as one of the discoverers of the function of the inner ear in the regulation of equilibrium. And, also, I participated in the discovery of an important respiratory regulatory process known as the Herring-Breuer reflex."

"Then, Josef, are you not a fortunate man? Have you not fulfilled your promise?"

Nietzsche's tone was puzzling. Was he truly asking for information? Or playing Socrates to Breuer's Alcibiades? Breuer decided to answer at face value.

"Fulfillment of goals—yes. But without satisfaction, Friedrich. At first, the flush of a new success lasted for months. But gradually it has grown more fleeting—weeks, then days, even hours—until now the feeling evaporates so quickly that it no longer even penetrates my skin. I now believe my goals were imposters—they were never the true destiny of the lad of infinite promise. Often I feel disoriented: the old goals don't work any more, and I've lost the knack of inventing new ones. When I think about the flow of my life, I feel betrayed or tricked, as though a celestial joke has been played on me, as though I've danced my life away to the wrong tune."

"Wrong tune?"

"The tune of the lad of infinite promise—the tune I've hummed all my life!"

"It was the right tune, Josef, but the wrong dance!"

"The right tune but the wrong dance? What do you mean?"

Nietzsche remained silent.

"You mean I interpreted the word 'promise' incorrectly?"

"And 'infinite' as well, Josef."

"I don't understand. Can you speak more clearly?"

"Perhaps you must learn to speak more clearly to yourself. In the last few days, I have realized that the philosophic cure consists of learning to listen to your own inner voice. Didn't you tell me that your patient, Bertha, cured herself through talking about every aspect of her thoughts? What was the term you used to describe that?"

"Chimneysweeping. Actually she invented the term—to sweep her chimney meant to unplug herself so that she could ventilate her brain, cleanse her mind of all disturbing thoughts."

"It's a good metaphor," Nietzsche said. "Perhaps we should try to use the method in our talks. Perhaps right now. Could you, for example, try to chimneysweep about the lad of infinite promise?"

Breuer leaned his head back in his chair. "I think I've said it all. That aging lad has reached the point in life when he can no longer see its point. His purpose for living—*my* purpose, my goals, the rewards that drove me through life—all seem absurd now. When I dwell on how I have pursued absurdities, how I have wasted the only life I have, a feeling of terrible desperation settles over me."

"What *should* you have pursued, instead?"

Breuer felt heartened by Nietzsche's tone, more kindly now, more assured, as if he were familiar with this terrain.

"That's the worst part! Life is an examination with no correct answers. If I had it to do all over again, I think I would do exactly the same thing, make the same mistakes. The other day I thought of a good plot for a novella. If only I could write! Imagine this: a middle-aged man, who has led an unsatisfying life, is approached by a genie, who offers him the opportunity to relive his life while maintaining full recall of his previous life. Of course, he leaps at the chance. But to his amazement and horror, he finds himself living the identical life—making the same choices, the same mistakes, embracing the same false goals and gods."

"And these goals you live by, where did they come from? How did you choose them?"

"How did I choose my goals? Choose, choose—your favorite word! Boys of five or ten or twenty don't *choose* their life. I don't know how to think about your question."

"Don't think," urged Nietzsche. "Just chimneysweep!"

"Goals? Goals are in the culture, the air. You breathe them in. Every young boy I grew up with inhaled the same goals. We all wanted to climb out of the Jewish ghetto, to rise in the world, to achieve success, wealth, respectability. That's what everybody wanted! No one of us ever set about deliberately choosing goals—they were just *there*, the natural consequences of my time, my people, my family."

"But they didn't work for you, Josef. They were not solid enough to support a life. Oh, perhaps they might be solid enough for some, for those with poor vision, or for the slow runners who chug all their lives after material objectives, or even for those who attain success but have the knack of continually setting new goals just out of their reach. But you, like me, have good eyes. You looked too far into life. You saw that it was futile to reach wrong goals and futile to set new wrong goals. Multiplications of zero are always zero!"

Breuer was entranced by these words. Everything else—walls, windows, fireplace, even the corpus of Nietzsche—faded. He had been waiting all his life for this exchange.

"Yes, everything you say is true, Friedrich—except for your insistence that one chooses one's life plan in a deliberate fashion. The individual doesn't consciously select his life goals: they are an accident of history—are they not?"

"Not to take possession of your life plan is to let your existence be an accident."

"But," Breuer protested, "no one has such freedom. You can't step outside the perspective of your time, your culture, your family, your——"

"Once," Nietzsche interrupted, "a wise Jewish teacher advised his followers to break with their mother and father and to seek perfection. *That* might be a step worthy of a lad of infinite promise! That might have been the right dance to the right tune."

The right dance to the right tune! Breuer tried to concentrate on the meaning of these words, but grew suddenly discouraged.

"Friedrich, I have a passion for such talk, but a voice inside keeps asking, 'Are we getting anywhere?' Our discussion is too ethereal—too distant from the pounding in my chest and the heaviness in my head."

"Patience, Josef. How long did you say your Anna O. chimneyswept?"

"Yes, it took time. Months! But you and I don't have months. And there was a difference: her chimneysweeping always focused on her pain. But our abstract talk about goals and life purpose feels irrelevant to *my* pain!"

Nietzsche, unperturbed, continued as if Breuer had not spoken. "Josef, you say all these life concerns intensified when you became forty?"

"What perseverance, Friedrich! You inspire me to be more patient with myself. If you have enough interest to ask about my fortieth year, then I must certainly find the resolve to answer you. The fortieth year—yes, that was a year of crisis, my *second* crisis. I had an earlier crisis at twenty-nine when Oppolzer, the chief of medicine at the university, died during a typhus epidemic. The sixteenth of April in eighteen seventy-one—I still remember the date. He was my teacher, my advocate, my second father."

"I'm interested in second fathers," said Nietzsche. "Tell me more."

"He was the great teacher of my life. Everyone knew he was grooming me to be his successor. I was the best candidate and should have been selected to fill his vacant chair. Yet it did not happen. Perhaps I didn't help it happen. An inferior appointment was made on political grounds, possibly on religious ones as well. There was no longer a place for me, and I moved my laboratory, even my research pigeons, into my home and entered full-time private practice. *That,*" Breuer said sadly, "was the end of my infinitely promising academic career."

"In saying you didn't help it happen, what do you mean?"

Breuer looked at Nietzsche with amazement. "What a transformation from philosopher to clinician! You have grown physician's ears. Nothing escapes you. I threw in that comment because I know I must be honest. Yet it's a sore point still. I hadn't wanted to talk about it, yet it was the very statement you picked up."

"You see, Josef, the very instant I urge you to talk about something against your will—*that's* the moment you choose to assume power by paying me a very fine compliment. *Now* can you still claim that the struggle for power is not an important part of our relationship?"

Breuer slumped back in his chair. "Oh, *that* again." He waved his hand in front of him. "Let's not reopen *that* debate. Please, let it go."

Then he added, "Wait! I've got one last comment: if you forbid the expression of any positive sentiments, then you *bring to pass* the very kind of relationship you predicted you would discover *in vivo*. That's bad science—you're tampering with the data."

"Bad science?" Nietzsche thought for a moment, then nodded. "You're right! Debate closed! Let's return to how you didn't help your own career."

"Well, the evidence is abundant. I procrastinated writing and publishing scientific articles. I refused to take the formal preliminary steps necessary for tenure. I didn't join the correct medical associations, or participate in university committees, or make the right political connections. I don't know why. Maybe *this* has to do with power. Maybe I shrink from the competitive struggle. It's easier for me to compete with the mystery of a pigeon's equilibrium system than with another man. I think it's my problems with competition that cause me such pain when I think of Bertha with another man."

"Maybe, Josef, you felt that a lad of infinite promise shouldn't *have* to scratch and claw his way upward."

"Yes, that, too, I've felt. But *whatever* the reason, it was the end of my academic career. It was the first wound of mortality, the first assault on my myth of infinite promise."

"So, that was at twenty-nine. And turning forty—the second crisis?"

"A deeper wound. Becoming forty shattered the idea that all things were possible for me. Suddenly I understood life's most obvious fact: that time is irreversible, that my life was running out. Of course, I knew that before, but knowing it at forty was a different kind of knowing. Now I *know* that 'the lad of infinite promise' was merely a marching banner, that 'promise' is an illusion, that 'infinite' is meaningless, and that I am in lockstep with all other men marching toward death."

Nietzsche shook his head emphatically. "You call clear vision a *wound*? Look at what you have learned, Josef: that time cannot be broken, that the will cannot will backward. Only the fortunate grasp such insights!"

"Fortunate? A strange word! I learn that death approaches, that I'm impotent and insignificant, that life has no real purpose or value—and you call that fortunate!"

"The fact that the will cannot will backward does *not* mean the will is impotent! Because, thank God, God is dead—that does *not* mean existence has no purpose! Because death comes—that does *not* mean that life has no value. These are all things I shall teach you in time. But we have done enough for today—perhaps too much. Before tomorrow, please review our discussion. Meditate upon it!"

Surprised by Nietzsche's sudden closure, Breuer looked at his watch and saw he had still another ten minutes available. But he offered no objection and left Nietzsche's room feeling the relief of a schoolboy released early from class.

Excerpts from Dr. Breuer's Case Notes on Eckart Müller, 7 December 1882

Patience, patience, patience. For the first time, I learn the meaning and the value of the word. I must keep in mind my long-range goal. All bold, premature steps at this stage fail. Think of the chess opening. Develop pieces slowly and systematically. Build a solid center. Don't move a piece more than once. Don't take out a queen too early!

And it is paying off! The big step forward today was the adoption of first names. He almost choked at my proposal; I could barely suppress my laughter. For all his free-thinking, he is a Viennese at heart and loves his titles—almost as much as his impersonality! After my Friedrich-ing him repeatedly, he began to reciprocate.

It made a difference in the atmosphere of the session. Within a few minutes, he opened the door a tiny crack. He alluded to having had more than his share of crises and of being forty when he was twenty! I let this pass—for now! But I must return to it!

Perhaps, for the time being, it is best if I forget about my attempts to help him—best if I simply flow with his efforts to help me. The more genuine I am, the less I try to manipulate, the better. He is like Sig—he has the eyes of a hawk and sees through any dissembling.

A stimulating discussion today, like the old days in Brentano's philosophy class. At times I got swept up in it. But was it productive? I repeated for him my concerns about aging, mortality, and purposelessness—all the morbid meditations of mine. He seemed strangely intrigued by my old refrain of the lad of infinite promise. I'm not sure I entirely understand his point yet—if there is one!

Today his method is clearer to me. Since he believes that my Bertha obsession serves to divert me from these Existenz concerns, his intent is to confront me with them, to stir them up, probably to make me more uncomfortable. Hence, he prods sharply and offers no support whatsoever. Given his personality, that, of course, is not difficult for him to do.

He appears to believe that a method of philosophic disputation will affect me. I try to let him know it does not touch me. But he, like me, keeps experimenting and improvising methods as he proceeds. His other meth-

odological innovation today was to employ my "chimneysweeping" technique. It feels odd for me to be the sweeper rather than the overseer—odd, but not unpleasant.

What is unpleasant and irritating is his grandiosity, which shines through repeatedly. Today he claimed that he will teach me about the meaning and value of life. Only not now! I'm not yet ready for it!!

Friedrich Nietzsche's Notes on Dr. Breuer, 7 December 1882

Finally! A discussion worthy of my attention—a discussion that proves much that I have thought. Here is a man so weighed down with gravity—his culture, his state, his family—as never to have known his own will. So kneaded into conformity is he that he looks astonished when I speak of choice, as though I were speaking some alien tongue. Perhaps conformity particularly constricts the Jews—external persecution binds a people so tight together that the single one cannot emerge.

When I confront him with the fact that he has allowed his life to be an accident, he denies the possibility of choice. He tells me that no one embedded in a culture can choose. When I gently confront him with Jesus' mandate to break with parents and culture in pursuit of perfection, he declares my method too ethereal and changes the subject.

It is curious how he had the concept in his grasp at an early age, but never developed the vision to see it. He was "the lad of infinite promise"—as are we all—but never understood the nature of his promise. He never understood that his duty was to perfect nature, to overcome himself, his culture, family, lust, his brutish animal nature, to become who he was, what he was. He never grew, he never shed his first skin: he mistook the promise to be the acquisition of material and professional objectives. And when he achieved these objectives without having ever quieted the voice that said, "Become yourself," he lapsed into despair and railed at the trick played on him. Even now he does not get the point!

Is there hope for him? He at least thinks about the right issues and does not resort to religious deceptions. But he has too much fear. How do I teach him to become hard? He once told that cold baths are good for toughening the skin. Is there a prescription for toughening resolve? He has arrived at the insight that we are ruled not by God's desire, but by time's desire. He realizes that the will is powerless against the "thus it was." Do I have the ability to teach him to transform the "thus it was" into the "thus I willed it"?

He insists on calling me by my first name, even though he knows it is not my preference. It is but a small torment; I am strong enough to permit him that little victory.

Letter to Lou Salomé from Friedrich Nietzsche, December 1882

Lou,

Whether I suffer a lot is inconsequential compared to the question of whether or not, dear Lou, you will find yourself again. I've never dealt with so poor a person as you are:

unknowing but sharp-witted
    rich in using up what's known
    without taste but naïve in this shortcoming
    honest and just in small matters, out of stubbornness usually
    On the larger scale, the entire stance toward life—dishonest
    without any sensitivity for giving or taking
    without spirit and incapable of love
    in affect always sick and near to madness
    without thankfulness, without shame toward benefactors

in particular
    undependable
    not well behaved
    crude in things of honor
    a brain with the first signs of a soul
    character of the cat—the predator clothed as a house pet
    nobleness as reminiscence of familiarity with nobler people
    a strong will, but not a large object
    without diligence and purity
    cruelly displaced sensuality
    childish egoism as a result of sexual atrophy and delay
    without love to people but love to God
    in need of expansion
    crafty, full of self-restraint in reference to the sexuality of men

Yours,
F.N.

CHAPTER 17

THE NURSES AT THE LAUZON CLINIC rarely talked about Herr Müller, Dr. Breuer's patient in room 13. There was little to say. To a busy, overworked nursing staff, Herr Müller was the ideal patient. During the first week, he had had no attacks of hemicrania. He made few demands and required little attention aside from the monitoring of vital signs—pulse, temperature, respiratory rate, and blood pressure—six times a day. The nurses regarded him—as had Frau Becker, Breuer's nurse—as a true gentleman.

It was clear, however, that he valued his privacy. He never initiated conversation. When called upon by the staff or other patients, he spoke amiably and briefly. He chose to take his meals in his room and, after his morning sessions with Dr. Breuer (which, the nurses assumed, consisted of massage and electrical treatments), he spent most of his day alone, writing in his room or, if weather permitted, scribbling notes while strolling around the garden. About his writing, Herr Müller courteously discouraged inquiries. It was known only that he was interested in Zarathustra, an ancient Persian prophet.

Breuer was impressed by the discrepancy between Nietzsche's gentle manner in the clinic and the shrill, often combative voice in his books. When he put the question to his patient, Nietzsche smiled and said, "It's no great mystery. If no one will listen, it's only natural to shout!"

He seemed content with his life in the clinic. He told Breuer not only that his days were pleasant and pain-free, but also that their daily talks together were productive for his philosophy. He had always been contemptuous of philosophers like Kant and Hegel, who wrote, he said, with an academic stylus solely for the academic community. His philosophy was *about* life and *for* life. The best truths, he always said, were bloody truths, ripped out of one's own life experience.

Before his connection with Breuer, he had never attempted to put his philosophy to practical use. He had casually dismissed the problem of application, claiming that those who could not understand him were not worth troubling with, whereas the superior specimens would find their way to his wisdom—if not now, then a hundred years later! But his daily encounters with Breuer were forcing him to take the matter more seriously.

Nevertheless, these carefree, productive Lauzon days were not so idyllic for Nietzsche as they seemed on the surface. Subterranean crosscurrents sapped his strength. Almost daily, he composed enraged, longing, desperate letters to Lou Salomé. Her image incessantly invaded his mind and diverted his energy from Breuer, from Zarathustra, and from the sheer joy of luxuriating in days free of pain.

Whether viewed from the surface or the depths, Breuer's life during the first week of Nietzsche's hospitalization was harried and tormented. The hours spend at the Lauzon taxed an already-burdened schedule. An invariable rule of Viennese medicine was that the worse the weather, the busier the physician. For weeks, a grim winter with unremitting gray skies, chilling blasts of northern wind, and heavy, soggy air sent patient after patient trudging in a steady stream into his examination room.

December diseases dominated Breuer's docket: bronchitis, pneumonitis, sinusitis, tonsillitis, otitis, pharyngitis, and emphysema. In addition, there were always patients with nervous diseases. That first week of December, two new young patients with disseminated sclerosis entered his office. Breuer especially hated this diagnosis: he had no treatment whatsoever to offer for the condition and dreaded the dilemma of whether to tell his young patients about the fate lying ahead of them: increasing disability, and episodes of weakness, paralysis, or blindness that could strike at any moment.

That first week as well, two new patients appeared who had no evidence of organic pathology and who, Breuer was certain, were suffering from hysteria. One, a middle-aged woman, had, during the past two years, experienced spastic seizures whenever she was left alone. The other patient, a girl of seventeen, had a spastic disorder of the legs and could walk only by using two umbrellas as canes. At irregular intervals, she had lapses in consciousness when she shouted such strange phrases as: "Leave me! Get gone! I'm not here! It's not me!"

Both patients, Breuer believed, were candidates for the Anna O. talking treatment. But that course of treatment had taken too heavy a toll—on his time, his professional reputation, his mental equilibrium, and his marriage. Even as he was vowing never to undertake it again, he found it demoralizing to turn to the conventional, ineffective therapeutic regimen—deep muscle massage and electrical stimulation according to the precise, yet unvalidated guidelines Wilhelm Erb had worked out in his widely used *Handbook of Electrical Therapeutics.*

If only he could have referred these two patients to another physician! But to whom? No one wanted such referrals. In December of 1882, there was, aside from him, no one in Vienna—no one in all of Europe—who knew how to treat hysteria.

But Breuer was exhausted not by the professional demands upon him, but by the self-imposed psychological torment he was suffering. Their fourth, fifth, and sixth sessions had followed the agenda established in their third meeting: Nietzsche pressed him to confront the *Existenz* issues in his life, especially his concerns about/purposelessness, his conformity and lack of freedom, and his fears of aging and death. If Nietzsche really wants me to become *more* uncomfortable, then, Breuer thought, he must be pleased by my progress.

Breuer felt truly miserable. He was growing even more estranged from Mathilde. Anxiety weighed him down. He could not free himself of the pressure in his thorax. It was as though a giant vise were crushing his ribs. His breathing was shallow. He kept reminding himself to breathe deeply; but no matter how hard he tried, he could not exhale the tension that constricted him. Surgeons had now learned to insert a thoracic tube in order to drain a patient's pleural fluid; sometimes he imagined plunging tubes into his chest and armpits and sucking out his *Angst.* Night after night, he suffered from dreadful dreams and severe insomnia. After several days, he was taking more chloral for sleep than was Nietzsche. He wondered how long he could continue. Was such a life worth living? Sometimes he thought about taking an overdose of Veronal. Several of his patients had endured suffering like this for years. Well, let them do it! Let them cling to a meaningless, miserable life. Not he!

Nietzsche, supposedly there to help him, gave him little comfort. When he described his anguish, Nietzsche dismissed it as a trifle. "Of course you suffer, it's the price of vision. Of course, you are fearful, living *means* to be in danger. Grow hard!" he exhorted. "You are not a cow, and I am no apostle of cud chewing."

By Monday night, one week after they had agreed upon their contract, Breuer knew that Nietzsche's plan had gone seriously awry. Nietzsche had theorized that the Bertha fantasies were a diversionary tactic on the part of the mind—one of the mind's "back alley" tactics to avoid facing the far more painful *Existenz* concerns clamoring for attention. Confront the important *Existenz* issues, Nietzsche had insisted, and the Bertha obsessions would simply fade away.

But they did not fade! The fantasies overran his resistance with ever greater ferocity! They demanded more from him: more of his attention, more of his future. Again, Breuer imagined changing his life, finding some way to break out of his prison—his marital-cultural-professional prison—and to flee from Vienna with Bertha in his arms.

One specific fantasy gathered strength. He imagined returning home one night to see a cluster of neighbors and firemen gathered in his street. His house is on fire! He throws his coat over his head and charges past restraining arms up the stairs into the burning house to save his family. But the flames and the smoke make rescue impossible. He loses consciousness and is rescued by firemen, who tell him his entire family have died in the fire: Mathilde, Robert, Bertha, Dora, Margarethe, and Johannes. Everyone praises his courageous attempt to save his family, everyone is aghast at his loss. He grieves deeply, his pain inexpressible. But he is free! Free for Bertha, free to escape with her, perhaps to Italy, perhaps to America, free to begin all over again.

But will it work? Is she too young for him? Are their interests the same? Will love stay? No sooner did these questions appear than the loop began again: once more he is on the street, watching his house consumed in flames!

The fantasy fiercely defended itself against interruption: once started, it had to be finished. Sometimes even in the brief interval between patients, Breuer would find himself in front of his burning house. If Frau Becker entered his office at this juncture, he pretended to be writing a note in a patient's chart and motioned for her to leave him for a moment.

While at home, he could not look at Mathilde without suffering paroxysms of guilt for having placed her in the burning house. So he looked at her less, spent more time in his laboratory doing research with his pigeons, more evenings at the coffeehouse, played tarock with friends twice a week, accepted more patients, and returned home very, very tired.

And the Nietzsche project? He was no longer actively struggling to help Nietzsche. He took refuge in a new thought: *maybe he could best help Nietzsche by letting Nietzsche help him!* Nietzsche seemed to be doing well. He was not abusing drugs, he slept soundly with only a half gram of chloral, his appetite was good, he had no gastric pains, and his migraine had not returned.

Breuer now fully acknowledged his own despair and his need for help. He stopped deceiving himself; stopped pretending he was talking to Nietzsche for *Nietzsche's* sake; that the talking sessions were a ploy, a clever strategy to induce him to talk about *his* despair. Breuer marveled at the seductiveness of the talking treatment. It drew him in; to *pretend* to be in treatment *was* to be in it. It was exhilarating to unburden himself, to share all his worst secrets, to have the undivided attention of someone who, for the most part, understood, accepted, and seemed even to forgive him. Even though some sessions made him feel worse, he unaccountably looked forward to the next with anticipation. His confidence in Nietzsche's abilities and wisdom increased. There was no longer doubt in his mind that Nietzsche had the power to heal him—if only he, Breuer, could find the path to that power!

And Nietzsche the person? Is our relationship, Breuer wondered, still solely professional? Certainly he knows me better—or, at least, knows more about me—than anyone in the world. Do I like him? Does he like me? Are we friends? Breuer wasn't sure about any of these questions—or about whether he could care for someone who remained so distant. Can I be loyal? Or will I, too, one day betray him?

Then something unexpected happened. After leaving Nietzsche one morning, Breuer arrived at his office to be greeted as usual by Frau Becker. She handed him a list of twelve patients, with red checks beside the names of those who had already arrived, and a crisp blue envelope on which he recognized Lou Salomé's handwriting. Breuer opened the sealed envelope and extracted a silver-bordered card:

11 December 1882

Dr. Breuer,

I hope to see you this afternoon.

Lou

Lou! No reservations about first names with her! Breuer thought, and then realized Frau Becker was speaking.

"The Russian Fräulein strolled in an hour ago asking to see you," explained Frau Becker, a frown creasing her usually smooth forehead. "I took the liberty of telling her about your heavy morning schedule, and she said she'd return at five. I let her know that your afternoon was just as heavily scheduled. Then she requested Professor Nietzsche's Vienna address, but I told her I knew nothing about it, and she'd have to talk to you about that. Did I do the right thing?"

"Of course, Frau Becker—as usual. But you seem perturbed?" Breuer knew that she had not only taken a great dislike to Lou Salomé during her first visit but also blamed her for the entire burdensome venture with Nietzsche. The daily visit to the Lauzon Clinic introduced such a strain into Breuer's office schedule that he now rarely had time to pay much attention to his nurse.

"To be honest, Doctor Breuer, I was irritated by her strolling into your office, so crowded with patients already, and expecting you'd be here waiting for her and that she should be ushered in ahead of everyone else. And, on top of that, asking me for the professor's address! Something not right about it—going behind your back and the professor's too!"

"That's why I say you did the right thing," said Breuer soothingly. "You were discreet, you referred her to me, and you protected our patient's privacy. No one could have handled it better. Now, send in Herr Wittner."

At around five fifteen, Frau Becker announced Fräulein Salomé's arrival and, in the same breath, reminded him that five patients were still waiting to be seen.

"Whom shall I send in next? Frau Mayer has been waiting almost two hours."

Breuer felt squeezed. He knew that Lou Salomé expected to be seen immediately.

"Send Frau Mayer in. I'll see Fräulein Salomé next."

Twenty minutes later, when Breuer was in the midst of writing his note on Frau Mayer, Frau Becker escorted Lou Salomé into the office. Breuer jumped to his feet and pressed to his lips the hand she offered. Since their last meeting, her image had dimmed for him. Now he was struck, once again, with what a beauty she was. How much brighter his office had suddenly become!

"Ah, *gnädiges* Fräulein, what a pleasure! I had forgotten!"

"Forgotten me already, Herr Doctor?"

"No, not you, just forgotten what a pleasure it is to see you."

"Then look more carefully this time. Here, I give you this side"—Lou Salomé turned her head flirtatiously first to the right, then to the left— "and now the other —I've been told this is my best side. Do you think so? But now tell me—I must know—you read my little note? Were you not perhaps offended by it?"

"Offended? No, of course not—though certainly chagrined at having so little time to offer you—perhaps just a quarter of an hour." He motioned to a chair and, as she settled herself—gracefully, slowly, as though she had at her disposal all the time in the world—Breuer took the chair next to her. "You saw my full waiting room. Unfortunately, there's no leeway in my time today."

Lou Salomé seemed unperturbed. Though she nodded sympathetically, she still gave the impression that Breuer's waiting room could not possibly have anything to do with her.

"I must," he added, "still visit several patients at home, and tonight I have a medical society meeting."

"Ah, the price of success, Herr Doctor Professor."

Breuer was still not content to leave the matter. "Tell me my dear Fräulein, why live so dangerously? Why not write ahead so I can arrange time for you? Some days I have not a free moment, and on others I am called out of town for consultation. You could have come to Vienna and been unable to meet with me at all. Why take the risk of making a trip in vain?"

"All my life people have warned me about such risks. And yet thus far I have never—not once—been disappointed. Look at today, this moment! Here I am, talking with you. And perhaps I shall stay over in Vienna, and we can meet again tomorrow. So tell me, Doctor, why should I change behavior that seems to work very well? Besides, I am too impetuous, I often cannot write ahead because I do not plan ahead. I make decisions quickly and act on them quickly.

"Still, my dear Doctor Breuer," Lou continued, serenely, "none of this is what I meant when I asked if you were offended by my note. I wondered whether you were offended by my informality, by my using my first name? Most Viennese feel threatened or naked without formal titles, but I *abhor* unnecessary distance. I should like you to address me as Lou."

My God, what a formidable—and provocative—woman, Breuer thought. Despite his discomfort, he saw no way to protest without allying himself with the stuffy Viennese. Suddenly he appreciated the nasty position into which he had placed Nietzsche a few days ago. Still, he and Nietzsche were contemporaries, while Lou Salomé was half his age.

"Of course, with pleasure. I shall never cast a vote for barriers between us."

"Good, then Lou it shall be. Now, as for your waiting patients, rest assured that I have nothing but respect for your profession. In fact my friend Paul Rée and I often discuss plans for entering medical school ourselves. Thus I appreciate obligations to patients, and shall rush to the point. You've guessed, no doubt, that I come today with questions and important information about our patient—if, that is, you are still meeting with him. I learned from Professor Overbeck only that Nietzsche left Basel to come to consult with you. I know nothing else."

"Yes, we have met. But tell me, Fräulein, what information do you bear?"

"Letters from Nietzsche—so wild, and enraged, and confused he sometimes sounds as if he's lost his mind. Here they are," and she handed Breuer a sheaf of papers. "While waiting to see you today, I copied excerpts for you."

Breuer looked at the first page, in Lou Salomé's neat hand:

> Oh the melancholy . . . where is there a sea in which one can really drown?
> I lost that little that I had: my good name, the trust of a few people. I shall lose my friend, Rée—I have lost the whole year due to the terrible tortures which have hold of me even now.
> One forgives one's friends with more difficulty than one's enemies.

Although there was much more, Breuer abruptly stopped. However fascinating Nietzsche's words, he knew that every line he read was a betrayal of his patient.

"Well, Doctor Breuer, what do you think of these letters?"

"Tell me again about why you felt I must see them."

"Well, I got them all at once. Paul had been withholding them from me but decided he had no right to do that."

"But why is it urgent that I see them?"

"Read on! Look what Nietzsche says! I thought certainly a physician *must* have this information. He mentions suicide. Also, many of the letters are very disorganized: perhaps his rational faculties are deteriorating. And also, I am only human, all these attacks on me—bitter and painful—I can't just shake them off. To be honest, I need your help!"

"What kind of help?"

"I respect your opinion—you're a trained observer. Do you regard me in this fashion?" She flipped through the letters. "Listen to these charges: 'A woman without sensitivity . . . without spirit . . . incapable of love . . . undependable . . . crude in things of honor.' Or to this one: 'a predator clothed as a house pet,' or to this: 'You are a small gallows bird, and I used to think you were the embodiment of virtue and honorableness.' "

Breuer shook his head vigorously. "No, no, of course I do not view you in this way. But in our few meetings—so brief and businesslike—how much value can my opinion be? Is that really the help you seek from me?"

"I know that much of what Nietzsche writes is impulsive, written in anger, written to punish me. You've talked to him. And you've talked about me, I'm sure. I must know what he *really* thinks about me. *That* is my request of you. What does he say about me? Does he really hate me? Does he regard me as such a monster?"

Breuer sat silent for a few moments, thinking through all the implications of Lou Salomé's questions.

"But, here I am," she continued, "asking you more questions, and you haven't yet answered my previous ones: Were you able to persuade him to talk to you? Do you still meet with him? Are you making progress? Have you learned to become a doctor of despair?"

She paused, staring directly into Breuer's eyes, waiting for a reply. He felt the pressure build, pressure from all sides—from her, from Nietzsche, from Mathilde, from his waiting patients, from Frau Becker. He wanted to scream.

At last, he took a deep breath and replied, *"Gnädiges* Fräulein, how very sorry I am to say that the only reply I can make is none at all."

"None at all!" she exclaimed in surprise. "Doctor Breuer, I don't understand."

"Consider my position. Although the questions you ask me are entirely reasonable, they cannot be answered without my violating a patient's privacy."

"That means, then, that he *is* your patient, and that you are continuing to see him?"

"Alas, I cannot even answer that question!"

"But surely it is different for *me,*" she said, growing indignant. "I'm not a stranger or a debt collector."

"The motives of the questioner are irrelevant. What *is* relevant is the patient's right to privacy."

"But this is no ordinary type of medical care! This entire project was my idea! I bear the responsibility for bringing Nietzsche to you to prevent his suicide. Surely I deserve to know the outcome of my efforts."

"Yes, it's like designing an experiment and wanting to know the outcome."

"Exactly. You'd not deprive me of that?"

"But what if my telling you the outcome jeopardizes the experiment?"

"How could that happen?"

"Trust my judgment in this matter. Remember, you sought me out because you deemed me an expert. Therefore I ask you to treat me as an expert."

"But Doctor Breuer, I'm not a disinterested bystander, not a mere witness at the site of an accident with morbid curiosity over the fate of the victim. Nietzsche was important to me—is still important. Also, as I mentioned, I believe I bear some responsibility for his distress." Her voice grew shrill. "I, too, am distressed. I have a *right* to know."

"Yes, I hear your distress. But as a physician, I must first be concerned with my patient and align myself with him. Perhaps some day, if you go through with your own plans to become a physician, you will appreciate my position."

"And *my* distress? Does that count for nothing?"

"I am distressed by your distress, but I can do nothing. I must suggest you go elsewhere for help."

"Can you supply me with Nietzsche's address? I can contact him only through Overbeck, who may not be passing my letters to him!"

Finally, Breuer grew irritated at Lou Salomé's insistence. The stand he must take became clearer. "You are raising difficult questions about a physician's duty to his patients. You force me to take positions I haven't reasoned through. But I believe, now, that I can tell you nothing—not where he lives, or the state of his condition, or even whether he is my patient. And, speaking of patients, Fräulein Salomé," he said, getting up from the chair, "I must return to those who await me."

As Lou Salomé, too, started to rise, Breuer handed her the letters she had brought. "I must return these to you. I understand your bringing them, but if, as you say, your name is poison to him, there is no way in which I may use these letters. I believe I erred in reading them at all."

Swiftly she took the letters, wheeled, and, without a word, stormed out.

Mopping his brow, Breuer sat down again. Had he seen the last of Lou Salomé? He doubted it! When Frau Becker entered the office to ask whether she could send in Herr Pfefferman, who was coughing violently in the waiting room, Breuer asked her to wait a few minutes.

"As long as you want, Doctor Breuer, just let me know. Maybe a nice cup of hot tea." But he shook his head and then, as she left him alone again, closed his eyes and hoped for rest. Visions of Bertha assailed him.

CHAPTER 18

THE MORE BREUER THOUGHT about Lou Salomé's visit, the angrier he became. Not angry at her—toward her he now felt mainly fear—but angry at Nietzsche. All the time that Nietzsche had been berating him for his preoccupation with Bertha, for—how did he put it?—"feeding at the trough of lust" or "rummaging through the trash of your mind," there, all the while, rummaging and guzzling alongside, had been Nietzsche!

No, he should not have read a word of those letters. But he had not thought of that quickly enough, and now what could he do with what he had seen? Nothing! None of it—neither the letters nor Lou Salomé's visit—could he share with Nietzsche.

Strange that Nietzsche and he shared the same lie, each concealing Lou Salomé from the other. Did dissimulation affect Nietzsche in the same way it did him? Did Nietzsche feel corrupt? Guilty? Might there be some way of using this guilt for Nietzsche's benefit?

Go slowly, Breuer said to himself on Saturday morning, as he walked up the wide marble stairway toward room 13. Don't make any radical moves! Something significant is taking place. Look how far we've come in just one week!

"Friedrich," Breuer said immediately after completing a brief physical examination, "I had a strange dream about you last night. I'm in a restaurant kitchen. Sloppy cooks have spilled oil all around on the floor. I slip on it and drop a razor which lodges in a crack. Then you come in—though not looking like yourself. You're wearing a general's uniform, but I know it's you. You want to help me retrieve the razor. I tell you not to, that you'd just drive it in deeper. But you try anyway, and you *do* drive it deeper. It's wedged tight in the crack, and every time I try to extract it, I cut my fingers." He stopped and looked expectantly at Nietzsche. "What do you make of this dream?"

"What do *you* make of it, Josef?"

"Most of it, like most of my dreams, is nonsense—except that part about you must mean something."

"Can you still see the dream in your mind?"

Breuer nodded.

"Keep looking at it and chimneysweep about it."

Breuer hesitated, looking dismayed, then tried to concentrate. "Let's see, I drop something, my razor, and you come along——"

"In a general's uniform."

"Yes, you come along dressed like a general and try to help me—but you don't help."

"In fact, I make things worse—I drive the blade in deeper."

"Well, all that fits with what I've been saying. Things are getting worse—my obsession with Bertha, the burning house fantasy, the insomnia. We've got to do something different!"

"And I'm dressed like a general?"

"Well, *that* part's easy. The uniform must refer to your lofty manner, your poetic speech, your proclamations." Emboldened by the new information he had obtained from Lou Salomé, Breuer continued, "It's symbolic of your unwillingness to join with me in a down-to-earth manner. Take, for example, my problem with Bertha. I know from my work with patients how common it is to have problems with the opposite sex. Virtually no one escapes the pain of love. Goethe knew that, and that's why *The Sorrows of Young Werther* is powerful: his love-sickness touched every man's truth. Surely it's happened to you."

Obtaining no response from Nietzsche, Breuer pressed further. "I'm willing to wager a large sum you've had a similar experience. Why not share it with me so the two of us can talk honestly, as equals?"

"And no longer as general and private, the powerful and powerless! Ach, sorry, Josef—I agreed not to talk about power, even when issues of power are so obvious they hit us on the head! As for love, I don't deny what you say; I don't deny that all of us—and that includes me—taste its pain.

"You mention *Young Werther*," Nietzsche continued, "but let me remind you of Goethe's words—'Be a man and do not follow me—but yourself! But yourself!' Did you know that he put that sentence into the second edition because so many young men had followed Werther's example and committed suicide? No, Josef, the important issue here is not for me to tell you about *my* way, but to help you find *your* way to grow out of your despair. Now, what about the razor in the dream?"

Breuer hesitated. Nietzsche's acknowledging that he, too, had tasted the pain of love was a major revelation. Should he pursue it further? No, it was enough for now. He allowed his attention to drift back to himself.

"I don't know why there should be a razor in the dream."

"Remember our rules, Josef. Don't try to reason it out. Just chimney-sweep. Say everything that occurs to you. Omit nothing." Nietzsche leaned back and closed his eyes, waiting for Breuer's answer.

"Razor, razor—last night I saw a friend, an ophthalmologist named Carl Koller, who is entirely clean-shaven. I thought this morning about getting *my* beard shaved off—but I often think about that."

"Keep sweeping!"

"Razor—wrists—I have a patient, a young man who's despondent about being a homosexual, and cut his wrists with a razor a couple of days ago. I shall see him later today. His name, incidentally, is Josef. Though I don't think about cutting my wrists, I *do* think, as I've told you, about suicide. It's lazy thinking—it's not planning. I feel very remote from the act of killing myself. It's probably no more likely than burning up my family or carrying Bertha off to America—yet I think about suicide more and more."

"All serious thinkers contemplate suicide," Nietzsche noted. "It's a comfort that helps us get through the night." He opened his eyes and turned to Breuer. "You say we must do something else to help you. What else?"

"Attack my obsession directly! It's ruining me. It's consuming my whole life. I'm not living *now*. I'm living in the past, or in a future that will never be."

"But sooner or later your obsession must yield, Josef. My model is so obviously correct. It's so clear that behind your obsession lie your primary fears about *Existenz*. It's also clear that the more we speak explicitly about these fears, the stronger your obsession gets. Don't you see how your obsession tries to divert your attention away from these deep facts of life? It's the only way you know to soothe your fears."

"But, Friedrich, we do *not* disagree. I'm being persuaded to your point of view, and I now believe your model is correct. But to attack my obsession directly is not to invalidate the model. You once described my obsession as a fungus or a weed. I agree, and I agree also that if I had cultivated my mind differently long ago, that obsession would never have taken root. But now that it's here, it must be eradicated, pulled out. The way you're going about it is too slow."

Nietzsche fidgeted in his chair, obviously uncomfortable with Breuer's criticism. "Do you have specific suggestions for eradication?"

"I'm a captive of the obsession: it'll never let me know how to escape. That's why I ask you about *your* experience with such pain and about the methods you've used to escape."

"But that was *exactly* what I was trying to do last week when I asked you to look at yourself from a great distance," Nietzsche replied. "A cosmic perspective always attenuates tragedy. If we climb high enough, we will reach a height from which tragedy ceases to look tragic."

"Yes, yes, yes." Breuer was growing increasingly annoyed. "I know that intellectually. Still, Friedrich, such a statement as 'a height from which tragedy ceases to look tragic' simply does not make me feel better. Forgive me if I sound impatient, but there is a gulf—a huge gulf—between knowing something intellectually and knowing it emotionally. Often when I lie awake at night frightened of dying, I recite to myself Lucretius' maxim: 'Where I am, death is not; where death is, I am not.' It's supremely rational and irrefutably true. But when I'm really frightened, *it never works*, it never calms my fears. This is where philosophy falls short. Teaching philosophy and *using* it in life are very different undertakings."

"The problem is, Josef, that whenever we abandon rationality and use lower faculties to influence men, we end up with a lower and cheaper man. When you say you want something that works, you mean you want something that can influence emotions. Well, there *are* experts in that! And who are they? The priests! They know the secrets of influence! They manipulate with inspiring music, they dwarf us with towering spires and soaring naves, they encourage the lust for submission, they proffer super-natural guidance, protection from death, even immortality. But look at the price they extract—religious thralldom; reverence for the weak; stasis; hatred of the body, of joy, of this world. No, we can't use these tranquiliz-ing, antihuman methods! We must find better ways of honing our powers of reason."

"The stage director of my mind," Breuer responded, "the one who decides to send me images of Bertha and my burning house, doesn't seem to be affected by reason."

"But *surely*"—and Nietzsche shook his clenched fists—"you must real-ize that there is *no reality* to any of your preoccupations! Your vision of Bertha, the halo of attraction and love that surround her—these don't really exist. These poor phantasms are not part of numinal reality. All seeing is relative, and so is all knowing. We invent what we experience. And what we have invented, we can destroy."

Breuer opened his mouth to protest that this was exactly the kind of exhortation that was pointless, but Nietzsche plunged on.

"Let me make it clearer, Josef. I have a friend—*had* one—Paul Rée, a philosopher. We both believe that God is dead. He concludes that a life without God is meaningless, and so great is his distress that he flirts with suicide: for convenience, he wears at all times a vial of poison around his neck. For me, however, godlessness is an occasion for rejoicing. I exalt in my freedom. I say to myself, 'What would there be to create if gods existed?' You see what I mean? The same situation, the same sense data—but two realities!"

Breuer slumped dejectedly in his chair, by now too dispirited even to rejoice in Nietzsche's mention of Paul Rée. "But I tell you that these arguments don't *move* me," he complained. "What good is this philoso-phizing? Even though we invent reality, our minds are devised in such a way as to conceal this from ourselves."

"But look at *your* reality!" Nietzsche protested. "One good look can show you how makeshift, how preposterous it is! Look at the object of your love—this cripple, Bertha—what rational man could love her? You tell me she often can't hear, becomes cross-eyed, twists her arms and shoulders into knots. She can't drink water, can't walk, can't talk German in the mornings; some days she talks English; some days, French. How does one know how to speak to her? She should have a sign posted, like a restaurant, advertising the *langue du jour.*" Nietzsche smiled broadly, much amused by his joke.

But Breuer did not smile. His expression darkened. "Why are you so insulting to her? You never mention her name without adding 'the cripple'!"

"I merely repeat what you have told me."

"It's true she is ill—but her illness is not *all* she is. She's also a very beautiful woman. Walk with her in the street, and all heads will turn in your direction. She's intelligent, talented, highly creative—a fine writer, a keen critic of the arts, gentle, sensitive, and, I believe, loving."

"Not *so* loving and sensitive, I think. Look at how she loves you! She attempts to seduce you into adultery."

Breuer shook his head. "No, that's not——"

Nietzsche interrupted. "Oh yes, oh yes! You can't deny it. Seduction is the correct word. She leans on you, pretending she cannot walk. She puts her head in your lap, her lips by your manhood. She tries to ruin your marriage. She humiliates you publicly by pretending to be pregnant with your child! Is this love? Spare *me* from such love!"

"I don't judge or attack my patients, nor do I laugh at their illnesses, Friedrich. I assure you, you don't know this woman."

"Thank God for *that* blessing! I've known some like her. *Believe me, Josef, this woman doesn't love you, she wants to destroy you!*" said Nietzsche fervently, rapping on his notebook at each word.

"You judge her by other women you've known. But you're mistaken—everyone who knows her feels as I do. What do you gain by ridiculing her?"

"In this, as in so many things, you are hobbled by your virtues. You, too, must learn to ridicule! That way lies health."

"When it comes to women, Friedrich, you are much too hard."

"And you, Josef, are much too soft. Why must you continue to defend her?"

Too agitated to sit any longer, Breuer arose and walked over to the window. He gazed out over the garden, where a man with bandaged eyes was shuffling: with one arm he clutched a nurse and, with the other, tapped the path before him with a cane.

"Release your feelings, Josef. Don't hold back."

Continuing to stare out the window, Breuer projected his voice over his shoulder. "It's easy for you to attack her. If you could see her, I assure you,

you'd sing a different tune. You'd be on your knees to her. She's a dazzling woman, a Helen of Troy, the very quintessence of womanhood. I told you already that her next physician has also fallen in love with her."

"Her next victim, you mean!"

"Friedrich"—Breuer turned around to face Nietzsche—"what are you doing? I've never seen you like this! Why are you pushing this so hard?"

"I'm doing exactly what you asked me to do—finding another way to attack your obsession. I believe, Josef, that part of your distress comes from buried resentment. There is something in you—some fear, some timidity—that won't permit you to express your anger. Instead, you take pride in your meekness. You make a virtue of necessity: you bury your feelings deep and then, because you experience no resentment, you assume that you are saintlike. You no longer assume the role of the understanding physician; you have *become* that role—you believe you are too fine to experience anger. Josef, a little revenge is a *good* thing. Swallowed resentment makes one sick!"

Breuer shook his head. "No, Friedrich, to understand is to forgive. I explored the roots of each of Bertha's symptoms. There is no *evil* in her. If anything, too much good. She is a generous, self-sacrificing daughter who fell ill because of her father's death."

"All fathers die—yours, mine, everyone's—*that's* no explanation for illness. I love actions, not excuses. The time for excuses—for Bertha, for yourself—has passed." Nietzsche shut his notebook. The meeting was over.

The next meeting began in equally stormy fashion. Breuer had requested a *direct attack* on his obsession. "Very well," said Nietzsche, who had always wanted to be a warrior. "If it's war you want, it's war you'll get!" And for the next three days he launched a mighty psychological campaign, one of the most creative—and one of the most bizarre—in Viennese medical history.

Nietzsche began by eliciting Breuer's promise to follow all directives without questions, without resistance. Then, Nietzsche instructed him to compose a list of ten insults and to imagine hurling them at Bertha. Next, Nietzsche encouraged him to imagine living with Bertha and then to visualize a series of scenes: sitting across the breakfast table and watching her with legs and arms in spasm, cross-eyed, mute, wry-necked, hallucinating, and stuttering. Nietzsche then suggested even more unpleasant images: Bertha vomiting, sitting on the toilet; Bertha with the labor pains of pseudocyesis. But none of these experiments succeeded in bleaching the magic out of Bertha's image.

At their next meeting, Nietzsche tried even more direct approaches. "Whenever you're alone and begin to think about Bertha, shout 'No!' or 'Stop!' as loud as you can. If you're not alone, pinch yourself hard whenever she enters your mind."

For two days, Breuer's private chambers echoed with "No!" and "Stop!" and his forearm was bruised from pinching. Once in the fiacre, he shouted "Stop!" so loud that Fischmann reined the horses in sharply and waited for further instructions. Another time, Frau Becker came rushing into the office at the sound of a particularly reverberating "No!" But these devices offered only tissue-thin resistance to his mind's desire. The obsessions kept coming!

On another day, Nietzsche instructed Breuer to monitor his thinking and, every thirty minutes, to record in his notebook how often and how long he thought about Bertha. Breuer was astounded to learn that rarely did an entire hour pass without his ruminating upon her. Nietzsche calculated that he spent approximately one hundred minutes a day on his obsession, over five hundred hours a year. This meant, he said, that in the next twenty years, Breuer would devote over six hundred precious waking days to the same boring, unimaginative fantasies. Breuer groaned at the prospect. And kept on obsessing.

Nietzsche then experimented with another strategy: he ordered Breuer to devote certain designated periods to thinking about Bertha, whether he wanted to or not.

"You insist on thinking about Bertha? Then I insist that you do it! I insist that you meditate about her for fifteen minutes six times a day. Let's go over your daily schedule and space the six periods throughout your day. Tell your nurse you need the uninterrupted time for writing or record keeping. If you want to think about Bertha at other times, that's fine—that's up to you. But during these six periods, you *must* think about Bertha. Later, as you accustom yourself to this practice, we will gradually decrease your time of forced meditation." Breuer followed Nietzsche's schedule—but his obsessions followed Bertha's.

Later, Nietzsche suggested Breuer carry a special purse in which to put five *Kreuzer* every time he thought about Bertha; he was then to donate that money to some charity. Breuer vetoed the plan. He knew it would be ineffective because he *liked* to give to charity. Nietzsche then suggested he give the money to Georg von Schönerer's anti-Semitic German National Association. Even that didn't work.

Nothing worked.

෴

Excerpts from Dr. Breuer's Case Notes on Eckart Müller, 9–14 December 1882

There is no longer any point in deceiving myself. There are two patients in our sessions and, of the two, I am the more urgent case. Strange, the more I acknowledge this to myself, the more amiably Nietzsche and I seem to work together. Perhaps the information I received from Lou Salomé has also changed the way we work.

I have, of course, said nothing to Nietzsche about her. Nor do I speak of my becoming a genuine patient. Yet I believe he senses these things. Perhaps in some unintentional, nonverbal way, I communicate things to him. Who knows? Perhaps in my voice, my tone or gestures. It's very mysterious. Sig is interested in such details of communication. I should talk about it with him.

The more I forget about trying to help him, the more he begins to open up to me. Look what he told me today! That Paul Rée was once a friend. That he, Nietzsche, had had his own love pain. That he had once known a woman like Bertha. Perhaps it's best for both of us if I just focus on myself and forget about trying to pry him open!

Also, he now alludes to the methods he uses to help himself—for example his "perspective-changing" approach in which he views himself from a more distant, cosmic perspective. He's right: if we view our trivial situation from the long skein of our lives, from the life of the whole race, from the evolution of consciousness, of course it loses its overarching significance.

But how to change my perspective? His instructions and exhortations to change perspective don't work, nor does trying to imagine myself stepping back. I can't remove myself emotionally from the center of my situation. I can't get far enough away. And judging from the letters he wrote Lou Salomé, I don't believe he can either!

. . . He also places great emphasis on the expression of anger. He made me insult Bertha ten different ways today. This method, at least, I can understand. Anger discharge makes sense from a physiological perspective: a buildup of cortical excitation must be periodically discharged. According to Lou Salomé's descriptions of his letters, that's his favorite method. I think he has within him a vast storehouse of anger. Why, I wonder? Because of his illness? Or his lack of professional recognition? Or because he has never enjoyed a woman's warmth?

He's good at insults. I wish I could remember some of his choicest ones. I loved his calling Lou Salomé a "predator clothed as a housecat."

It comes easy to him—but not to me. He's precisely right about my inability to express my anger. It runs in my family. My father, my uncles. For Jews, repression of anger is a survival trait. I can't even locate the anger. He insists it's there toward Bertha—but I'm sure he's confusing it with his own anger toward Lou Salomé.

How unfortunate for him to have gotten entangled with her! I wish I could offer him my sympathy. Think of it! This man has almost no experience with women. And whom does he choose to involve himself with? Certainly the most powerful woman I've ever seen. And she's only twenty-one! God help us all when she's fully grown! And the one other woman in his life, his sister, Elisabeth—I hope never to meet her. She sounds as forceful as Lou Salomé and probably meaner!

. . . Today he asked me to imagine Bertha as a baby with a bowel movement in her diapers—and to tell her how beautiful she is while imagining her gazing at me cross-eyed and wry-necked.

. . . Today he told me to put a Kreuzer in my shoe for every fantasy and to walk on it all day. Where does he get these ideas? He seems to have an endless store of them!

. . . shouting "No!" and pinching myself, counting every fantasy and recording it in a ledger, walking with coins in my shoe, giving money to Schönerer . . . punishing myself for tormenting myself. Madness!

I have heard that they teach bears to dance and to stand on two legs by heating the bricks of the floor under them. Is that so different from this approach? He tries to train my mind with these ingenious little methods of punishment.

Yet I am no bear and my mind is too rich for animal-trainer techniques. These efforts are ineffective—and they are demeaning!

But I cannot blame him. I asked him to attack my symptoms directly. He humors me. His heart is not in these efforts. All along he has insisted that growth is more important than comfort.

There must be another way.

Excerpts from Friedrich Nietzsche's Notes on Dr. Breuer, 9–14 December 1882

The lure of a "system"! I fell prey to it for a time today! I believed that Josef's suppression of anger was behind all of his difficulties, and I exhausted myself trying to incite him. Perhaps long repression of passions alters and enervates them.

. . . He presents himself as good—he does no harm—other than to himself and to nature! I must stop him from being one of those who call themselves good because they have no claws.

I believe he needs to learn to curse before I can trust his generosity. He feels no anger! Is he so afraid someone will hurt him? Is this why he does not dare to be himself? Why he desires only small happinesses? And he calls this virtue. Its real name is cowardice!

He is civilized, polite, a man of manners. He has tamed his wild nature, turned his wolf into a spaniel. And he calls this moderation. Its real name is mediocrity!

. . . He trusts me now and believes in me. I have given my word that I will endeavor to heal him. But the physician must first, like the sage, heal himself. Only then can his patient behold with his eyes a man who heals himself. Yet I have not healed myself. Worse, I suffer the very afflictions that beset Josef. Do I, by my silence, do that which I have sworn never to do: betray a friend?

Shall I speak of my affliction? He will lose confidence in me. Will that not harm him? Will he not say that, if I have not healed myself, I cannot heal him? Or will he become so concerned with my affliction that he will abandon the task of wrestling with his own? Do I serve him best through silence? Or through acknowledging that the two of us are similarly afflicted and must join forces to find a solution?

. . . Today I see how much he has changed . . . less devious . . . and he no longer wheedles, no longer attempts to strengthen himself by demonstrating my weakness.

. . . This frontal attack on his symptoms, which he has asked me to launch, is the most dreadful wallowing in shallow waters I have ever done. I should be a raiser, not a lowerer! Treating him as a child whose mind must be slapped when it misbehaves is lowering him. And lowering me as well! IF A HEALING LOWERS THE HEALER, CAN IT POSSIBLY RAISE THE PATIENT?

There must be a higher way.

Letter to Lou Salomé from Friedrich Nietzsche, December 1882

My dear Lou,

Don't write letters like that to me! What do I have to do with this wretchedness? I wish you could raise yourself up before me so that I didn't have to despise you.

But, Lou! What kind of letters are you writing? Revengeful-lustful schoolgirls write like that! What do I have to do with this pitifulness? Please understand, I want you to raise up before me, not that you reduce yourself. How can I forgive you if I don't recognize that being in you again for which you could ever possibly be forgiven?

No, my dear Lou, we are a long way still from forgiving. I can't shake forgiving out of my shirtsleeves after the offense had four months' time to work its way into me.

Goodbye, my dear Lou, I won't see you again. Protect your soul from such actions and make good to others and especially my friend Rée what you couldn't make good to me.

I didn't create the world and, Lou, I wish I had—then I would be able to bear all the guilt that things turned out between us the way they did.

Goodbye, dear Lou, I didn't read your letter to its end but I'd read too much already. . . .

F.N.

CHAPTER 19

"WE'RE NOT GETTING ANYWHERE, Friedrich. I'm getting worse."

Nietzsche, who had been writing at his desk, had not heard Breuer enter. Now he turned around, opened his mouth to speak, yet remained silent.

"Do I startle you, Friedrich? It must be confusing to have your physician enter your room and complain that he is worse! Especially when he is impeccably attired and carries his black medical bag with professional assurance!

"But, trust me, my outward appearance is all deception. Underneath, my clothes are wet, my shirt clings to my skin. This obsession with Bertha—it's a whirlpool in my mind. It sucks up my every clean thought!

"I don't blame *you!*" Breuer sat down next to the desk. "Our lack of progress is *my* fault. It was *I* who urged you to attack the obsession directly. You're right—we do not go deep enough. We merely trim leaves when we should be uprooting the weed."

"Yes, we uproot nothing!" Nietzsche replied. "We must reconsider our approach. I, too, feel discouraged. Our last sessions have been false and superficial. Look at what we tried to do: discipline your thoughts, control your behavior! Thought training and behavior shaping! These methods are not for the human realm! Ach, we're not animal trainers!"

"Yes, yes! After the last session I felt like a bear being trained to stand and dance."

"Precisely! A teacher should be a raiser of men. Instead, in the last few meetings, I've lowered you and myself as well. We cannot approach human concerns with animal methods."

Nietzsche rose and gestured toward the fireplace, the waiting chairs. "Shall we?" It occurred to Breuer, as he took his seat, that though the future "doctors of despair" might discard traditional medical tools—stethoscope, otoscope, ophthalmoscope—they would in time develop their own accoutrements, beginning with two comfortable fireside chairs.

"So," Breuer began, "let's return to where we were before this ill-advised direct campaign upon my obsession. You had advanced a theory that Bertha is a diversion, not a cause, and that the real center of my *Angst* is my fear of death and godlessness. Maybe so! I think you may be right! Certainly it's true that my obsession about Bertha keeps me pasted to the surface of things, leaving me no time for deeper or darker thoughts.

"Yet, Friedrich, I don't find your explanation entirely satisfying. First, there's still the riddle of 'Why Bertha?' Of all the possible ways to defend myself against *Angst,* why choose this particular, stupid obsession? Why not some *other* method, some *other* fantasy?

"Second, you say Bertha is merely a diversion to misdirect my attention from my core *Angst.* Yet 'diversion' is a pale word. It's not enough to explain the *power* of my obsession. Thinking about Bertha is preternaturally compelling; it contains some hidden, powerful meaning."

"*Meaning!*" Nietzsche slapped his hand sharply against the arm of his chair. "Exactly! I've been thinking along identical lines since you left yesterday. Your final word, 'meaning,' may be the key. Perhaps our mistake from the beginning has been to neglect the *meaning* of your obsession. You claimed you cured each of Bertha's hysterical symptoms by discovering its origin. And also that this 'origin' method was not relevant to your own case because the origin of your Bertha obsession was already known—having begun after you met her and intensifying after you stopped seeing her.

"But perhaps," Nietzsche continued, "you've been using the wrong word. Perhaps what matters is not the *origin*—that is, the first appearance of symptoms—but the *meaning* of a symptom! Perhaps you were mistaken. Perhaps you cured Bertha by discovering not the origin, but the meaning of each symptom! *Perhaps*"—here Nietzsche almost whispered as if he were conveying a secret of great significance—"*perhaps symptoms are messengers of a meaning and will vanish only when their message is com-*

prehended. If so, our next step is obvious: if we are to conquer the symptoms, we must determine what the Bertha obsession *means* to you!"

What next? Breuer wondered. How does one go about discovering the *meaning* of an obsession? He was affected by Nietzsche's excitement and awaited instructions. But Nietzsche had settled back in his chair, taken out his comb, and begun to groom his mustache. Breuer grew tense and cranky.

"Well, Friedrich? I'm waiting!" He rubbed his chest, breathing deeply. "This tension here, in my chest, grows every minute I sit here. Soon it will explode. I can't reason it away. Tell me how to start! How can I discover a meaning that I myself have concealed?"

"Don't try to discover or solve anything!" Nietzsche responded, still combing his mustache. "That will be my job! Your job is just to chimney-sweep. Talk about what Bertha *means* to you."

"Haven't I already talked too much about her? Shall I wallow once again in my Bertha ruminations? You've heard them all—touching her, undressing her, caressing her, my house on fire, everyone dead, eloping to America. Do you really want to hear all that garbage again?" Getting up abruptly, Breuer paced back and forth behind Nietzsche's chair.

Nietzsche continued to speak in a calm and measured manner. "It's the *tenacity* of your obsession that intrigues me. Like a barnacle clinging to its rock. Can we not, Josef, just for a moment, pry it away and peer underneath? Chimneysweep for me, I say! Chimneysweep about this question: What would life—your life—be like without Bertha? Just talk. Don't try to make sense, even to make sentences. Say anything that comes to your mind!"

"I can't. I'm wound up, I'm a coiled spring."

"Stop pacing. Close your eyes and try to describe what you see on the back of your eyelids. Just let the thoughts flow—don't control them."

Breuer stopped behind Nietzsche's chair and clutched its back. His eyes closed, he rocked to and fro, as his father had when he prayed, and slowly began to mumble his thoughts:

"A life without Bertha—a charcoal life, no colors—calipers—scales—funerary marbles—everything decided, now and for always—I'd be here, you'd find me here—always! Right here, this spot, with this medical bag, in these clothes, with this face which, day by day, will grow darker and more gaunt."

Breuer breathed deep, feeling less agitated, and sat down. "Life without

Bertha?—What else?—I'm a scientist, but science has no color. One should only *work* in science, not try to live in it—I need magic—and passion—you can't live without magic. *That's* what Bertha means, *passion and magic.* Life without passion—who can live such a life?" He opened his eyes suddenly. "Can you? Can anyone?"

"Please chimneysweep about passion and living," Nietzsche prodded him.

"One of my patients is a midwife," Breuer went on. "She's old, wizened, alone. Her heart is failing. But still she's passionate about living. Once I asked her about the source of her passion. She said it was that moment between lifting a silent newborn and giving it the slap of life. She was renewed, she said, by immersion in that moment of mystery, that moment that straddles existence and oblivion."

"And *you,* Josef?"

"I'm like that midwife! I want to be close to mystery. My passion for Bertha isn't natural—it's supernatural, I know that—but I need magic. I can't live in black and white."

"We all need passion, Josef," Nietzsche said. "Dionysian passion *is* life. But does passion have to be magical and debasing? Can't one find a way to be the *master* of passion?

"Let me tell you about a Buddhist monk I met last year in the Engadine. He lives a spare life. He meditates half his waking hours and spends weeks without exchanging a word with anyone. His diet is simple, only a single meal a day, whatever he can beg, perhaps only an apple. But he meditates upon that apple until it's bursting with redness, succulence, and crispness. By the end of the day, he *passionately* anticipates his meal. The point is, Josef, you don't have to relinquish passion. *But you have to change your conditions for passion.*"

Breuer nodded.

"Keep going," Nietzsche urged. "Chimneysweep more about Bertha—what she means to you."

Breuer closed his eyes. "I see myself running with her. Running away. Bertha means *escape*—dangerous escape!"

"How so?"

"Bertha is danger. Before her, I lived within the rules. Today I flirt with the limits of those rules—perhaps that's what the midwife meant. I think about exploding my life, sacrificing my career, committing adultery, losing my family, emigrating, beginning life again with Bertha." Breuer slapped himself lightly on the head. "Stupid! Stupid! I know I'll never do it!"

"But there's a lure to this dangerous teeter-tottering on the edge?"

"A lure? I don't know. I can't answer that. I don't like danger! If there's a lure, it's not danger—I think the lure is *escape*, not from danger but *from safety*. Maybe I've lived too safely!"

"Maybe, Josef, living safely *is* dangerous. Dangerous and deadly."

"Living safely *is* dangerous." Breuer mumbled the words to himself several times. "Living safely *is* dangerous. Living safely *is* dangerous. A powerful thought, Friedrich. So is that the meaning of Bertha: to escape the dangerously deadly life? Is Bertha my freedom wish—my escape from the trap of time?"

"Perhaps from the trap of *your* time, your historical moment. But, Josef," he said solemnly, "do not make the mistake of thinking she will lead you out of time! Time cannot be broken; that is our greatest burden. And our greatest challenge is to live *in spite of* that burden."

For once, Breuer did not protest Nietzsche's assumption of his philosopher's tone. This philosophizing was different. He didn't know what to *do* with Nietzsche's words, but he knew they reached him, moved him.

"Be assured," he said, "I have no dreams of immortality. The life I want to escape is the life of the eighteen eighty-two Viennese medical bourgeoisie. Others, I know, envy my life—but I dread it. Dread its sameness and predictability. Dread it so much that sometimes I think of my life as a death sentence. Do you know what I mean, Friedrich?"

Nietzsche nodded. "Do you remember asking me, perhaps the first time we talked, whether there were any advantages to having migraine? It was a good question. It helped me think about my life differently. And do you remember my answer? That my migraine forced me to resign my university professorship? Everyone—family, friends, even colleagues—lamented my misfortune, and I am certain history will record that Nietzsche's illness tragically ended his career. But not so! The reverse is true! The professorship at the University of Basel was *my* death sentence. It sentenced me to the hollow life of the academy and to spend the rest of my days providing for the economic support of my mother and sister. I was fatally trapped."

"And then, Friedrich, migraine—the great liberator—descended upon you!"

"Not so different is it, Josef, from this obsession that descends upon you? Perhaps we are more alike than we think!"

Breuer closed his eyes. How good to feel so close to Nietzsche. Tears welled up; he pretended a coughing fit in order to turn his head away.

"Let us continue," said Nietzsche impassively. "We're making progress. We understand that Bertha represents passion, mystery, dangerous escape. What else, Josef? What other meanings are packed into her?"

"Beauty! Bertha's beauty is an important part of the mystery. Here, I brought this for you to see."

He opened his bag and held out a photograph. Putting on his thick glasses, Nietzsche walked to the window to inspect it in better light. Bertha, clothed from head to toe in black, was dressed for riding. Her jacket constricted her: a double row of small buttons, stretching from her tiny waist to her chin, struggled to contain her mighty bosom. Her left hand daintily clasped both her skirt and a long riding whip. From her other hand, gloves dangled. Her nose was forceful, her hair short and severe; and on it perched an insouciant black cap. Her eyes were large and dark. She did not trouble to look into the camera, but stared far into the distance.

"A formidable woman, Josef," said Nietzsche, returning the photograph and sitting down again. "Yes, she has great beauty—but I don't like women who carry whips."

"Beauty," Breuer said, "is an important part of Bertha's meaning. I'm easily captured by such beauty. More easily than most men, I think. Beauty is a mystery. I hardly know how to speak about it, but a woman who has a certain combination of flesh, breasts, ears, large dark eyes, nose, lips—especially lips—simply awes me. This sounds stupid, but I almost believe such women have superhuman powers!"

"To do what?"

"It's too stupid!" Breuer hid his face in his hands.

"Just chimneysweep, Josef. Suspend your judgment—and speak! You have my word I do not judge you!"

"I can't put it into language."

"Try to finish this sentence: 'In the presence of Bertha's beauty, I feel——' "

" 'In the presence of Bertha's beauty, I feel—I feel—' What do I feel? I feel I'm in the bowels of the earth—in the center of existence. I'm just where I should be. I'm in the place where there are no questions about life or purpose—the center—the place of safety. Her beauty offers infinite safety." He lifted his head. "See, I tell you this makes no sense!"

"Go on," said Nietzsche imperturbably.

"For me to be captured, the woman must have a certain look. It's an adoring look—I can see it in my mind now—wide-open, glistening eyes, lips closed in an affectionate half-smile. She seems to be saying—oh, I don't know——"

"Continue, Josef, please! Keep imagining the smile! Can you still see it?" Breuer closed his eyes and nodded.

"What does it say to you?"

"It says, 'You're adorable. *Anything* you do is all right. Oh, you darling, you get out of control, but one expects that of a boy.' Now I see her turning to the other women around her, and she says, 'Isn't he something? Isn't he dear? I'll take him into my arms and comfort him.' "

"Can you say more about that smile?"

"It says to me I can play, do whatever I want. I can get into trouble—but, no matter what, she'll continue to be delighted by me, to find me adorable."

"Does the smile have a personal history for you, Josef?"

"What do you mean?"

"Reach back. Does your memory contain such a smile?"

Breuer shook his head. "No, no memories."

"You answer too quickly!" Nietzsche insisted. "You started to shake your head before I finished my question. Search! Just keep watching that smile in your mind's eye and see what comes."

Breuer closed his eyes and gazed at the scroll of his memory. "I've seen Mathilde give that smile to our son, Johannes. Also, when I was ten or eleven, I was infatuated by a girl named Mary Gomperz—she gave me that smile! That exact smile! I was desolate when her family moved away. I haven't seen her for thirty years, yet I still dream about Mary."

"Who else? Have you forgotten your mother's smile?"

"Haven't I told you? My mother died when I was three. She was only twenty-eight, and she died after giving birth to my younger brother. I'm told she was beautiful, but I have no memories of her, not one."

"And your wife? Does Mathilde have that magical smile?"

"No. Of *that* I can be certain. Mathilde is beautiful, but her smile has no power for me. I know it's stupid to think that Mary, at age ten, has power, while Mathilde has none. But that's the way I experience it. In our marriage, it is *I* who have power over *her*, and it is she who desires *my* protection. No, Mathilde has no magic, I don't know why."

"Magic requires darkness and mystery," Nietzsche said. "Perhaps her mystery has been annihilated by the familiarity of fourteen years of marriage. Do you know her too well? Perhaps you cannot bear the truth of a relationship to a beautiful woman."

"I begin to think I need another word than beauty. Mathilde has all the components of beauty. She has the aesthetics, but not the power, of beauty. Perhaps you're right—it is too familiar. Too often I see the flesh and blood under the skin. Another factor is that there's no competition; no other men have ever been in Mathilde's life. It was an arranged marriage."

"It puzzles me that you would want competition, Josef. Just a few days ago, you spoke of dreading it."

"I want competition, and I don't. Remember, you said I didn't have to make sense. I'm just expressing words as they occur to me. Let me see—let me collect my thoughts—*Yes,* the woman of beauty has more power if she is desired by other men. But such a woman is too dangerous—she will scald me. Maybe Bertha is the perfect compromise—she's not yet fully formed! She is beauty in embryo, still incomplete."

"So," Nietzsche asked, "she's safer because she has no other men competing for her?"

"That's not quite it. She's safer because I have the inside track. Any man would want her, but I can easily defeat competitors. She is—or, rather, was—completely dependent on me. For weeks she refused to eat unless I personally fed her every meal.

"Naturally, as her physician, I deplored my patient's regression. Tsk, tsk, I clucked my tongue. Tsk, tsk, what a pity! I expressed my professional concern to her family, but secretly, as a man—and I'd never admit this to anyone but you—*I relished my conquest.* When she told me, one day, that she had dreamed of me, I was ecstatic. What a victory—to enter her innermost chamber, a place where no other man had ever gained entry! And since dream images do not die, it was a place where I would endure forever!"

"So, Josef, you win the competition without having had to compete!"

"Yes, that is another meaning of Bertha—*safe contest, certain victory.* But a beautiful woman *without* safety—that is something else." Breuer fell silent.

"Keep going, Josef. Where do your thoughts go now?"

"I was thinking about an unsafe woman, a fully formed beauty about Bertha's age who came to see me in my office a couple of weeks ago, a woman to whom many men have paid homage. I was charmed by her—and terrified! I was so unable to oppose her that I could not keep her waiting and saw her out of turn before my other patients. And when she made an inappropriate medical request of me, it was all I could to resist her wishes."

"Ah, I know that dilemma," said Nietzsche. "The most desirable woman is the most frightening one. And not, of course, because of what she *is,* but because of what we make of her. Very sad!"

"Sad, Friedrich?"

"Sad for the woman who is never known, and sad, too, for the man. I know that sadness."

"You, too, have known a Bertha?"

"No, but I have known a woman like that other patient you describe—the one who cannot be denied."

Lou Salomé, thought Breuer. Lou Salomé, without a doubt! *At last,* he speaks of her! Though reluctant to relinquish the focus on himself, Breuer nonetheless pressed the inquiry.

"So, Friedrich, what happened to that lady you could not deny?"

Nietzsche hesitated, then took out his watch. "We have struck a rich vein today—who knows, perhaps a rich vein for both of us. But we are running out of time and I am certain you still have much to say. Please continue to tell me what Bertha means to you."

Breuer knew that Nietzsche was closer than ever before to disclosing his own problems. Perhaps a gentle inquiry at this point would have been all that was necessary. Yet when he heard Nietzsche prod him again: "Don't stop: your ideas are flowing," Breuer was only too glad to continue.

"I lament the complexity of the double life, the secret life. Yet I treasure it. The surface bourgeois life is deadly—it's too visible, one can see the end too clearly and all the acts, leading right to the end. It sounds mad, I know, but the double life *is* an additional life. It holds the promise of a lifetime extended."

Nietzsche nodded. "You feel that time devours the possibilities of the surface life, whereas the secret life is inexhaustible?"

"Yes, that's not exactly what I said, but it's what I mean. Another thing, perhaps the most important thing, is the ineffable feeling I had when I was with Bertha or that I have now when I think about her. Bliss! That's the closest word."

"I've always believed, Josef, that we are more in love with desire than with the desired!"

" *'More in love with desire than with the desired!'* " Breuer repeated. "Please give me some paper. I want to remember that."

Nietzsche tore a sheet from the back of his notebook and waited while Breuer wrote the line, folded the paper, and put it in his jacket pocket.

"And another thing," Breuer continued, "Bertha eases my aloneness. As far back as I can remember, I've been frightened by the empty spaces inside of me. And my aloneness has nothing to do with the presence, or absence, of people. Do you know what I mean?"

"Ach, who could understand you better? At times I think I'm the most alone man in existence. And, like you, it has nothing to do with the presence of others—in fact, I hate others who rob me of my solitude and yet do not truly offer me company."

"What do you mean, Friedrich? How do they not offer company?"

"By not holding dear the things I hold dear! Sometimes I gaze so far into life that I suddenly look around and see that no one has accompanied me, and that my sole companion is time."

"I'm not sure if my aloneness is like yours. Perhaps I've never dared to enter it as deeply as you."

"Perhaps," Nietzsche suggested, "Bertha stops you from entering it more deeply."

"I don't think I want to enter it more. In fact, *I feel grateful to Bertha for removing my loneliness.* That's *another* thing she means to me. In the last two years, I've never been alone—Bertha was always there at her home, or in the hospital, waiting for my visit. And now she's always inside of me, still waiting."

"You attribute to Bertha something that is your own achievement."

"What do you mean?"

"That you're still as alone as before, as alone as each person is sentenced to be. You've manufactured your own icon and then are warmed by its company. *Perhaps you are more religious than you think!*"

"But," Breuer replied, "in a sense she *is* always there. Or *was,* for a year and a half. Bad as it was, that was the best, the most vital, time of my life. I saw her every day, I thought about her all the time, I dreamed about her at night."

"You told me of one time she was *not* there, Josef—in that dream that keeps returning. How does it go—that you're searching for her——?"

"It begins with something fearful happening. The ground starts to liquefy under my feet, and I search for Bertha and cannot find her——"

"Yes, I'm convinced there is some important clue in that dream. What was the fearful event that happened—the ground opening up?"

Breuer nodded.

"Why, Josef, at that moment, should you search for Bertha? To protect her? Or for her to protect you?"

There was a long silence. Twice Breuer snapped his head back as though to order himself to attention. "I can't go further. It's astounding, but my mind won't work anymore. Never have I felt so fatigued. It's only mid-morning, but I feel as though I've been laboring without stop for days and days."

"I feel it, too. Hard work today."

"But the right work, I think. Now I must go. Until tomorrow, Friedrich."

Excerpts from Dr. Breuer's Case Notes on Eckart Müller, 15 December 1882

Can it have been only a few days ago that I pleaded with Nietzsche to reveal himself? Today, finally, he was ready, eager. He wanted to tell me that he felt trapped by his university career, that he resented supporting his mother and sister, that he was lonely and suffered because of a beautiful woman.

Yes, finally he wanted to reveal himself to me. And yet, it's quite astounding—I did not encourage him! It was not that I had no desire to listen. No, worse than that! I resented his talking! I resented his intruding upon my time!

Was it only two weeks ago I tried to manipulate him into revealing some tiny scrap of himself, that I complained to Max and Frau Becker about his secretiveness, that I bent my ear to his lips to hear him say, "Help me, help me," that I promised him, "Count on me"?

Why, then, did I neglect him today? Have I grown greedy? This counsel-

ing process—the longer it goes, the less I understand it. Yet it is compelling. More and more, I think about my talks with Nietzsche; sometimes they even interrupt a Bertha fantasy. These sessions have become the center of my day. I feel greedy for my time and often can hardly wait until our next one. Is that why I let Nietzsche put me off today?

In the future—who knows when, maybe fifty years hence?—this talking treatment could become commonplace. "Angst doctors" will become a standard specialty. And medical schools—or perhaps philosophy departments—will train them.

What should the curriculum of the future "Angst doctor" contain? At present, I can be certain of one essential course: "relationship"! That's where the complexity arises. Just as surgeons must first learn anatomy, the future "Angst doctor" must first understand the relationship between the one who counsels and the one who is counseled. And, if I am to contribute to the science of such counseling, I must learn to observe the counseling relationship just as objectively as the pigeon's brain.

Observing a relationship is not easy when I myself am part of it. Still, I note striking trends.

I used to be critical of Nietzsche, but no longer. On the contrary, I now cherish his every word and, day by day, grow more convinced that he can help me.

I used to believe I could help him. No longer. I have little to offer him. He has everything to offer me.

I used to compete with him, to devise chess traps for him. No longer! His insight is extraordinary. His intellect soars. I gaze at him as a hen at a hawk. Do I revere him too much! Do I want him to soar above me? Perhaps that is why I do not want to hear him talk. Perhaps I do not want to know of his pain, his fallibility.

I used to think about how to "handle" him. No longer! Often I feel great surges of warmth toward him. That's a change. Once I compared our situation to Robert's training his kitten: "Stand back, let him drink his milk. Later he'll let you touch him." Today, midway through our talk, another image flitted through my mind: two tiger-striped kittens, head touching head, lapping milk from the same bowl.

Another strange thing. Why did I mention that a "fully formed beauty" recently visited my office? Do I want him to learn of my meeting with Lou Salomé? Was I flirting with danger? Silently teasing him? Trying to drive a wedge between us?

And why did Nietzsche say he doesn't like women with whips? He must have been referring to that picture of Lou Salomé that he doesn't know I saw. He must realize his feelings for her are not so different from my feelings toward Bertha. So, was he silently teasing me? A little private joke? Here we are, two men trying to be honest with one another—yet both prodded by the imp of duplicity.

Another new insight! What Nietzsche is to me, I was to Bertha. She magnified my wisdom, revered my every word, cherished our sessions, could scarcely wait until the next—indeed, prevailed upon me to see her twice daily!

And the more blatantly she idealized me, the more I imbued her with power. She was the anodyne for all my anguish. Her merest glance cured my loneliness. She gave my life purpose and significance. Her simple smile anointed me as desirable, granted me absolution for all bestial impulses. A strange love: we each bask in the radiance of one another's magic!

Yet I grow hopeful. There is power in my dialogue with Nietzsche, and I am convinced that this power is not illusory.

Strange that, only hours later, I have forgotten much of our discussion. A strange forgetting, not like the evaporation of an ordinary coffeehouse conversation. Could there be such a thing as an active forgetting—forgetting something not because it is unimportant, but because it is too important?

I wrote down one shocking phrase: "We are more in love with desire than with the desired."

And another: "Living safely is dangerous." Nietzsche says that my entire bürgerlich life has been lived dangerously. I think he means I am in danger of losing my true self, or of not becoming who I am. But who am I?

Friedrich Nietzsche's Notes on Dr. Breuer, 15 December 1882

Finally, *an outing worthy of us. Deep water, quick dips in and out. Cold water*, refreshing *water. I love a living philosophy! I love a philosophy chiseled out of raw experience. His courage grows. His will and his ordeal lead the way. But is it not time for me to share the risks?*

The time for an applied philosophy is not yet ripe. When? Fifty years, a hundred years hence? The time will come when men will cease to fear knowledge, will no longer disguise weakness as "moral law," will find the courage to break the bond of "thou shalt." Then shall men hunger for my living wisdom. Then shall men need my guidance to an honest *life, a life of unbelief and discovery. A life of overcoming. Of lust overcome. And what greater lust than the lust to submit?*

I have other songs that must be sung. My mind is pregnant with melodies, and Zarathustra calls me ever more loudly. My métier is not that of technician. Still, I must put my hand to the task and record all blind alleys and all fair trails.

Today the entire direction of our work changed. And the key? The idea of meaning *rather than "origin"!*

Two weeks ago, Josef told me he cured each of Bertha's symptoms by discovering its original cause. *For example, he cured her fear of drinking water by helping her remember that she had once observed her chambermaid allowing the dog to lap water from Bertha's glass. I was skeptical at first, even more so now. The sight of a dog drinking from one's glass—unpleasant? To some, yes! Catastrophic? Hardly! The cause of hysteria? Impossible!*

No, that was not "cause" but manifestation—*of some deeper persisting* Angst! *That is why Josef's cure was so evanescent.*

We must look to meaning. *The symptom is but a messenger carrying the news that Angst is erupting from the innermost realm! Deep concerns about finitude, the death of God, isolation, purpose, freedom—deep concerns locked away for a lifetime—now break their bonds and bang at the doors and windows of the mind. They demand to be heard. And not only heard, but lived!*

That strange Russian book about the Underground Man continues to haunt me. Dostoevsky writes that some things are not to be told, except to friends; other things are not to be told even to friends; finally, there are things one does not tell even oneself! *Surely it is the things Josef has never told even himself that now erupt within him.*

Consider what Bertha means to Josef. She is escape, dangerous escape, escape from the danger of the safe life. And passion as well, and mystery and magic. She is the great liberator bearing the reprieve from his death sentence. She has superhuman powers; she is the cradle of life, the great mother confessor: she pardons all that is savage and bestial in him. She provides him with guaranteed victory over all competitors, with perduring love, eternal companionship, and everlasting existence in her dreams. She is a shield against the teeth of time, offering rescue from the abyss within, safety from the abyss below.

Bertha is a cornucopia of mystery, protection, and salvation! Josef Breuer calls this love. But its real name is prayer.

Parish priests, like my father, have always protected their flock from Satan. They teach that Satan is the enemy of faith, that in order to undermine faith, Satan may assume any guise—and none more dangerous and insidious than the cloak of skepticism and doubt.

But who will protect us—the holy skeptics? Who will warn us of threats to the love of wisdom and hatred of servitude? Shall that be my calling? We skeptics have our enemies, our Satans who undermine our doubting and plant the seeds of faith in the most cunning places. Thus we kill gods, but we sanctify their replacements—teachers, artists, beautiful women. And Josef Breuer, a renowned scientist, beatifies, for forty years, the adoring smile of a little girl named Mary.

We doubters must be vigilant. And strong. The religious drive is ferocious. Look how Breuer, an atheist, yearns to persist, to be forever observed, forgiven, adored, and protected. Shall my calling be that of the doubter's priest? Shall I spend myself in detecting and destroying religious wishes, whatever their disguise? The enemy is formidable; the flame of belief is fueled inexhaustibly by the fears of death, oblivion, and meaninglessness.

Where will meaning take us? If I uncover the meaning of the obsession, then what? Will Josef's symptoms abate? And mine? When? Will a quick dip in and out of "understanding" be sufficient? Or must it be a prolonged submersion?

And which *meaning? There seem to be many meanings to the same symptom, and Josef has not begun to exhaust the meanings of his Bertha obsession.*

Perhaps we must peel the meanings off one by one until Bertha ceases to mean anything but Bertha herself. Once she is stripped of surplus meanings, he will see her as the frightened naked human, all too human, that she and he and all of us really are.

CHAPTER 20

THE FOLLOWING MORNING Breuer entered Nietzsche's room still wearing his fur-lined greatcoat and holding a black top hat. "Friedrich, look out the window! That shy orange globe low in the sky—do you recognize it? Our Viennese sun has finally made an appearance. Shall we celebrate by taking a walk today? We both say we think best while walking."

Nietzsche bounced up from his desk as though he had springs on his feet. Breuer had never seen him move so quickly. "Nothing would please me more. The nurses haven't permitted me to set foot outdoors for three days. Where can we walk? Have we sufficient time to escape the cobblestones?"

"Here's my plan. I visit my parents' grave on the Sabbath, once a month. Come with me today—the cemetery is less than an hour's ride. I'll make a short stop, just enough time to lay some flowers, and from there we'll go on to the Simmeringer Haide for an hour's walk in the forest and meadow. We'll be back in time for dinner. On the Sabbath, I schedule no appointments until afternoon."

Breuer waited while Nietzsche dressed. He often said that though he liked cold weather, it did not like him—and so, to protect himself from migraine, he donned two heavy sweaters and twisted a five-foot wool scarf several times around his neck before struggling into his overcoat. Putting on a green eyeshade to protect his eyes from the light, he topped it with a green Bavarian felt hat.

During the ride, Nietzsche inquired about the stack of clinical charts, medical texts, and journals crammed in the door pockets and scattered over the empty seats. Breuer explained that his fiacre was his second office.

"There are days that I spend more time riding in here than in the Bäckerstrasse office. Some time ago, a young medical student, Sigmund Freud, wished to obtain a first-hand view of the everyday life of the physician and asked to accompany me for an entire day. He was aghast at the number of hours I spent in this fiacre and resolved, then and there, to pursue a research career rather than a clinical one."

In the fiacre, they circled the southern part of the city on the Ringstrasse, crossed the Wien River on the Schwarzenberg Bridge, passed the summer palace and, following the Renweg and then the Simmering Hauptstrasse, soon arrived at the City of Vienna Central Cemetery. Entering the third large gate, the Jewish division of the cemetery, Fischmann, who had been driving Breuer to his parents' grave for a decade, unerringly traversed a maze of small paths, some barely wide enough for the fiacre to pass, and stopped before the large mausoleum of the Rothschild family. As Breuer and Nietzsche alighted, Fischmann handed Breuer a large bouquet of flowers that had been stored beneath his seat. The two men walked silently along a dirt path through rows of monuments. Some simply bore a name and death date; others had a brief statement of remembrance; others were adorned with a Star of David or with a relief of hands with outstretched fingers to denote the dead of the Cohen, the holiest tribe.

Breuer gestured toward the bouquets of fresh-cut flowers that lay before many graves. "In this land of the dead, *these* are the dead, and *those*"—he pointed to an old untended and abandoned section of the cemetery— "those are the truly dead. No one now tends their graves because no one living has ever known them. *They* know what it means to be dead."

Reaching his destination, Breuer stood before a large family plot encircled by a thin carved stone rail. Within lay two headstones: a small upright one reading, "Adolf Breuer 1844–1874"; and a large, flat, gray marble slab on which had been carved two inscriptions:

LEOPOLD BREUER 1791–1872
Beloved Teacher and Father
Not Forgotten by His Sons

BERTHA BREUER 1818–1845
Beloved Mother and Wife
Died in the Blossom of Youth and Beauty

Breuer picked up the small stone vase sitting on the marble slab, emptied last month's dried blossoms, and gently inserted the flowers he had brought, flouncing them into fullness. After placing a small, smooth pebble on both his parents' slab and his brother's headstone, he stood in silence, head bowed.

Nietzsche, respecting Breuer's need for solitude, wandered down a path lined with granite and marble tombstones. Soon he entered the neighborhood of the wealthy Viennese Jews—Goldschmidts, Gomperzes, Altmanns, Wertheimers—who, in death as in life, sought assimilation into Christian Viennese society. Large mausoleums housing entire families, their entrances barricaded by heavy wrought-iron grills adorned with clinging iron vines, were guarded by elaborate funerary statues. Farther down the path were massive headstones upon which stood interdenominational angels, their outstretched stony arms pleading, Nietzsche imagined, for attention and remembrance.

Ten minutes later, Breuer caught up with him. "It was easy to find you, Friedrich. I heard you humming."

"I amuse myself by composing doggerel as I stroll. Listen," he said, as Breuer fell into step beside him. "My latest:

Though no stones hear and none can see
Each sobs softly, 'Remember me. Remember me.' "

Then, without waiting for a response from Breuer, he asked, "Who was Adolf, the third Breuer next to your parents?"

"Adolf was my only sibling. He died eight years ago. My mother died, I'm told, as a consequence of his birth. My grandmother moved into our home to raise us, but she died long ago. Now," Breuer said softly, "they are all gone and I am next in line."

"And the pebbles? I see many tombstones here with pebbles on them."

"A very old Jewish custom—simply to honor the dead, to signify memory."

"Signify to whom? Excuse me, Josef, if I cross the line of propriety."

Breuer reached into his coat to loosen his collar. "No, it's all right. In fact, you ask *my* type of iconoclastic question, Friedrich. How strange to squirm in the way I make others squirm! But I have no answer. I leave the pebbles for no one. Not for the sake of social form, for others to see—I have no other family and am the only one who ever visits this grave. Not for superstition or fear. Certainly not for hope of reward hereafter: since childhood, I have believed that life is a spark between two identical voids, the darkness before birth and the one after death."

"Life—a spark between two voids. A nice image, Josef. And isn't it strange how we are so preoccupied with the second void and never think upon the first?"

Breuer nodded appreciatively and, after a few moments, continued, "But the pebbles. You ask, for whom I leave these pebbles? Perhaps my hand is tempted by Pascal's wager. After all, what's to be lost? It's a small pebble, a small effort."

"And a small question, too, Josef. One I asked merely to gain time to ponder a much greater question!"

"Which question?"

"Why you never told me your mother's name was Bertha!"

Breuer had never expected this question. He turned to look at Nietzsche. "Why should I have? I never thought of it. I never told you that my eldest daughter is *also* named Bertha. It's not relevant. As I told you, my mother died when I was three, and I have no memories of her."

"No *conscious* memories," said Nietzsche, correcting him. "But most of our memories exist in the subconscious. You've no doubt seen Hartmann's *Philosophy of the Unconscious?* It's in every bookstore."

Breuer nodded. "I know it well. Our café table group has spent many hours discussing it."

"There is a real genius behind that book—but it is the publisher, not the author. Hartmann is, at best, a journeyman philosopher who has merely appropriated the thoughts of Goethe, Schopenhauer, and Shelling. But to the publisher, Duncker, I say, *'Chapeau!'* "—and Nietzsche flourished his green hat in the air. "*There's* a man who knows how to put a book before the nose of every reader in Europe. It's in its ninth edition! Overbeck tells me that over a hundred thousand copies have been sold! Can you imagine! And I'm grateful if one of my books sells two hundred!"

He sighed and replaced his hat on his head.

"But to go back to Hartmann, he discusses two dozen different aspects of the unconscious and leaves no doubt that the greatest part of our memory and mental processes is outside consciousness. I agree, except that he doesn't go far enough: It's difficult, I believe, to overestimate the degree to which life—real life—is lived by the unconscious. Consciousness is only the translucent skin covering existence: the trained eye can see through it—to primitive forces, instincts, to the very engine of the will to power.

"In fact, Josef, you alluded to the unconscious yesterday when you imagined entering Bertha's dreams. How did you put it—that you had gained access to her innermost chamber, that sanctuary in which nothing ever decays? If your image dwells eternally in her mind, then where is it housed during the moments she's thinking of something else? Obviously there *must* be a vast reservoir of unconscious memories."

At that moment, they came upon a small group of mourners congregated near a canopy covering an open grave. Four burly cemetery journeymen, using heavy ropes, had lowered the casket; and the mourners, even the frail and elderly, now lined up to drop a small shovelful of soil into the grave. Breuer and Nietzsche walked in silence for several minutes, inhaling the dank, sweet-sour odor of newly turned earth. They came to a fork. Breuer touched Nietzsche's arm to signal they must take the path to the right.

"In respect to unconscious memories," Breuer resumed when they could no longer hear the gravel pelting the wooden coffin, "I agree entirely with you. In fact, my hypnotic work with Bertha produced much evidence of their existence. But, Friedrich, what are you suggesting? Surely not that I love Bertha because she and my mother have the same name?"

"Don't you find it remarkable, Josef, that though we've talked for many hours about your patient Bertha, it wasn't till this morning that you told me that was your mother's name?"

"I haven't concealed it from you. I've simply never connected my mother and Bertha. Even now, it seems strained and far-fetched. To me, Bertha is Bertha Pappenheim. I never think about my mother. No image of her ever enters my mind."

"Yet all your life you place flowers on her grave."

"On my whole family's grave!"

Breuer sensed he was being obstinate but was, nonetheless, determined to continue speaking his mind truthfully. He felt a wave of admiration for Nietzsche's stamina as he persisted, uncomplaining and undaunted, in his psychological investigation.

"Yesterday we worked on every possible meaning of Bertha. Your chimneysweeping stirred many memories. How can it be that your mother's name never came to mind?"

"How can I answer that? Nonconscious memories are beyond my conscious control. I don't know where they are. They have a life of their own. I can only talk about what I experience, what's *real*. And Bertha *qua* Bertha is the most real thing in my life."

"But, Josef, that's exactly the point. What did we learn yesterday if not that your relationship to Bertha is *unreal,* an illusion woven from images and longings that have nothing to do with the real Bertha?

"Yesterday we learned that your Bertha fantasy protects you from the *future,* from the terrors of aging, death, oblivion. Today I realize that your vision of Bertha is also contaminated by ghosts from the *past*. Josef, only this instant is real. In the end, we experience only ourselves in the present moment. Bertha's not real. She's but a phantom who comes from both the future and the past."

Breuer had never seen Nietzsche so confident—certain of every word.

"Let me put it another way!" he continued. "You think you and Bertha are an intimate twosome—the most intimate, private relationship imaginable. Not so?"

Breuer nodded.

"Yet," Nietzsche said emphatically, "I am convinced that *in no way do you and Bertha have a private relationship*. I believe that your obsession will be resolved when you can answer one pivotal question: 'How many people are in this relationship?' "

The fiacre waited just ahead. They got in, and Breuer instructed Fischmann to take them to the Simmeringer Haide.

Once inside, Breuer took up the question. "I've lost your meaning, Friedrich."

"Surely, you can see that you and Bertha have no private tête-à-tête. It's never you and she alone. Your fantasy teems with others: beautiful women with redemptive and protective abilities; faceless men whom you defeat for Bertha's favors; Bertha Breuer, your mother; and a ten-year-old girl with an adoring smile. If we have learned anything at all, Josef, it is that your obsession with Bertha is *not about Bertha!*"

Breuer nodded and sank into thought. Nietzsche, too, fell silent and stared out the window for the remainder of the ride. When they alighted, Breuer asked Fischmann to pick them up in an hour.

The sun had now disappeared behind a monstrous slate-gray cloud, and the two men leaned into an icy wind, which only yesterday had swept the Russian steppes. They buttoned up to their necks and started off at a brisk pace. Nietzsche was the first to break the silence.

"It's strange, Josef, how I'm always soothed by a cemetery. I told you my father was a Lutheran minister. But did I also tell you that my backyard and play area was the village churchyard? Incidentally, do you know Montaigne's essay on death—where he advises us to live in a room with a window overlooking a cemetery? It clears one's head, he claims, and keeps life's priorities in perspective. Do cemeteries do that for you?"

Breuer nodded. "I love that essay! There was a time when cemetery visits *were* restorative for me. A few years ago, when I felt crushed by the end of my university career, I sought solace among the dead. Somehow the tombs soothed me, allowed me to trivialize the trivial in my life. But then suddenly it changed!"

"How so?"

"I don't know why, but somehow the calming, enlightening effect of the cemetery disappeared. I lost my reverence and began to regard the funerary angels, and the epitaphs about sleeping in the arms of God, as foolish, even pathetic. A couple of years ago, I underwent another change. Everything about the cemetery—the headstones, the statues, the family houses of the dead—began to frighten me. Like a child, I felt the cemetery haunted by ghosts, and I walked to my parents' grave swiveling my head continuously, looking around and behind me. I began to procrastinate about coming and sought someone to accompany me. Nowadays my visits get shorter and shorter. I often dread the sight of my parents' grave and sometimes, when I stand there, fear I'll sink into the earth and be swallowed up."

"Like your nightmare of the ground liquefying beneath you."

"How eerie your speaking of that, Friedrich! Just a few minutes ago, that very dream passed through my mind."

"Perhaps it *is* a cemetery dream. In the dream, as I remember, you fell forty feet and came to rest upon a slab—wasn't 'slab' your word?"

"A *marble* slab! A headstone!" Breuer replied. "One with writing on it that I could not read! And there's something else I don't think I've told you. This young student, also a friend, Sigmund Freud, whom I mentioned before—the one who rode with me all day on my house calls . . ."

"Yes?"

"Well, dreams are his hobby. He often asks friends about their dreams. Precise numbers or phrases in dreams intrigue him, and when I described my nightmare, he proposed a novel hypothesis about falling precisely forty feet. Since I first dreamed this dream near my fortieth birthday, he suggested that the forty feet really stood for forty years!"

"Ingenious!" Nietzsche slowed his pace and clapped his hands together. "Not feet, but years! Now the riddle of the dream begins to yield! Upon reaching your fortieth year, you imagine falling into the earth and ending up on a marble slab. But is the slab the end? Is it death? Or does it, in some way, signify a break in the fall—a rescue?"

Without waiting for an answer, Nietzsche rushed on. "And still another question: The Bertha you searched for when the ground began to liquefy— which Bertha was that? The young Bertha, who offers the illusion of protection? Or the mother, who once offered real safety, and whose name is written on the slab? Or a fusion of the two Berthas? After all, in a way they are near in age, your mother dying when she was not much older than Bertha!"

"Which Bertha?" Breuer shook his head. "How can I ever answer that? To think that only a few months ago I imagined that the talking cure might eventually develop into a precise science! But how to be precise about such questions? Perhaps correctness should be gauged by sheer power: your words seem powerful, they move me, they *feel* right. Yet can *feelings* be trusted? Everywhere, religious zealots *feel* a divine presence. Shall I consider their feelings less trustworthy than mine?"

"I wonder," Nietzsche mused, "whether our dreams are closer to who we are than either rationality or feelings."

"Your interest in dreams surprises me, Friedrich. Your two books barely mention them. I remember only your speculation that the mental life of primitive man still operates in dreams."

"I think our entire prehistory can be found in the text of our dreams. But dreams fascinate me from a distance only: unfortunately, I recall very few of my own—though one recently had great clarity."

The two men walked without speaking, cracking twigs and leaves underfoot. Would Nietzsche describe his dream? Breuer had learned by now that the less he asked, the more Nietzsche gave of himself. Silence was best.

Several minutes later, Nietzsche continued. "It's short and, like yours, involves both women and death. I dreamed I was in bed with a woman, and there was a struggle. Perhaps we each tugged at the sheets. At any rate, a couple of minutes later, I found myself tightly bound in the sheets, so tightly that I could not move and began to suffocate. I awoke in a sweat, gasping for air and calling out, 'Live, live!' "

Breuer tried to help Nietzsche recall more of the dream, but to no avail. Nietzsche's only association to the dream was that being wrapped in sheets was like Egyptian embalming. He had become a mummy.

"It strikes me," Breuer said, "that our dreams are diametrically opposite. I dream about a woman rescuing me from death, while in your dream the woman is the instrument of death!"

"Yes, that's what my dream says. And I believe it's so! To love woman is to hate life!"

"I don't understand, Friedrich. You're speaking cryptically again."

"I mean that one can't love a woman without blinding oneself to the ugliness beneath the fair skin: blood, veins, fat, mucus, feces—the physiological horrors. The lover must put out his own eyes, must forsake truth. And, for me, an untrue life is a living death!"

"So there can never be a place for love in your life?" Breuer sighed deeply. "Even though love is ruining *my* life, your statement makes me sad for you, my friend."

"I dream of a love that is more than two people craving to possess one another. Once, not long ago, I thought I had found it. But I was mistaken."

"What happened?"

Thinking that Nietzsche had shaken his head slightly, Breuer did not press him. They walked together on until Nietzsche resumed: "I dream of a love in which two people share a passion to search together for some higher truth. Perhaps I should not call it love. Perhaps it's real name is friendship."

How different their discussion was that day! Breuer felt close to Nietzsche, even wished to walk arm in arm with him. Yet he also felt disappointed. He knew he would not get the help he needed on this day. There was not enough compressed intensity during such a walking conversation. It was too easy, in an uncomfortable moment, to slip into silence and to let one's attention be caught by the clouds of exhaled breath and the crackling of bare branches trembling in the wind.

Once Breuer fell behind. Nietzsche, turning to look for him, was surprised to see his companion, hat in hand, standing and bowing before a small plant of ordinary appearance.

"Foxglove," Breuer explained. "I have at least forty patients with heart failure whose life depends upon the largesse of that plebeian plant."

For both men, the cemetery visit had opened old childhood wounds; and, as they strolled, they reminisced. Nietzsche recounted a dream he remembered from the age of six, a year after his father had died.

"It's as vivid today as if I'd dreamed it last night. A grave opens and my father, dressed in a shroud, arises, enters a church, and soon returns carrying a small child in his arms. He climbs back into his grave with the child. The earth closes on top of them, and the gravestone slides over the opening.

"The truly horrible thing was that shortly after I had that dream, my younger brother was taken ill and died of convulsions."

"How ghastly!" Breuer said. "How eerie to have had such a pre-vision! How do you explain it?"

"I can't. For a long time, the supernatural terrified me, and I said my prayers with great earnestness. Over the last few years, however, I've begun to suspect that the dream was unrelated to my brother, that it was *me* my father had come for, and that the dream was expressing my fear of death."

At ease with one another in a way they had not been before, both men continued to reminisce. Breuer recalled a dream of some calamity occurring in his old home: his father standing helplessly, praying and rocking, wrapped in his blue-and-white prayer shawl. And Nietzsche described a nightmare in which, entering his bedroom, he saw, lying in his bed, an old man dying, a death rattle in his throat.

"We both encountered death very early," said Breuer thoughtfully, "and we both suffered a terrible early loss. I believe, speaking for myself, I've never recovered. But you, what about *your* loss? What about having had no father to protect you?"

"To protect me—or to *oppress* me? Was it a loss? I'm not so sure. Or it may have been a loss for the child, but not for the man."

"Meaning?" Breuer asked.

"Meaning that I was never weighed down by carrying my father on my back, never suffocated by the burden of his judgment, never taught that the object of life was to fulfill his thwarted ambitions. His death may well have been a blessing, a liberation. His whims never became my law. I was left alone to discover my own path, one not trodden before. Think about it! Could I, the antichrist, have exorcized false beliefs and sought new truths with a parson-father wincing with pain at my every achievement, a father who would have regarded my campaigns against illusion as a personal attack against *him*?"

"But," Breuer rejoined, "if you had had his protection when you needed it, would you have *had* to be the antichrist?"

Nietzsche did not respond, and Breuer pressed no further. He was learning to accommodate to Nietzsche's rhythm: any truth-seeking inquiries were permissible, even welcomed; but added force would be resisted. Breuer took out his watch, the one given him by his father. It was time to turn back to the fiacre, where Fischmann awaited. With the wind at their backs, the walking was easier.

"You may be more honest than I," speculated Breuer. "Perhaps my father's judgments weighed me down more than I realized. But most of the time I miss him a great deal."

"What do you miss?"

Breuer thought about his father and sampled the memories passing before his eyes. The old man, yarmulke on head, chanting a blessing before he tasted his supper of boiled potatoes and herring. His smile as he sat in the synagogue and watched his son wrapping his fingers in the tassels of his prayer shawl. His refusal to let his son take back a move in chess: "Josef, I cannot permit myself to teach you bad habits." His deep baritone voice, which filled the house as he sang passages for the young students he was preparing for their bar mitzvah.

"Most of all, I think I miss his attention. He was always my chief audience, even at the very end of his life, when he suffered considerable confusion and memory loss. I made sure to tell him of my successes, my diagnostic triumphs, my research discoveries, even my charitable donations. And even after he died, he was still my audience. For years I imagined him peering over my shoulder, observing and approving my achievements. The more his image fades, the more I struggle with the feeling that my activities and successes are all evanescent, that they have no real meaning."

"Are you saying, Josef, that if your successes could be recorded in the ephemeral mind of your father, *then* they would possess meaning?"

"I know it's irrational. It's much like the question of the sound of a tree falling in an empty forest. Does unobserved activity have meaning?"

"The difference is, of course, that the tree has no ears, whereas it is you, yourself, who bestow meaning."

"Friedrich, you're more self-sufficient than I—more than any one I've known! I remember marveling, in our very first meeting, at your ability to thrive with no recognition whatsoever from your colleagues."

"Long ago, Josef, I learned that it is easier to cope with a bad reputation than with a bad conscience. Besides, I'm not greedy; I don't write for the crowd. And I know how to be patient. Perhaps my students are not yet alive. Only the day after tomorrow belongs to me. Some philosophers are born posthumously!"

"But, Friedrich—believing you will be born posthumously—is that *so* different from my longing for my father's attention? You can wait, even until the day after tomorrow, but you, too, yearn for an audience."

A long pause. Nietzsche nodded finally and then said softly, "Perhaps. Perhaps I have within me pockets of vanity yet to be purged."

Breuer merely nodded. It did not escape his notice that this was the first time one of his observations had been acknowledged by Nietzsche. Was this to be a turning point in their relationship?

No, not yet! After a moment, Nietzsche added, "Still, there is a difference between coveting a parent's approval and striving to elevate those who will follow in the future."

Breuer did not respond, though it was obvious to him that Nietzsche's motives were not purely self-transcendent; he had his own back-alley ways of courting remembrance. Today it seemed to Breuer as if *all motives*, his and Nietzsche's, sprang from a single source—the drive to escape death's oblivion. Was he growing too morbid? Maybe it was the effect of the cemetery. Maybe even one visit a month was too frequent.

But not even morbidity could spoil the mood of this walk. He thought of Nietzsche's definition of friendship: two who join together in a search for some higher truth. Was that not precisely what he and Nietzsche were doing that day? Yes, they were friends.

That was a consoling thought, even though Breuer knew that their deepening relationship and their engrossing discussion brought him no closer to relief from his pain. For the sake of friendship, he tried to ignore this disturbing idea.

Yet, as a friend, Nietzsche must have read his mind. "I like this walk we take together, Josef, but we must not forget the raison d'être of our meetings—your psychological state."

Breuer slipped and grabbed a sapling for support as they descended a hill. "Careful, Friedrich, this shale is slick." Nietzsche gave Breuer his hand, and they continued their descent.

"I've been thinking," Nietzsche continued, "that, though our discussions appear to be diffuse, we, nonetheless, steadily grow closer to a solution. It's true that our direct attacks on your Bertha obsession have been futile. Yet in the last couple of days we have found out *why:* because the obsession involves not Bertha, or not only her, but a series of meanings folded into Bertha. We agree on this?"

Breuer nodded, wanting to suggest politely that help was not going to come by way of such intellectual formulations. But Nietzsche hurried on. "It's clear now that our primary error has been in considering Bertha the target. *We have not chosen the right enemy."*

"And that is—?"

"You know, Josef! Why make *me* say it? The right enemy is the underlying *meaning* of your obsession. Think of our talk today—again and again, we've returned to your fears of the void, of oblivion, of death. It's there in your nightmare, in the ground liquefying, in your plunge downward to the marble slab. It's there in your cemetery dread, in your concerns about meaningless, in your wish to be observed and remembered. The paradox, *your* paradox, is that you dedicate yourself to the search for truth but cannot bear the sight of what you discover."

"But you, too, Friedrich, must be frightened by death and by godlessness. From the very beginning, I have asked, 'How do you bear it? How have *you* come to terms with such horrors?' "

"It may be time to tell you," Nietzsche replied, his manner becoming portentous. "Before, I did not think that you were ready to hear me."

Breuer, curious about Nietzsche's message, chose, for once, not to object to his prophet voice.

"I do not teach, Josef, that one should 'bear' death, or 'come to terms' with it. That way lies life-betrayal! Here is my lesson to you: *Die at the right time!"*

"Die at the right time!" The phrase jolted Breuer. The pleasant afternoon stroll had turned deadly serious. "Die at the right time? What do you mean? Please, Friedrich, I can't stand it, as I tell you again and again, when you say something important in such an enigmatic way. Why do you do that?"

"You pose two questions. Which shall I answer?"

"Today, tell me about dying at the right time."

"Live when you live! Death loses its terror if one dies when one has consummated one's life! If one does not live in the right time, then one can never die at the right time."

"What does *that* mean?" Breuer asked again, feeling ever more frustrated.

"Ask yourself, Josef: *Have you consummated your life?*"

"You answer questions with questions, Friedrich!"

"You ask questions to which you know the answer," Nietzsche countered.

"If I knew the answer, why would I ask?"

"To avoid knowing your own answer!"

Breuer paused. He knew Nietzsche was right. He stopped resisting and turned his attention within. "Have I consummated my life? I have achieved a great deal, more than anyone could have expected of me. Material success, scientific achievement, family, children—but we've gone over all that before."

"Still, Josef, you avoid my question. Have you lived your life? Or been lived by it? Chosen it? Or did it choose you? Loved it? Or regretted it? That is what I mean when I ask whether you have consummated your life. Have you used it up? Remember that dream in which your father stood by helplessly praying while something calamitous was happening to his family? Are you not like him? Do you not stand by helplessly, grieving for the life you never lived?"

Breuer felt the pressure mounting. Nietzsche's questions bore into him; he had no defense against them. He could hardly breathe. His chest seemed about to burst. He stopped walking for a moment and took three deep breaths before answering.

"These questions—you know the answer! No, I've not chosen! No, I've not lived the life I've wanted! I've lived the life assigned me. I—the real I—have been encased in my life."

"And *that*, Josef is, I am convinced, the primary source of your *Angst*. That precordial pressure—it's because your chest is bursting with unlived life. And your heart ticks away the time. And time's covetousness is forever. Time devours and devours—and gives back nothing. How terrible to hear you say that you lived the life assigned to you! And how terrible to face death without ever having claimed freedom, even in all its danger!"

Nietzsche was firmly in his pulpit, his prophet's voice ringing. A wave of disappointment swept over Breuer; he knew now that there was no help for him.

"Friedrich," he said, "these are grand-sounding phrases. I admire them. They stir my soul. But they are far, far away from my life. What does claiming freedom mean to my everyday situation? How can I be free? It's not the same as you, a young single man giving up a suffocating university career. It's too late for me! I have a family, employees, patients, students. It's far too late! We can talk forever, but I cannot change my life—it is woven too tight with the thread of other lives."

There was a long silence, which Breuer broke, his voice weary. "But I cannot sleep, and now I cannot stand the pain of this pressure in my chest." The icy wind piercing his greatcoat, he shivered and wrapped his scarf more tightly around his neck.

Nietzsche, in a rare gesture, took his arm. "My friend," he whispered, "I *cannot* tell you how to live differently because, if I did, you would *still* be living another's design. But, Josef, there is something I *can* do. I can give you a gift, the gift of my mightiest thought, my thought of thoughts. Perhaps it may already be somewhat familiar to you, since I sketched it briefly in *Human, All Too Human*. This thought will be the guiding force of my next book, perhaps of all my future books."

His voice had lowered, assuming a solemn, stately tone, as if to signify the culmination of everything that had gone before. The two men walked arm in arm. Breuer looked straight ahead as he awaited Nietzsche's words.

"Josef, try to clear your mind. Imagine this thought experiment! What if some demon were to say to you that this life—as you now live it and have lived it in the past—you will have to live once more, and innumerable times more; and there will be nothing new in it, but every pain and every joy and everything unutterably small or great in your life will return to you, all in the same succession and sequence—even this wind and those trees and that slippery shale, even the graveyard and the dread, even this gentle moment and you and I, arm in arm, murmuring these words?"

As Breuer remained silent, Nietzsche continued, "Imagine the eternal hourglass of existence turned upside down again and again and again. And each time, also turned upside down are you and I, mere specks that we are."

Breuer made an effort to understand him. "How is this—this—this fantasy——"

"It's more than a fantasy," Nietzsche insisted, "more really than a thought experiment. Listen only to my words! Block out everything else! Think about infinity. Look behind you—imagine looking infinitely far into the past. Time stretches backward for all eternity. And, if time infinitely stretches backward, must not everything that *can* happen have *already* happened? Must not all that passes *now* have passed this way before? Whatever walks here, mustn't it have walked this path before? And if everything has passed before in time's infinity, then what do you think, Josef, of *this* moment, of our whispering together under this arch of trees? Must not *this,* too, have come before? And time that stretches back infinitely, must it not also stretch ahead infinitely? Must not we, in this moment, in every moment, recur eternally?"

Nietzsche fell silent, to give Breuer time to absorb his message. It was midday, but the sky had darkened. A light snow began to fall. The fiacre and Fischmann loomed into sight.

On the ride back to the clinic, the two men resumed their discussion. Nietzsche claimed that, though he had termed it a thought experiment, his assumption of eternal recurrence could be scientifically proven. Breuer was skeptical about Nietzsche's proof, which was based on two metaphysical principles: that time is infinite, and force (the basic stuff of the universe) is finite. Given a finite number of potential states of the world and an infinite amount of time that has passed, it follows, Nietzsche claimed, that all possible states must have already occurred; and that the present state must be a repetition; and, likewise, the one that gave birth to it and the one that arises out of it and so on, backward into the past and forward into the future.

Breuer's perplexity grew. "You mean that through sheer random occurrences this precise moment would have occurred previously?"

"Think of time that has always been, time stretching back forever. In such infinite time, must not recombinations of all events constituting the world have repeated themselves an infinite number of times?"

"Like a great dice game?"

"Precisely! The great dice game of existence!"

Breuer continued to question Nietzsche's cosmological proof of eternal recurrence. Though Nietzsche responded to each question, he eventually grew impatient and finally threw up his hands.

"Time and time again, Josef, you have asked for concrete help. How many times have you asked me to be relevant, to offer something that can change you? *Now* I give you what you request, and you ignore it by picking away at details. Listen to me, my friend, listen to my words—this is the most important thing I will ever say to you: *let this thought take possession of you, and I promise you it will change you forever!*"

Breuer was unmoved. "But how can I believe without proof? I cannot conjure up belief. Have I given up one religion simply to embrace another?"

"The proof is extremely complex. It is still unfinished and will require years of work. And now, as a result of our discussion, I'm not sure I should even bother to devote the time to working out the cosmological proof— perhaps others, too, will use it as a distraction. Perhaps they, like you, will pick away at the intricacies of the proof and ignore the important point— the psychological *consequences* of eternal recurrence."

Breuer said nothing. He looked out the window of the fiacre and shook his head slightly.

"Let me put it another way," Nietzsche continued. "Will you not grant me that eternal recurrence is *probable*? No, wait, I don't need even that! Let us say simply that it is *possible*, or *merely* possible. That is enough. Certainly it is more possible and more provable than the fairy tale of eternal damnation! What do you have to lose by considering it a possibility? Can you not think of it, then, as 'Nietzsche's wager'?"

Breuer nodded.

"I urge you, then, to consider the *implications* of eternal recurrence for your life—not abstractly, but now, *today,* in the most concrete sense!"

"You suggest," said Breuer, "that every action I make, every pain I experience, will be experienced through all infinity?"

"Yes, eternal recurrence means that every time you choose an action you must be willing to choose it *for all eternity.* And it is the same for every action *not* made, every stillborn thought, every choice avoided. And all unlived life will remain bulging inside you, unlived through all eternity. And the unheeded voice of your conscience will cry out to you forever."

Breuer felt dizzy; it was hard to listen. He tried to concentrate on Nietzsche's mammoth mustache pounding up and down at each word. Since his mouth and lips were entirely obscured, there was no forewarning of the words to come. Occasionally his glance would catch Nietzsche's eyes, but they were too sharp, and he shifted his attention down to the fleshy but powerful nose, or up to the heavy overhanging eyebrows which resembled ocular mustaches.

Breuer finally managed a question: "So, as I understand it, eternal recurrence promises a form of immortality?"

"No!" Nietzsche was vehement. "I teach that life should never be modified, or squelched, because of the promise of some other kind of life in the future. What is immortal is *this* life, *this* moment. There is no afterlife, no goal toward which this life points, no apocalyptic tribunal or judgment. *This moment exists forever,* and you, alone, are your only audience."

Breuer shivered. As the chilling implications of Nietzsche's proposal grew more clear, he stopped resisting and, instead, entered a state of uncanny concentration.

"So, Josef, once again I say, let this thought take possession of you. Now I have a question for you: *Do you hate the idea? Or do you love it?*"

"*I hate it!*" Breuer almost shouted. "To live *forever* with the sense that I have *not* lived, have *not* tasted freedom—the idea fills me with horror."

"*Then,*" Nietzsche exhorted, "*live in such a way that you love the idea!*"

"All that I love *now,* Friedrich, is the thought that I have fulfilled my duty toward others."

"Duty? Can duty take precedence over your love for *yourself* and for your own quest for unconditional freedom? If you have not attained yourself, then 'duty' is merely a euphemism for using others for your own enlargement."

Breuer summoned the energy for one further rebuttal. "There *is* such a thing as a duty to others, and I have been faithful to that duty. There, at least, I have the courage of my convictions."

"Better, Josef, far better, to have the courage to *change* your convictions. Duty and faithfulness are shams, curtains to hide behind. Self-liberation means a sacred *no,* even to duty."

Frightened, Breuer stared at Nietzsche.

"You want to become *yourself,*" Nietzsche continued. "How often have I heard you say that? How often have you lamented that you have never known your freedom? Your goodness, your duty, your faithfulness—these are the bars of your prison. You will perish from such small virtues. You must learn to know your wickedness. You cannot be *partially* free: your instincts, too, thirst for freedom; your wild dogs in the cellar—they bark for freedom. Listen harder, can't you hear them?"

"But I *cannot* be free," Breuer implored. "I have made sacred marriage vows. I have a duty to my children, my students, my patients."

"To build children you must first be built yourself. Otherwise, you'll seek children out of animal needs, or loneliness, or to patch the holes in yourself. Your task as a parent is to produce not another self, another Josef, but something higher. It's to produce a creator.

"And your wife?" Nietzsche went on inexorably. "Is she not as imprisoned in this marriage as you? Marriage should be no prison, but a garden in which something higher is cultivated. *Perhaps the only way to save your marriage is to give it up.*"

"I have made sacred vows of wedlock."

"Marriage is a something large. It is a large thing to always be two, to remain in love. Yes, wedlock *is* sacred. And yet . . ." Nietzsche's voice trailed off.

"And yet?" Breuer asked.

"Wedlock *is* sacred. Yet"—Nietzsche's voice was harsh—"*it is better to break wedlock than to be broken by it!*"

Breuer closed his eyes and sank into deep thought. Neither man spoke for the remainder of their journey.

∽

Friedrich Nietzsche's Notes on Dr. Breuer, 16 December 1882

A stroll that began in sunlight and ended darkly. Perhaps we journeyed too far into the graveyard. Should we have turned back earlier? Have I given him too powerful a thought? Eternal recurrence is a mighty hammer. It will break those who are not yet ready for it.

No! A psychologist, an unriddler of souls, needs hardness more than anyone. Else he will bloat with pity. And his student drown in shallow water.

Yet at the end of our walk, Josef seemed sorely pressed, barely able to converse. Some are not born hard. A true psychologist, like an artist, must love his palette. Perhaps more kindness, more patience was needed. Do I strip before teaching how to weave new clothing? Have I taught him "freedom from" without teaching "freedom for"?

No, a guide must be a railing by the torrent, but he must not be a crutch. The guide must lay bare the trails that lie before the student. But he must not choose the path.

"Become my teacher," he asks. "Help me overcome despair." Shall I conceal my wisdom? And the student's responsibility? He must harden himself to the cold, his fingers must grip the railing, he must lose himself many times on wrong paths before finding the right one.

In the mountains alone, I travel the shortest way—from peak to peak. But students lose their way when I walk too far ahead. I must learn to shorten my stride. Today, we may have traveled too fast. I unraveled a dream, separated one Bertha from another, reburied the dead, and taught dying at the right time. And all of this was but the overture to the mighty theme of recurrence.

Have I pushed him too deep into misery? Often he seemed too upset to hear me. Yet what did I challenge? What destroy? Only empty values and tottering beliefs! That which is tottering, one should also push!

Today I understood that the best teacher is one who learns from his student. Perhaps he is right about my father. How different my life would be had I not lost him! Can it be true that I hammer so hard because I hate him for dying? And hammer so loud because I still crave an audience?

I worry about his silence at the end. His eyes were open, but he seemed not to see. He scarcely breathed.

Yet I know the dew falls heaviest when the night is most silent.

CHAPTER 21

RELEASING THE PIGEONS was almost as hard as saying farewell to his family. Breuer wept as he unclasped the wire doors and hoisted the cages up to the open window. At first the pigeons seemed not to understand. They looked up from the golden grain in their food dish and stared uncomprehendingly at Breuer, whose gesticulating arms enjoined them to fly for their freedom.

It was only when he jostled and banged their cages that the pigeons fluttered through the open jaws of their prison and, without once looking back at their keeper, flew into the blood-streaked early morning sky. Breuer watched their flight with sorrow: every silver-blue wing flap signified the ending of his scientific research career.

Long after the sky had emptied, he continued to stare out the window. It had been the most painful day of his life, and he was still numb from his confrontation with Mathilde earlier that morning. Again and again, he repeated the scene in his mind and searched for more graceful and painless ways he might have informed her that he was leaving.

"Mathilde," he had told her, "there is no way to say this but simply to say it: I must have my freedom. I feel trapped—not by you, but by destiny. And a destiny not of my choosing."

Astonished and frightened, Mathilde had merely stared at him.

He had continued. "Suddenly I am old. I find myself an old man entombed in a life—a profession, a career, a family, a culture. Everything has been assigned to me. I chose nothing. I must give myself a chance! I must have an opportunity to find myself."

"A chance?" Mathilde replied. "Find yourself? Josef, what are you saying? I don't understand. What is it you ask?"

"I ask nothing from you! I ask something of myself. I *have* to change my life! Otherwise, I shall face my death without ever feeling I have lived."

"Josef, this is madness!" Mathilde's voice rose. Her eyes grew wide with fear. "What has happened to you? Since when is there a *your* life and a *my* life? We share a life; we made a covenant to combine our lives."

"But how could I give something before it was mine to give?"

"I don't understand you any longer. 'Freedom,' 'finding yourself,' 'never having lived'—your words make no sense to me. What is happening to you, Josef? To us?" Mathilde could speak no further. She crammed both fists into her mouth, whirled away from him, and began to sob.

Josef had watched her body heave. He moved closer to her. She fought for breath, her head bent down on the sofa arm, her tears falling to her lap, her breasts rippling with her sobs. Wishing to console her, he placed his hand on her shoulder—only to feel her recoil. It was then, at that moment, that he realized he had come to a fork in the course of his life. He had turned off, away from the crowd. He had made the break. His wife's shoulder, her back, her breasts, were no longer his; he had relinquished the right to touch her, and now he would have to face the world without the shelter of her flesh.

"It's best if I go immediately, Mathilde. I can't tell you where I'm going. It's better if I don't know myself. I shall leave instructions for all business matters with Max. I leave you everything and shall take nothing with me except the clothes on my back, a small valise, and enough money to feed myself."

Mathilde continued to cry. She seemed unable to respond. Had she even heard his words?

"When I know where I am, I'll contact you."

Still no response.

"I must go away. I must make a change and take control of my life. I think that when I am able to choose my destiny, we will both be better off. Perhaps I will choose the same life, but it has to be a choice, my choice."

Still there had been no response from the weeping Mathilde. Breuer had left the room in a daze.

The whole conversation had been a cruel mistake, he thought, as he closed the pigeon cages and carried them back to his laboratory shelf. There remained in one cage four pigeons unable to fly because surgical experiments had damaged their equilibrium. He knew he should sacrifice them before he left, but he wanted no more responsibility for anyone or anything. Instead, he replenished their water and food and left them to their fate.

No, I should never have talked to her about freedom, choice, entrapment, destiny, finding myself. How *could* she understand me? I scarcely understand myself. When Friedrich first spoke to me in that language, I couldn't comprehend him. Other words would have been better—perhaps "brief sabbatical," "professional exhaustion," "an extended visit to a North African spa." Words she could understand. And she could offer them as explanation to the family, to the community.

My God, what will she say to everyone? In what kind of position is she left? No, stop! That's *her* responsibility! Not mine. To annex the responsibility of others—that way lies entrapment, for me *and* for them.

Breuer's meditations were interrupted by the sound of footsteps coming up the stairs. Mathilde flung the door open, slamming it against the wall. She looked ghastly, her face pale, her hair hanging down in disarray, her eyes inflamed.

"I've stopped crying, Josef. And *now* I shall answer you. There is something *wrong*, something *evil*, in what you just said to me. And something simple-minded, too. Freedom! Freedom! You speak of freedom. What a cruel joke to me! I wish *I* had had *your* freedom—the freedom of a man to obtain an education, to choose a profession. Never before have I wished so hard for an education—I wish I had the vocabulary, the logic, to demonstrate to you just how foolish you sound!"

Mathilde stopped and pulled a chair away from the desk. Refusing Breuer's help, she sat silently for a moment to catch her breath.

"You want to leave? You want to make new life choices? Have you forgotten the choices you *have already* made? You chose to marry me. And do you *truly* not understand that you chose to commit yourself—to me, to us? What is choice if you refuse to honor it? I don't know what it is—maybe whim or impulse, but it is *not* choice."

It was frightening to see Mathilde like this. But Breuer knew he had to stand his ground. "I should have become an 'I' before I became a 'we.' I made choices before I was formed enough to make choices."

"Then that, *too*, is a choice," Mathilde snapped back. "Who is this *'I'* that didn't become an I? A year from now you'll say this 'I' of *today* wasn't yet formed, and that the choices you make today don't count. This is just self-trickery, a way to weasel out of responsibility for your choices. At our wedding, when we said *yes* to the rabbi, we said *no* to other choices. I could have married others. Easily! There were many who desired me. Wasn't it you who said I was the most beautiful woman in Vienna?"

"I still say it."

Mathilde hesitated for a moment. Then, brushing away his statement, she continued. "Don't you understand that you cannot enter a covenant with me and then suddenly say, 'No, I take it back, I'm not sure after all.' That's *immoral. Evil.*"

Breuer did not answer. He held his breath and imagined flattening his ears, like Robert's kitten. He knew Mathilde was right. And he knew Mathilde was wrong.

"You want to be able to choose and, at the same time, keep all choices open. You asked me to give up *my* freedom, what little I had, at least the freedom to choose a husband, and yet you want to keep your precious freedom open—open to satisfy your lust with a twenty-one-year-old patient."

Josef flushed. "So *that's* what you think? No, this does not involve Bertha or any other woman."

"Your words say one thing, your face another. I have no education, Josef—through no choice of mine. But I'm not a fool!"

"Mathilde, don't belittle my struggle. I'm grappling with the meaning of *my whole life*. A man has a duty to others, but he has a higher one to himself. He——"

"And a woman? What about her meaning, her freedom?"

"I don't mean *men*, I mean *person*—men *and* women—each of us has to choose."

"I'm not like you. I can't choose freedom when my choice enslaves others. Have you thought about what your freedom means for me? What kind of choices does a widow, or a deserted wife, have?"

"You are free, just like me. You are young, rich, attractive, healthy."

"Free? Where is your head today, Josef? Think about it! Where is a woman's freedom? I was not permitted an education. I went from my father's house to your house. I had to fight my mother and grandmother even for the freedom to choose my rugs and furniture."

"Mathilde, it's not reality, but only your attitude toward your culture that imprisons you! A couple of weeks ago I saw a young Russian woman in consultation. Russian women have no greater independence than Viennese women, yet this young woman has claimed her freedom: she defies her family, she demands an education, she exercises her right to choose the life she wants. And so can you! You're free to do anything you want. You're rich! You can change your name and move to Italy!"

"Words, words, words! A thirty-six-year-old Jewess traveling free. Josef, you talk like a fool! Wake up! Live in reality, not in words! What about the children? Change my name! Shall each of them, too, choose a new name?"

"Remember, Mathilde, *you* wanted nothing more than to have children, as soon as we were married. Children and more children. I pleaded with you to wait."

She held back her angry words and turned her head away from him.

"I can't tell you how to be free, Mathilde. I can't design your path for you because then it would no longer be *your* path. But, if you have the courage, I know you can find the way."

She rose and walked to the door. Turning to face him, she spoke in measured terms: "Listen to me, Josef! You want to find freedom and make choices? Then know that this very moment is a choice. You tell me that you need to choose your life—and that, in time, you may choose to resume your life here.

"But Josef, *I choose my life, too.* And I choose to say to you *there is no return.* You can *never* resume your life with me as your wife because when you walk out of this house today I will *no longer be your wife.* You cannot choose to return to this home because it will *no longer be your home!*"

Josef closed his eyes and bowed his head. The next sounds he heard were the door slamming and Mathilde's steps descending the stairs. He felt staggered by the blows he had absorbed, but also strangely exhilarated. Mathilde's words were terrible. But she was right! This decision *had* to be irreversible.

Now it is done, he thought. Something is finally happening to me, something *real,* not just thoughts, but something in the real world. Over and over, I've envisioned this scene. Now I *feel* it! Now I know what it's like to take control of my destiny. It is terrible, and wonderful.

He finished his packing, then kissed each of his sleeping children, and softly whispered goodbye to them. Only Robert stirred, murmuring, "Where are you going, Father?" but immediately fell back to sleep. How strangely painless it was! Breuer marveled at the way he had numbed his feelings to protect himself. He lifted his valise and descended the stairs to his office, where he spent the remainder of the morning writing long notes of instruction to Frau Becker and to the three physicians to whom he would turn over his patients.

Should he write letters of explanation to his friends? He wavered. Wasn't this the time to break all ties with his former life? Nietzsche had said that a new self has to be built on the ashes of his old life. But then he recalled that Nietzsche himself had continued to correspond with a few old friends. If even Nietzsche could not cope with complete isolation, why should he ask more of himself?

So he wrote letters of farewell to his closest friends: to Freud, Ernst Fleishl, and Franz Brentano. To each he described his motivations for leaving while acknowledging that these reasons, sketched in a brief letter, might seem insufficient or incomprehensible. "Trust me," he urged each, "this is not a frivolous act. I have significant grounds for my actions, all of which I shall reveal to you at a later date." Toward Fleishl, his pathologist friend who had seriously infected himself while dissecting a cadaver, Breuer felt particular guilt: for years he had offered him medical and psychological support and now would be removing it. He also felt guilty toward Freud, who depended on him not only for friendship and professional advice but also for financial support. Even though Sig was fond of Mathilde, Breuer hoped that, in time, he would understand and forgive his decision. To his letter, Breuer added a separate note officially canceling all of Freud's debts to the Breuers.

He wept as he descended the stairs of Bäckerstrasse 7 for the last time. While he waited for the district *Dientsmann* to fetch Fischmann, he meditated on the brass plaque by the front door: DOCTOR JOSEF BREUER, CONSULTANT—SECOND FLOOR. The plaque would not be there when he next visited Vienna. Nor would his office. Oh, the granite and bricks and the second floor would be there, but they would no longer be *his* bricks; his office would soon lose the odor of his existence. He had experienced the same feeling of dislocation whenever he had visited his childhood home—the small house which reeked of both intense familiarity and the most painful indifference. It housed another struggling family, perhaps another boy of great promise who many years hence might grow up to be a physician.

But he, Josef, was not *necessary*: he would be forgotten, his place swallowed by time and the existence of others. He would die sometime in the next ten to twenty years. And he would die alone: no matter the companionship, he thought, one always dies alone.

He cheered himself with the thought that if man is alone and necessity an illusion, then he is *free!* Yet as he boarded his fiacre, his cheer gave way to a sense of oppression. He looked at the other apartments on the street. Was he being watched? Were his neighbors staring out of every window? Surely they must be aware of this momentous event taking place! Would they know tomorrow? Would Mathilde, assisted by her sisters and her mother, throw his clothes into the street? He had heard of angry wives doing that.

His first stop was Max's home. Max was expecting him because, the day before, immediately after his cemetery discussion with Nietzsche, Breuer had confided in him his decision to leave his life in Vienna and had asked him to handle Mathilde's financial affairs.

Again, Max strenuously attempted to dissuade him from this impetuous and ruinous course of action. To no avail; Breuer was resolute. Finally Max tired and appeared resigned to his brother-in-law's decision. For an hour the two men huddled over the file of the family financial records. When Breuer prepared to leave, however, Max suddenly stood up and blocked the doorway with his huge body. For a moment, especially when Max spread his arms, Breuer feared an attempt to restrain him physically. But Max simply wanted to embrace him. His voice broke as he croaked, "So, it's no chess tonight? My life will never be the same, Josef. I'll miss you horribly. You're the best friend I've ever had."

Too overcome to respond in words, Breuer hugged Max and quickly left the house. In the fiacre, he instructed Fischmann to drive him to the train station and, just before they arrived, told him that he was off on a very long trip. He gave him two months' wages and promised to contact him when he returned to Vienna.

As he waited to board the train, Breuer scolded himself for not telling Fischmann that he would never be returning. "To treat him so casually— how could you? After ten years together?" Then he pardoned himself. There was only so much he could bear in a single day.

He was heading to the small town of Kreuzlingen in Switzerland, where Bertha had been hospitalized at the Bellevue Sanatorium for the past few months. He was puzzled by his dazed mental state. Just when and how had he made the decision to visit Bertha?

As the train rumbled into movement, he put his head back on the cushion, closed his eyes, and meditated on the events of the day.

Friedrich was right: All along, my freedom has been here for the taking! I could have seized my life years ago. Vienna is still standing. Life will go on without me. My absence would have happened anyway, ten or twenty years from now. From a cosmic perspective, what difference does it make? I am already forty years old: my younger brother has been dead for eight years, my father for ten, my mother for thirty-six. Now, while I can still see and walk, I shall take some small fraction of my life for myself—is that too much to demand? I am so tired of service, so tired of taking care of others. Yes, Friedrich was right. Shall I remain yoked to the plow of duty forever? Shall I, throughout all eternity, live a life I regret?

He tried to sleep, but each time he nodded off, visions of the children drifted into his mind. He winced with pain to think of them without a father. Friedrich is right, he reminded himself, when he says, "Do not create children until one is ready to *be* a creator and to *spawn* creators." It is wrong to bear children out of need, wrong to use a child to alleviate loneliness, wrong to provide purpose in life by reproducing another copy of oneself. It is wrong also to seek immortality by spewing one's germ into the future—as though sperm contains your consciousness!

Still, what about the children? They were a mistake, they were forced upon me, begotten before I was aware of my choices. Yet they are *here*, they exist! About them Nietzsche is silent. And Mathilde has warned that I may never again see them.

Breuer slumped into despair but quickly roused himself. No! Away with such thoughts! Friedrich is right: duty, propriety, faithfulness, selflessness, kindness—these are soporifics that lull one to sleep, a sleep so deep that one awakens, if at all, only at the very end of life. And then only to learn that one has never really lived.

I have only one life, a life that may recur forever. I do not want to regret for all eternity that I lost myself while pursuing my duty to my children.

Now is my chance to build a new self on the ashes of my old life! Then, when I have done that, I shall find my way to my children. Then I shall no longer be tyrannized by Mathilde's notions of what is socially permitted! Who can block a father's path to his children? I shall become an axe. I shall hew and slash my way to them! As for today, God help them. I can do nothing. I am drowning and must first save myself.

And Mathilde? Friedrich says that the only way to save this marriage is to give it up! And "Better to break wedlock than be broken by it." Perhaps Mathilde, too, was broken by wedlock. Perhaps she will be better off without me. Perhaps she was as imprisoned as I. Lou Salomé would say so. How did she put it: that she would never be enslaved by the frailties of another? Perhaps my absence will liberate Mathilde!

It was late in the evening when the train reached Konstanz. Breuer got off and spent the night at a modest train-station hotel; it was time, he told himself, to become acclimated to second- and third-class accommodations. In the morning, he hired a carriage to Kreuzlingen, and the Bellevue Sanatorium. Arriving, he informed the director, Robert Binswanger, that an unexpected consultation request had brought him to Geneva, close enough to the Bellevue to pay a visit to his former patient, Fräulein Pappenheim.

There was nothing unusual about Breuer's request: he was well known to the Bellevue as a long-time friend of the former director, Ludwig Binswanger, Sr., who had recently died. Dr. Binswanger offered to send for Fräulein Pappenheim immediately. "She's taking a walk now and discussing her condition with her new physician, Doctor Durkin." Binswanger stood and walked to the window. "There, in the garden, you can see them."

"No, no, Doctor Binswanger, do not interrupt them. I feel strongly that nothing should take priority over patient-doctor sessions. Besides, the sun is glorious today, I've seen too little of it in Vienna lately. If you have no objection, I'll wait for her in your garden. Also, it would be interesting for me to observe Fräulein Pappenheim's condition, especially her gait, from an unobtrusive position."

On a lower terrace of the extensive Bellevue gardens, Breuer saw Bertha and her physician strolling back and forth along a path bordered by high, carefully trimmed boxwoods. He chose his observation perch carefully: a white bench on the upper terrace, almost entirely hidden by the bare branches of an encircling lilac arbor. From there, he could look down and see Bertha clearly; perhaps, when she strolled by, he would be able to hear her words.

Bertha and Durkin had just passed below his bench and were walking down the path away from him. Her lavender scent wafted up to him. He inhaled it greedily and felt the ache of deep longing coursing through his body. How frail she seemed! Suddenly she stopped. Her right leg was in contracture; he remembered how often this had happened when he had strolled with her. She clung to Durkin for support. How tightly she was clasping him, precisely as she had once clasped Breuer. Now both of her arms were clutching Durkin's, and she was pressing against him! Breuer remembered her pressing her body against *him*. Oh, how he loved the feel of her breasts! Like the princess feeling the pea through many mattresses, he could feel her velvet, yielding breasts through all obstacles—her Persian lamb cape and his fur-lined greatcoat only gossamer-thin barriers to his pleasure.

There, Bertha's right quadriceps was now in severe spasm! She grabbed at her thigh. Breuer knew what would come next. Durkin quickly lifted her, carried her to the next bench, and laid her down. Now would come the massage. Yes, Durkin was taking off his gloves, carefully slipping his hands under her coat, and now beginning to massage her thigh. Would Bertha now moan with pain? Yes, softly! Breuer could hear her! Now won't she close her eyes, as if in trance, stretch her arms over her head, arch her back, and thrust her breasts upward? Yes, yes, there she goes! Now her coat will fall open—yes, he saw her hand unobtrusively slip down and unbutton it. He knew her dress would creep up, it always did. There! She's bending her knees—Breuer had never seen her do *that* before—and her dress slides up, almost to her waist. Durkin stands stark still, gazing at her pink silk underpants and the faint outline of a dusky triangle.

From his distant perch, Breuer stares over Durkin's shoulder, equally transfixed. Cover her up, you poor fool! Durkin tries to pull down her dress and close her coat. Bertha's hands interfere. Her eyes are closed. Is she in trance? Durkin appears agitated—as well he might be, Breuer thought—and looks nervously about him. No one there, thank God! The leg contracture has eased. He helps Bertha up, and she tries to walk.

Breuer feels dazed, as though he were no longer in his own body. There is something unreal about the scene before him, as though he were watching a drama from the last balcony row of an enormous theater. What is he feeling? Perhaps jealousy toward Dr. Durkin? He's young and handsome and single, and Bertha is hanging on to him more closely than she ever did him. But no! He feels no jealousy, no animosity—none at all. On the contrary, he feels warm and close to Durkin. Bertha does not divide them, but draws them together into a brotherhood of agitation.

The young couple continued their stroll. Breuer smiled to see that it was now the doctor, and not the patient, who walked with an awkward, shuffling gait. He felt great empathy for his successor: how many times had *he* had to stroll with Bertha while dealing with the inconvenience of a throbbing erection! "Lucky for you, Doctor Durkin, that it's winter," Breuer said to himself. "It's much worse in summer with no coat to conceal yourself. Then you have to tuck it under your belt!"

The couple, having reached the end of the path, had now turned back in his direction. Bertha put her hand to her cheek. Breuer could see that her orbital muscles were in spasm, and that she was in agony; her facial pain, tic douloureux, was a daily occurrence and so severe that only morphine could relieve it. Bertha stopped. He knew exactly what would come next. It was eerie. Once again it felt like the theater, and he the director or prompter coaching the cast on their next lines. Put your hands on her face, your palms on her cheeks, your thumbs touching on the bridge of her nose. That's right. Now press down lightly and stroke her eyebrows, again and again. Good! He could see Bertha's face relax. She reached up, took Durkin by the wrists, and held each hand to her lips. *Now* Breuer felt a stab. Only once had she kissed his hands like that: it had been their closest moment. She came closer. He could hear her voice. "Little father, my dear little father." That smarted. It was what she used to call *him*.

This was all he heard. It was enough. He rose and, without a word to the puzzled nursing staff, walked out of the Bellevue and into his waiting carriage. In a daze, he returned to Konstanz, where he somehow managed to board the train. The sound of the locomotive whistle brought him back to himself. His heart pounding, he sank his head back into the cushion and began to think about what he had seen.

That brass plaque, my office in Vienna, my childhood home, and now Bertha, too—all continue to be what they are: none of them require *me* for their existence. I'm incidental, interchangeable. I'm not *necessary* for Bertha's drama. None of us is—not even the leading men. Neither I, nor Durkin, nor those yet to come.

He felt overwhelmed: perhaps he needed more time to absorb all this. He was tired; he leaned back, closed his eyes and sought refuge in a Bertha reverie. But nothing happened! He had proceeded through his usual steps: he focused upon the stage of his mind, he set the initial scene of the reverie, he was open to what would develop—that had always been up to Bertha to decide, not him—and he had stepped back waiting for the action to begin. But there was no action. Nothing moved. The stage remained a still-life awaiting his direction.

Experimenting, Breuer found he could now summon Bertha's image or dismiss her at will. When he called on her, she readily appeared in any form or posture he wished. But she no longer had autonomy: her image was frozen until he willed her to move. The fittings had come loose: his tie to her, her hold on him!

Breuer marveled at this transformation. Never before had he thought about Bertha with such *indifference*. No, not indifference—such calmness, such self-possession. There was no great passion or longing, but no rancor either. For the first time, he understood that he and Bertha were fellow sufferers. She was as trapped as he had been. She also had not become who she was. She had not chosen her life but instead was witness to the same scenes playing themselves endlessly.

In fact, as he thought about it, Breuer realized the full tragedy of Bertha's life. Perhaps she did not know these things. Perhaps she had forgone not only choice, but *awareness* as well. She so often was in "absence," in a trance, not even *experiencing* her life. He knew that in this matter Nietzsche had been wrong! *He was not Bertha's victim*. They were *both* victims.

How much he had learned! If only he could begin again and become her physician now. The day at Bellevue had shown him how evanescent had been the effects of his treatment. How foolish to have spent month after month attacking symptoms—the silly, superficial skirmishes—while neglecting the real battle, the mortal struggle underneath.

With a roar the train emerged from a long tunnel. The blast of bright sunlight snapped Breuer's attention back to his current predicament. He was returning to Vienna to see Eva Berger, his former nurse. He looked dazedly around the train compartment. I've done it again, he thought. Here I sit on the train, hurling myself toward Eva, yet confounded about when and how I made the decision to see her.

When he arrived in Vienna, he took a fiacre to Eva's home and approached her door.

It was four in the afternoon, and he almost turned away, certain—and then hoping—that she would be at work. But she *was* at home. She seemed shocked to see him and stood staring at him, not saying a word. When he asked if he could enter, she admitted him, after glancing uneasily at her neighbors' doors. He felt immediately comforted by her presence. Six months had passed since he had seen her, but it was easy as ever for him to unburden himself to her. He told her everything that had happened since he had dismissed her: his meeting with Nietzsche, his gradual transformation, his decision to claim his freedom and to leave Mathilde and the children, his silent, final encounter with Bertha.

"And now, Eva, I'm free. For the first time in my life, I can do anything, go anywhere I wish. Soon, probably right after we talk, I shall go to the train station and choose a destination. Even now I don't know where I'll head, perhaps south, toward the sun—perhaps Italy."

Eva, ordinarily an effusive woman who used to respond with paragraphs to his every sentence, was now strangely silent.

"Of course," Breuer continued, "I'll be lonely. You know how I am. But I'll be free to meet anyone I choose."

Still no response from Eva.

"Or invite an old friend to travel with me to Italy."

Breuer could not believe his own words. Suddenly he imagined a skyful of his pigeons swarming through his laboratory window, *back into* their wire cages.

To his dismay, but also relief, Eva did not respond to his innuendos. Instead, she began to question him.

"What kind of freedom do you mean? What do you mean by 'unlived life'?" She shook her head incredulously. "Josef, none of this makes much sense to me. I've always wished I had *your* freedom. What kind of freedom have *I* had? When you have to worry about the rent and the butcher's bill, you don't worry much about freedom. You want freedom from your profession? Look at *my* profession! When you fired me, I had to accept any job I could find, and right now the only freedom I wish for is the freedom not to work the night shift at the Vienna General Hospital."

The night shift! That's why she's home at this hour, Breuer thought.

"I offered to help you find another position. You didn't answer any of my messages."

"I was in shock," Eva replied. "I learned a hard lesson—that you can count on no one but yourself." Here, for the first time, she raised her glance and stared directly into Breuer's eyes.

Flushed with shame at not having protected her, he began to ask her forgiveness—but Eva rushed on, talking about her new job, her sister's wedding, her mother's health, and then her relationship with Gerhardt, the young lawyer whom she had first met when he was a patient at the hospital.

Breuer knew he was compromising her by his visit, and rose to leave. As he neared the door, he reached awkwardly for her hand and started to ask a question, but hesitated—did he still have the right to say anything familiar to her? He decided to risk it. Though it was obvious that the intimate bond between them was frayed, still, fifteen years of friendship are not so easily obliterated.

"Eva, I shall go now. But, please, one last question."

"Ask your question, Josef."

"I can't forget the times when we were close. Do you remember when, late one evening, we sat in my office and talked for an hour? I told you how desperately and irresistibly I felt drawn to Bertha. You said you were frightened for me, that you were my friend, that you didn't want me to ruin myself. Then you took my hand, as I'm taking yours now, and said that you would do *anything*, anything I wanted, if it would save me. Eva, I can't tell you how often, perhaps hundreds of times, I've relived that conversation, how much it has meant to me, how often I have regretted being so obsessed with Bertha that I did not respond more directly to you. And my question is—perhaps it is simply—Were you sincere? Should I have responded?"

Eva withdrew her hand, placed it lightly on his shoulder, and spoke haltingly. "Josef, I don't know what to say. I shall be honest—I am sorry to answer your question in this way, but for the sake of our old friendship I must be honest. Josef, I do not remember that conversation!"

Two hours later, Breuer found himself slumped in a second-class seat on the train to Italy.

He realized how important it had been for him, this last year, to have had Eva as insurance. He had counted on her. He had always been certain she would be there when he needed her. How could she have forgotten?

"But, Josef, what did you expect?" he asked himself. "That she'd be frozen in a closet, waiting for you to open the door and reanimate her? You're forty years old, time to understand that your women exist apart from you: they have a life of their own, they grow, they go on with their lives, they age, they make new relationships. Only the dead don't change. Only your mother, Bertha, lies suspended in time, waiting for you."

Suddenly the awful thought burst forth that it was not only Bertha's and Eva's lives that would go on, but Mathilde's as well—that she would exist without him, that the day would come when she would care for another. Mathilde, his Mathilde, with another man—that pain was hard to bear. Now his tears flowed. He looked up at the luggage rack for his valise. There it was, in easy reach, the brass handle stretching eagerly toward him. Yes, he knew precisely what he should do: grab the handle, lift the valise over the metal rail of the rack, pull it down, get off at the next stop, wherever it was, take the first train back to Vienna, and throw himself on Mathilde's mercy. It was not too late—surely, she would take him in.

But he imagined Nietzsche's powerful presence blocking him.

"Friedrich, how could I have given up everything? What a fool I was to have followed your advice!"

"You had already given up everything of importance before you ever met me, Josef. That was why you were in despair. Do you remember how you lamented the loss of the lad of infinite promise?"

"But now I have nothing."

"Nothing is everything! In order to grow strong you must first sink your roots deep into nothingness and learn to face your loneliest loneliness."

"My wife, my family! I love them. How could I have left them? I shall get off at the next stop."

"You flee only from yourself. Remember that every moment eternally recurs. Think of it: think of flying from your freedom for all eternity!"

"I have a duty to——"

"Only a duty to become who you are. Become strong: otherwise, you will forever use others for your own enlargement."

"But Mathilde. My vows! My duty to——"

"Duty, duty! You will perish from such small virtues. Learn to become wicked. Build a new self on the ashes of your old life."

All the way to Italy, Nietzsche's words pursued him.

"Eternal recurrence."

"The eternal hourglass of existence turning upside down, again and again."

"Let this idea take possession of you, and I promise that it will change you forever."

"Do you love the idea or hate it?"

"Live in such a way that you love the idea."

"Nietzsche's wager."

"Consummate your life."

"Die at the right time."

"The courage to change your convictions!"

"This life is your eternal life."

♦ ♦ ♦

Everything had begun, two months ago, in Venice. Now it was back to the city of gondolas he was heading. As the train crossed the Swiss-Italian border and conversations in Italian reached his ears, his thoughts turned from eternal possibility to tomorrow's reality.

Where should he go when he got off the train in Venice? Where would he sleep tonight? What would he do tomorrow? And the day after tomorrow? What would he do with his time? What did Nietzsche do? When he was not sick, he walked and thought and wrote. But that was *his* way. How———?

First, Breuer knew, he had to earn a living. The cash in his moneybelt would last for only a few weeks: thereafter the bank, at Max's instruction, would send him only a modest monthly draft. He could, of course, continue to doctor. At least three of his former students are practicing medicine in Venice. He should have no difficulty building a practice. Nor would the language present a problem: he had a good ear and some English, French, and Spanish; he could pick up Italian quickly. But had he sacrificed so much simply in order to reproduce his Viennese life in Venice? No, that life was behind him!

Perhaps some work in a restaurant. Because of his mother's death and his grandmother's frailty, Breuer had learned to cook and often assisted in the preparation of the family meals. Though Mathilde teased him and chased him out of the kitchen, when she was not around he used to wander in to observe and to instruct the cook. Yes, the more he thought about it, the stronger he felt that restaurant work might be just the thing. Not just managing or cashiering: he wanted to touch the food—to prepare it, to serve it.

He arrived late in Venice and again spent the night at a train-station hotel. In the morning, he took a gondola into the central city and walked and thought for hours. Many of the local Venetians turned to look at him. He understood why when he caught sight of his image in the reflection of a shop window: long beard, hat, coat, suit, tie—all in forbidding black. He looked foreign, precisely like an aging, wealthy Jewish Viennese medical consultant! Last night at the train station, he had noticed a cluster of Italian prostitutes soliciting customers. None had approached him, and no wonder! The beard and the funereal clothes would have to go.

Slowly his plan took shape: first, a visit to a barber and a working-class clothing store. Then he would begin intensive Italian instruction. Perhaps after two or three weeks, he could begin to explore the restaurant business:

Venice might need a good Austrian restaurant or even an Austrian-Jewish one—he had seen several synagogues during his walk.

The barber's dull razor jerked his head back and forth as it attacked his twenty-one-year-old beard. Occasionally it sheared off patches of beard cleanly, but more often it grabbed and tugged out divots of the wiry auburn hair. The barber was dour and impatient. Understandably so, Breuer thought. Sixty lira is too little for the size of this beard. Motioning to him to slow down, he reached in his pocket and offered two hundred lira for a gentler shave.

Twenty minutes later, as he stared into the barber's cracked mirror, a wave of compassion for his own face swept over him. In the decades since he had seen it, he had forgotten the battle with time it had been waging under the darkness of his beard. Naked now, he saw that it was weary and battered. Only his forehead and brows had held firm and were resolutely supporting the loose, defeated flaccid sheets of his facial flesh. An enormous crevice stretched out from each nostril to separate his cheeks from his lips. Smaller wrinkles spread down from both eyes. Turkey-gullet folds draped from his jaw. And his chin—he had forgotten that his beard had concealed the shame of his puny chin, which now, even weaker, hid timidly, as best it could, below his moist, hanging lower lip.

On his way to a clothing store, Breuer looked at the dress of passers-by and decided to purchase a heavy short navy coat, some solid boots, and a thick striped sweater. Yet everyone who passed him was younger than he. What did the older men wear? Where *were* they, anyway? Everyone seemed so young. How would he make friends? How would he meet women? Perhaps a waitress in the restaurant, or an Italian teacher. But, he thought, I don't want another woman! I'll never find a woman like Mathilde. I love her. This is insane. Why did I leave her? I'm too old to start over. I'm the oldest person on this street—perhaps that old woman there with the cane is older, or that stooped man selling vegetables. Suddenly he felt dizzy. He could barely stand. Behind him he heard a voice.

"Josef, Josef!"

Whose voice is that? It sounds familiar!

"Doctor Breuer! Josef Breuer!"

Who knows where I am?

"Josef, listen to me! I'm counting backward from ten to one. When I reach five, your eyes will open. When I reach one, you'll be fully awake. Ten, nine, eight, . . ."

I know that voice!

"Seven, six, five . . ."

His eyes opened. He looked up into Freud's smiling face.

"Four, three, two, one! You're wide awake! Now!"

Breuer was alarmed. "What's happened? Where am I, Sig?"

"Everything's all right, Josef. Wake up!" Freud's voice was firm but soothing.

"What's happened?"

"Give yourself a couple of minutes, Josef. It will all come back."

He saw he had been lying on the sofa in his library. He sat up. Again, he asked, "What's happened?"

"You tell *me* what happened, Josef. I did exactly as you instructed."

As Breuer still appeared dazed, Freud explained, "Don't you remember? You came over last night and asked me to be here this morning at eleven to assist you in a psychological experiment. When I arrived, you asked me to hypnotize you, using your watch as a pendulum."

Breuer reached into his waistcoat pocket.

"There it is, Josef, on the coffee table. Then, remember, you asked me to instruct you to sleep deeply and to visualize a series of experiences. You told me that the first part of the experiment would be devoted to leavetaking—from your family, friends, even patients; and that I should, if it seemed necessary, give you suggestions like: 'Say goodbye,' or 'You can't go home again.' The next part was to be devoted to establishing a new life, and I was to make suggestions like: 'Keep on going,' or 'What do you want to do next?' "

"Yes, yes, Sig, I'm waking up. It's all coming back to me. What time is it now?"

"One o'clock Sunday afternoon. You've been out for two hours, just as we planned. Everyone will be arriving soon for dinner."

"Tell me exactly what happened. What did you observe?"

"You quickly entered a trance, Josef, and for the most part stayed hypnotized. I could tell some active drama was being played out—but silently, in your own inner theater. There were two or three times when you seemed to be coming out of the trance, and I deepened it by suggesting you were traveling and feeling the rocking motion of the train, and that you put your head back into the seat cushion and fall deeper asleep. Each time, it seemed to be effective. I can't tell you much more. You seemed very unhappy; a couple of times you wept and once or twice looked frightened.

I asked if you wanted to stop, but you shook your head, so I kept urging you forward."

"Did I speak aloud?" Breuer rubbed his eyes, still trying to rouse himself.

"Rarely. Your lips moved a great deal, so I guessed you were imagining conversations. I could make out only a few words. Several times you called for Mathilde, and I also heard the name Bertha. Were you speaking of your daughter?"

Breuer hesitated. How to answer? He was tempted to tell Sig everything, yet his intuition warned him not to. After all, Sig was only twenty-six, and regarded him as a father or an older brother. Both were accustomed to that relationship, and Breuer was not prepared for the discomfort of abruptly altering it.

Furthermore, Breuer knew how inexperienced and narrow-minded his young friend was in matters involving love or carnality. He recalled how he had embarrassed and puzzled him recently by pronouncing that all neuroses begin in the marital bed! And just a few days ago, Sig had indignantly condemned the young Schnitzler for his erotic affairs. How much understanding, then, could Sig be expected to have for a forty-year-old husband infatuated with a twenty-one-year-old patient? Especially when Sig absolutely worshiped Mathilde! No, confiding in him would be an error. Better to talk to Max or Friedrich!

"My daughter? I'm not sure, Sig. I can't remember. But my mother's name also was Bertha, did you know that?"

"Oh yes, I forgot! But she died when you were very young, Josef. Why would you be saying goodbye to her now?"

"Perhaps I never really let her go before. I think some adult figures enter a child's mind and refuse to leave. Maybe one has to force them out before one can be master of one's own thoughts!"

"Hmm—interesting. Let's see, what else did you say? I heard, 'No more doctoring,' and then, just before I woke you, you said, 'Too old to start over!' Josef, I'm burning with curiosity. What does all this mean?"

Breuer chose his words carefully. "Here's what I can tell you, Sig. It's all related to that Professor Müller, Sig. He forced me to think about my life, and I realized I've reached a point where most of my choices are behind me. Yet I wondered what it would have been like to have chosen differently—to have lived another life without medicine, family, Viennese culture. So I tried a thought experiment to have the experience of freeing myself from these arbitrary constructs—to face formlessness, even to enter some alternative life."

"And what did you learn?"

"I'm still dazed. I'll need time to sort everything out. One thing I feel clear about is that it's important not to let your life live you. Otherwise, you end up at forty feeling you haven't really lived. What have I learned? Perhaps to live *now*, so that at fifty I won't look back upon my forties with regret. It's important for you, too. Everyone who knows you well, Sig, realizes that you have extraordinary gifts. You have a burden: the richer the soil, the more unforgivable the failure to cultivate it."

"You *are* different, Josef. Maybe the trance changed you. You never talked to me like this before. Thank you, your faith inspires me—but perhaps it burdens me, too."

"And I also learned," Breuer said, "—or maybe it's the same thing, I'm not sure—that we must live *as though* we were free. Even though we can't escape fate, we must still butt our heads against it—we must *will* our destiny to happen. We must love our fate. It's as though——"

There was a knock on the door.

"Are you two still in there?" asked Mathilde. "Can I come in?"

Breuer went quickly to open the door, and Mathilde entered with a plate of steaming, tiny wursts, each wrapped in flaky filo dough. "Your favorite, Josef. I realized this morning that I haven't made these for you in a long time. Dinner's ready. Max and Rachel are here, and the others are on the way. And Sigi, you're staying. I've already set your place. Your patients will wait another hour."

Taking his cue from Breuer's nod to him, Freud left the room. Breuer put his arm around Mathilde. "You know, my dear, it's strange you asked if we were still in the room. I'll tell you about our talk later, but it was like taking a distant journey. I feel I've been away for a very long time. And now I've come back."

"That's good, Josef." She put her hand on his cheek and rubbed his beard affectionately. "I am glad to welcome you back. I've missed you."

Dinner, by the Breuer family standards, was a small affair, with only nine adults at the table: Mathilde's parents; Ruth, another of Mathilde's sisters, and her husband, Meyer; Rachel and Max; and Freud. The eight children sat at a separate table in the foyer.

"Why are you looking at me?" Mathilde murmured to Breuer, as she carried out a large tureen of potato-carrot soup. "You're embarrassing me,

Josef," she whispered later, as she set down the large platter of braised veal tongue and raisins. "Stop it, Josef, stop staring!" she said again, as she helped to clear the table before bringing in dessert.

But Josef didn't stop. As if for the first time, he scrutinized his wife's face. It wrenched him to realize that she, too, was a combatant in the war against time. Her cheeks had no crevices—she had refused to permit that—but she could not defend all fronts, and a fine crinkling flared out from the corners of her eyes and mouth. Her hair, stretched up and back and swirled into a gleaming bun, had been heavily infiltrated by columns of gray. When had that happened? Was he partly to blame? United, he and she might have suffered less damage.

"Why should I stop?" Josef put his arm lightly around her waist, as she reached to take his plate. Later, he followed her into the kitchen. "Why shouldn't I look at you? I—but, Mathilde, I've made you cry!"

"A good cry, Josef. But sad, too, when I think of how long it's been. This whole day is strange. What did you and Sigi talk about, anyway? Do you know what he told me at dinner? That he's going to name his first daughter after me! He says he wants to have two Mathildes in his life."

"We've always suspected Sig was clever, and now we are certain. It *is* a strange day. But an important one—I've decided to marry you."

Mathilde set down her tray of coffee cups, put her hands on his head, and drew him to her, kissing his forehead. "Did you drink schnapps, Josef? You're talking nonsense." She picked up the tray again. "But I like it." Just before pushing open the swinging door into the dining room, she turned. "I thought you decided to marry me fourteen years ago."

"What's important is that I choose to do it *today*, Mathilde. And every day."

After coffee and Mathilde's *Linzertorte*, Freud hurried off to the hospital. Breuer and Max each took a glass of slivovitz into the library and sat down to chess. After a mercifully short game—Max quickly crushing a French defense with a withering queen's side attack—Breuer stayed Max's hand as he started to set up the next game. "I need to talk," he told his brother-in-law. Max quickly overcame his disappointment, put away the chess pieces, lit another cigar, blew out a long fume of smoke, and waited.

Since their brief contretemps a couple of weeks before, when Breuer had first told Max about Nietzsche, the two men had grown much closer. Now a patient and sympathetic listener, Max had over the past two weeks followed Breuer's accounts of his meetings with Eckart Müller with great interest. Today he seemed transfixed by Breuer's detailed description of yesterday's cemetery discussion and this morning's extraordinary trance session.

"So, in your trance you first thought I'd try to block the door to stop you from leaving? I probably would have. Who else would I have to beat at chess? But seriously, Josef, you look different. You really think you've gotten Bertha out of your mind?"

"It's amazing, Max. Now I can think about her as I think of anyone else. It's as though I've had surgery to separate Bertha's image from all the emotion that used to adhere to it! And I'm absolutely certain that this surgery occurred the moment I observed her in the garden with her new doctor!"

"I don't understand." Max shook his head. "Or is it best not to understand?"

"We have to try. Maybe it's wrong to say that my infatuation with Bertha died the moment I observed her with Doctor Durkin—I mean my *fantasy* of her with Doctor Durkin, which is so vivid I regard it still as a real event. I'm sure the infatuation had already been weakened by Müller, especially by his making me understand how I had given her such enormous power. The trance fantasy of Bertha and Doctor Durkin came along at the opportune time to dislodge it completely. All her power disappeared when I saw her repeating those familiar scenes with him, as if by rote. Suddenly I realized she has no power. She can't control her own actions—in fact, she's just as helpless and driven as I was. We were both just fill-in performers in each other's obsessive drama, Max."

Breuer grinned. "But, you know, something even more important is happening to me, and that's my change in feelings for Mathilde. I felt it a little during the trance, but it's settling in even more strongly now. All during dinner I looked at her and kept feeling this surge of warmth toward her."

"Yes," Max smiled, "I saw you looking at her. It was fun to see Mathilde flustered. It was like the old days to see some play between the two of you. Maybe it's very simple: you appreciate her now because you got close to experiencing what it would be like to lose her."

"Yes, that's part of it, but there are other parts, too. You know, for years, I've bridled at the bit I thought Mathilde had placed in my mouth. I felt imprisoned by her and longed for my freedom—to experience other women, to have another, entirely different life.

"Yet when I did what Müller asked me to do, when I grasped my freedom, I panicked. In the trance, I tried to give freedom away. I held out the bit, first to Bertha and then to Eva. I opened my mouth and said, 'Please, please, bridle me. Jam this into my mouth. I don't want to be free.' The truth is, I was terrified of freedom."

Max nodded gravely.

"Remember," Breuer continued, "what I told you of my trance visit to Venice—the barbershop where I discovered my aging face? The street of clothing stores where I found myself the oldest person? Something Müller said comes back right now: *'Choose the right enemy.'* I think that's the key! All these years I've been fighting the wrong enemy. The real enemy was, all along, not Mathilde, but destiny. The real enemy was aging, death, and my own terror of freedom. I blamed Mathilde for not allowing me to face what I was really unwilling to face! I wonder how many other husbands do that to their wives?"

"I expect I'm one of them," Max said. "You know, I often daydream about our childhood together, our days at the university. 'Ah, what a loss!' I say to myself. 'How did I ever let those times slip away?' And then secretly I blame Rachel—as if it were *her* fault that childhood ends, *her* fault that I grow old!"

"Yes, Müller said that the real enemy is 'time's devouring jaws.' But somehow now I don't feel so helpless before those jaws. Today, perhaps for the first time, I feel like I'm *willing* my life. I accept the life I've chosen. Right now, Max, I don't wish I had done anything differently."

"As clever as your professor is, Josef, it seems to me that in designing this trance experiment you outwitted him. You found a way to experience an irreversible decision without making it irreversible. But there's something I still don't understand. Where was the part of you that designed the trance experiment *during* the trance? While you were *in* the trance, some part of you must have been aware of what was really happening."

"You're right, Max. Where was the witness, the 'I' that was tricking the rest of my 'me'? I get dizzy thinking about it. Someday someone far brighter than I will come along to unravel that conundrum. But, no, I don't think I have outwitted Müller. In fact, I feel something quite different: I feel I've let him down. I've refused to follow his prescription. Or perhaps, simply, I've acknowledged my limitations. He often says, 'Every person must choose how much truth he can stand.' I guess I've chosen.

And, Max, I've also let him down as a physician. I've given him nothing. In fact, I no longer even think of helping him."

"Don't knock yourself, Josef. You're always so hard on yourself. You're different from him. Do you remember that course we took together on religious thinkers—Professor Jodl, wasn't it?—and the term he had for them—'visionaries.' That's what your Müller is—a visionary! I've long lost sight of who's the physician and who's the patient, but if you *were* his physician, and even if you *could* change him—and you can't—would you *want* to change him? Have you ever heard of a married or domesticated visionary? No, it would ruin him. I think his destiny is to be a lonely seer.

"You know what I think?" Max opened the box of chess pieces. "I think there's been enough treatment. Maybe it's over. Maybe a little more of this treatment would kill both the patient and the doctor!"

AX WAS RIGHT. It *was* time to stop. Even so, Josef astonished himself when on Monday morning he walked into room 13 and declared himself fully recovered.

Nietzsche, sitting on his bed grooming his mustache, appeared even more astonished.

"Recovered?" he exclaimed, dropping his tortoiseshell mustache comb on the bed. "Can this be true? How is it possible? You seemed in such distress when we parted on Saturday. I worried about you. Had I been too hard? Too challenging? I wondered if you would discontinue our treatment project. I wondered many things, but never once did I expect to hear that you were fully recovered!"

"Yes, Friedrich, I, too, am surprised. It happened suddenly—a direct result of our session yesterday."

"Yesterday? But yesterday was Sunday. We had no session."

"We had a session, Friedrich. Only you weren't there! It's a long story."

"Tell me that story," said Nietzsche, as he rose from the bed. "Tell me every detail! I want to learn about recovery."

"Here, to our talking chairs," said Breuer, taking his accustomed place.

"There's so much to tell . . ." he began, while next to him Nietzsche leaned forward eagerly, literally on the edge of his chair.

"Begin with Saturday afternoon," Nietzsche said quickly, "after our walk in the Simmeringer Haide."

"Yes, that wild walk in the wind! That walk was wonderful. And terrible! You're right—when we returned to the fiacre, I was in great distress. I felt like an anvil: your words were hammer blows. Long afterward, they still reverberated, especially one phrase."

"Which was———"

"That *the only way I could save my marriage was to give it up*. One of your more confusing pronouncements: the more I thought about it, the dizzier I got!"

"Then I should have been more clear, Josef. I meant only to say that an ideal marriage relationship exists only when it is not *necessary* for each person's survival."

Seeing no sign of enlightenment on Breuer's face, Nietzsche added, "I meant only that, to fully relate to another, one must first relate to oneself. If we cannot embrace our own aloneness, we will simply use the other as a shield against isolation. Only when one can live like the eagle—with no audience whatsoever—can one turn to another in love; only then is one able to care about the enlargement of the other's being. *Ergo, if one is unable to give up a marriage, then the marriage is doomed.*"

"So, you mean, Friedrich, that the only way to save the marriage is *to be able* to give it up? That's clearer." Breuer thought for a moment. "That edict is wonderfully instructive for a bachelor, but it presents a monumental quandary for the married man. What use can I make of it? It's like attempting to rebuild a ship at sea. For a long time on Saturday, I was staggered by the paradox of having to irretrievably give up my marriage in order to save it. Then, suddenly, I had an inspiration."

Nietzsche, his curiosity ignited, took off his spectacles and leaned perilously forward. Another inch or two, Breuer thought, and he'll slip right off the chair. "How much do you know about hypnosis?"

"Animal magnetism? Mesmerism? Very little," Nietzsche replied. "I know that Mesmer himself was a scoundrel, but a short time ago I read that several well-known French doctors are now using mesmerism to treat many different medical ailments. And, of course, you employed it in your treatment of Bertha. I understand only that it's a sleeplike state in which one becomes highly suggestible."

"More than that, Friedrich. It's a state in which one is capable of experiencing intensely vivid hallucinatory phenomena. My inspiration was that in a hypnotic trance I could approximate the *experience* of giving up my marriage and yet, in real life, preserve it."

Breuer proceeded to tell Nietzsche everything that had happened to him. Almost everything! He started to describe his observation of Bertha and Dr. Durkin in the Bellevue garden, but suddenly decided to keep that secret. Instead, he described only the journey to the Bellevue Sanatorium and his impulsive departure.

Nietzsche listened, his head nodding faster and faster, his eyes bulging with concentration. When Breuer's narrative ended, he sat silently, as though disappointed.

"Friedrich, are you at a loss for words? It's the first time. I, too, am confused, but I do know I feel good today. Alive. Better than I have felt in years! I feel *present*—here with you, rather than *pretending* to be here, while secretly thinking of Bertha."

Nietzsche was still listening intensely, but said nothing.

Breuer continued, "Friedrich, I feel sadness, too. I hate to think our talks will end. You know more about me than anyone in the world, and I treasure the bond between us. And I have another feeling—shame! Despite my recovery, I am ashamed. I feel that, by using hypnosis, I've tricked you. I've taken a risk-free risk! You must be disappointed with me."

Nietzsche vigorously shook his head. "No. Not at all."

"I know your standards," Breuer protested. "You *must* feel I've fallen short! More than once I've heard you ask, 'How much truth can you stand?' I know that's how you measure a person. I'm afraid *my* answer is, 'Not very much!' Even in my trance, I fell short. I imagined trying to follow you to Italy, to go as far as you, as far as you wished me to—but my courage flagged."

Continuing to shake his head, Nietzsche leaned forward, rested his hand on the arm of Breuer's chair, and said, "No, Josef, you went far—farther than most."

"Perhaps as far as the farthest limits of my limited ability," Breuer responded. "You always said I must find my own way and not search for *the* way or *your* way. Perhaps work, community, family are my way to a meaningful life. Still, I feel I've fallen short, that I've settled for comfort, that I cannot stare at the sun of truth as you do."

"And I, at times, wish I could find the shade."

Nietzsche's voice was sad and wistful. His deep sighs reminded Breuer that two patients were involved in their treatment contract, and that only one had been helped. Perhaps, Breuer thought, it's not too late.

"Though I pronounce myself healed, Friedrich, I don't want to stop meeting with you."

Nietzsche shook his head slowly and determinedly. "No. It has run its course. It's time."

"It would be selfish to stop," said Breuer. "I've taken so much and given you little in return. Yet I also know I've had little opportunity to give help—you've been too uncooperative even to have a migraine."

"The best gift would be to help me understand recovery."

"I believe," Breuer responded, "that the most powerful factor was my identification of the right enemy. Once I understood that I must wrestle with the *real* enemy—time, aging, death—then I came to realize that Mathilde is neither adversary nor rescuer, but simply a fellow traveler trudging through the cycle of life. Somehow that simple step released all my fettered love for her. Today, Friedrich, I love the idea of repeating my life eternally. Finally, I feel I can say, 'Yes, I *have* chosen my life. And chosen well.' "

"Yes, yes," said Nietzsche, hurrying Breuer along. "I understand you've changed. But I want to know the *mechanism—how* it happened!"

"I can only say that in the last two years I was very frightened by my own aging or, as you put it, by 'time's appetite.' I fought back—but blindly. I attacked my wife rather than the real enemy and finally, in desperation, sought rescue in the arms of one who had no rescue to give."

Breuer paused, scratching his head. "I don't know what else to say except that, thanks to you, I know that the key to living well is *first to will that which is necessary and then to love that which is willed.*"

Overcoming his agitation, Nietzsche was struck by Breuer's words.

"*Amor fati*—love your fate. It's eerie, Josef, how twin-minded we are! I had planned to make *Amor fati* my next, and final, lesson in your instruction. I was going to teach you to overcome despair by transforming '*thus it was*' into '*thus I willed it.*' But you've anticipated me. You've grown strong, perhaps even ripe—but"—he paused, suddenly agitated, "this Bertha who invaded and possessed your mind, who gave you no peace— you haven't told me how you banished her."

"It's not important, Friedrich. It's more important for me to stop grieving for the past and——"

"You said you wanted to give me something. Remember?" Nietzsche cried, his desperate tone alarming Breuer. "Then give me something concrete. *Tell me how you cast her out!* I want every detail!"

Only two weeks ago, Breuer recalled, it was I who was pleading to Nietzsche for explicit steps to follow, and Nietzsche who was insisting on there being no *the* way, that each person has to find his own truth. Nietzsche's suffering must be terrible indeed for him now to be denying his own teaching and hoping to find in my healing the precise path to his own. Such a request, Breuer resolved, must not be granted.

"I want nothing more, Friedrich," he said, "than to give you something—but it must be a gift of real substance. There is urgency in your voice, but you conceal your true wishes. Trust me, this one time! Tell me exactly what you want. If it's in my power to give, it shall be yours."

Jumping out of his chair, Nietzsche paced back and forth for a few minutes, then went to the window and stood, looking out, his back to Breuer.

"A deep man needs friends," he began, as if speaking more to himself than to Breuer. "All else failing, he still has his gods. But I have neither friends nor gods. I, like you, have lusts, and no greater lust than for the perfect friendship, a friendship *inter pares*—among equals. What intoxicating words, *inter pares,* words containing so much comfort and hope for one such as me, who has always been alone, who has always sought but never met one who belonged precisely to him.

"Sometimes I have unburdened myself in letters, to my sister, to friends. But when I meet others face to face I am ashamed and turn away."

"Just as you turn away from me now?" Breuer interrupted.

"Yes." And Nietzsche fell silent.

"Do you have something to unburden now, Friedrich?"

Nietzsche, still gazing out the window, shook his head. "On the rare occasions when I have been overcome with loneliness and given vent to public outbursts of misery, I have loathed myself an hour later and grown strange to myself, as if I'd fallen from my own company.

"Nor have I ever allowed others to unburden themselves to me—I was unwilling to incur the debt of reciprocation. I avoided all this—until the day, of course"—he turned to face Breuer—"that I shook your hand and agreed to our strange contract. You are the first person with whom I have ever stayed the course. And even with you, at first, I anticipated betrayal."

"And then?"

"In the beginning," Nietzsche replied, "I was embarrassed for you—never had I heard such candid revelations. Next I grew impatient, then critical and judgmental. Later I turned again: I grew to admire your courage and honesty. Turning still further, I felt touched by your trust in me. And now, today, I am left with great melancholy at the thought of leaving you. I dreamed of you last night—a sad dream."

"What was your dream, Friedrich?"

Returning from the window, Nietzsche sat and faced Breuer. "In the dream, I wake up here in the clinic. It is dark and cold. Everyone is gone. I want to find you. I light a lamp and search in vain through empty room after empty room. Then I descend the stairs to the common room where I see a strange sight: a fire—not in the fireplace, but a neat wood fire in the center of the room—and around that fire are eight tall stones, sitting as if they are warming themselves. Suddenly I feel tremendous sadness and start to weep. That's when I really woke up."

"A strange dream," Breuer said. "Any ideas about it?"

"I have just a feeling of great sadness, a deep longing. I've never wept in a dream before. Can you help?"

Breuer silently repeated Nietzsche's simple phrase, "Can you help?" It was what he had longed for. Three weeks ago could he ever have imagined such words from Nietzsche? He must not waste this opportunity.

"Eight stones warmed by the fire," he replied. "A curious image. Let me tell you what occurs to me. You remember, of course, your severe migraine in Herr Schlegel's *Gasthaus?*"

Nietzsche nodded. "Most of it. For some of it, I was not present!"

"There's something I haven't told you," Breuer said. "When you were comatose, you uttered some sad phrases. One of them was, 'No slot, no slot.'"

Nietzsche looked blank. "'No slot'? What could I have meant?"

"I think 'no slot' meant that you had no place in any friendship or any community. I think, Friedrich, you long for a hearth but fear your longing!"

Breuer softened his voice. "This must be a lonely time of the year for you. Already many of the other patients here are leaving to rejoin their families for the Christmas holidays. Perhaps that's why the rooms are empty in your dream. When searching for me, you find a fire warming eight stones. I think I know what that means: around my hearth my family is seven—my five children, my wife, and I. Might you not be the eighth stone? Perhaps the dream is a wish for my friendship and my hearth. If so, I welcome you."

Breuer leaned forward to clasp Nietzsche's arm. "Come home with me,

Friedrich. Even though my despair is alleviated, we have no need to part. Be my guest for the holiday season—or better, stay for the entire winter. It would give me the greatest pleasure."

Nietzsche rested his hand on top of Breuer's for a moment—just for a moment. Then he rose and walked again to the window. Rain, driven by the northeastern wind, violently lashed the glass. He turned.

"Thank you, my friend, for inviting me into your home. Yet I cannot accept."

"But why? I'm convinced it would benefit you, Friedrich, and me as well. I have an empty room about the size of this one. And a library in which you could write."

Nietzsche shook his head gently but firmly. "A few minutes ago when you said you had gone to the outermost limits of your limited ability, you were referring to facing isolation. I, too, face my limits—the limits of relatedness. Here, with you, even now as we talk face to face, soul to soul, I abut against these limits."

"Limits can be stretched, Friedrich. Let us try!"

Nietzsche paced back and forth. "The moment I say, 'I cannot bear loneliness any longer,' I fall to untold depths in my own estimation—for I've deserted the highest that is in me. My appointed path requires me to resist the dangers that may lure me away."

"But, Friedrich, joining another is not the same as abandoning yourself! Once you said there was much you could learn from me about relationships. Then allow me to teach you! At times it's right to be suspicious and vigilant, but at other times one must be able to relax one's guard and permit oneself to be touched." He stretched his arm out to him. "Come, Friedrich, sit."

Obediently, Nietzsche returned to his chair and, closing his eyes, took several deep breaths. Then he opened his eyes and plunged. "The problem, Josef, is not that you might betray me: it is that *I* have been betraying *you*. I've been dishonest with you. And now, as you invite me into your home, as we grow closer, my deceit eats away at me. It is time to change that! No more deceit between us! Permit me to unburden myself. Hear my confession, my friend."

Turning his head away, Nietzsche fixed his gaze on a small floral cluster in the Kashan rug and, in a quavering voice, began. "Several months ago, I became deeply involved with a remarkable young Russian woman named Lou Salomé. Before then I had never allowed myself to love a woman.

Perhaps because I was inundated with women early in life. After my father died, I was surrounded by cold, distant women—my mother, my sister, my grandmother and aunts. Some deep noxious attitudes must have been laid down because ever since I have regarded with horror a liaison with a woman. Sensuality—a woman's flesh—seems to me the ultimate distraction, a barrier between me and my life mission. But Lou Salomé was different, or so I thought. Though she was beautiful, she also appeared a true soulmate, my twin brain. She understood me, pointed me in new directions—toward dizzying heights I had never before had the courage to explore. I thought she would be my student, my protégée, my disciple.

"But then, catastrophe! My lust emerged. She used it to play me off against Paul Rée, my close friend who had first introduced us. She led me to believe I was the man for whom she was destined, but when I offered myself, she spurned me. I was betrayed by everyone—by her, by Rée, and by my sister, who attempted to destroy our relationship. Now everything has turned to ashes, and I live in exile from all whom I once held dear."

"When you and I first talked," Breuer interjected, "you alluded to *three* betrayals."

"The first was Richard Wagner, who betrayed me long ago. That sting has now faded. The others were Lou Salomé and Paul Rée. Yes, I *did* allude to them. But I pretended that I had resolved the crisis. *That* was my deception. The truth is that I have never, *even to this moment,* resolved it. This woman, this Lou Salomé, invaded my mind and set up housekeeping there. I still cannot dislodge her. Not a day passes, sometimes not an hour, without my thinking of her. Most of the time I hate her. I think of striking out at her, of publicly humiliating her. I want to see her grovel, beg me to take her back! Sometimes the opposite—I long for her, I think of taking her hand, of our sailing on Lake Orta, of greeting an Adriatic sunrise together——"

"She is your Bertha!"

"Yes, she is my Bertha! Whenever you described your obsession, whenever you tried to root it out from your mind, whenever you tried to understand its meaning, you were speaking for me as well! You were doing double work—mine as well as yours! I concealed myself—like a woman—then crawled out after you had left, placed my feet in your footprints, and attempted to follow your path. Coward that I was, I crouched behind you and allowed you alone to face the dangers and humiliations of the trail."

Tears were running down Nietzsche's cheeks, and he wiped them dry with a handkerchief.

Now he raised his head and faced Breuer directly. "*That* is my confession and my shame. Now you understand my intense interest in your liberation. Your liberation can be *my* liberation. Now you know why it is important for me to know precisely how you cleansed Bertha from your mind! *Now* will you tell me?"

But Breuer shook his head. "My trance experience is now hazy. But even if I were able to recall precise details, what value would they be to you, Friedrich? You yourself told me that there is no *the* way, that the only great truth is the truth we discover for ourselves."

Bowing his head, Nietzsche whispered, "Yes, yes, you are right."

Breuer cleared his throat and took a deep breath. "I can't tell you what you wish to hear, but, Friedrich"—he paused, his heart racing. Now it was his turn to plunge—"there *is* something I must tell you. I, too, have not been honest, and it is time now for *me* to confess."

Breuer had a sudden awful premonition that, no matter what he said or did, Nietzsche would regard this as the fourth great betrayal in his life. Yet it was too late to turn back.

"I fear, Friedrich, that this confession may cost me your friendship. I pray it does not. Please believe that I confess out of devotion, for I cannot bear the thought of your learning from another what I am about to say, of your feeling once again—a fourth time—betrayed."

Nietzsche's face froze into deathmask stillness. He sucked in his breath as Breuer began: "In October, a few weeks before you and I first met, I took a brief holiday with Mathilde to Venice, where there was a strange note waiting for me at the hotel."

Reaching into his jacket pocket, Breuer handed Nietzsche Lou Salomé's note. He watched Nietzsche's eyes widen in disbelief as he read.

21 October 1882

Doctor Breuer,

I must see you on a matter of great urgency. The future of German philosophy hangs in the balance. Meet me at nine tomorrow morning at the Café Sorrento.

Lou Salomé

Holding the note in his trembling hand, Nietzsche stammered, "I don't understand. What—what——"

"Sit back, Friedrich, it's a long story, and I must tell it from the beginning."

For the next twenty minutes, Breuer related everything—the meetings with Lou Salomé; her learning about Anna O.'s treatment from her brother, Jenia; her plea on Nietzsche's behalf; and his own agreeing to her request for help.

"You must be wondering, Friedrich, whether a physician has ever agreed to a more bizarre consultation. Indeed, when I look back on my talk with Lou Salomé, I find it hard to believe I agreed to her request. Imagine! She was asking me to invent a treatment for a nonmedical ailment and to apply it surreptitiously to an unwilling patient. But somehow she persuaded me. In fact, she regarded herself a full partner in this endeavor and, in our last meeting, demanded a report of the progress of 'our' patient."

"What!" exclaimed Nietzsche. "You saw her recently?"

"She appeared unannounced in my office a few days ago, and insisted I provide her with information about the progress of the treatment. Of course, I gave her nothing, and she left in a huff."

Breuer continued, revealing all his perceptions about the course of their work together: his frustrated attempts to help Nietzsche; his knowing that Nietzsche concealed his despair about the loss of Lou Salomé. He even shared his master plan—how he pretended to seek treatment for his own despair in order to keep Nietzsche in Vienna.

Nietzsche jerked upright at this revelation. "So, all this has been pretense?"

"At first," Breuer acknowledged. "My plan was to 'handle' you, to play the cooperative patient while I gradually reversed the roles and eased *you* into becoming a patient. But then the real irony occurred when I *became* my role, when my pretense of patienthood became reality."

What else was there to tell? Searching his mind for other details, Breuer found none. He had confessed all.

Eyes closed, Nietzsche bowed his head and clutched it with both hands.

"Friedrich, are you all right?" asked Breuer in concern.

"My head—I'm seeing flashing lights—both eyes! My visual aura——"

Breuer immediately assumed his professional persona. "A migraine is trying to materialize. At this stage, we can stop it. The best thing is caffeine and ergotamine. Don't move! I'll be right back."

Rushing from the room, he dashed downstairs to the central nursing desk and then to the kitchen. He returned in a few minutes carrying a tray with a cup, a pot of strong coffee, water, and some tablets. "First, swallow these pills—ergot and some magnesium salts to protect your stomach from the coffee. Then I want you to drink this entire pot of coffee."

Once Nietzsche swallowed the pills, Breuer asked, "Do you want to lie down?"

"No, no, we must talk this through!"

"Lean your head back in your chair. I'll darken the room. The less visual stimulation, the better." Breuer lowered the shades on the three windows and then prepared a cold wet compress, which he draped over Nietzsche's eyes. They sat silent for a few minutes in the dusk. Then Nietzsche spoke, his voice hushed.

"So Byzantine, Josef—everything between us—all so Byzantine, so dishonest, so doubly dishonest!"

"What else could I have done?" Breuer spoke softly and slowly so as not to rouse the migraine. "Perhaps I should never have agreed in the first place. Should I have told you earlier? You would have turned on your heel and walked away forever!"

No response.

"Not true?" Breuer asked.

"Yes, I'd have caught the next train out of Vienna. But you lied to me. You made promises to me——"

"And I honored every promise, Friedrich. I promised to conceal your name, and I kept that promise. And when Lou Salomé inquired about you—*demanded to know* is more accurate—I refused to speak of you. I refused even to let her know we were meeting. And one other promise I kept, Friedrich. Remember I said that when you were comatose you uttered some phrases?"

Nietzsche nodded.

"The other phrase was 'Help me!' You repeated it over and over."

" 'Help me!' I said *that*?"

"Again and again! Keep drinking, Friedrich."

Nietzsche having emptied his cup, Breuer filled it once more with the thick black coffee.

"I remember nothing. Neither 'Help me' nor that other phrase, 'No slot'—that wasn't *me* talking."

"But it was your voice, Friedrich. Some part of you spoke to me, and

I gave *that* 'you' my promise to help. *And I never betrayed that promise.* Drink some more coffee. Four full cups is my prescription."

As Nietzsche drank the bitter coffee, Breuer rearranged the cold compress on his brow. "How does your head feel? The flashing lights? Do you want to stop talking for a while and rest?"

"I'm better, much better," said Nietzsche in a weak voice. "No, I don't want to stop. Stopping would agitate me more than talking. I'm used to working while feeling like this. But first let me try to relax the muscles in my temples and scalp." For three or four minutes, he breathed slowly and deeply while counting softly, and then spoke. "There, that's better. Often I count my breaths and imagine my muscles relaxing with each count. Sometimes I keep focused by concentrating only on the breathing. Have you ever noticed that the air you breathe in is always cooler than the air you breathe out?"

Breuer watched and waited. Thank God for the migraine! he thought. It forces Nietzsche, even for a short time, to remain where he is. Under the cold compress, only his mouth was visible. The mustache quivered as if he were on the verge of saying something and then, apparently, thought better of it.

Finally, Nietzsche smiled. "You thought to manipulate me, and all the while I thought I was manipulating you."

"But, Friedrich, what was conceived in manipulation has now been delivered into honesty."

"And—ach!—behind everything there was Lou Salomé, in her favorite position, holding the reins, whip in hand, controlling both of us. You've told me a great deal, Josef, but one thing you've left out."

Breuer stretched out his hands, palms up. "I have nothing more to hide."

"Your motives! All of this—this plotting, this deviousness, the time consumed, the energy. You're a busy physician. Why did you do this? Why did you ever agree to become involved?"

"That's a question I have often asked myself," said Breuer. "I don't know the answer other than to say it was to please Lou Salomé. Somehow she enchanted me. I could not refuse her."

"Yet you refused her the last time she appeared in your office."

"Yes—but by then I had met you, made promises to you. Believe me, Friedrich, she was not pleased."

"I salute you for standing up to her—you did something I never could. But tell me, at the beginning, in Venice, *how* did she enchant you?"

"I'm not sure I can answer that. I only know that after half an hour with her I felt I could refuse her nothing."

"Yes, she had the same effect on me."

"You should have seen the bold way she strode to my table in the café."

"I know that walk," said Nietzsche. "Her imperial Roman march. She doesn't bother to watch for obstacles, as though nothing would dare block her path."

"Yes, and such an air of unmistakable confidence! And something so free about her—her clothes, her hair, her dress. She's entirely released from convention."

Nietzsche nodded. "Yes, her freedom is striking—and admirable! In that one thing we can all learn from her." He slowly turned his head and appeared pleased at the absence of pain. "I've sometimes thought of Lou Salomé as a mutation, especially when one considers that her freedom blossomed in the midst of a dense bourgeois thicket. Her father was a Russian general, you know." He looked sharply at Breuer. "I imagine she was immediately personal with you? Suggested you call her by her first name?"

"Exactly. And she gazed directly into my eyes and touched my hand as we spoke."

"Oh yes, that sounds familiar. The first time we met, Josef, she disarmed me completely by taking my arm when I was leaving and offering to walk me back to my hotel."

"She did precisely the same thing with me!"

Nietzsche stiffened, but went on. "She told me that she didn't want to leave me so quickly, that she had to have more time with me."

"Her precise words to me, Friedrich. And then she bristled when I suggested my wife might be unsettled by seeing me walking with a young woman."

Nietzsche chuckled. "I know how she'd have reacted to that. She doesn't look kindly on conventional marriage—she considers it a euphemism for female indenture."

"Her very words to me!"

Nietzsche slumped down in the chair. "She flaunts all convention, except one—when it comes to men and sex, she's as chaste as a Carmelite!"

Breuer nodded. "Yes, but I think perhaps we misinterpret the messages she sends. She's a young girl, a child, unaware of the impact of her beauty upon men."

"There we disagree, Josef. She is entirely aware of her beauty. She uses it to dominate, to suck men dry, and then move on to the next one."

Breuer pressed on. "Another thing—she flaunts convention with such charm that one can't help becoming an accomplice. I surprised myself by agreeing to read a letter Wagner wrote you, even though I suspected she had no right to possess it!"

"What! A letter from Wagner? I never noticed one was missing. She must have taken it during her Tautenberg visit. Nothing is beneath her!"

"She even showed me some of *your* letters, Friedrich. I felt immediately drawn into her deepest confidence." Here Breuer felt he was taking perhaps the greatest risk of all.

Nietzsche jerked upright. The cold compress fell from his eyes. "She showed you *my* letters? That vixen!"

"Please, Friedrich, let's not awaken the migraine. Here, drink this last cup and then lean back and let me replace the compress."

"All right, Doctor, on these matters I follow your advice. But I think the danger is over—the visual flashes have disappeared. Your drug must be taking effect."

Nietzsche drank the remaining lukewarm coffee in one swallow. "Finished—enough of that—that's more coffee than I drink in six months!" After slowly twisting his head around, he handed Breuer the compress. "I don't need this now. My attack seems to be gone. Amazing! Without your help it would have progressed into several days of torment. A pity"—he ventured a glance at Breuer—"I can't carry you with me!"

Breuer nodded.

"But how *dare* she show you my letters, Josef! And how *could* you have read them?"

Breuer opened his mouth, but Nietzsche held up his hand to silence him. "No need to answer. I understand your position, even the way you felt flattered by being chosen as her confidant. I had the identical reaction when she showed me love letters from Rée and from Gillot, one of her teachers in Russia who also fell in love with her."

"Still," Breuer said, "it must be painful for you, I know. I would be devastated to learn that Bertha had shared our most intimate moments with another man."

"It *is* painful. Yet it's good medicine. Tell me everything else about your meeting with Lou. Spare me nothing!"

Now Breuer knew why he had not told Nietzsche about his trance vision of Bertha walking with Dr. Durkin. That powerful emotional experience had released him from her. And that was precisely what Nietzsche needed—not a description of someone else's experience, not an intellectual understanding, but his own emotional experience, strong enough to rip away the illusory meanings he had heaped upon this twenty-one-year-old Russian woman.

And what more powerful emotional experience than for Nietzsche to "eavesdrop" upon Lou Salomé as she entranced another man with the same artifices she had once turned on him? Accordingly, Breuer searched his memory for every minute detail of his encounter with her. He began to recount to Nietzsche her words: her wish to become his student and protégée, her flattery, and her desire to include Breuer in her collection of great minds. He described her actions: her preening, her turning her head first one way, then the other, her smile, her cocked head, her open and adoring gaze, the play of her tongue as she moistened her lips, the touch of her hand as she rested it on his.

Listening with his great head rolled back, his deep eyes closed, Nietzsche seemed overcome by emotion.

"Friedrich, what were you feeling as I spoke?"

"So many things, Josef."

"Describe them to me."

"Too much to make sense of."

"Don't try. Just chimneysweep."

Nietzsche opened his eyes and looked at Breuer, as though to reassure himself that there would be no further duplicity.

"Do it," Breuer urged. "Consider it a physician's orders. I am well acquainted with someone similarly afflicted who says it helped."

Haltingly, Nietzsche began. "As you talked about Lou, I remembered my own experiences with her, my own impressions—identical—uncannily identical. She was the same with you as she was with me—I feel stripped of all those pungent moments, those sacred memories."

He opened his eyes. "It's hard to let your thoughts talk—embarrassing!"

"Trust me, I can personally testify that embarrassment is rarely fatal! Go on! Be hard by being tender!"

"I trust you. I know you speak from strength. I feel——" Nietzsche stopped, his face flushed.

Breuer urged him on. "Close your eyes again. Perhaps it will be easier to talk without looking at me. Or lie down on the bed."

"No, I'll stay here. What I wanted to say is that I'm glad you met Lou. Now you know me. And I feel a kinship with you. But at the same time, I feel anger, outrage." Nietzsche opened his eyes as if to ascertain that he had not offended Breuer, and then he continued, in a soft voice, "I feel outraged by your desecration. You've trampled on my love, ground it into the dust. It's painful, right here." He tapped his fist upon his chest.

"I know that spot, Friedrich. I, too, felt that pain. Remember how upset I got every time you called Bertha a cripple? Remember——"

"Today I am the anvil," Nietzsche interrupted, "and it is *your* words that are hammer blows—crumbling the citadel of my love."

"Keep going, Friedrich."

"That's all my feelings—except sadness. And loss, much loss."

"What have you lost today?"

"All those sweet, those precious private moments with Lou—gone. That love we shared—where is it now? Lost! Everything ground down to dust. Now I know I've lost her forever!"

"But, Friedrich, possession must precede loss."

"Near the Lake of Orta"—Nietzsche's tone grew softer yet, as if to keep his words from trampling his delicate thoughts—"she and I once climbed to the top of the Sacro Monte to watch a golden sunset. Two luminous coral-tinted clouds that looked like merging faces sailed by. We touched softly. We kissed. We shared a holy moment—the only holy moment I have ever known."

"Did you and she ever speak again of that moment?"

"She knew of that moment! I often wrote her cards from afar referring to Orta sunsets, Orta breezes, Orta clouds."

"But," Breuer persisted, "did *she* ever speak of Orta? Was it for her also a holy moment?"

"She knew what Orta was!"

"Lou Salomé believed I should know everything about her relationship to you, and therefore took pains to describe each of your meetings in the greatest detail. She omitted nothing, she claimed. She spoke at length of Lucerne, Leipzig, Rome, Tautenberg. But Orta—I swear to you!—she mentioned only in passing. It made no particular impression on her. And one other thing, Friedrich. She tried to recall, but she said that she didn't remember if she had ever kissed you!"

Nietzsche was silent. His eyes flooded with tears, his head hung down.

Breuer knew he was being cruel. But he knew that not to be cruel now would be crueler yet. This was a singular opportunity, one that would never come again.

"Forgive my hard words, Friedrich, but I follow the advice of a great teacher. 'Offer a suffering friend a resting place,' he said, 'but take care it be a hard bed or field cot.' "

"You've listened well," Nietzsche replied. "And the bed *is* hard. Let me tell you *how* hard. Can I make you understand how much I have lost! For fifteen years, you've shared a bed with Mathilde. You're the central person in her life. She cares about you, touches you, knows what you like to eat, worries if you're late. When I extrude Lou Salomé from my mind—and I realize that nothing less than this is now taking place—do you know what I have left?"

Nietzsche's eyes focused not on Breuer but rather inward, as if he were reading from some internal text.

"Do you know that no other woman has ever touched me? Not to be loved or touched—ever? To live an absolutely unobserved life—do you know what that is like? Often I go for days without saying a word to anyone, except perhaps *'Guten Morgen'* and *'Guten Abend'* to my *Gasthaus* owner. Yes, Josef, you were right in your interpretation of 'no slot.' I belong nowhere. I have no home, no circle of friends to whom I speak daily, no closet full of belongings, no family hearth. I don't even have a state, for I have given up my German citizenship and never remain in one place long enough to get a Swiss passport."

Nietzsche looked piercingly at Breuer, as if he wished to be stopped. But Breuer was silent.

"Oh, I have my pretenses, Josef, my secret ways of tolerating aloneness, even glorifying it. I say that I must be separate from others to think my own thoughts. I say that the great minds of the past are my companions, that they crawl out of their hiding places into *my* sunshine. I scoff at the fear of solitude. I profess that great men must undergo great pain, that I have flown too far into the future, and that none can accompany me. I crow that if I am misunderstood or feared or rejected, then so much the better—it means I am on target! I say that my courage in facing aloneness without the herd, without the illusion of a divine provider, is proof of my greatness.

"Yet over and over I am haunted by one fear——" He hesitated for a moment, then plunged ahead. "Despite my bravado about being the posthumous philosopher, despite my certitude that my day will come, despite even my knowledge of eternal return—I am haunted by the thought of dying alone. Do you know what it's like to know that when you die, your body may not be discovered for days or weeks, not until the aroma beckons some stranger? I try to soothe myself. Often, in my deepest isolation, I speak to myself. Yet not too loudly, for I fear my own hollow echo. The one, the only one, who filled this hollowness was Lou Salomé."

Breuer, finding no voice for his sorrow, or for his gratitude that Nietzsche had chosen to confide these great secrets in him, listened silently. Within him, the hope grew stronger that he might, after all, still succeed in being the doctor for Nietzsche's despair.

"And now, thanks to you," Nietzsche wound up, "I know that Lou was merely illusion." He shook his head and stared out the window. "Bitter medicine, Doctor."

"But, Friedrich, to pursue truth, don't we scientists have to renounce all illusion?"

"TRUTH with capital letters!" Nietzsche exclaimed. "I forget, Josef, that scientists have still to learn that TRUTH, too, is an illusion—but an illusion without which we can't survive. So I shall renounce Lou Salomé for some other, yet unknown, illusion. It's hard to realize she's gone, that there's nothing left."

"Nothing left of Lou Salomé?"

"Nothing good." Nietzsche's face was pinched in disgust.

"Think about her," Breuer urged. "Let images appear to you. What do you see?"

"A bird of prey—an eagle with bloody claws. A wolfpack, led by Lou, my sister, my mother."

"Bloody claws? Yet she sought help for you. All that effort, Friedrich—a trip to Venice, another to Vienna."

"Not for me!" Nietzsche replied. "Maybe for her own sake, for atonement, for her guilt."

"She doesn't strike me as one burdened by guilt."

"Then perhaps for the sake of art. She values art—and she valued my work, work already done and work yet to come. She has a good eye—I'll credit her with that.

"It's strange," Nietzsche mused. "I met her in April, almost exactly nine months ago, and now I feel a great work quickening. My son, Zarathustra, stirs to be born. Perhaps nine months ago, she sowed the seed of Zarathustra in the furrows of my brain. Perhaps *that's* her destiny—to impregnate fertile minds with great books."

"So," Breuer ventured, "in appealing to me in your behalf, Lou Salomé may not be the enemy, after all."

"No!" Nietzsche pounded the arm of his chair. "You said that, I didn't. You're wrong! I'll *never* agree that she had concern for me. She appealed to you on her own behalf, to fulfill *her* destiny. She never knew *me*. She *used* me. What you've told me today verifies that."

"How?" Breuer asked, though he knew the answer.

"How? It's obvious. You told me yourself, Lou is like your Bertha— she's an automaton, playing her role, the same role, with me, with you, with one man after the other. The particular man is incidental. She seduced both of us in the same way, with the same female deviousness, the same guile, the same gestures, the same promises!"

"And yet this automaton controls you. She dominates your mind: you worry about her opinion, you pine for her touch."

"No. No pining. No longer. What I feel now is rage."

"At Lou Salomé?"

"No! She's unworthy of my anger. I feel self-loathing, anger at the lust that forced me to crave such a woman."

Is this bitterness, Breuer wondered, any better than obsession or loneliness? Banishing Lou Salomé from Nietzsche's mind is only part of the procedure. I need also to cauterize the raw wound left in her place.

"Why such anger at yourself?" he asked. "I remember your saying we all have our wild dogs barking in the cellar. How I wish you could be kinder, more generous to your own humanity!"

"Remember my first granite sentence—I've recited it to you many times, Josef—'Become who you are'? That means not only to perfect yourself but also not to fall prey to another's designs for you. But even falling in battle to another's power is preferable to falling prey to the woman-automaton who never even sees you! That is unforgivable!"

"And you, Friedrich, did *you* ever really see *Lou Salomé*?"

Nietzsche jerked his head.

"What do you mean?" he asked.

"She may have played *her* role, but you, what role did *you* play? Were you, and I, so different from her? Did you see *her*? Or did you, instead, see only prey—a disciple, a plowland for your thoughts, a successor? Or perhaps, like me, you saw beauty, youth, a satin pillow, a vessel into which to drain your lust. And wasn't she also a spoil of victory in the grunting competition with Paul Rée? Did you really see her *or* Paul Rée when, after you met her for the first time, you asked him to propose marriage to her in your behalf? I think it wasn't Lou Salomé you wanted, but someone *like her.*"

Nietzsche was silent. Breuer continued, "I shall never forget our walk in the Simmeringer Haide. That walk changed my life in so many ways. Of all that I learned that day, perhaps the most powerful insight was that I had not related to *Bertha*, but instead to all the private meanings I had attached to her—meanings that had nothing at all to do with her. You made me realize that I never saw her as she really was—that neither of us truly saw one another. Friedrich, *isn't that true for you as well?* Perhaps no one is at fault. Perhaps Lou Salomé has been used as much as you. Perhaps we're all fellow sufferers unable to see each other's truth."

"It is not my desire to understand what women wish." Nietzsche's tone was sharp and brittle. "It's my wish to avoid them. Women corrupt and spoil. Perhaps it is simply enough to say that I am ill suited for them, and leave it at that. And, in time, that may be my loss. From time to time, a man needs a woman, just as he needs a home-cooked meal."

Nietzsche's twisted, implacable answer plunged Breuer into reverie. He thought of the pleasure he drew from Mathilde and his family, even the satisfaction he drew from his new perception of Bertha. How sad to think that his friend would be forever denied such experiences! Yet he could think of no way to alter Nietzsche's distorted view of women. Perhaps it was too much to expect. Perhaps Nietzsche was right when he said that his attitudes toward women had been laid down in the first few years of his life. Perhaps these attitudes were so deeply embedded as to remain forever beyond the reach of any talking treatment. With this thought, he realized he had run out of ideas. Moreover, there was little time left. Nietzsche would not remain approachable much longer.

Suddenly, in the chair beside him, Nietzsche took off his spectacles, buried his face in his handkerchief, and burst into sobs.

Breuer was stunned. He must say something.

"I wept too when I knew I had to give up Bertha. So hard to give up that vision, that magic. You weep for Lou Salomé?"

Nietzsche, his face still buried in the handkerchief, blew his nose and shook his head vigorously.

"Then, for your loneliness?"

Again, Nietzsche shook his head.

"Do you know why you weep, Friedrich?"

"Not certain," came the muffled reply.

A fanciful idea occurred to Breuer. "Friedrich, please try an experiment with me. Can you imagine your tears having a voice?"

Lowering his handkerchief, Nietzsche looked at him, red-eyed and puzzled.

"Just try it for a minute or two," Breuer urged gently. "Give your tears a voice. What would they say?"

"I feel too foolish."

"I felt foolish, too, trying all the strange experiments *you* suggested. Indulge me. Try."

Without looking at him, Nietzsche began, "If one of my tears were sentient, it would say—it would say"—here he spoke in a loud, hissing whisper—" 'Free at last! Bottled up all these years! This man, this tight dry man, has never let me flow before.' Is that what you mean?" he asked, reverting to his own voice.

"Yes, good, very good. Keep going. What else?"

"What else? The tears would say"—again the hissing whisper—" 'Good to be liberated! Forty years in a stagnant pool. Finally, finally, the old man has a housecleaning! Oh, how I've wanted to escape before! But no way out—not until this Viennese doctor opened the rusty gate.' " Nietzsche stopped and daubed his eyes with his handkerchief.

"Thank you," said Breuer. "An opener of rusty gates—a splendid compliment. Now, in your own voice, tell me more about the sadness behind these tears."

"No, not sadness! On the contrary, when I talked to you a few minutes ago about dying alone, I felt a powerful surge of relief. Not so much *what* I said, but *that* I said it, that I finally, finally shared what I felt."

"Tell me more about *that* feeling."

"Powerful. Moving. A holy moment! *That's* why I wept. That's why I weep now. I've never done this before. Look at me! I can't stop the tears."

"It's good, Friedrich. Strong tears are cleansing."

Nietzsche, his face buried in his hands, nodded. "It's strange, but at the very moment when I, for the first time in my life, reveal my loneliness in all its depth, in all its despair—at that precise moment, loneliness melts away! The moment I told you I had never been touched was the very moment I first allowed myself to *be* touched. An extraordinary moment, as though some vast, interior icepack suddenly cracked and shattered."

"A paradox!" said Breuer. "Isolation exists only in isolation. Once shared, it evaporates."

Nietzsche raised his head and slowly wiped the tear tracks from his face. He ran his comb through his mustache five or six times and once again donned his thick spectacles. After a brief pause, he said, "And I have still another confession. Perhaps," he looked at his watch, "the final one. When you came into my room today and announced your recovery, Josef, I was devastated! I was so wretchedly self-absorbed, so disappointed at losing my raison d'être for being with you, that I could not bring myself to rejoice in your good news. That kind of selfishness is unforgivable."

"Not unforgivable," replied Breuer. "You yourself taught me that we are each composed of many parts, each clamoring for expression. We can be held responsible only for the final compromise, not for the wayward impulses of each of the parts. Your so-called selfishness is forgivable *precisely* because you care enough about me to share it with me now. My parting wish for you, my dear friend, is that the word 'unforgivable' be banished from your lexicon."

Nietzsche's eyes once again filled with tears, and again he pulled out his handkerchief.

"And *these* tears, Friedrich?"

"The way you said 'my dear friend.' I've often used the word 'friend' before, but not until this moment has the word ever been wholly *mine*. I've always dreamed of a friendship in which two people join together to attain some higher ideal. And here, now, it has arrived! You and I have joined together precisely in such a way! We've participated in the other's self-overcoming. I *am* your friend. You are mine. We are friends. We—are—friends." For an instant, Nietzsche seemed almost gay. "I love the sound of that phrase, Josef. I want to say it over and over."

"Then, Friedrich, accept my invitation to stay with me. Remember the dream: your slot is at my hearth."

At Breuer's invitation, Nietzsche froze. He sat slowly shaking his head before answering. "That dream both entices and torments me. I'm like you. I want to warm myself by a family hearth. But I'm frightened by giving in to comfort. That would be to abandon myself and my mission. For me, it would be a type of death. Perhaps that explains the symbol of an inert stone warming itself."

Nietzsche rose, paced for a moment or two, and then stopped behind his chair. "No, my friend, my destiny is to search for truth on the far side of loneliness. My son, my Zarathustra, will be ripe with wisdom, but his only companion will be an eagle. He will be the loneliest man in the world."

Nietzsche looked again at his watch. "I know your schedule well enough by this time, Josef, to realize your other patients are waiting for you. I can't keep you much longer. Each of us must go our own way."

Breuer shook his head. "It crushes me that we have to part. It's unfair! You've done so much for me and received so little in return. Perhaps Lou's image has lost its power over you. Perhaps not. Time will tell. But there seems much more we could do."

"Don't underestimate what you have given me, Josef. Don't underestimate the value of friendship, of my knowing I'm not a freak, of my knowing I'm capable of touching and being touched. Before, I only half embraced my concept of *Amor fati:* I had trained myself—*resigned* myself is a better term—to love my fate. But now, thanks to you, thanks to your open hearth, I realize I have a choice. I shall always remain alone, but what a difference, what a wonderful difference, to *choose* what I do. *Amor fati*—choose your fate, love your fate."

Breuer stood and faced Nietzsche, the chair between them. Breuer walked around the chair. For a moment, Nietzsche looked frightened, cornered. But, at Breuer's approach, arms spread, he, too, opened his arms.

At noon, on 18 December 1882, Josef Breuer returned to his office, to Frau Becker and his waiting patients. Later he dined with his wife, his children, his father- and mother-in-law, young Freud, and Max and his family. After dinner, he napped and dreamed about chess and the queening of a pawn. He continued the comfortable practice of medicine for thirty more years but never again made use of the talking cure.

That same afternoon, the patient in room 13 at the Lauzon Clinic, Eckart Müller, boarded a fiacre to the train station and thence traveled south, alone, to Italy, to the warm sun, the still air, and to a rendezvous, an honest rendezvous, with a Persian prophet named Zarathustra.

AFTERWORD

Years ago in an essay about the writing of *When Nietzsche Wept* I cited a phrase by André Gide; "History is fiction that *did* happen. Whereas fiction is history that *might have* happened."

A felicitous phrase, I thought, and wrote,

> Fiction is history that might have happened. Perfect! That was precisely the fiction I wanted to write. My novel, *When Nietzsche Wept*, could have happened. Given the very improbable history of the field of psychotherapy, all the events of this book could have come to pass if history had rotated only slightly on its axis. (from *The Yalom Reader*, Basic Books, NY, 1998)

In February 2003 an event occurred which gave these words an eerie prescience. Renate Müller-Buck forwarded me a remarkable letter she had discovered while working on the commentary volumes for Nietzsche's correspondence within the historical critical edition of Nietzsche's works and letters founded by Montinari and Giorgio Colli. In the Weimar Nietzsche Archives, she came across a 1878 letter in which Siegfried Lipiner tries to convince Heinrich Köselitz to send Nietzsche to Vienna where he would be treated by Breuer!

Siegfried Lipiner was a Viennese poet and philosopher and a friend of Nietzsche, Freud, Mahler, and Breuer. At one time they were all members, along with Freud, of the Pernerstorfer Circle, a group of students and intellectuals interested in philosophy and social democratic literature. Heinrich Köselitz, (a musician with the pseudonym of Peter Gast) was Nietzsche's close friend, disciple, and amanuensis.

In other words, the very fictional event which I had imagined and used as the foundation to my novel came close to having been history. Certainly, as the letter below indicates, Siegfried Lipiner was doing his utmost to persuade Nietzsche's friend to arrange for Nietzsche to visit Vienna and consult with his friend, Josef Breuer. He had found funds to pay for Nietzsche's several-months stay in Vienna, had arranged with Dr. Breuer, had discussed the plan with some of Nietzsche's friends, and had even given thought to the neighborhood where Nietzsche might reside.

The plan never became history. Köselitz replied that he personally found the offer enticing and even entertained the fantasy of abducting Nietzsche and bringing him to Vienna. But, after consulting Nietzsche's sister, Elisabeth, and his friend, Franz Overbeck, decided it would be best to decline the offer. Nietzsche was too ill to undergo the agitation of a major move. Besides, he was just about to leave for a cold-water cure at Baden-Baden. Furthermore, he had suffered harm by changing physicians too often, and had just entered the care of two eminent physicians and it was felt that he should not change again. Some of Nietzsche's letters written before this proposal indicate that Nietzsche had taken a dislike to Siegfried Lipiner's inclination to tell him what to do and it is possible that Nietzsche himself may have turned down the proposal.

Here is the letter from Lipiner and the reply from Köselitz.

Praterstrasse, Vienna,
22nd February 1878

My dear friend Köselitz!

I must thank you so much for your letter which made me very happy.—Could you be so kind as to give my respects to Mr. P. Widemann. It will be a great pleasure to review his works. How are you progressing with your cultural activities? Is there anything I can do to assist you? Do not be shy to ask me, I will ask friends to help wherever possible.

What you wrote about Overbeck confirms my impression of him after reading the paper on discord and accord. Are you familiar with Paul de Lagarde? If not—you should make up for this as soon as possible. His paper "On the Present State of the German Reich" (Göttingen, Dieterich, 1876) is brilliant; I love and adore him in the highest. But now to the essence. Fräulein von Meysenburg has written alarming things about Nietzsche. I was, as you know, at that time in Salzburg, invited by von Seydlitz. Her telegram also did not contain anything reassuring. One thing is certain: Nietzsche must be forced to concentrate in the next few months only on his cure. I have the following plan: He should come to Vienna; if necessary, I will pick him up; we will not travel in one [sic] tour, instead we will make interruptions—then he might as well consult our efficient physicians in Vienna, under their constant supervision and care adhere to a rigorous and continuous healing process; a highly competent nerve pathologist, Dr. Breuer, a personal friend of mine, will look after him with utmost care; Professor Bamberger will have overall supervision of the treatment, an efficient, highly experienced young doctor (specialist and assistant doctor in general hospital) will assist him; I have been provided with the necessary funds to keep N. here for several months living without any worries, except those regarding his health—these will not cause Nietzsche any troubles whatsoever, will and shall not evoke a single doubt. N. shall, if he wishes, not live in, but in the vicinity of Vienna, in our mild climate and in quite healthy and open surroundings; however, he can also have absolutely quiet living quarters in town. Of course I will purchase the whole lot; he need not worry about a thing, will find everything prepared.—Not one word shall be uttered that could upset or excite him,—he will enjoy the most gentle, caring, protecting, soothing treatment. He has here, once a convalescent, the best distraction available. In short: there is no reason in existence nor conceivable that could prevent him from coming here, everything seems to be quite clear. Baron Seydlitz is just delighted about this plan; Hans Richter, to whom I had spoken, also thinks it is highly recommendable.

Meanwhile I have requested to obtain [sic] medical advice on that question, the result of which will leave no doubt. Please, dear friend, write me immediately of what you think about this matter, talk to Fräulein Nietzsche, try to dissipate all doubts and create a favourable atmosphere. To name it, help me overcome a hindrance: N. should not believe that he is a burden to anybody nor that he should have a bad conscience. He should know that we all who love him would feel hurt if he rejected because of these reasons. Gratitude is also a bit of principii individuationis.

Everything that I have said is meant word for word. Also, N. should not believe that any of his admirers would bother him; no one will approach him unless he is in good health [sic]. I myself will know how to treat him; you can rely on that, I know that tranquility is most important to him.—If N. is in Lucerne, kindly give me his address. Otherwise, give him my best regards, read to him the letter if you wish and work in any case towards my plan, that is for his sake [sic].—Please also extend my sincerest regards to highly esteemed Fräulein Nietzsche. I will write to Nietzsche as soon as I am in receipt of your reply.

From the bottom of my heart.

Yours truly,
Lipiner

My dear Sir!

I could not reply to your kind letter until now since I had been consulting with many an expert. By this delay your patience has been put hard to the test despite my efforts to hasten things.

All of us are of the utmost admiration for your friendship that you show whilst explaining your wonderful plan. Upon reading your letter for the first time, I was of the impression that Nietzsche could hardly resist this invitation; but before showing it to him personally, I needed to ask various friends for their advice. Overbeck and Nietzsche's sister felt that even though they are moved by your overwhelming concern it would be more advisable with respect to N[ietzsche]'s present state of health not to mention anything about your plans. First of all, this would excite him far too much, this should be actually avoided as we could make him sick again for a month—and then this suggestion came, unfortunately, a little too late. 4 months ago N[ietzsche] might have been persuaded to accept your invitation; but now he has his own doctors here, very good doctors, even though they are by no means from Vienna. He is being treated by Prof. Immermann (the son of Münchhausen-I[mmermann]) and Prof. Massini, 2 highly intelligent men, whose care he cannot be taken from without running a risk now. N[ietzsche]'s illness goes back in part to the frequent change of doctors, all of whom experimented with him and not actually knowing what he was suffering from. But now he has in fact outstanding doctors whose causality abilities have been acquired by their aptitude and studies. Therefore we are convinced that N[ietzsche] should stay under their care. Of course it is easy to say this long distance, i.e. Vienna which can be very proud of its famous physicians; however, it is rather doubtful that you, who devotes every thought and all your love to finally restoring our poor, poor friend's health, will be satisfied. However, I hope I can reassure you by formulating what all of us close to N[ietzsche] are primarily concerned about: N[ietzsche]'s fast recovery; how every individual wants to lend a hand and help and, how each and every one of us is stunned at whatever stage by the dreadful mercilessness and inaccessibility of organic nature; how we did everything, what kind of suggestions and contributions for recovery came into mind; how we even thought of abducting N[ietzsche], finally I say to you: hopefully I can convince you that despite of and after all things said, the present treatment by the doctors, and especially in anticipation of its results, seems to be the most appropriate for N[ietzsche]'s state of health.—The trip to Lucerne didn't take place after all; but next Monday (4th March) N[ietzsche] will travel to Baden-Baden for a cold water cure. I will let you know his address which I hope to acquire on Tuesday . . .

AUTHOR'S NOTE

Friedrich Nietzsche and Josef Breuer never met. And, of course, psychotherapy was not invented as a result of their encounter. Nonetheless, the life situation of the major characters is grounded in fact, and the essential components of this novel—Breuer's mental anguish, Nietzsche's despair, Anna O., Lou Salomé, Freud's relationship with Breuer, the ticking embryo of psychotherapy—were all historically in place in 1882.

Friedrich Nietzsche had been introduced by Paul Rée to the young Lou Salomé in the spring of 1882 and, over the next months, had had a brief, intense, and chaste love affair with her. She would go on to have a distinguished career as both a brilliant woman of letters and a practicing psychoanalyst; she would also be known for her close friendship with Freud and for her romantic liaisons, especially with the German poet Rainer Maria Rilke.

Nietzsche's relationship with Lou Salomé, complicated by the presence of Paul Rée and sabotaged by Nietzsche's sister, Elisabeth, ended disastrously for him; for years he was anguished by his lost love and by his belief that he had been betrayed. During the latter months of 1882—those in which this book is set—Nietzsche was deeply depressed, even suicidal. His despairing letters to Lou Salomé, parts of which are quoted throughout the book, are authentic, though there is uncertainty about which were merely drafts and which were actually sent. Wagner's letter to Nietzsche cited in chapter 1 is also authentic.

Josef Breuer's medical treatment of Bertha Pappenheim, known as Anna O., occupied much of his attention in 1882. In November of that year, he began to discuss the case with his young protégé and friend, Sigmund Freud, who was, as the novel describes, a frequent visitor to the Breuer home. A dozen years later, Anna O. was to be the first case described in Freud and Breuer's *Studies on Hysteria*, the book that launched the psychoanalytic revolution.

Bertha Pappenheim was, like Lou Salomé, a remarkable woman. Years after her treatment with Breuer, she went on to a career as a pioneering social worker so distinguished as to be posthumously honored by West Germany in 1954 in a commemorative postage stamp. Her identity as Anna O. was not public knowledge until Ernest Jones revealed it in his 1953 biography, *The Life and Work of Sigmund Freud*.

Was the historical Josef Breuer obsessed with erotic desire for Bertha Pappenheim? Little is known of Breuer's internal life, but the relevant scholarship does not rule out that possibility. Conflicting historical accounts agree only that Breuer's treatment of Bertha Pappenheim evoked complex and powerful feelings in both parties. Breuer was so preoccupied with his young patient and spent so much time visiting her that his wife, Mathilde, did grow resentful and jealous. Freud spoke explicitly to Ernest Jones, his biographer, of Breuer's emotional overinvolvement with his young patient and in a letter to his fiancée, Martha Bernays, written at the time, reassured her that nothing of that sort would ever happen with him. The psychoanalyst George Pollock has suggested that Breuer's strong response to Bertha may have had its roots in his having lost his mother, also named Bertha, at an early age.

The account of Anna O.'s dramatic delusional pregnancy and Breuer's panic and precipitous termination of therapy has long been part of psychoanalytic lore. Freud first described the incident in a 1932 letter to the Austrian novelist Stefan Zweig, and Ernest Jones repeated it in his Freud biography. Only recently has the account been questioned, and Albrecht Hirschmüller's 1990 biography of Breuer suggests that the entire incident was a myth of Freud's making. Breuer himself never clarified the point and, in his published 1895 case history, compounded the confusion surrounding the Anna O. case by grossly and unaccountably exaggerating the efficacy of his treatment.

It is remarkable, considering Breuer's vast influence on the development of psychotherapy, that he turned his attention to psychology for only a short segment of his career. Medicine best remembers Josef Breuer not only as an important research investigator in the physiology of respiration and equilibrium, but also as a brilliant diagnostician who was physician to an entire generation of great figures in *fin de siècle* Vienna.

Nietzsche suffered from poor health for most of his life. Although, in 1889, he collapsed and slipped irrevocably into the severe dementia of paresis (a form of tertiary syphilis, from which he died in 1900), there is general consensus that for most of his earlier life he suffered from another illness. It is likely that Nietzsche (whose clinical picture I have portrayed following Stefan Zweig's vivid 1939 biographical sketch) suffered from severe migraine. For this condition, Nietzsche had consulted many physicians throughout Europe and might easily have been persuaded to seek medical consultation with the eminent Josef Breuer.

It would have been out of character for a distressed Lou Salomé to have applied to Breuer to help Nietzsche. She was not, according to her biographers, a woman significantly burdened by guilt and is known to have ended many love affairs with apparently little remorse. In most matters, she guarded her privacy and did not, as far as I can ascertain, speak publicly of her personal relationship with Nietzsche. Her letters to him have not survived. Most likely they were destroyed by Elisabeth, Nietzsche's sister, whose feud with Lou Salomé lasted a lifetime. Lou Salomé did indeed have a brother, Jenia, who was studying medicine in Vienna in 1882. It is highly unlikely, however, that Breuer would have presented the case of Anna O. at a student conference in that year. Nietzsche's letter (following chapter 12) to Peter Gast, a friend and editor, and Elisabeth Nietzsche's letter (following chapter 7) to Nietzsche are fictional, as is the Lauzon Clinic and the characters of Fischmann and Breuer's brother-in-law Max. (Breuer was, however, an avid chess player.) All of the dreams reported are fictional, except two of Nietzsche's: those of his father rising from the grave and the old man's death rattle.

In 1882, psychotherapy had not yet been born; and Nietzsche, of course, never formally turned his attention in that direction. Yet in my reading of Nietzsche, he was deeply and significantly concerned with self-understanding and personal change. For chronological consistency, I have confined myself to citing Nietzsche's pre-1882 works, primarily *Human, All Too Human, Untimely Meditations, Dawn,* and *The Gay Science.* I have, however, assumed as well that the great thoughts of *Thus Spake Zarathustra,* much of which he wrote a few months after the close of this book, were already percolating in Nietzsche's mind.

I am indebted to Van Harvey, Professor of Religious Studies at Stanford University, for permitting me to attend his superb Nietzsche course, for many hours of collegial discussion, and for a critical reading of my manuscript. My gratitude to colleagues in the Department of Philosophy, especially Eckart Förster and Dagfinn Føllesdal, for permitting me to attend related courses in German philosophy and phenomenology. Many have given suggestions on this manuscript: Morton Rose, Herbert Kotz, David Spiegel, Gertrud and George Blau, Kurt Steiner, Isabel Davis, Ben Yalom, Joseph Frank, members of the Stanford Biography Seminar under the guidance of Barbara Babcock and Diane Middlebrook—to all my thanks. Betty Vadeboncoeur, Stanford University history of medicine librarian, was invaluable in my research. Timothy K. Donahue-Bombosch translated the letters cited from Nietzsche to Lou Salomé. Many offered editorial instruction and assistance along the way: Alan Rinzler, Sara Blackburn, Richard Ellman, and Leslie Becker. The Basic Books staff, especially Jo Ann Miller, offered enormous support; Phoebe Hoss, in this as in previous books, was an enabling editor. My wife, Marilyn, who has always been my first, most thorough, and most merciless critic, surpassed herself in this book—providing not only continuous critique from the first to the final draft, but also suggesting the book's title.

About the Author

IRVIN D. YALOM is the author of *The Schopenhauer Cure, Lying on the Couch,* and *Love's Executioner,* as well as several classic textbooks on psychotherapy. He is professor emeritus of psychiatry at Stanford University, and lives and practices in Palo Alto, California.

BOOKS BY IRVIN D. YALOM

THE NOVELS:

LYING ON THE COUCH: *A Novel*
ISBN 0-06-092851-4 (paperback)
A tantalizing, almost illicit, glimpse at what therapists might really be thinking during their sessions, exposing many of the lies that are told on and off the couch.
"A dazzling, psychiatric whodunit . . . a real genius." —*Los Angeles Times*

WHEN NIETZSCHE WEPT: *A Novel of Obsession*
ISBN 0-06-074812-5 (Perennial Classics paperback)
This richly evocative novel portrays an astutely imagined relationship between Europe's greatest philosopher and one of the founding fathers of psychoanalysis.
"The best dramatization of a great thinker's thought since Sartre." —*Chicago Tribune*

THE SCHOPENHAUER CURE: *A Novel*
ISBN 0-06-621441-6 (NEW in hardcover)
A cast of memorably wounded characters struggles to heal pain and change lives in this novel of group therapy.

THE NON-FICTION:

THE GIFT OF THERAPY
An Open Letter to a New Generation of Therapists and Their Patients
ISBN 0-06-093811-0 (paperback)

At once startlingly profound and irresistibly practical, Yalom's insights will help enrich the therapeutic process for a new generation of both patients and counselors.
"For both the professional and the lay reader. . . . In 85 short chapters, [Yalom] presents little pearls of ideas shaped from 35 years in practice." —*Library Journal*

LOVE'S EXECUTIONER: *And Other Tales of Psychotherapy*
ISBN 0-06-095834-0 (Perennial Classics paperback)

Ten riveting true narratives based on Yalom's psychotherapist practice that reveal an intimate and unusual view of the relationship between patient and therapist.
"The fascinating, moving, enervating, inspiring, unexpected stuff of psychotherapy is told with economy and . . . humor." —*Washington Post Book World*

MOMMA AND THE MEANING OF LIFE: *Tales of Psychotherapy*
ISBN 0-06-095838-3 (paperback)
Yalom probes the mysteries and marvels at the heart of the therapeutic encounter, revealing his own and his patient's confrontations with life's most profound challenges.
"These six engrossing narratives are very valuable gleanings from a master therapist's professional and personal experience." —*Kirkus Reviews*